Reclamation

Book Four of

Best Laid Plans

By Nathan Jones

The events depicted in this novel are fictional. The characters in this story are also fictional, and any resemblance to anyone living or dead is entirely unintentional. While most locations are real some creative license has been taken in describing them, and a few locations are entirely fictional.

ISBN: 9798611535271

Books by Nathan Jones

BEST LAID PLANS
Fuel
Shortage
Invasion
Reclamation
Determination

NUCLEAR WINTER
First Winter
First Spring
Chain Breakers
Going Home

Fallen City

MOUNTAIN MAN
Badlands
Homecoming
Homeland
Mountain War
Final Stand
Lone Valley

ISOLATION
Shut In
Going Out (upcoming)

Dedication

This book is dedicated to my brother Seth, for his invaluable help with the technical challenges I couldn't handle on my own. Thanks to him I was able to focus on writing, and words cannot express my sincere gratitude.

Table of Contents

Dedication iv
Prologue: Retaliation 1
Chapter One: Hospitality 26
Chapter Two: High Price 41
Chapter Three: Meadows 71
Chapter Four: Herding 91
Chapter Five: Convoy 107
Chapter Six: A Few Final Steps 132
Chapter Seven: Homecoming 150
Chapter Eight: Settling In 170
Chapter Nine: Abuzz 188
Chapter Ten: Upset 205
Chapter Eleven: Volunteers 229
Chapter Twelve: Joining Up 255
Chapter Thirteen: Confusion 274
Chapter Fourteen: Unpleasant Arrival 301
Chapter Fifteen: Necessity 320
Chapter Sixteen: First Strike 340
Chapter Seventeen: Aftermath 366
Chapter Eighteen: Reassigned 387
Epilogue: A Closer Look 410

Prologue

Retaliation

A bigger jolt than usual shook Trev out of his fitful sleep, nearly jostling him off his place on the bench in the back of the truck. Leaning against him Jim *did* start to fall, and still half asleep Trev reached out and caught his brother, pulling him back up.

They were slowing down, and by the crunch of gravel under the tires they'd left the asphalt road and were pulling onto a shoulder to stop. "Finally," he mumbled.

Around him his other family members, most of whom had also been asleep, began to stir and expressed their own relief as they stretched and worked out kinks in their muscles from the awkward sitting positions. Trev retrieved his captured AK-47 from where he'd stowed it between two diesel cans and made his way to the back of the truck, where he made sure his weapon was ready to fire before leaning out the opening in the canvas tarp.

His bladder felt like it was going to explode, and behind him his siblings and cousin were whining for him to get out of the way for similar reasons, but he refused to hop down until he was certain the area was safe.

It was after dark. That meant they'd been driving for a long time without stopping, since they'd stolen the truck from the internment camp in the early afternoon. Trev couldn't be sure what his uncle Lucas, who'd been behind the wheel this entire time, had been thinking during the drive, but it was obvious he refused to take any chances until they were well away from the danger they'd left behind.

Trev didn't blame him.

"It's safe," he finally said, the pronouncement driven more by his desperate biological need than his careful inspection. And his trust in Lucas's care when it came to picking a stopping point.

It looked safe at a glance, at least, with them on a small road in the middle of a peaceful looking countryside, not a single source of light to be seen in the darkness aside from the truck's headlights and taillights. At least until the truck's engine abruptly turned off and the lights died, probably so the vehicle would be harder to spot while they were stopped.

Without another moment's hesitation he hopped down and trotted towards the nearest bushes, slinging his rifle as he went. Behind him he heard the rest of his family similarly escaping from the back of the truck and scattering in all directions to answer the call of nature. A few door slams from the cab suggested his mom, aunt, and likely his uncle as well had similar goals in mind.

"Does anyone have toilet paper?" Linda called from somewhere off to his left.

"Doubt it," his dad called back sympathetically. "Find a tree or bush with lots of leaves."

"Great," his sister muttered, loud enough for everyone to hear. After spending so long on the road and roughing it in less than ideal locations Trev could sympathize, but there wasn't much to be done about it now that they'd left the internment camp far behind; they might've been held against their will there, but if nothing else it *had* offered those sorts of basic amenities.

At least they had the luxury of privacy now. During the drive there'd been a few times when his family members trapped in the back of the truck hadn't been able to wait any longer, and they'd had to find creative solutions to the unpleasant situation. Trev's dad had done his best to encourage them to look on the bright side of things, since it was better to be tackling the problem riding in a truck headed for home than using the latrines in the internment camp with fallout raining on their heads. That was dubious encouragement, since none of them wanted to be reminded about what had happened earlier that day.

Half a minute later, feeling almost human again, Trev paused to get a better look at the landscape around him. It was surprisingly peaceful and quiet, with no sign of the devastation the world had suffered over the last twelve hours. After their harrowing escape from the internment camp he almost expected to see mushroom clouds on the horizon in every direction.

Shivering slightly, he pushed down those grim thoughts and made his way over to where his uncle had a book of maps spread over the hood, reading it by the light of a small flashlight. "Was this with the truck?" he asked.

Lucas shook his head. "One of the few possessions Eva and Mary were able to pack up to bring along in all the confusion. I was fine leaving furniture and extra clothes behind, but maps of all the lower 48 States were pretty much a must."

"So where are we?"

His uncle pointed at the map of Wisconsin he'd opened the book to as he answered. "Nearly to the border, maybe an hour or two away from La Crosse."

Trev whistled. The truck couldn't go much faster than 50 and they'd been driving nonstop, but even so that was pretty good time. They'd made it all the way across Michigan's Upper Peninsula and through most of Wisconsin, and had nearly reached the border into Minnesota. "So how long have we been driving for?"

"About ten hours." Lucas grimaced and stretched, popping his back. "Been a long time since the road trips of my youth. That was a pretty brutal drive."

"Not just for the driver," Trev's mom said as she appeared at Trev's side, giving him a hug and a kiss on the cheek before leaning over to frown at the map, then at her brother. "Did we really have to go through all that without even bathroom breaks? We could've changed drivers at the same time."

"I don't know about you, Clair, but I was kind of in a hurry to leave the fallout behind."

Trev's aunt arrived at the scene in time to hear the exchange, and she came over to lean against her husband as she aired her own complaints. "We all were, but we had to have outrun that in the first few hours, right?"

Lucas gave Trev a long-suffering look. For the most part everyone in the family was pretty reasonable, but when they were in the mood to be unreasonable they had a tendency to dog pile. Not that they didn't have a good excuse to be on edge, after the horrific events of the day.

"Fallout's the most pressing reason, but it definitely isn't the only one," his uncle said. "The Gold Bloc troops have ventured almost as far into Wisconsin as into Michigan, so we face potential trouble with every mile until we can get past their lines, hopefully in the next few hours."

He turned to Trev. "You probably didn't see it since you were in the back, but we passed a second internment camp not long after leaving the Upper Peninsula, this one intact by all appearances. We didn't get close enough to see more than that the fences were still up and there were people inside, and I took pains to avoid getting close enough for a second glimpse, but it was definitely up."

Trev felt a surge of sympathy for the people still in that camp. Living in the Mackinac camp had been bad enough, but after seeing the brutality of the Gold Bloc soldiers after the nukes flew he guessed things had to be much, much worse for anyone still unlucky enough to be their prisoners.

Eva wrapped her arms around her husband, and the complaint had left her voice when she answered. "It was harrowing enough just being a passenger spending hours weaving a path on backroads to avoid any vehicles, and even then running into more than a few. Your uncle did a great job bluffing his way past any trucks we did encounter by driving innocuously. There were a few close calls when I was sure we'd be stopped, but we never were."

Lucas nodded. "In the confusion of a nuclear war, the Gold Bloc soldiers were probably too worried about their own problems to harass other trucks for routine inspections. But even those brushes were enough to get my heart pounding." He took a final look at the map, then reluctantly shut and folded the flimsy book and tucked it under one arm. "We should keep going. I'm going to refill the diesel tanks while we get everyone in."

Trev nodded too. "All right. I'll take the wheel this time." He raised his voice to a quiet shout to call everyone back to the truck.

His dad materialized not far away in the dim light of stars and a crescent moon. "Hold on," he said quietly. "We're in a hurry to get home, and the sooner the better as far as I'm concerned, but have we thought about what we're going to do for water, food, and rest? We've still got a long ways to go, and I'd prefer not to have the drivers falling asleep at the wheel and delirious from thirst, exhaustion, and hunger."

"It's just another thirty or so hours," Lucas argued. "We can make that pushing, and all get a nice long drink, meal, and sleep back in Aspen Hill."

Trev thought of his disastrous first day's hike right after the Gulf refineries attack, when he'd pushed himself too hard and ended up getting injured on a pothole a few inches deep. "If we've left the blockheads and fallout behind there's no reason to push that hard. We'd just set ourselves up to be in a disaster we're not equipped to handle for no good reason. Besides, we have a truck now. Maybe we should think about what we could do to make our situation better before getting home."

His uncle gave him a thoughtful look. "What did you have in mind? Scavenging, foraging?"

"Newtown," George guessed.

Trev clapped his dad on the shoulder in confirmation. He'd talked about the town a bit with his family while they'd been stuck in the internment camp waiting for an opportunity to escape, and it was hard to ignore so much wheat and other necessities available for trade for almost absurdly reasonable prices. "We could do a lot of good for the town, and make sure we have enough food to last us a long time."

"I'm not sure how much I like that," his mom said, pausing in feeling her way along the truck to the back. Trev could hear the frown in her voice. "We were so fortunate to all get out alive together, and we've got the truck and enough fuel to get to Aspen Hill. Why tempt fate?"

"We haven't got much more than the clothes on our backs," Trev argued. "And when I left the town it was in big trouble in more ways than one, especially with food. Newtown could provide us with a lot of the things we need, and even some things to make life more comfortable."

To his surprise his dad spoke up against the idea too. "How exactly would we pay for any of this? We can't afford to sell the truck or any fuel, which just leaves the three guns you captured, some spare magazines and ammo, and the flak jackets and a set of riot gear. We might get something out of that, but do we really want to sell what we need to defend ourselves in a bad situation?"

Eva cleared her throat. "Lucas?"

"Right," his uncle patted his belt, a vague motion in the darkness. "I've got a dozen one-ounce gold coins sewn into the waistband of these pants. They started out as an "in case of emergency" thing while we were in Norway, but I've held on to them since."

Trev couldn't help but grin. "Like father, like son."

Lucas's voice turned somber. "I'm not throwing my weight behind the idea though, Trev. We could just as easily buy things in Aspen Hill, from people we trust more and with much less risk."

"No, you can't. Nobody has anything to sell, and even if they did they wouldn't be taking gold when most people are trying to just get by and feed themselves. Newtown's the only place in a good enough shape to be trading for precious metals."

There was a long, thoughtful pause, which was broken by the hair-raising sound of a vehicle engine in the distance. His mom made an alarmed noise, and they all listened intently for a few seconds until they could reassure themselves that the noise wasn't heading their way.

"This is a bad place and time to debate this," Lucas said. "Let's get back on the road. We can all think it through as we drive."

Trev nodded and followed his uncle to the back of the truck to haul some diesel up and refill the tanks. While he did that his parents and aunt got everyone up into the back of the truck, leaving him, his dad, and Mary in the cab for the next leg of the trip. Both had gotten enough rest that they thought they could take over if he started to get too tired to keep driving, and they also looked more than a little eager to be sitting on the slightly more comfortable stiff leather front seat for a change.

In just a few minutes they were back on the road, Trev behind the wheel doing his best to reacquaint himself with driving a vehicle for the first time in what seemed like an eternity. He also didn't have the most experience with stick shifts, and embarrassed himself by riding the clutch and jostling them all the first few times he shifted gears.

At least he didn't kill the engine, and no one called him out on his bad driving. Even Mary, who might've hummed a teasing song in other circumstances, kept quiet as they drove, eyes straining into the blackness beyond the headlights.

They breathed a sigh of relief when they crossed the Mississippi River into Minnesota less than two hours later, although there was a bit of worry that the bridge might be guarded. Trev approached cautiously in the darkness with the headlights on and had everyone duck low in the seats.

There was no point trying to be stealthy since the engine would've given away their presence anyway, and it was likely any Gold Bloc sentries would have night vision. So the only way to make the best of a bad situation was to keep their eyes open, and be ready to get out of there fast if there was trouble.

There wasn't. Either the invading forces hadn't made it this far yet or the confusion of the previous day had disrupted their security. Either way Trev crossed the bridge at a safe but fast speed and barreled on into the night.

With no food, water, or real need to rest just yet there was no reason to stop, and in a way it was a tremendous relief to see the miles rolling away under the truck's tires. Each minute that passed meant they were that much farther from the troubles behind, and that much closer to home and an end to the insanity they'd fled.

Since his dad and Mary were sleeping there wasn't much to do to fill the time but think, so he did. Mostly about Newtown, since the alternative was thinking about the Gold Bloc invasion and the global thermonuclear war mankind had finally succumbed to earlier that day. He'd already been thinking about that for most of the drive, so it was a relief to focus on their immediate future instead.

For Trev it wasn't so much an issue of whether they should visit the town as how they should approach it. There was no question they needed to stop somewhere, at least for water, unless they wanted to drive straight through to Utah for more than a full day. Whatever his uncle might claim, thirst and exhaustion would make driving hazardous well before then, especially after the frantic time they'd had escaping the internment camp and the stress it had put on their minds and bodies.

Newtown was the only safe place Trev knew about, and it was a realistic goal to set. They'd have to drive another fifteen or so hours to reach it, but they could manage that without putting themselves in too terrible a position. Which left the main question whether they wanted to risk revealing they had a truck, or just go in on foot at first.

Trev honestly wasn't sure, although he did know that eventually they'd probably have to give away the fact that they had a vehicle; if they did visit the town it would be stupid not to buy as much wheat as the truck could carry, since the good it could do for the family and the rest of Aspen Hill couldn't be argued.

Lugging several thousand pounds of grain out of town would be suspicious enough that only an idiot wouldn't see what they were doing, at which point they may as well not insult their hosts by trying to hide the existence of the truck. Of course that risk depended on Trev's assurance of Vernon's integrity, which he couldn't be completely confident about.

They'd either have to cache their AK-47s or check them in to the sheriff, leaving them at his mercy with a very tempting target. Trev could understand his family's concerns, and he shared them. But at the same time at the end of Trev's first visit there Vernon had returned the silver rounds the barflies had shaken him down for, as well as his checked gun.

A few ounces of silver and a .45 couldn't come close to comparing to a truck with enough fuel to travel hundreds of miles. That might tempt even a saint these days. But could they afford not to take the chance, when so much good could come from it?

Trev mulled that over as he drove on, through the first faint predawn glow until it was light enough that he could turn off the headlights so the truck would be harder to see. He considered it lucky that they hadn't run into any roadblocks or ambushes up to this point; while in Gold Bloc territory the enemy would've kept the roads safe for their own vehicles, but now that he and his family were back out in territory that was still firmly US there was no telling what they might run into.

He'd need to be more cautious than he had been.

Just after dawn they stopped for another bathroom break, this one not causing quite the stampede the last one had. Afterwards they huddled together around the hood to seriously discuss whether or not to risk Newtown.

Almost everyone was against the idea, but they were also for it. There was just too much to be gained, and lost, from the risk. Finally, as Lucas began getting antsy about getting back on the road, they agreed to drive in that direction and make a final decision once they got closer to the town.

His dad took the wheel, and Trev settled back in the passenger seat to get what sleep he could on a padded leather bench that didn't recline and only had one armrest.

He couldn't wait for the trip to be over.

*****

April 26th, the day the world ended.

On the radio they'd already settled on calling yesterday's nuclear war the Retaliation. Lewis wasn't sure the name worked for him. It seemed too simple, too . . . plain, to properly describe the horror that had taken place the day before. The unimaginable loss of life and certainty of future suffering caused by a few hundred of the most fearsome weapons humanity had ever produced.

But he supposed it was human nature to reduce the scope of the unimaginable down to a simple term, something people could bear to say and think about.

It had been nearly a full day since the nukes fell. He'd spent most of the morning trying to put the event from his mind by working hard on the coop, rabbit hutch, his traps around the gardens, and other projects. But his curiosity had finally gotten the better of him when Chauncey radioed in about good, solid information about the previous day's events coming over his shortwave.

Lewis had hurried to the storehouse, joining a few dozen people clustered around the retired teacher, who sat at his usual place behind the counter tweaking the feed on his radio. No one seemed to notice his arrival as he made his way over to stand next to Matt and Rick near the counter, all too intent on the message coming from the old shortwave.

From what he was able to gather through context, it seemed to be a rebroadcast from Hill Air Force Base up in northern Utah, where the remnants of the military in the area had retreated after the Antelope Island camp riots the previous fall. They'd hunkered down there for the winter, struggling to keep themselves and a handful of refugees alive with limited success, and then in the spring had tentatively set out to restore order in the immediate area.

The base was glowing dust now, after being the target of a nuclear strike, but before then they claimed to have been in direct contact with the President's bunker in the hours before the missiles flew.

It turned out that the President and his cabinet, who'd seemed to disappear in the first week after the Gulf refineries attack as riots spread across the nation, had been around all along. They'd retreated to a secret, safe location, and from there spent the next several months coordinating with the remnants of the US military, FETF administrators, and the civic leaders of any remaining pockets of civilization big enough to notice via satellite surveillance, for as long as possible as their resources ran out and riots tore apart their efforts.

After that the President and his remaining staff had turned their focus away from domestic crises, to address the increasing threat of the Gold Bloc and the deal they were strong-arming Canada into. As his position steadily weakened he did his best to find diplomatic solutions that would prevent the failing US from being invaded, and give them some hope of being able to rebuild in the near future.

It had been his decision to keep the troops in Canada guarding the crude oil being produced there, held ready in the event of the US finally restoring refining capability. He was also the one who'd overseen the construction of those refineries until those efforts, too, fell apart. Then at that point he'd scrambled to prevent the incomplete structures from being looted or vandalized, while trying to negotiate help for the construction projects from other countries with ever more generous promises of shares of the refined gasoline and diesel.

Most importantly, he was the one who'd kept up peace and trade negotiations with the rest of the world, searching for aid and trying to keep the vultures from circling. The threats to the Gold Bloc, with all out nuclear war as the only card the nation had left to play, had all come from him.

If the rebroadcast from Hill Air Force Base could be believed, yesterday's catastrophe had all started when the President issued yet another ultimatum. This one held the same message as the others, i.e. "do what we say or we'll nuke you", but the tone had been far more dire.

The US's final threat to the Gold Bloc had given them one day to pull their forces out of the US entirely, or at least make a convincing enough show of it that the US could trust they'd be gone before too much longer. The President had made it clear that even though the Gold Bloc had called his bluff the previous instances, with the country being invaded and his citizens in the northern states suffering mass incarceration he could no longer afford to bluff and this time he *would* carry out his threats.

As part of his ultimatum the remaining US satellites would be watching the withdrawal of invasion forces carefully, and lack of compliance or any sign of foul play would see every single warhead the US possessed launched in a full spectrum strike at Gold Bloc countries to wipe them completely off the face of the earth.

The Gold Bloc response had been to claim that their forces were engaged in peacekeeping and humanitarian missions, and they flat out didn't believe that the US would trigger global thermonuclear war as a reaction to their presence. They considered the failing country's position to be far too weak.

Their leaders were so dismissive of this newest ultimatum, in fact, that they didn't even bother to broadcast it to the world, and prevented other sources from reporting on it as well to avoid drawing attention to the Gold Bloc forces invading the US and forming massive prison camps. For their part the US government in exile did their best to spread news of the ultimatum, but they didn't have the resources with the Gold Bloc hampering their efforts.

What had followed was a 24 hour period of heated debates as the President held firm on his stance, making it clear that this time he would be ignored at peril to the world. The US literally had nothing left to lose, with what little they had being snatched up by an invading force estimated to number in the millions, or even tens of millions if Gold Bloc settlers were included in the count.

The Gold Bloc leaders, meanwhile, kept confident in their assertion that his desperation showed he was only moments from folding, and that after he failed to live up to his threats following the deadline then real negotiations could begin. For the unequivocal surrender of the United States and the President's aid in calming the populace in lieu of a total takeover by Gold Bloc forces.

Only it hadn't been a bluff. When the deadline arrived the Gold Bloc leadership watched in horrified surprise along with the rest of the world as hundreds of US nukes flew. They hadn't given even the slightest hint of pulling their forces out, and if they'd prepared for an actual nuclear strike beyond launching their own nukes at any worthwhile US targets their preparations hadn't been enough.

The rest was, tragically, history.

The rebroadcast ended, and a subdued voice came on to add the few details that he'd managed to gather since Hill Air Force Base went silent. By all accounts the President's bunker and several other remaining military targets had been obliterated, along with every single nuclear silo, just in case the US had held any of their nukes back. Any remaining population centers of over ten thousand people, mostly along the coasts or in the South, had similarly been targeted. The estimated loss of life was in the tens of millions, and roughly ten percent of the nation was now uninhabitable due to radiation from fallout.

The broadcaster continued on to list losses on the Gold Bloc side, and collateral damage to neutral targets, and here the tally was far more horrific. Unimaginably so. The list of destroyed capitol cities alone seemed to last forever.

To his credit, whoever it was on the other end of the radio hadn't gone the lazy route of just looking at a map and reading off locations; he actually seemed to be giving information he'd gathered over a day of painstaking effort, after getting in contact with anyone he could who knew anything at all. A lot of it had been passed on from other sources, but his report was still an impressive example of careful fact finding.

Such as it was. It was too soon afterwards, and things were far too chaotic, for anyone to have a complete picture on exactly how great the devastation had been. Also there probably wasn't anyone left on the planet who had the sort of birds-eye view through satellites and other communications equipment to give a detailed report.

At best the people he'd been able to contact knew the broad strokes of the situation, and more specifically what had happened closer to home that they could see with their own eyes or report through a trusted source.

One piece of solid information from numerous sources, though, was of a confirmed nuclear strike on the Gold Bloc military camp south of Sault Ste. Marie. That was hundreds of miles away from Greenbush and where Lewis expected Trev and his family to be, but even so it was far too close for comfort. With worry for his loved ones filling his thoughts it was hard to focus on the rest of the report after that.

Lewis had never really stopped to consider how terrifying nukes were. Sure, intellectually he knew the devastation they could cause, and he'd seen the videos of Hiroshima and Nagasaki in his high school history class. He'd watched the horror of the Middle East Crisis unfold in every detail and grieved along with the rest of the world.

But the terror of it was new, fanned to life with the realization that there were, in fact, situations in which humanity was insane enough to unleash that kind of devastation on a global scale. He could no longer sleep easy in the knowledge that the people with their finger on the button would go to any lengths, seek any compromise, to avoid that fate.

Because they hadn't.

And what did that mean? An explosive big enough to destroy an entire city, which could kill him before he even realized it had gone off. And in a horrific way that wasn't even the most frightening aspect of the nuclear blast, because the explosion would spray radiation into the surrounding area for miles.

Sometimes that fallout could be seen, but the smaller particles were often hard to detect with the naked eye, bringing lingering sickness that could lead to a slow agonizing death or an even more agonizing recovery that could take years, if it ever fully happened at all.

The broadcaster on the radio returned to the more local aftermath of the Retaliation after a while, specifically how the Gold Bloc invading forces had responded to it all. Whatever Lewis might think of the name, here at least it was fitting, and that was in the response it had provoked. In the last day the surviving blockheads who'd escaped the targeted strikes on their camps had regrouped, and in many cases began pursuing retribution on the prisoners they'd captured.

In the chaos many of the prison camps had erupted into mass riots and a large number of people had escaped. Those prisoners who hadn't managed to get free had either been left behind to succumb to the fallout, gunned down if they tried to flee to safer territory still in Gold Bloc hands, or simply killed outright in mass executions.

Not satisfied with that horrific bloodshed, the Gold Bloc soldiers had begun chasing down the fleeing prisoners and shooting them on sight. They'd also stopped their efforts of searching for any US citizens still remaining in the areas they moved into, to capture and take to the internment camps, and begun murdering them in cold blood instead. The death toll from these atrocities was already estimated in the hundreds of thousands.

As the horrific details kept coming Lewis looked away, sickened. A lot of those prisoners were people captured in Michigan, and Trev and his family could've gotten caught up in that. The thought was almost too horrible to contemplate, but at the same time he firmly told himself he had to be prepared for the possibility he might never see his cousins or aunt and uncle again.

He wasn't sure how long the broadcast lasted, but at some point he realized with a start that he was hearing things he'd already heard before. His suspicions were confirmed as the crowd around him, which had been still and silent as they listened to the news, began to shift around and murmur to each other, verifying that the message had looped.

Matt turned to look at him, eyebrows raised in question, and Lewis shrugged and nodded. He'd come late to this, but he was pretty sure he'd heard all this before. Before too long just about everyone agreed they'd heard everything they were going to.

Chauncey leaned forward and turned off the radio, hand shaking slightly. Even that effort seemed to tire him, and he seemed relieved to sink back into his chair, scratching at the bandage around the stump of his leg.

"It's awful, but I'm glad that at least we're far away from all of that," Matt said after a short silence.

Lewis shook his head. In some ways they were far away, but in others they were pretty close to smack dab in the middle. And with Gold Bloc forces to the east and west of them the trouble would probably be heading their way before too long, until they really *were* smack dab in the middle.

The mood was already bleak enough, and most of the people here had likely already come to the same realization, so he kept his pessimistic thoughts to himself.

Unfortunately Chauncey decided to speak up in his place. "Not so far," he muttered, gritting his teeth as his scratching fingers moved onto the stump itself. "Closer than any of us would like, and headed our way."

The room sank into an even grimmer silence, and Matt sighed. "I'd sort of hoped the Retaliation would stop their invasion."

Chauncey shook his head. "If anything it forced them into a position where they have no choice but to keep going." He abruptly yanked his hand away from his leg, clenching it into a fist on the armrest of his chair. "Which means at some point we might have to deal with them right here. They're far away at the moment, but that could change fast with the vehicles they have."

Lewis nodded, although he was too lost in thought to speak up. After a short silence Matt turned and stared out the window, as if imagining a convoy of enemy troops driving right down Main Street. "So what do we do about it?"

"Keep our ear to the ground, I suppose," the retired teacher answered. "Be alert for trouble heading our way, and when it comes have the best plans we can think of for how to deal with it."

"Right," Lewis agreed, straightening. "And one of those plans should be for evacuating everyone up Aspen Hill Canyon if need be. We should get everyone together and talk it through."

Matt turned to him. "You mean a town meeting?"

"Eventually. Although first things first we should talk it through with the Mayor and the other town leaders." Lewis glanced at Chauncey. "Should we gather them all up here?"

Their friend grimaced and glanced down at the stump of his leg. "Sure, I'll be around." He tried to make the words humorous, but more than a little bitterness crept in.

Chauncey had made it clear on previous visits that his bitterness was for his situation, not Lewis for suggesting they hit the raider camps or Matt for leading the disastrous attack. Lewis didn't know about his friend, but that didn't help much with the guilt. He knew rationally that the retired teacher had made his own decision and was facing the consequences of it as well as he could, but still . . .

It *had* been Lewis's idea. He would always shoulder a bit of the burden for what had happened because of it.

In the face of Chauncey's bad mood the crowd sort of naturally broke up after that. Lewis said his goodbyes along with Matt, then followed his friend out the door in the direction of town hall. About halfway there Matt abruptly straightened, a grin breaking out across his weary features, and bolted up the street to where Sam had just come outside through the auditorium door, leaving the combined clinic and storeroom that had taken over the large space.

Matt filled his wife in on what they'd heard over the radio, at least until Sam begged him to stop, clearly distressed by the grim news. So as they sought out the Mayor they talked about the work they'd done that morning instead, filling the conversation with more pleasant, hopeful things.

At least until they had to broach Lewis's idea to prepare the town for evacuation in case it was ever necessary. Catherine had been listening to the news on her own radio, since Chauncey had retransmitted it on the town frequency. She clearly wasn't pleased by the idea of another evacuation, remembering the chaos of the one they'd carried out when the raiders first showed up, but she reluctantly agreed that planning the next one in advance would make it go much smoother.

So they began preparing a checklist of things the townspeople would want to do to get ready, as well as dates and times for a few drills so everyone could practice. It was a shame to have to take people from their other necessary tasks for this, and Lewis expected some grumbling. But if a Gold Bloc push into the area was a "when" rather than an "if" the time wouldn't be wasted, and could save lives and leave everyone in a much better position if they did have to abandon their homes and flee up Aspen Hill Canyon into the mountains.

During the planning Jane arrived, finished with her shift at the gardens. She'd spent part of the time caring for their remaining crops as best she could, and part of it on sentry duty in case of thieves or vandals or, more likely since the raiders were defeated, four-legged varmints that were too big for the traps or managed to avoid them.

She came over to stand beside him, content to listen in on the discussion. Although she did have a few tips to give about how to pack and what to bring from her days as a refugee, although she hated being called that and instead described it as "Before my group found a home here."

After the meeting Matt and Sam made their way over to the clinic to visit Terry and April, while Lewis and Jane headed back to the shelter to sleep. They may have gone to bed early yesterday by some standards, but with their schedule of sleeping during the day to patrol at night the rest hadn't been great, even if they'd skipped their patrol to get it. Still, they agreed they should try to sleep now so this night's patrol wouldn't be quite as painful.

Now that they were by themselves Jane felt more comfortable showing signs of affection. She took his hand, and as they walked occasionally leaned her shoulder against his. Lewis enjoyed the opportunity to be close to his wife, filled with equal parts gratitude and disbelief that things had turned out the way they had with her.

Matt and Sam caught up to them halfway home, for some reason hurrying to do so. "Hey," Sam called as the two came in shouting distance.

Jane casually slipped her hand out of his, and together they slowed down to meet their friends. "Hey," Lewis said back. Then he caught their expressions. "What's up?"

"You promised us dinner and a movie, remember?" Matt asked, smiling. Sam nodded emphatically. "How about this evening?"

Lewis bit back a groan. It wasn't that he was too exhausted for the activity, and it did sound nice, but hearing the suggestion while thinking of their impending nightly shift made him feel tired. He was about to answer that, but before he could Jane cut in. "We're going to catch some sleep before our shift starts."

Matt didn't lose his smile. "Yeah, about that. Asking you to do a full shift every night when there are plenty of people who could do it doesn't seem very fair. I know you guys volunteered for it, but I'm officially unvolunteering you. From now on you'll take a shift at most once every three nights. After all, you've got your own stuff to do."

"Like dinner and a movie," Sam said, grinning.

Jane glanced at him, seeming okay with the idea, so Lewis nodded. Patrolling every night *was* a bit much, especially after sleepless days like the last few. "Dinner and a movie sounds nice," he said. "As long as you don't mind us falling asleep halfway through."

Matt laughed. "Are you kidding? If it means you'll finally be able to get some decent rest I'll be happy to tuck you in myself."

Chapter One

Hospitality

The distance from Newtown to Michigan that had taken Trev a bit over 8 days to travel took just a bit under 27 hours driving almost nonstop. That included brief restroom breaks and slowing down cautiously at hills and bends in the road, or any other obstacle that obstructed their sight and could provide an ambush spot.

There was also a heated debate between the driver and the passengers in the cab at every city, and even the smaller towns, about whether to circle around them on side roads or blast through at high speeds in the center of the road and hope for the best. Since they were following Lewis's route for the last half of the trip, which Trev had already traveled once, he was able to say with some confidence which areas they should avoid and which had been abandoned when he came through and were probably still safe.

On the longer stretches they were able to make up time, going the heavy truck's top speed of just over 50 miles an hour some of the way, and averaged maybe 35 or 40mph over the entire trip. Trev spent most of that time in the cab, even when he was too exhausted to stay awake and ended up sleeping, since he knew the route and aside from Lucas was the only one who really knew how to shoot a rifle. There was a bit of grumbling about him commandeering one of the most comfortable seats the entire trip, but everyone agreed he should be up there in case they ran into trouble.

When he wasn't sleeping or driving he spent the time watching the terrain zip by outside. Maybe it was lingering exhaustion, but a sight that should've been familiar somehow felt unreal; after all, he'd spent his entire life driving at these high speeds along highways. And yet in less than a year, much of it spent traveling by foot, this sort of mobility had become unfamiliar and almost miraculous.

He'd taken cars for granted for a long time, even when he'd finally got one himself and could enjoy the freedom it offered. But now, riding in this truck that was carrying his family safely home, he didn't think he'd ever take driving for granted again. Even if things got back to normal, and gas became as cheap as it had been when his parents fondly reminisced of the days of filling up their tank for less than a dollar a gallon.

Trev supposed the old adage was true, that you couldn't truly appreciate something until you'd lost it.

About ten miles south of Newtown they pulled the truck off Highway 83 to have their final debate about whether or not to stop at the town, and if so how they'd go about doing it. It was late afternoon by that point, and the exhausted and deprived group was a lot more amenable to the idea than they had been that morning. Even Mary, who usually just listened and hummed through these sorts of family shouting matches, took a break from some song about taking the plunge to toss in her support of the idea.

In the end they agreed that the gain was worth the risk. It probably helped that Trev had described his hamburger in detail to people who, even before this grueling trip, had been making do on barely edible internment camp rations for weeks, and food storage or fish and game all winter before that.

It never paid to underestimate the persuasive power of a half-pound of well-seasoned and grilled meat.

The only thing left to decide was whether to trust in the sheriff's integrity. They eventually agreed that if they were going in, there was no reason to hide the truck and go in on foot. For one thing there was the risk that someone might discover the vehicle, more than likely a Newtown patrol, and take it from them.

At that point the family could claim it was theirs, but finders keepers would make that claim pretty weak. Especially in light of such a prize. They also didn't want to split up the group by leaving anyone behind to guard it, even though his parents and uncle liked that idea.

The main issue was, again, that if they were going into Newtown they pretty much had to take the opportunity to buy enough supplies to fill the truck. The family need something to survive on, and any surplus they could spare for the town would save lives.

Unfortunately there was no way to purchase that much wheat without rousing suspicions, so they might as well be forthright. If they went in on foot to buy everything and haul it out to some hidden location outside of town, and the people of Newtown decided to go scour the area and found the vehicle, there would be plenty of cause for both sides to point fingers at the other. At that point Newtown had the firepower to back up their side of the argument and they might decide to take the truck anyway.

It was a situation with no ideal outcome. Under the circumstances they were desperate enough that if it came down to it, the family was willing to trust in the integrity of a man who'd done right by Trev in the past.

Although not completely. The one thing they *could* do to make the truck a less tempting target, and offer themselves an alternative if Newtown did steal the vehicle, was hide as much fuel as they could. They'd leave enough in the truck to drive a hundred miles, which hopefully would be enough to avoid suspicion that they'd hidden any extra diesel, and cache the rest.

If Vernon ended up stealing the truck with that amount of fuel it would be a problem but not a disaster, since with any luck they'd be able to find another working diesel vehicle to take them the rest of the way home. They decided to cache the weapons and other captured gear as well, since Vernon would just ask them to check them anyway, and if he ended up stealing the truck it wasn't very likely he'd return them.

They buried everything at the edge of a meadow several hundred yards off the road, carrying it all by foot and being careful not to make a trail. They had to dig with their hands and rocks and cover it with leaves and clumps of dirt once they finished, and it wasn't anywhere close to the best cache Trev had done. But this far from town out in the middle of nowhere he hoped it would be good enough.

Once that task was complete the family continued on to town, with Lucas driving and Trev next to the window with his siblings riding in the space between them. Oddly enough, even though he was no longer alone and had already had a chance to meet the sheriff, Trev felt far more vulnerable than he had during his first visit as they made their way up the old road towards the grain silos shining up ahead.

"Holy cow, they're huge!" Jim said.

Normally Linda would've come down on her younger brother with pure disgust for stating the obvious like that, but she was too busy gaping herself. "Are they really full of food?" she asked hopefully.

"Maybe not full, but close enough," Trev replied. He pointed out the window. "There's one of the sentry posts. They do a pretty good job of protecting the town."

Lucas slowed down, eyeing the spot cautiously. They could barely see the top of a hunched man with a weapon aimed their way. "Should we stop here until they decide what to do with us, so we don't spook them?"

Trev hesitated. "The sentries didn't bother me last time I came in. They let me ride right into town. I guess they don't want to spoil a potential customer's impression of an open trading post too much."

As if to confirm that, the man they were looking at abruptly stood and lowered his rifle, waving them on into town. Trev waved back as his uncle continued forward, still driving slowly.

However friendly the town might've wanted to look, when they reached Fred Vernon's house at the edge they found four men waiting with the sheriff behind a portable riot control barricade of reinforced Plexiglas. A quick glance around showed several more men in ideal sniper spots. A tack strip had also been laid across the road, looking oddly out of place.

When they were still twenty feet out Vernon stepped forward and held out one hand, and Lucas slowed the truck to a stop as the sheriff cautiously approached the driver's side window. Vernon's expression and posture were friendly enough, but he kept his hand on his weapon the entire time.

"Been a while since I saw a running vehicle," he called, giving a low whistle as he looked the truck over. "Lucky my boys aren't the sort to shoot first and ask questions later; you caused quite a stir driving up in a blockhead truck. It *is* Gold Bloc, right?"

"Captured," Lucas answered. "We're US citizens, and we're not planning on causing any trouble."

"That's good to hear." Vernon reached the window and looked past Lucas at Linda and Jim, eyes softening slightly at the sight of the younger passengers. Then he saw Trev and gave a start of surprise, peering closer. "Hey, didn't you stop here a few weeks ago? Came on a bicycle, checked that .45?"

Trev nodded. "Yeah. Trevor Smith. Good to see you again, Sheriff. We're on the trip back and want to buy some supplies."

"Well I see you've upgraded from your last ride!" Vernon tucked his thumbs behind his belt and grinned as he looked the truck over again.

"Yeah," Trev answered. He tried to think of something else to say, but before he could the sheriff turned back to his uncle.

"That's probably a story worth hearing. Later." He offered his hand. "Fred Vernon, Sheriff of Newtown."

Trev's uncle quickly shook. "Lucas Halsson, Trev's uncle. These are my other niece and nephew. My wife, sister, and brother-in-law are in the back with my daughter."

"Well I'll be honest, you folks look pretty rough." Vernon sniffed slightly. "And smell it too. We can offer you hot water, clean clothes, food, and beds for reasonable prices. First, though . . ." His eyes strayed towards the northeast. "You folks have any news? We've got what people are saying over the radio, but given everything that's happened it just doesn't seem like much in the way of information."

"Not much news, but some stories," Trev answered, ignoring his uncle's warning look. "We saw a mushroom cloud, from closer than any of us would like."

Vernon casually but hastily dropped his arm away from the dusty vehicle, giving it a cautious look. "We've got Geiger counters and iodine tablets too, if you need it. We'll probably want to sweep you before you go any farther to make sure you're not bringing in any contaminants."

"Right," Lucas said. "I hadn't considered that possibility, sorry."

"That's fine." The sheriff turned and called an order to one of his deputies, who immediately turned and ran off down the street. "Shouldn't take long. While we wait we can get the formalities taken care of, then maybe you'd be willing to share some of those stories you've got."

With Vernon's encouragement they got everyone out of the truck and Lucas introduced the family to the sheriff, who insisted they call him Fred. The man had his other deputy bring a couple jugs of water, which they quickly passed around the group taking eager, grateful gulps until their thirst had slackened. As they emptied the jugs Fred laid down the town's rules and checked them and the truck for weapons.

Not too long after that the deputy showed up with an ancient looking Geiger counter and ran it over them. To Trev's immense relief they barely registered above background, and the truck also checked out. Everyone else looked relieved as well, especially his aunt, who'd admitted that she'd been looking for symptoms of radiation sickness in every discomfort over the last day or so.

"Looks like you won't need those iodine tablets after all," the sheriff said, waving his men away now that he was satisfied the newcomers didn't pose a danger to the town in any way. "Unless of course you wanted to stock up on some in case of future need. Which wouldn't be the worst idea under the circumstances."

"We just might," Trev's dad answered. "We had to leave a lot of things behind and have lots of stuff we'll need to buy, if it's available."

Fred grinned. "That's what I like to hear." He turned and waved towards his house. "Why don't you folks stay with me tonight? I can make up some extra beds, and have Westman bring you over a hot meal from his grill."

"We don't know how to thank you," Clair said, looking overwhelmed.

The sheriff's grin broadened. "You can thank me by making big purchases tomorrow. Welcome to Newtown."

*****

Fred proved to be an ideal host. After a flurry of activity getting everyone their own beds set up in a comfortable number of rooms, he saw that they got enough grilled steaks and instant mashed potatoes, complete with fresh butter, to satisfy them.

While they ate he boiled up water on a wood burning stove in the kitchen, providing them with soap and clean washcloths so they could wash up. He also handed out enough t-shirts and sweatpants for all of them, and offered the services of one of the townspeople to wash their clothes and dry them overnight. Last of all he pointed the way to his bathroom, which was a similar setup to the one Trev had used in the Newtown Bar and Grill.

Once all those tasks were taken care of the sheriff politely invited them to let him know if they needed anything else and retired to his study, where he'd set up his own bed. He good-naturedly waved off their effusive thanks, and aside from promising to take their dirty clothes to be washed once they'd washed up and changed they didn't hear from him for the rest of the night.

More comfortable in the presence of just family, everyone took care of all their basic needs and indulged in the unexpected luxury of washing themselves and putting on clean clothes. The mood of the group that had been tense and borderline argumentative all day finally lifted, and there were a lot more smiles. Even laughter, especially when Trev, his siblings, and their cousin caught sight of their parents looking unfamiliar in their new pajamas.

Although everyone admitted they were a huge improvement on the coveralls they'd been forced to wear in the internment camp.

As everyone else settled into bed Trev headed out to check on the truck and make sure everything was secure for the night. Lucas had locked the doors and the gas tanks before they went inside, but it didn't hurt to double check.

His dad announced he would come along, and together they went over the vehicle. Afterwards Trev took a moment to stand on the porch, watching the sun lowering towards the horizon over the unkempt fields beyond the town. Even exhausted as he was it felt good to be on his feet after sitting for so long, and his dad seemed to have the same idea as he came over to stand beside him with his hands on the railing. "Hard to believe the sun still rises and sets after yesterday," he said quietly.

Trev nodded, letting a contented silence stretch on for a few minutes.

After a while his dad turned to rest a hand on his shoulder. "It's hard to say what needs to be said sometimes, but I just wanted you to know how much it means to all of us that you risked your life to come and find us. When that machine gun was tearing after you yesterday, when it seemed impossible you could survive-"

His dad sucked in a sharp breath, mild features twisting in sudden grief, and he pulled Trev into a fierce hug. "I'm just glad you're okay, son." Trev hugged him back, tears pricking at his eyes. Especially when his dad continued. "Everything you've been through, everything you've accomplished . . . you can't believe how proud I am of you. I just wanted you to know."

Trev tried to reply, but the words wouldn't come through the lump in his throat. After a bit his dad pulled away, and together they watched the sun sink towards the ruined fields. By mutual unspoken agreement they went in to sleep not long afterwards, before the sun had fully set, and as Trev pulled Vernon's gifted blankets around him his exhaustion hit him with the weight of the truck parked outside.

He slept like the dead for almost ten hours, and still felt like he could go back to sleep if he wanted when he opened his eyes to a predawn glow trickling in through the window. It wasn't much, barely enough to see his hand in front of his eyes, but he resisted the temptation of his comfortable bed and pulled himself into a sitting position.

As far as he knew he was the first one awake. He sat in the predawn darkness for a while, savoring the quiet outside and the peaceful sounds of breathing and soft snores from his siblings, before finally reaching over to pull on his boots.

Careful not to wake Jim and Linda he got to his feet as quietly as possible and slipped out of the room, then down the stairs and through the front door into a morning so early most would still call it night.

The air was crisp and chilly, and as far as he could see no one but him was up yet and no lights were on in the town. He shivered slightly, wishing he had a jacket, and hurried over to check on the truck and make sure none of the diesel had been siphoned.

As far as he could tell it hadn't, and the clumsy inspection he made, mostly by touch, reassured him that nothing had been stolen and the vehicle hadn't been tampered with. He had half feared he might find Westman and his barflies poking around while the town slept, and it was a relief to see that nothing was amiss.

"Not much fuel in there."

Trev jumped a full foot, and it took all his willpower to not shout in surprise as he whirled towards the front porch he'd just walked across. The sheriff was there reclined on his porch swing, a dark shape in the darkness. It was no wonder he'd missed him on his way out.

"Yeah," he said cautiously. "Enough to make it home, I hope."

Fred's voice came from the darkness again, sounding thoughtful. "Hard to scout in all directions with no vehicles, but we've followed all the roads hereabouts for at least a hundred miles while scavenging. Must've missed where you live in all that."

He wasn't about to take that bait. "I suppose if we can't make it the entire distance, we'll find a way to haul our supplies the rest of the way."

"Fair enough. Got to do what you have to in the world, way it is now." A sudden twinkle of flame appeared with a metallic clink as the sheriff cupped a lighter to a cigarette, and when the flame disappeared the end glowed orange as he took a deep drag. "Suppose it's useless to ask, but would you consider selling? We mostly want the fuel, but we'd give you good money for the vehicle too. Your choice of precious metals or supplies, enough to set up your entire family here in town for years."

Trev fought an uneasy surge of suspicion, telling himself it was a fair offer and he couldn't blame the man for trying. "Newtown seems like one of the better places to live," he admitted. "But we've got family and friends who need us."

"Yeah, I can understand that too." Fred took another drag, an exhaled plume hiding the glowing tip for a moment. Trev could smell the smoke drifting his way in the darkness. The sheriff abruptly patted the bench next to him, which Trev heard more than saw; a thump of hand on padding. "Not much else to do this early in the morning. How about you tell me the story of how you came by this Godsend? I'll admit, I've been dying to hear."

With a shrug Trev made his way over and sat. Fred offered him a cigarette and he shook his head. "No thanks." With an easy nod the sheriff settled back into an expectant silence, so Trev settled back too and told his story.

He couldn't think of any reason not to. The Gold Bloc was Newtown's enemy as much as everyone else's, and he felt he should do something to repay the kindness Fred had showed in inviting them into his house and feeding and clothing them. That was almost unheard of generosity in these times.

The sun was just moments from rising when Trev finally finished. Fred had a few questions about Gold Bloc movements he'd noticed, and the way the enemy treated their prisoners. He was obviously really worried about news on the radio that the Gold Bloc were continuing their invasion, and concerned about the danger to Newtown.

It didn't seem like it would be a problem any time soon, this far out in the middle of nowhere. But who knew how fast the blockheads would move?

They were interrupted by the sounds of people stirring inside, and the older man sighed. "The Retaliation, they're calling it on the radios. April 26th, a day no one will ever forget."

Trev hadn't known either of those things. He could've asked Lucas the date while in the internment camp, he just hadn't bothered. "One we shouldn't," he agreed.

Fred gave him a sharp look. "The blockheads definitely won't. They're already tearing through the poor people they had trapped in their camps, and hunting down any who escaped in the confusion like you and your family. Most all those folks don't have the luxury of a vehicle, and it doesn't look good for them."

Trev nodded and looked away. He'd had a good idea of what the others who'd escaped the internment camp would be facing, but he'd avoided thinking about it.

"Doesn't look good for us either, if we stay put," the older man continued in a softer voice. He abruptly stood up, looking rumpled and tired in the wan predawn light. "But that's neither here nor there. Let's see about getting you folks breakfast, then we'll head on over to the General Store and see about getting this truck of yours stuffed with goodies."

That suggestion improved Trev's mood slightly. He appreciated the sheriff's hospitality, but the sooner they were on their way back home with what they needed the better he'd feel. He stood as well and followed the man inside.

Chapter Two

High Price

Fred treated the family to a generous breakfast of pancakes with butter and syrup, as well as fried strips of potted meat. Then, after everyone had changed into the freshly laundered clothes he'd taken care of for them last night, he once again proved himself a good host by offering to walk along with the family up to the General Store, while giving them a tour of the town along the way.

"It'll be a good chance to stretch your legs before you go out on the road again, and Lucas can bring the truck up to meet us there," he said with a smile.

Trev's parents and aunt and uncle exchanged glances. "We wouldn't want to keep you from your duties," his dad said.

The sheriff waved that off. "Are you kidding? With the purchases you guys plan to make you're VIPs, the town wants to roll out the red carpet for you. Besides, it's only neighborly." He started ushering them out the door, grabbing his cowboy hat as he went. "My boys can handle the town for a few hours on their own. I'm pretty much just a glorified greeter as it is." He said that last with a chuckle.

To Trev's surprise the town had completely woken up since his early morning conversation with Fred, going from deserted to bustling in just a few hour's time. Townspeople were out and about doing morning chores, chatting, or buying and selling. More than a few had set out their wares on blankets and were acting as impromptu vendors. He even saw Westman out in front of his bar, grilling hamburgers and hot dogs for a few waiting customers.

The sheriff noticed him staring at the crowds and grinned. "Bet you thought the place was a ghost town during your last visit."

"Sort of," Trev admitted. "I know there's enough houses for hundreds of people, but I didn't see anyone but you."

The sheriff shrugged. "Timing, that's all. We keep a pretty strict work schedule to make sure everyone's pulling their weight, and you just happened to show up during the middle of the day's main shift. Pretty much everyone was busy, aside from the few layabouts you ran into at the bar."

"Makes sense."

Fred waved at the vendors and townspeople going about their business. "Morning and evening is when we do the most trade. Travelers tend to arrive late and stay the night, so it works out best for everyone. In fact, we've got a few groups in who arrived yesterday evening to trade."

"Trev mentioned the town's gained a solid reputation," Lucas observed, glancing around as he headed for the truck to meet them at the store.

"Yeah, we have," the sheriff answered, looking slightly annoyed. Maybe he thought that reputation was being questioned. "In fact, we don't get many people just passing through these days, since almost all our visitors come specifically to trade with us. Your nephew was actually one of the rare exceptions on his last visit." He smiled. "And your visit this time supports the trend. Let's get started, shall we?"

They drew more than a few stares as they made their way down the street, and many of the townspeople called out their wares as they passed. It was mostly scavenged junk by the looks of it, but there were a few things that caught their eye. Fred didn't give them a chance to browse, though, briskly continuing on towards the store as he gave them a bit of the new town's history and pointed out a few of the more notable buildings.

As Trev followed the sheriff up the street his eyes were drawn past the early morning bustle to the defensible positions Newtown had set up around the town. Maybe it was just his time spent taking shifts at the roadblocks back in Aspen Hill, but it seemed natural to double-check the town's defenses.

Oddly enough most of the positions were abandoned, with only two lookouts that he could see. The last time he'd come through they'd all been manned, an odd contrast to the previously deserted town, and now it was the opposite. Maybe this was how they ran their shifts in the morning. Either way he trusted Fred knew what he was doing, so he put it out of his mind.

By the time they reached the General Store near the silos they'd drawn a crowd of dozens of townspeople trailing along after them, drawn by the spectacle. The crowd's main attention was the truck, though, and as Lucas drove it up the street and into the General Store's parking lot he even drew a few cheers, like it was a parade. Trev supposed a vehicle was a rare sight these days, worth gawking at, but he hoped the crowd didn't get any ideas as Fred led the family inside to help them find what they needed.

A few people did, drifting into the store after them. Those curious and hopeful townspeople introduced themselves, struck up conversations, offered valuable personal possessions to sell, or subtly probed the family about the possibility of buying their way onto the truck when they left. Fred put a stop to that pretty quick by shooing everyone else out and having a few of his men wait by the doors to keep order, leaving them to make their purchases in peace.

Trev had noticed those deputies hanging around outside the store, maybe to keep order with the morning bustle. Aside from the lookouts he'd spotted earlier they were the only ones he'd seen. Another oddity of the morning shift probably.

His family wasted no time in spreading through the store searching for specific items to meet their needs, although he saw more than one stop to look closer at something that had caught the eye. Trev never thought he'd be along for a shopping spree after the end of the world, but this came pretty close.

The first thing Lucas did was head over to where Deb and Clara waited behind the counter. Deb looked excited by the morning's events, and had waved to Trev and called out a greeting when he came in, while Clara seemed more impatient at all the bother.

After his uncle introduced himself to the two women he got right down to business confirming the value of his gold coins. It turned out, like Trev had learned before, they were still trading pretty well. After that it wasn't so much a matter of deciding what they could afford but of what they needed and had room to take with them.

Wheat came first. Trev and his dad went out to the truck to do some simple calculations on how much space a sack of wheat took. They decided to use sacks rather than buckets, even though they wouldn't store as well long term that way, because it was way easier to fill every square inch of space with grain in cloth sacks. Besides, there were plenty of empty buckets available at home. As for weight, they were pretty confident the rugged vehicle could handle whatever they put in there, short of something like a full load of lead bars.

It turned out they could fit thousands of pounds in the back, stacking sacks right up to the tarp at the front half of the truck bed and halfway up the rest of the way. That created a fairly flat surface where the people who'd have to ride in the back could sprawl, packing the other things they planned to buy around them.

Definitely claustrophobic, but in a way comfier than the hard benches over long periods of time. While the rest of the family got everything else Trev and his dad started hauling the wheat out and packing it in, helped by Max and a couple other General Store employees. Even Fred pitched in for a few trips.

With the wheat taking up most of the space they had to be selective about what else they bought. They focused on getting a few sets of rugged clothes each, complete with boots, socks, and underwear, along with coats, gloves, and warm hats for when it got colder. They also got backpacks, tents, sleeping bags, several full 5-gallon water jugs, a water purifier, and other useful camping supplies.

Lucas purchased the only AK-47 the store had available. Then, or so it must've looked to Clara who was assisting him, he went way overboard buying ammunition, magazines, cleaning supplies, and spare parts for the rifle. That was probably a bit suspicious, but Trev couldn't argue that those things would all be useful for their three other captured weapons. Especially the ammo, which his uncle bought the store out of.

Trev's mom had made a find of her own, several dozen packets of heirloom seeds. Coming back from one trip carrying wheat out to the truck Trev paused to admire her discovery and compliment her own it.

She beamed, although she looked a bit wistful. "It's a shame we lost everything back at the house. I had all the seeds I'd purchased ahead of time, all the way before the Gulf refineries attack, for this year's garden. And I had all the seeds I managed to harvest myself from the garden last fall. And all the extras I had laying around in case I wanted to expand the garden or plant a different variety of crops." She shook her head in frustration. "A lot of potential left behind."

No arguing that. His mom's garden had spanned over a quarter of an acre, complete with stone paths and a bench tucked away in a bower beneath an arched grape trellis. She'd spent hours and hours working on it, while Jim and Linda had complained about being roped into working on it too a few times when he talked to them.

Her dream had been to learn enough to make it self-sustaining, so she could maintain it without needing to buy new seeds and plant everything again every year. She'd gotten very good at harvesting seeds and getting cuttings, and from what he'd heard on his rare visits their neighbors often came to her for help with their own gardens. Or to harvest the fresh produce she generously offered them.

It was probably the most significant thing their family had been forced to leave in Greenbush. Those lost seeds were worth their weight in gold, and the garden could've fed them all with a bit of fish and game to supplement their diets. But there was no point looking back.

"Lewis has a pretty good stock of heirloom seeds," he offered. "We've got our own garden plot going back in Aspen Hill." He gestured to the packets she held. "These will definitely help, too."

She nodded and tucked them into her cart, then paused to hug him and kiss him on the cheek before continuing on to search for more sundries that would be useful when they got home. Trev's siblings, cousin, and aunt were doing the same, although he was amused to notice that Jim and Linda had dragged Mary into a conspiracy to fill a cart with seriously overpriced snacks for the trip.

The blond young woman went along gamely, although she was nervously humming a song he didn't recognize. From context it probably involved kids getting a whupping from their parents after they got caught misbehaving.

Finally, even though there were plenty of other things worth buying and they all glanced wistfully at what they'd have to leave behind, the family filed out of the store to finish loading the truck while Lucas tallied up their purchases and paid up.

They still had to consider the remaining containers of diesel they'd left behind that they needed to go back for, which would take up some space. And while they could stand being packed to the gills if they had to, having a bit of room to stretch their legs wasn't the worst thing in the world.

Fred continued to pitch in as they finished the loading, then stood back and whistled while Trev and his dad made a few final adjustments and shifted some things around. "Looks like you got her just about full up."

"Pretty much, once we've got ourselves in there," Trev agreed, hopping down to stand beside him looking at their handiwork.

The sheriff squinted up at the truck bed, then sauntered over to the cab to peer inside at the stuff they'd packed into the foot space. "I'd say you did a good job of gathering up the necessities. Just the sort of stuff I'd pack along if I was going to head to greener pastures." He paused. "In fact, it looks like we won't have to add much to what you've loaded."

The comment was so offhand, spoken in the same friendly tone that Trev didn't get it at first. Then he stiffened. "What?"

Fred rapped the truck's hood with his knuckles. "I want to buy this. By which I mean I'm going to buy this. I'd like to give you one last chance to say yes of your own free will."

That knock seemed to have been some sort of signal, because a dozen of his deputies, all heavily armed, abruptly converged on the truck. They weren't quite waving their weapons around, but they definitely had their eye on Trev's family and the crowd of townspeople.

Most of the men went to the locked boxes in front of the store, where customers could safely stow their belongings while they shopped, and began pulling out fully loaded duffels to toss into the vehicle. Others climbed into the back of the truck and began tossing out a few of the sacks of wheat to make room for their things, also dumping the clothes his family had purchased that they didn't seem to need. Everything else in the truck they kept.

The men who'd been keeping the peace in front of the store had disappeared inside, and before too long one emerged herding Lucas, Deb, Clara, Max, and the other employees who'd helped load the trunk in front of him at gunpoint. Inside the store the rest were hastily stuffing more duffels with anything of value.

That seemed like pretty solid confirmation that it wasn't just Trev's family Fred Vernon had betrayed. When the crowd of on looking townspeople realized it they broke into murmurs of confusion and growing anger, and a few shouted out accusing questions.

Vernon ignored them, eyes still on Trev. He looked back miserably, unable to find any anger or outrage within the overwhelming numbness that had enveloped him. The man's honesty in returning his silver at the end of the last visit, his hospitality in taking them into his house, his generosity feeding them and helping them get the things they need and load them into the truck, all ultimately served to make this theft seem almost inevitable. Like this was the way the world was, now.

"I can't believe you decided to rob us after all," he said, trying to hide his bitterness. "We were your guests."

The sheriff's eyes narrowed. "Not robbery. I'm making a purchase, and I'll give you a fair price for it. I'm just not giving you a choice in the matter." He casually drew his 9mm, not quite pointing it directly at Trev as he jerked his head towards where Lucas and the employees waited near the front of the store. "If you and your family will head on over there, please?"

Trev reluctantly complied, giving Vernon's men space to continue their work. "Why the pretense of letting us buy everything and load the truck?" he demanded. "Too lazy to do it yourself?" It probably wasn't a good idea to antagonize the man, but he couldn't help himself.

It was Clara who answered, spitting off to one side as she did. "That playacting was for us, wasn't it Fred? So you could get the truck mostly loaded without tipping off the town that you meant to rob and abandon us, same as you're doing to these poor travelers. Where's all your other deputies, the ones who aren't complete cronies? Got 'em locked away somewhere while you skedaddle?"

So not all of Newtown's defenders were in on the sheriff's plot. That would explain why the town's defenses had been unmanned. Trev silently cursed himself for not paying more attention to that when he'd noticed it. They'd probably been at Vernon's mercy from the moment they entered the town, but with a little forewarning they might have found some way out of this.

Vernon scowled at Clara's question, although beneath the fierce expression it almost looked like his conscience was acting up. "The Gold Bloc is about to swarm all over this country, madder than a swarm from a kicked beehive after the nukes destroyed their homes. Anyone with half a brain will be making for Mexico as quick as they can. Nothing personal, but I wanted to get out ahead of that and this truck's the perfect opportunity."

"What about your reputation as an honest, law-abiding sheriff?" Lucas asked. He was obviously angry, but he managed to keep his tone somewhat even.

The sheriff, or Trev supposed former sheriff, shrugged. "Doesn't mean much to have a reputation as sheriff of a ghost town. Which is what this place will be if you take my advice and get while the getting's good."

As Vernon continued he reached into his pocket and pulled out a heavy clinking sack. "But I do pride myself on fairness and honesty, so here: twenty 1oz. gold coins as payment. No idea how much a truck like this is actually worth, but I'd say that's a generous price for it. Especially since by your nephew's own admission it's stolen." His eyes narrowed. "Now, considering that I could've just taken it and booted you all out of town with nothing I'd say I'm being pretty fair. So don't make this any more difficult than it has to be."

Lucas accepted the money, looking resigned. "I guess we should've expected that a working vehicle would be too big a temptation for even an honest person to pass up. Although you won't get more than a hundred miles with the fuel in it." Trev couldn't help but admire his uncle for making one last effort to dissuade the man from robbing them.

"Don't push my buttons, Halsson," the former sheriff snapped. "You think I'm stupid? You all show up in a stolen truck with no weapons and barely enough diesel to get out of spitting distance of this town, looking to buy enough supplies to set yourself up wherever you're going. Don't think I didn't notice you in there buying enough ammunition, spare mags, and other stuff for three more AK-47s."

Trev felt his heart sink. That number was suspiciously specific.

Sure enough Vernon continued and confirmed his fears. "Last night I had my boys head down the way you came up, scouring every square foot within a hundred yards of the road. Took most of the night, but we found the extra fuel you'd hidden, along with the weapons, body armor, and riot gear."

So that was it. Their last precaution in case of just this situation hadn't been enough. If Vernon had the diesel he had every reason to steal the truck and take it as far south as he could. He might even be able to reach Mexico with the remaining fuel.

Vernon turned away to oversee the last of the loading. Once he was gone Lucas slumped down to lean against the front of the General Store, opening the sack to check the coins inside but showing little real interest in them. "They look real," he mumbled.

"It's a joke, paying us for something he's stealing from us." Trev kicked at the shed's corrugated steel wall, making it ring with a dull *poing*. "This is my fault. I'm the one who guaranteed this town was safe."

"It was, when it was just you." His uncle shook his head. "It's easier to find trustworthy people when you have nothing major to steal. We knew this was a risk when we came here."

Trev's dad sighed and slumped down beside his brother-in-law. "Best to accept it's all lost and figure out what to do next. We've still got 700 miles to go, on foot it's looking like. We need the supplies to make it that distance and some way to carry them."

Eva started to cry, and Clara came over to put an arm around her. The store employee looked like she was on the verge of tears herself. "I'm sorry this happened," she mumbled. "I just can't believe he would do this."

Trev looked at her, and at Deb and the other employees in their own little huddle nearby, then to the crowd of townspeople that had doubled in size and was still growing. Vernon's sudden turn had been bad for Trev's group, but for the people of Newtown it had to really be pulling the rug out from under them.

The man they'd trusted to defend them was taking all their most valuable possessions and leaving them to fend for themselves. Trev tried to imagine if Matt and some of the Aspen Hill defenders had done this, and just couldn't. He couldn't believe his friends and neighbors were capable of it.

These people had probably thought the same up until fifteen minutes ago.

A few braver or more foolish townspeople in the crowd called out curses and threats as Vernon and his men finished loading the truck and began piling inside. The former sheriff did his best to ignore the resentment directed his way as he made his way over to Trev. "I'm glad to see you didn't try anything."

Trev couldn't hide his glare. Try anything . . . as opposed to what? They'd left their weapons behind, but even if they hadn't they would've had to check them in to get into town. And if somehow neither of those were the case there was no way they could fight so many people, especially when it would put the rest of the family in danger. Their only option had been to trust in Vernon's integrity.

When he didn't respond Vernon continued. "We'll be going now, but before we do I wanted to wish you luck with whatever you decide to do. I'm sorry things had to turn out like this."

Seriously? Trev couldn't believe the guy could still stand there and pretend to be reasonable after what he'd done. He knew it was pointless, and possibly a bad idea since he might anger the sheriff turned thief, but he couldn't help himself. "You think apologizing matters when you do it anyway?"

Just about everyone in his family shot him warning looks at that, and Vernon's eyes narrowed. "It's not all bad, now," he said. "Maybe after this you'll decide to stay in Newtown after all. You're welcome to have my house, I won't be needing it." He tried for a hearty chuckle and failed miserably. "Heck, you can even take over as sheriff if you want. You've got all that machine gun dodging experience you told me about, right?"

Trev grit his teeth. "I thought you were one of the few people left with some integrity."

The sheriff's eyes narrowed in a sudden flash of annoyance, although his voice remained amiable. "Guess you thought wrong. It wasn't an easy decision, mind you. I was up most of the night debating it, but in the end I couldn't pass up the opportunity of a truck and fuel. Not with the blockheads swarming south towards us. Don't you remember me telling you you got to do what you have to, way the world is now?" Trev had obviously pricked the older man's conscience, because he quickly looked away and turned to leave.

Deb abruptly bolted forward from where she'd been standing with the other employees. "What about us?" she demanded. "We trusted you!"

The former sheriff paused for a moment, giving the woman a look of equal parts guilt and annoyance. "The town still has plenty, and everything we're taking is what we've earned. You should be grateful we looked after you as long as we did, kept you alive through the winter. And if you have any brains you'll pack up and follow us south as quick as you can."

He opened the driver's side door and hauled himself behind the wheel, slamming it behind him. The engine rumbled to life a moment later, and Vernon began carefully backing it around the piled sacks of wheat and other things his men had tossed out to make room for them and their stuff.

Before driving off, though, he paused for one final word to Trev's family. "I'm no thief!" he called, in defiance of all evidence to the contrary. "We'll be taking your fuel because we need it, but the AKs and other stuff we'll leave behind. You're free to hike out and grab it."

The truck lurched into motion rumbling down the street towards the highway, leaving the town behind. Trev watched them go, still doing his best to keep all the helpless rage he felt at the situation bottled up.

They had 700 or so miles to go, with the invading Gold Bloc forces getting closer by the minute. The former sheriff hadn't just taken their vehicle, he might have sentenced them to their deaths.

And it was all Trev's fault for vouching for the man.

*****

"He left us," Clara said numbly, staring south as if she could still see the departed truck. "After swearing to protect us, he and his men took everything useful and ran off. How could he do that?"

The General Store employees had wandered over to join the rest of the townspeople, who for the most part were still shocked and disbelieving at what had just happened. They'd left Trev and his family to gather up the few things Vernon had dumped from the truck, along with what they'd been carrying on them, which the former sheriff had allowed them to keep. Those were all the possessions they had left.

Some members of Trev's family had shaken off their daze quicker than Newtown's residents. "He took our *truck*," his mom said, finally releasing her pent up anger as she rummaged through the spare clothes they'd purchased. There were a few small things there, like the packets of seeds she'd put in a pocket for safekeeping, but not many.

Even though she didn't look his way Trev still hunched his shoulders slightly at her outburst. She may not have meant it as an accusation but it might as well have been one, since this had been his idea and he'd pushed for it.

Lucas had started piling up the few sacks of wheat, the motions calm and deliberate. But when he replied his voice also shook with anger. "We knew it was a risk. We did our best to minimize that risk but it wasn't enough. So now we forget about it and focus on what we're going to do now."

Trev wasn't willing to let it go like that. His family had been safe in Greenbush all winter, and the Halssons had been in Norway, so they wouldn't have known better. But he should've. How many times had he been robbed? How many times had people tried to rob him? He should've known better.

"We need to go get our guns," his dad said, letting the sack he'd halfheartedly lifted sink back to the ground. "If he was telling the truth about leaving everything but the fuel behind we should go after it."

That was a good point, although the weapons wouldn't be nearly as useful since Vernon had taken their new AK-47 and all the spare magazines, ammo, and other stuff Lucas had purchased. One of the former sheriff's men had been toting an AK, and he'd wanted all of that stuff for it.

Which reminded him. Trev glanced across the street at the townspeople. It looked like no one had stepped forward to take charge in the confused mass of people. The main emotions in the crowd remained uncertainty and fear, as well as the growing groundswell of outrage and resentment. With Vernon gone it seemed as if they'd lost their sense of purpose, and maybe their backbone too. He wasn't sure what they were going to do now.

"Do you think they've thought to release the deputies Vernon locked up?" he asked.

Lucas shrugged. "If so that's their business, not ours. I doubt they'd appreciate us sticking our noses in. Besides, we have our own problems to worry about."

True enough. Trev abruptly stood. "I'll go after the guns."

His uncle nodded and reached into the parcel of extra goods he'd been holding onto when Vernon's man kicked him out of the store. He pulled out a full water bottle, handing it over. "You'll be walking half the day to get there and back, but I suppose we don't have a choice."

"Thanks." Trev hadn't thought of water, but with twenty miles to go he was glad Lucas had before he could take off and regret his lack of foresight a few miles down the road.

His dad was also nodding his approval of the plan, even as he turned to look behind him at the General Store. "In the meantime this is still a trading post, or at least I hope it is if Newtown's people will cooperate, and Vernon left us quite a bit of money. We'll try to purchase new supplies and see what we can do about transportation. Hopefully when you get back we'll be ready to go."

Trev grimaced. He wasn't looking forward to walking the 700 miles to Aspen Hill, including going over the mountains west of Denver and retracing the most brutal part of his trip. A few weeks of spring might've melted some of the winter snows away by now, but probably not enough. Good thing Vernon had at least left their winter gear.

As he started down the street in the direction the truck had vanished Deb broke away from the townspeople and came over to him. Her eyes were slightly red, as if she'd been crying or at least fighting not to. "Hey," she said. "You okay?"

Under the circumstances? "Yeah," he answered. "Are *you* okay?"

She nodded, although her expression grew even more miserable. "I'm so sorry. I was so proud of this town for the way we treated newcomers. For the way we treated each other. And you know, from the very beginning Fred was the example that inspired us all to be better. Then he did this!" A tear finally slipped free, and she wiped it away almost angrily.

"I'm sorry too," Trev said. He felt like there was more he should say, but he couldn't think of it. "What will you do now?"

"How should I know?" she said, rubbing at her eyes again. "I looks like we need to go, but I don't know where. Or how. I guess we'll have to talk it over and figure it out."

Trev nodded, again trying to imagine if Catherine and Matt and Chauncey and more of Aspen Hill's best people had suddenly abandoned the town. Aspen Hill might just shatter if that happened, especially during a crisis.

Since he couldn't figure out what to say or do he awkwardly extricated himself and continued on. At first at a walk, but before he'd even left town he found himself jogging, and having to consciously make the effort to not break into an outright run. Most of what spurred him on was his frustration at the situation, although the knowledge of the distance he had to travel and the fact that they couldn't continue on for home until he returned helped keep him going.

Anger and urgency both faded after the first mile, and he finally allowed himself to slow to a walk for a while until he could catch his breath to jog again. He might not've been in tiptop shape after the stress of the last couple days, but at least the two meals Vernon had fed them before the former sheriff pulled his stunt had given him the strength to keep up a good pace.

He alternated jogging and walking as the sun rose higher in the sky, marching on toward noon. It took him about two hours to reach the poorly hidden cache at the edge of the meadow, and by the time he got there he was tired enough to stop and take a serious rest.

Which took the form of him plopping onto his back halfway across the meadow, staring up at the clear blue sky above him until it stopped wobbling at the edges of his vision and his breath sounded a bit less like a rasping wheeze.

Then he got up and strode the rest of the way to the meadow's edge.

Vernon hadn't been lying about finding the cache through their poor job of disguising the spot where they'd buried it; the hole had been dug up again and everything taken out and strewn across the grass. The cans of diesel were gone, of course, but once again true to the former sheriff's dubious word everything else they'd hidden was still there.

Trev wearily began gathering things up, then put his mind to the unexpected task of figuring out a way to carry it all. Like with the water, he hadn't really thought through how he was going to lug 3 rifles, 2 flak jackets loaded with gear, and a full suit of riot gear including crowd control tools the 10 miles back to town.

"Fantastic," he muttered. "It's just one thing after another." And the worst part was he couldn't blame anyone but himself for the situation, since it was all thanks to his own poor judgement. Not to mention lack of planning and foresight. If Lewis was here he'd be facepalming himself into a concussion at what a mess his cousin had made of things.

After what felt like way too long he managed to rig one flak jacket with various straps and belts to tie everything else onto it, in a cobbled together mess that could almost charitably be called a backpack. It certainly weighed enough to remind him of his overloaded backpack on that disastrous first trip after the Gulf refineries attack.

To make matters even worse the weight was poorly balanced and the left shoulder of the jacket dug into his skin more and more with every step, no matter how many times he adjusted it. Before too long the skin was rubbed raw, and he sincerely hoped the trickles he felt under his shirt were from sweat. Eventually he bunched the shirt under the strap in a way that was tolerable enough to continue.

Tiring himself out running to the cache meant he went even slower on the way back, and was forced to take a ludicrous number of breaks to rest and remove the jury rigged pack. Thanks to that the trip that had taken a couple hours there took almost five to get back, which meant midafternoon was getting on towards late afternoon by the time he left the highway and trudged up the old worn road leading to Newtown.

He noticed that the town's defenders were back in their emplacements outside the town, so they must've been freed from wherever Vernon had stowed them. Trev was glad to see they were still taking their duties seriously even after their leader's betrayal. A few waved as he passed, although from the way some stood just staring at him he had to guess they had mixed feelings for the guy who'd brought the truck that had let their sheriff ditch them.

His first view of Newtown was a bit of a surprise, although maybe it shouldn't have been. It looked as if a whirlwind had torn through the town while he'd been gone, with a chaotic jumble of items strewn around where the townspeople had emptied their shanties and crudely built homes of any possessions small enough to take with them, or necessary enough to be worth the extra effort.

The Newtown General Store looked as if it had been completely stripped of its goods, anything useful taken away and everything else tossed in a pile in front with people poking through the rubbish searching for whatever had been overlooked that might be worth taking. And the large silos looming over the town were swarming with figures that looked tiny in comparison, who seemed to be emptying out the grain into sacks and other containers to take with them.

None of that was unexpected. Vernon bailing on his own people would paint a pretty clear picture of just how much danger the town was in, so it figured that the townspeople would be preparing to evacuate.

What *was* unexpected was that the people of Newtown were loading their possessions into dozens of handcarts, which looked as if they'd been crudely built from car trailers or from the chassis of stripped vehicles to make crude wagons.

Trev hadn't seen any of these carts and wagons the last time he'd been here, but it could be they'd been available and he just hadn't been looking. After all, a town that was setting itself up as a trading post and offering tons of grain for sale would want to have a way for customers to haul their purchases away in a world where fuel was scarce to the point of nonexistence. He could actually admire the ingenuity required to get good use out of useless cars and trucks.

To his delight, his family had managed to purchase two of those makeshift handcarts for themselves, along with two smaller wagons. He found them waiting in the parking lot of the General Store, organizing a few last things in the carts. From the looks of it they'd managed to purchase more wheat, at least as much as they could carry, along with a few tarps to protect the sacks from the elements.

Lucas winced when he saw Trev limping into the parking lot. "Ouch. I didn't stop to think how much all that stuff weighed. I should've gone with you."

"It's okay," Trev said, wearily letting the pack slide off his shoulders to lean against the cart. He could probably lift it up inside, but he really didn't want to go to the effort at the moment. Instead he leaned against the makeshift aluminum siding of the cart and rubbed at his left shoulder.

"It's not okay," Linda protested. "We need you able to push a cart!"

Trev couldn't help but shoot his sister a dirty look. It was true, sure, but she could've put it more tactfully after he'd just got finished lugging almost a hundred pounds for 10 miles. "All by myself, huh? What do those weigh, a thousand pounds each?"

"Just with the wheat alone," his dad confirmed.

Trev winced. The carts had been cleverly made but they still looked fairly heavy. Which meant all told they'd be lucky if two people could manage one for any amount of time, and it would probably require at least three people. Meanwhile the smaller wagons weren't nearly as large or sturdily built as Lewis's, and were each holding 4 sacks of wheat or 200lbs. That weight wouldn't be terrific to haul, but compared to the carts he could almost envy whoever had the job.

Eight people should be enough to manage all that, barely, although they wouldn't be able to rotate out anyone for rests and would all have to take more breaks. But even if it was doable Trev didn't look forward to the grind.

Going on paved, mostly level roads would help with that a lot, but he remembered how difficult the trip up to the hideout had been and couldn't hope that good roads would be enough to make the difference. None of his family were used to walking long distances or hauling heavy loads the way he was, and while they'd adjust in time the first days were going to be brutal.

Still, there was no time like the present to get to it. Trev groaned slightly as he grabbed the makeshift pack he'd lugged all this way and heaved it up onto the cart. "Okay. Let's get going."

"It's not a race," his mom said, half stern and half concerned. "We've got a long way to go and you look like you can barely stand." She handed him a strip of jerky, which must've been hard to trade for with the entire town packing up to move, as well as another water bottle.

Trev knew that. He'd already learned the lesson about not pushing himself numerous times, he just hadn't been thinking clearly since Vernon took the truck. So he accepted the food and sat down against the rubber tire of the cart to get what rest he could as his family continued with the final preparations.

While he was eating a small group of townspeople approached them, including Clara and Deb. "We're getting the caravan together," the man in the lead called as they closed the final ten yards. "We just wanted to know if you'd be joining us."

His parents and aunt and uncle stepped forward to meet them halfway. "Depends on where you're headed," Lucas replied.

The man grimaced. "South. Not following Vernon, though . . . wouldn't mind it if I never saw that guy again. But he was at least right that the blockheads are coming from the north."

"We're heading west," Trev's mom said. "We've got family to get to. Although I suppose if any of your people are planning on going that way we'd be happy to travel with them."

The man glanced back at his neighbors questioningly, then shrugged. "Haven't heard of anyone. I think most of us are going to stick together if we can. Safety in numbers, and even if Vernon tarnished Newtown's reputation I'd still say we've got a good community. One worth keeping together. If anyone is headed west we'll send them your way."

There were handshakes all around. "I hope you manage to find a safe place to rebuild," Trev's dad said by way of farewell. "Thank you for your kindness and generosity."

The town's spokesman grimaced again. "It's an unpleasant situation all around, but you folks seem decent enough. I'm sorry you got dragged into all this, especially when you gave us your trust."

*****

Fifteen minutes later the family set out, dispirited but determined.

Trev and Jim started out pulling one handcart, aided by Linda pushing from behind, while his dad and uncle hauled the other with Mary pushing from behind and his mom and aunt did their best with the wagons.

It was a somewhat imbalanced setup, skewed on the idea that Trev was the strongest and had the best endurance out of the group and needed to handle more of the load. His two siblings gave it all they had, but they weren't quite strong enough to make up the difference and Trev ended up with a lot of the weight. That was something he was willing to handle, but it meant that in spite of the help the job was far more difficult than even towing Lewis's wagon last fall had been.

Unfortunately it was just as difficult for the rest of his family, meaning their progress was slow and painful even starting out.

Trev learned from Jim and Linda as they went that there'd been a fierce debate among their family about whether to go for the handcarts or purchase bicycles. Newtown had enough decent ones for their family to ride, but doing so would've meant leaving behind just about everything since no bicycle trailers were available and Vernon had taken all the store's backpacks. It would be a faster trip, but in many ways a more difficult one.

In spite of that Lucas had argued for the bikes. If the rumors they'd heard in Newtown were true then the surviving Gold Bloc forces were pushing southwestwards hard behind them, trampling the fleeing internment camp prisoners in their path as they rushed to capture objectives before any sort of resistance to their invasion could be mounted.

Their uncle didn't want to be stuck on the road pulling wagons with the idea of enemy soldiers close behind, which is why he'd pushed for the bicycles. Even though they couldn't outrun trucks, at least they gave enough speed to possibly outrun an army that had to deal with complex logistics.

Mary and Jim agreed with him, while Trev's dad was on the fence. But his mom and aunt insisted that they'd have a tough time of things if they arrived in Aspen Hill with no food, and if the town was already suffering then at best they couldn't expect any help, and at worst they'd be an added burden. Besides, they'd already purchased the supplies Vernon had left them with and it would be a waste to leave them all behind.

Linda agreed with them, and also argued that with so many bikes something could go wrong with one, which would make the rest useless since they could only go as fast as the slowest person in the group. Everyone who supported going on foot could also point out that ultimately they'd already sacrificed speed by losing the truck trying to get these supplies, and it didn't make any sense to abandon that purpose now when the handcarts were available.

Eventually the rest of the family came around to the position of going on foot. The time they'd made in the truck had put a healthy buffer between them and the chaos behind them, and even Lucas admitted that the Gold Bloc soldiers would be dramatically slowed down if they tried to take and hold territory as they went, no matter how they rushed to take things quickly. As long as the family pushed hard every day they should be able to get to Aspen Hill long before there was any danger from the enemy behind them.

Trev was kind of irked that he hadn't had a say in the decision, especially since he probably would've voted on the side of taking bikes. But the family had needed to decide on something and he wasn't around, so they'd picked the best choice they could.

Now, watching their maddeningly slow progress as they reached Highway 23 and started west, he saw even more confirmation that they should've gone with the other option. At least to his mind, although it seemed like the realization of just what they had in store for them sinking in on the faces of his loved ones as well. They had an almost unfathomably long distance to go like this, and while they might get stronger as time went on they also had to worry about possible injuries or illness that would slow them down. Not to mention sheer exhaustion.

It would be pointless to say he'd told them so when he hadn't had a say in the matter at all, even though he was the only one with any real experience going on difficult journeys with bikes *and* on foot hauling wagons. With the decision already made throwing in his opinion now would just make everyone more miserable. All he could do was shoulder his burden and do his best to keep everyone's spirits up as he got them physically and mentally prepared for a long, long trip.

At the very least he could estimate that in the month and a half or so it would take them to get home at this pace they'd only eat through a quarter of their 2,400 pounds of wheat, leaving them with roughly 1,800 if all went well. They'd have to work much, much harder to get that food home, but once they did they'd be in a better position than if they'd made the journey on bikes with nothing at all.

He just hoped Aspen Hill didn't desperately need them for something before then, and the pursuing Gold Bloc troops really were so bogged down by their conquests that they didn't have time to trawl smaller roads out in the middle of nowhere.

But it was pointless to worry about anything but the trip ahead, so he positioned his right shoulder more firmly on the push bar and continued on, each laborious step taking him and his family closer to home and safety.

Chapter Three

Meadows

It was Lewis's idea to go out the third day after the Retaliation.

He and Jane were more rested than they'd been in over a month. The evening they'd spent with Matt and Sam had turned into binge watching movies until he and Jane both fell asleep on their beanbag chair and, he assumed, his friends shut everything down and headed off to bed themselves.

Knowing that they didn't have to worry about a patrol anytime soon had led to a surprisingly restful night, where he slept far longer than he usually would have, and when he woke up in the morning he found Jane going over her gear and happily joined her doing the necessary repairs and maintenance on his own, a much more thorough job than he'd been able to do for a while.

That was just the beginning of the day, since being free from patrols didn't mean that there weren't still plenty of things to do. Stuff they hadn't been able to give their full attention to before now, since most of their time had been spent sleeping or walking their routes outside of town.

The gardens needed work, and looking after the traps while they were there, and they had the rabbit hutch to work on and hunting that could be done. There was also plenty still to do to make the shed a bit more comfortable and secure to live in. And while they were at it, it couldn't hurt to think about building a new structure to relieve the crowded conditions inside the shelter itself. Matt's family and Jane's group were enduring the situation with good grace, but there were definitely no objections to the idea of expanding the living space.

And it would be nice to spend more personal time with his wife without feeling like it was being stolen from more pressing issues. He cherished the time they spent patrolling together but it wasn't exactly restful or relaxing. The previous night had been a nice change from that, definitely something he could get used to.

If nothing else he had his radio and current events to keep up on, although that was a depressing way to spend the time these days. Or he could delve into his hard drives for a book to read or listen to.

All of that was far too much to do in one day, and a lot of it would require ongoing effort. But he'd gotten a good start on it, enough that he felt a bit more comfortable setting everything aside for a full day to do something else. Something he and Jane had both been wanting to do, and now that they had time to work with they agreed to give it a try.

So after another full night of sleep they got up early, collected the bicycles he'd purchased from the storehouse as part of his payment for the cache he and Trev had sold to the town, lightly packed only the most necessary gear for a short trip, and got ready to head up Aspen Hill Canyon.

There were plenty of reasons to go. They wanted to look for good hunting spots, they wanted to do some more long range and thorough scouting above the town for things they and the townspeople would find useful or might be a threat, and most of all they wanted to venture farther afield and find the Norman family's lost herd of sheep, which seemed to have disappeared after the raiders scared them off.

The plan was to travel light and put some real miles behind them, exploring the smaller backroads in the mountains west of town. If the snow had cleared off the higher roads they might even try traveling all the way to Highway 31 to check on the hideout, with the plan of returning to live there again at some future point if necessary.

Jane really liked the idea of wintering there after hearing him describe his time spent in the mountains with Trev. And much as Lewis loved his cousin and enjoyed his company, he had to admit that the prospect of spending the frigid months confined in that small space with his wife instead was a lot more appealing.

Finding the sheep was the main priority for this trip, though. The herd had a big head start on the people searching for them, and had likely retreated up to familiar grazing grounds in the high mountains to escape whatever fright had accompanied the violent capture of their shepherds. No one knew exactly where those grazing grounds were, but Lewis knew the area fairly well and had some ideas.

Now that he and Jane had the free time and some bicycles they wanted to check those spots out.

They invited Pete Childress to come as well, since the young man had devoted so much time to finding the lost animals after they'd beaten the raiders, and Tom Harding and his son Alvin were familiar companions from other hunting trips and seemed happy to come along. They also invited Matt, half expecting their overworked and overburdened friend to refuse, but surprisingly Matt almost ran to retrieve his old bike from the shed at his family's house and get it working.

Lewis could tell by Sam's obvious disappointment that she wanted to go, too, but they were going to be pushing themselves hard to cover ground and he wanted to spare her that in her condition. Not to mention there was no telling what sort of work they had to look forward to if they actually found the herd, facing the prospect of bringing it back down the canyon.

Which was all rational, but Lewis was still relieved when Sam took the news with good grace, admitting that she really was feeling too tired to be biking dozens of miles up steep mountain switchbacks. She assured them she was happy to keep to her original plan for the day, getting the new hens and rooster they were getting from Jack Dawson settled in with Henrietta in the chicken coop Lewis and Matt had finished the day before yesterday.

The group set out not long after breakfast, the reminder of their dwindling food stores serving as an incentive to get something done today. Almost immediately Pete rode ahead and set the pace up the canyon, determined to find the animals that had eluded him for so long. He was familiar enough on his bike that he spent almost as much time waiting for them to catch up as he did making his way up the steep winding road.

Lewis considered himself in the best shape of his life in spite of lingering weariness and slight malnutrition, but even he found the pace brutal. As for Tom, the older man was looking gray in the face by the time they reached the top, and from Matt's frequent concerned glances it was obvious his friend was on the verge of telling him to turn back.

"Maybe we should slow down," Lewis suggested as they took a breather and admired the view. He didn't do it completely for Tom's sake, but because they were well away from Aspen Hill now and needed to spend a bit more time searching the area. Not only for possible threats but also for anything the town could find useful. Scouting was one of their goals up here, after all, and that was hard to do while zipping around on a bike.

Pete didn't seem happy about the suggestion, although he stuck with the group when they set out again. At least until they reached the first fork in the road, where he pulled off and stopped several feet along the dirt path that branched off to the left.

"Maybe we should split up to get more searching done," he suggested. Then, almost before the words were out of his mouth, he took off.

Matt stared after him, not looking too happy himself. "Well there he goes," he muttered.

Tom scratched at his stubbly chin. "Should one of us go with him?" he asked. "We shouldn't be letting anyone run off alone."

"He's been alone on most of his trips searching for the sheep," Jane pointed out.

The younger man was already nearly out of sight. Lewis grimaced. "I'm not sure any of us could keep up with him."

Matt shook his head firmly. "I'm with Tom, we don't want anyone up here alone. Even if it means chasing him around all day." His friend looked over at him and Jane. "You two want to go?"

Not the worst idea. The two of them probably had the best chance of keeping up, and with any luck they'd be able to keep the more reckless youth out of trouble. "Sure. Keep your radio handy." Lewis nodded to his wife and they took off down the dirt path.

The road was still mostly uphill, but compared to the slope up the canyon it felt practically level. Lewis actually enjoyed giving in to his impulse to pedal fast and feel the crisp mountain air whistle around him, a grin spreading across his face. The day was cool and nearly perfect for light exercise, and the snow had receded from the slopes surrounding them. Wildflowers were starting to peek out through green grass that would rarely reach that deep shade of color throughout the rest of the year, even when it was rainy.

This was the sort of thing he'd loved to do before the world went crazy, spending an entire day or even multiple days as he left his shelter on foot and hiked and camped wherever his mood took him. If he was really in the mood to get lost in nature he'd take his truck up to some higher point and go from there, or go all the way to the hideout and roam beyond familiar territory to explore the steep mountain slopes that seemed to go on and on.

In spite of that constant roaming he'd been a relative tenderfoot when it came to survival skills, but he'd done his best to prepare for any disasters he might encounter, and hadn't let his inexperience keep him from doing what he enjoyed.

A bit of guilt niggled at the back of his mind, telling him he shouldn't be this content after the horror of the Retaliation. He accepted that guilt, and the genuine grief and sympathy he felt for those who had suffered in the last few days, but he also decided to put it all aside for the moment. He'd been in a fog of grim purpose since the raiders arrived, faced with death every day and struggling to his limits to do what needed to be done.

Now, with something as simple as riding a bike beside his wife on a mountain road, that fog had lifted. It would probably come back, when they returned home and the weight of how profoundly the world had changed and everything they'd need to do to survive those changes settled on him again. But for now it was a relief to be free of it.

He looked over at Jane and saw a wide grin on her face as well, and when her light blue eyes met his he had a feeling she felt the same. She'd needed this as much as he had.

Since Jane had started out slightly ahead of him she soon naturally assumed point, as if they were on patrol. Which was a good mindset to have these days. She set the pace and scanned the way ahead for possible dangers, as well as any sign of Pete, while Lewis rode a bit behind and to her left and focused on the landscape to the sides, as well as the occasional glance behind.

There wasn't much to see aside from slopes lined with scrub brush, and the occasional stands of trees growing along meadows blooming into spring growth. But he didn't let the enjoyable view dull his caution as their pursuit of their wayward friend dragged on for fifteen or so minutes with no sight of him.

At that point Lewis saw a 6-point buck partially obscured by trees in the meadow to their right. He gave a low whistle, doing his best not to let the sound carry, and Jane glanced over her shoulder at him while slowing. When she saw what he was looking at she came to a stop entirely and let him catch up.

"That's tempting," she said.

Lewis nodded. His and Trev's remaining food storage had entirely run out a few days ago, and he and Jane also had everyone else living at the shelter to worry about. That meat would provide a few good meals for all of them.

It would also be a huge hassle to move with them on their bikes, not to mention it would signal the end of their search for Pete, as well as for the elusive herd of sheep. He shook his head regretfully. It was tempting, but not tempting enough. "Maybe it'll still be there on the way back."

His wife nodded in agreement, and without another word started off again. Lewis caught up and got back to scanning the area to the sides and behind them.

A few minutes later they finally caught up to their friend at the top of a high point along the road, where the young man's bike lay on its side in an awkward place. Pete was sprawled on his back beside it, and Lewis couldn't tell if he'd crashed, had finally gotten winded and decided to take a breather, or had just decided the spot would be a good place to have a look around.

Either way, he was glad they'd caught up to the idiot before he ran them a merry chase around the mountains.

Jane slowed down, glancing back at him, and Lewis took the cue and continued on to his friend while she stopped nearby and got out her binoculars to inspect the area. He dropped his new bike on its kickstand beside the downed one and went over to stand with his shadow covering the young man's face.

"About time," Pete said, opening his eyes and squinting up at him. "You decide to have a picnic or something?"

Lewis was pretty sure they hadn't been more than a minute or so behind, and he wasn't in the mood for banter. "Go ahead and ditch us without a word if you want, but it'll make me think twice about inviting you along next time."

"All right, I get it," his friend snapped, then sighed and sat up, brushing reddish-brown hair out of his eyes. He hadn't had a haircut in a while and was getting pretty shaggy. Lewis wondered if that was because, with the young man's parents gone, there wasn't anyone to give him one and he was too shy or proud to ask.

That simple reminder of what their friend had gone through recently was enough to take the edge off his annoyance, and he resolved to offer Pete a mirror and some scissors when they got back. He'd also try to find a circumspect way to see if April might be willing to give the young man a haircut: Matt's sister had been helping with that when it came to everyone living in the shelter, and she didn't do too bad a job.

While he was at it, it might not hurt to look into other needs his friend had neglected since being left alone. Pete did a good enough job of acting independent that it was easy to forget he was still practically a kid; Alice, about his age, had immediately been taken in by another family in the same situation, but somehow Pete had been overlooked.

As far as Lewis knew he was still officially sleeping in the storehouse, with the few remaining defenders who'd been left homeless after Turner's missile barrage and the families the town had temporarily moved there. Although more often he slept out in the wilds in his search for the missing sheep.

Lewis reached into his pack and pulled out a couple strips of dried meat, offering one to the young man while he began gnawing on the other. Pete was almost too quick to accept it, and immediately began gnawing on his as well. "Have you searched this area before?" he asked.

Pete nodded. "Although it took way longer without a bike. That's why I'm in such a hurry to get past where I've already been while I have one."

"Let's get going, then." Lewis started for his bicycle.

He'd just hopped on and Pete was in the middle of getting on his own when Jane abruptly made a warning sound. "Shh! Listen."

Lewis froze, straining to hear past the soft susurration of wind in his ears and the rustling of the grass and trees around him to catch the elusive sound. Almost before his brain recognized it as a truck engine he found himself riding hard across the bumpy meadow towards the nearest source of cover, a small thicket of scrub oak. Pete was almost as quick to react, while Jane had a head start of ten feet on them.

Weeks of being terrorized by raiders in vehicles had left them all with an instinctual caution bordering on paranoia when it came to that noise.

Within 30 seconds they'd got themselves concealed, weapons prepared as they listened to decide whether they should stay hidden or if they could risk making a break for it without being noticed. During that time Lewis whispered into the radio to let Matt and the others know what was going on, and alert them to the possible danger they might be in if they were anywhere in the area or there was more than one vehicle out there.

After a brief pause Matt replied. "We don't hear anything from where we are."

Lewis nodded, although his friend couldn't see. "Not surprising. It sounds like it's coming from farther ahead, well away from the road you guys took."

"Do you think they're Gold Bloc?"

"I really doubt it. From what we've heard, even with the ground they've taken since the Retaliation the invading forces are still at least a state away from us in either direction, and anyway this sounds like only one vehicle. I don't think they'd overextend that far just to explore backroads in the mountains of central Utah." Lewis fell silent, straining his ears. He could still hear the engine noise, but was the vehicle still getting closer? There was a nearby road that came close to this one but went off a different way.

"Whoever it is, we should assume they're unfriendly," Matt stated. "You guys are a bit closer to town than us, can you radio in a warning?"

"From this distance?" Lewis turned to look doubtfully down at the valley far below. "Maybe if we had a direct line of sight."

"Try to get it, then. If there are trucks driving around the area then Aspen Hill needs to be warned."

"The noise is getting farther away," Jane reported. She had a look of intense concentration mingled with slight annoyance, as she did her best to listen to the vehicle over the racket of his radio conversation. Lewis doubted his wife would appreciate him telling her the expression was really cute, but darn it, it was.

He listened to verify her statement for himself, then nodded in agreement and relayed the information to Matt, finishing with, "We're going to backtrack, and maybe do some trailblazing to find a good radio spot. If we have to we'll send someone down the canyon, but I doubt we'll need to go that far."

"All right. We'll keep going along this road until we have some solid reason to turn back. Maybe once you guys finish warning the town you can head after us so we're all together in case there's a threat."

Lewis wanted to suggest his friends just abandon their search and head back, but if the vehicle was on the road he thought it was on then it wouldn't come anywhere near them or the town in either direction it went. Not unless it drove twenty or so miles out of the way to reach a connecting road. "Be careful."

They waited until the noise of the engine had faded entirely, then pushed their bikes back to the dirt road and hopped on. The slight uphill slope he'd had no complaints about on the way there was even better as a slight downhill, and they coasted a good deal of the way, keeping their eyes out for any sign of a solid line of sight to the town below.

After ten minutes or so they found one, a spar of rock thrusting out of the hillside in the middle of another scrub oak thicket above a steep slope. Pete volunteered to brave the dense brush, which had a tendency to catch on clothes and skin with branches and roots that barely bent and were nearly impossible to break without serious effort or tools.

Lewis was only too happy to let his friend make the climb, and Jane made no objections either. They watched from the road as Pete slowly and laboriously wove his way through the thicket, at one point cursing and holding up his forearm to display a long scratch. After what seemed like forever he finally reached the spar and clambered out to the point, where he stood holding out his radio for long enough that Lewis was afraid the effort had been wasted.

More to feel like he was in the loop than anything Lewis swapped to the town frequency. He could hear his friend's voice loud and clear, but there were no replies.

At least as far as he could hear. To his relief, from the way Pete was talking he was either playing a prank on them or he'd managed to contact someone down below. Their friend gave the pertinent details, then repeated them a bit impatiently as if the reception was bad, and finally said a few farewells and signed off. Once that was done the young man lowered his radio and turned to give them a thumbs up, then picked his way back down the spar and through the thicket to rejoin them.

“You reach Chauncey?” Lewis asked as their friend crouch to grab his bike.

“Nope. Ben was on patrol west of town, up on a hilltop taking a breather. He passed the news on to the Mayor.”

“Well that's taken care of, then,” Jane said. “Unless the Mayor wanted us to do something.”

“Nah.” Pete grinned. “Just to be careful. And find the sheep.”

They set off, making their way the remainder of the distance to the fork in the road and heading up the branch Matt and the Hardings had taken. They rode hard, and even with the head start their friends had on them Lewis was confident they could catch up. Tom would slow the other group down a bit, and Matt was good about conserving strength with a realistic pace. It might take a while, though, and until then they kept their own eye out for anything worth noticing as they rode along.

A half hour passed, then an hour. With the noon sun hovering overhead Lewis was just about to suggest they stop for lunch and a rest when his radio crackled with Matt's voice, distorted by distance or interference from the hills between them.

". . . news! We . . . signs of sheep!"

Lewis glanced at his companions and grinned as he replied. "Nice! How old?"

"Hard . . . say, but maybe . . . days. We can . . . faster than . . . though. Catch them . . . end of the day."

"All right, see you soon." Lewis paused to get a drink from his water bottle, glad to see that the other two did the same, and then they set off again at the same pace.

Pete, unable to contain himself, let out a few exultant whoops as they rode.

*****

It turned out Lewis underestimated Tom's endurance.

Sure, the other group had a huge lead on them. Even so, it took the better part of the afternoon of steady riding at a strong pace to catch up, following the landmarks Matt described and closing the gap foot by foot. They got to the point where Lewis found himself looking at the lowering sun and, even accounting for a better pace on the downhill return trip, concluding it would be after dark by the time they got home if they turned back now.

That wasn't the worst thing in the world. They'd all brought their camping gear just in case, well aware that they might have to roam far to find the Norman family's missing herd. In a way Lewis looked forward to the prospect of camping in the mountains, even with the temperature already starting to drop and bound to get pretty chilly by morning. There was a peace and contentment up here that reminded him of good days in the past.

In fact, he was a little tempted to suggest that their third wheel continue on alone and catch up to the rest of the group, so he and Jane could set up their own camp and enjoy an evening together out in nature. But since they had no concrete idea of how far ahead Matt and the others were he kept the idea to himself.

Besides, they needed to find the sheep and get them back to Aspen Hill. Now wasn't the time for a relaxed camping trip.

They encountered the signs their friend had mentioned around midafternoon: swaths of trampled, short cropped grass where the sheep had grazed, scattered dung, and broken branches in thickets they'd passed through. From that point Matt's landmarks weren't really necessary, although he kept calling them in so they could measure their progress catching up.

The sun was only a few lengths above a higher peak to the west, an early sunset that would lead to a long twilight, when Matt finally called in that he'd found the herd. Lewis put on a burst of speed, ignoring his exhaustion, and Jane and Pete didn't complain as they kept pace.

Just after sunset they reached a rise in the road, which overlooked a nice sheltered meadow full of grayish-white sheep with a handful of brown ones standing out among the herd. The Normans had gotten around to shearing them all before the raiders came, and the short wool hadn't snagged nearly as much dirt and debris as it otherwise would've so they all looked fairly clean and healthy.

Lewis counted 19, which meant roughly a third of the Normans' herd had been killed or lost in the last few weeks since the raiders scattered them. That was less than he could've hoped for, but more than he'd expected.

They walked their bikes down to where Matt and the Hardings were waiting a reasonable distance from the herd, so as not to spook the sheep. There they quietly congratulated each other, especially Pete, who'd been searching longer and harder than anyone in town.

Finding the animals was good news for Aspen Hill, but it was also good news for them personally. Catherine had agreed that anyone who found the flock or aided in bringing it back to town would be given one sheep each as a reward. There was some grumbling at the announcement, about finder's keepers and the town claiming the remaining animals, but it couldn't be argued that anyone had a better claim. Or for that matter that everyone wouldn't benefit more equally if the herd was cared for by the community.

It was also a fair assumption that it would take multiple people to bring the herd in, so it was possible the town wouldn't get quite as many of the sheep after all was said and done.

"It looks like we've got 2 rams, one adult and the other a few months old," Tom said. The older man didn't have more than a passing knowledge of sheep, but he'd raised goats for a few years and that experience was better than none. "The rest are ewes, all still young enough for breeding I think. Not too surprising since usually only one or so rams is kept to maintain the herd, and the Normans sold the wethers and older ewes to the town for meat over a month ago."

Alvin nearly danced with excitement as his father spoke. "Dad thinks a few might be pregnant, too!" he said. "That means the herd is really a bit bigger than it looks, right? Or it will be soon?"

All of that was good news, since it meant every one of the sheep was potentially useful for growing the herd. The Normans had been raising them for wool, which would be their best use, but if need be they could also provide meat in an emergency. Maybe even milk, although ewes weren't supposed to be great producers unless they'd been selectively bred for it.

Lewis wondered how the Mayor would feel about rewarding them with the pregnant ewes. That would be an unexpected boon, especially since ideally at least one of them would need to take one of the rams as their reward if they wanted to start their own herd.

Of course, it was probably not the best idea to count their eggs before they hatched. They still had to get the herd back to Aspen Hill, with only Tom's limited experience with goats to go on. At least the older man had assured them that sheep were for the most part more docile than goats and would tend to stick together.

"What's their mood?" Lewis asked. At Matt's confused look he motioned to the generous distance between them and the nearest animals. "Have you tried getting closer?"

"Not yet," Matt admitted. He glanced at Tom. "We agreed that since it's so close to nightfall we'd set up camp now and start moving the herd back to town in the morning."

Lewis could get behind that idea. The idea of trying to figure out shepherding during the twilight hours sounded just awful, and they wouldn't get the herd very far before they'd have to stop anyway. There was also the fact that the sheep seemed to be settling down for the night themselves, clumping together for warmth with the few lambs stubbornly frolicking away then returning to the group until they, too, settled down.

"Why don't we set up camp next to the herd?" Jane suggested. "If we're careful we can give the sheep an opportunity to get used to us being around without spooking them, which should make things easier in the morning."

Lewis glanced at Tom, noticing the others doing the same. The older man shrugged. "Worth a shot. We can at least see how close they'll let us get and set up there. Get that water heating up under the frog before we bring it to a boil."

Decided, they slowly approached the sheep, calling out friendly and inane greetings in low, calm tones. Whenever one of the animals spooked, usually by scrambling to its feet and standing there with ears pricked ready to bolt, they'd stop where they were and keep talking to each other in the same calm tones.

The Normans had done a good job caring for their animals, and while the sheep were skittish at first they didn't seem overly frightened of humans. The bolder of the lambs, the young ram, even came over to nose at them as they reached what they decided was a reasonable distance. The little guy scampered back to his mom as they began lowering their bikes and getting out their tents, but soon he was back nosing at the cloth and nibbling on the tent poles.

Jane soon had the lamb nuzzling her hand as she petted it, and Alvin and Pete managed to keep it in place long enough to pet it as well. That was a reassuring sight to see, and gave Lewis some hope that getting the sheep back to Aspen Hill the next day wouldn't be too hard after all.

After a quick meal they all agreed to turn in early, tired from the ride, and split off to their tents for the night. Lewis fell asleep to the soft rustle of animals moving nearby and the occasional *baa*. They were some of the sweetest sounds he'd ever heard.

Chapter Four

Herding

Lewis's group started early the next morning, wakened by the noise of sheep grazing around their tents. The animals still didn't seem bothered by the presence of humans as everyone ate breakfast and broke camp, and once they were ready and holding their bikes they all looked at each other in silent question.

Finally Tom snorted, wheeled his bike around to the side of the herd opposite the direction of Aspen Hill, and began slowly and calmly walking towards the animals.

At first the sheep didn't seem to care, but after the older man whistled a few times they finally started drifting away from him towards the road, *baaing* to each other in mild complaint. A few started drifting off to one side to continue grazing, and Alvin wheeled his bike around to usher them back towards the herd.

Once the sheep reached the road they started to cross it, and Lewis pedaled over to try to steer them back towards the road. Unfortunately he moved too quickly and too close and spooked the animals, so before he could get where he wanted to be they began trotting off at a diagonal from him and the road both.

Jane, observing from farther up the road, circled far around to get in front and to the side of the oncoming animals and with some whistling managed to get them headed towards the road again, where Pete and Alvin waited to hem them in and keep them from crossing back to the original meadow. It took a bit of finagling, but finally they managed to get the herd moving down the road the direction they wanted at a decent pace.

Herding sheep wasn't exactly rocket science, but that didn't make it easy, either. They had to be in constant motion around the edges of the small herd, keeping the strays from breaking away and bolting off, which at best meant the stray had to be rounded up, and at worst could lead to more of the sheep making a break after the stray to keep together.

Jane proved to have the temperament for that sort of task, keeping cool and calm even when the animals balked, and more importantly keeping her tone soothing as she talked to the sheep. Lewis wasn't able to stay quite that levelheaded, but at least he managed to keep his temper bottled in so he wouldn't spook the herd.

Matt . . . not so much. The first time a stray got past their friend he made the mistake of chasing it rather than trying to circle around and head it off back towards the rest of the herd. Which caused the sheep to bolt in fright, leading him on a merry chase for several minutes as he shouted after it angrily.

Even on his bike he had trouble keeping up with the running animal, and whenever he closed the distance the stray would veer away in an unexpected direction. He'd have to brake hard, unable to skid on the grass, and then pedal even harder to catch up again. From what Lewis could see Matt's efforts weren't doing any good, and probably quite a bit of harm as the fleeing sheep got more and more frightened and exhausted.

Finally the animal rejoined the herd on its own. Once Matt realized it he hopped off his bike and pushed it back towards them, stomping and muttering angrily about whether it was even worth it to bring in all of them. Their friend's bad mood was so apparent that even the sheep noticed it, and he couldn't get to within twice the distance of the rest of them before the herd started shying away nervously. Which led to other strays breaking away and even more hassle.

Finally Lewis pulled his friend aside. “Someone needs to ride ahead and let Aspen Hill know we're bringing the herd in. They'll need a fenced in area, fodder, that sort of thing.”

Matt glared at him. “Are you just trying to get rid of me because I'm making a mess of this?”

“A bit of both,” Lewis admitted, trying not to smile.

His friend didn't share his amusement. “One of these ewes is going to be mine, and we'll probably keep our own herd together. I need to learn how to handle them so I can help you.”

“There's plenty of time to learn. For the moment you should probably give them some space until you can earn their trust again.” Lewis leaned far off his bike and clapped him on the shoulder. “It *is* important that the town gets a place ready for them. And if you've got any spare time you could maybe see about getting your family and Jane's group busy building an enclosure for our animals when they arrive."

Matt sighed. "I guess you're right. To be honest riding ahead sounds pretty tempting, so I don't really mind admitting defeat this time. I'll see you guys back at home. Tomorrow or the day after at the latest, right?"

Lewis nodded, then watched as his friend circled cautiously around the herd, keeping well away to avoid further spooking them, and took off down the road. The combination of hard pedaling and a downhill slope got him to an almost dangerous pace within a few hundred feet, and Matt was soon out of sight around the next bend.

"Where's he off to?" Pete called from near the front of the herd.

With a start Lewis stepped up onto his pedals and rode back to his place, just in time to turn back a few opportunistic strays. "He's going ahead to let Aspen Hill know we're coming."

"Probably a good thing," Alvin said from the other side of the road. "When it comes to being a shepherd he was pretty *baa*d."

"Ugh no, we're not doing that," Pete said, glaring over his shoulder.

"Doing what?" Alvin asked innocently. "When it comes to bad puns I never feel sheepish."

Lewis shook his head. "Sheep puns are too easy to even be funny."

The young man shrugged. “Sorry. They're just something I herd.”

Jane snickered and Tom guffawed loudly. Lewis couldn't help his own smile. Pete glanced backwards again, still glaring. “I should've gone with Matt,” he muttered loud enough for everyone to hear.

Herding the sheep they had to go much slower than they had yesterday, but not quite at the constant walk Lewis had feared as an intolerable pace. The sheep could move faster than that for short periods, which allowed them to ride faster for brief stretches as they herded the animals along the road. The main thing that slowed them wasn't the pace the animals could manage but their tendency to wander, slowing the group down as they were rounded up again.

Last night they'd all anticipated that even going from sunup to sundown there was no way they'd reach Aspen Hill that day, and possibly not the next either. Even the slightly increased pace only gave them hope of reaching home before sundown tomorrow, but at least it was something.

One major delay, and a major concern as well, was making sure the animals had enough time to graze and places to water. With Matt gone on ahead to alert the town, as well as get a place ready for the herd once it arrived, they decided Pete would be the next best candidate for scouting ahead for water sources and ideal areas to stop and rest. He'd shown he had the energy to ride circles around them, and he actually seemed relieved at the chance to move faster going on ahead.

Getting away from Alvin's puns was probably also an incentive.

Near noon they descended down into the single ravine they'd encountered on this mostly uphill road, not nearly as low elevation as Aspen Hill at the base of the canyon but low enough that the spring weather was milder. Pete had also briefly returned to report the stream flowing along the bottom, even though they all remembered the distinctive landmark from the previous day's ride.

It was an ideal place to stop and give the sheep a chance to graze and water, and themselves an opportunity to rest and eat a decent meal. Lewis ran the stream water through his filter, and everyone seemed to appreciate a chance to drink their fill of the cool, crisp water and refill their canteens.

The slow pace hadn't really tired Lewis out, and Jane was feeling up to a hike, so while Tom rested and Alvin kept an eye on the herd they made their way upstream to look for signs of game. It was a good hunting spot, if a bit far from the town, and if things dried up in the valley below it might be worth considering for future expeditions.

The ground to either side of the ravine was steep enough to make footing awkward, and often densely overgrown with underbrush. At some points they even found themselves hopping stones in the stream or leaping from bank to bank as the easiest way forward. The going got easier after a few minutes when they came across a game trail, and although neither of them had planned to make the hike a long one they agreed to go a bit farther.

Lewis was glad they had a few minutes later, when the stream cut through a grove of mingled aspen and evergreens that was almost completely choked with undergrowth that would make further travel impossible. Although that wasn't what had cheered him up.

"Guess this is where we turn back," Jane said, eyeing the tangle.

He nodded absently, eyes on a large split evergreen that had died recently enough that brown needles still hung on its branches.

"What is it?" Jane asked, coming up alongside him and following his gaze.

Lewis pointed. "See that? Up where it splits."

His wife frowned, squinting. "A swarm of bugs? Buzzing around a . . ." her confusion abruptly cleared. "Beehive!"

He grinned. "Right. Never thought I'd see one out in the wild. This is lucky."

She glanced back downstream to where they could see the road winding up the opposite side of the ravine, although their friends watching the herd were obscured by a thicket. "Do we want to try harvesting it?" she asked, obviously reluctant at the thought.

"That too." At her wary look his grin widened. "Why just take the honey when we can also take the bees?" Her wary look turned alarmed, and he hesitated in sudden realization. "Oh. You're not allergic, are you?"

"No." Jane frowned at the misshapen lump of the hive. "It's just, well, we don't know anything about keeping bees. Do we really want to have a swarm of them around stinging everyone when we might mess it up and end up accidentally letting the queen die or something?"

Lewis hesitated. He was well aware of how tricky it could be to handle bees, and the consequences for messing up could be pretty severe. Still, it was hard to ignore any potential source of food, and honey would provide a nice treat as well as a great trade item.

"Maybe we can ask around town to see if anyone has any experience," he said. "Or I can check my books and see if I've got any on beekeeping. I'm pretty sure I grabbed at least a few. If nothing else we can at least think about coming back and just harvesting the honey, now that we know where the hive is."

She gave him a relieved look, as if she'd been afraid he was going to suggest they wade in without any sort of protective clothing and tangle with the bees right then and there. "Sounds like a plan," she said, then glanced downstream. A stray had ambled into view around the thicket, soon followed by another, and they saw Alvin circling to try to head them off as another stray broke away in the opposite direction.

Looked as if their break was over. "Back to work," he said with a last longing look at the beehive. His wife nodded, and they began picking their way back downstream.

*****

The remainder of the day was fairly uneventful. Any soreness remaining after the previous day's more strenuous ride faded with the easier pace, which involved walking their bikes more often than not. And there was an almost soothing quality to the constant *baaing* of the sheep that Lewis soon became familiar with.

He could get used to having his own herd with Jane. A nomadic life in the mountains didn't sound all that terrible at the moment, and it fit both their natures well.

As the sun began to set the sheep began getting more balky. They didn't stray as often, but they began wandering off the road to graze and became more and more indifferent to any efforts to get them going again. A few even plopped down in the grass to rest.

At that point Tom suggested they call it an early night. Lewis agreed that they didn't know enough about herding to justify pushing limits that didn't need to be pushed, and anyway the sheep hadn't seemed to mind an early start that morning. Getting a strong early start would make up any time they lost by not trying to drive the weary animals onward at a slower pace.

They waited until the next time Pete made his way back to report in, and with his agreement set up camp in a decent meadow where the sheep could graze. It wasn't far from a little trickle of a stream, which made its way down the hillside in a surprisingly deep cut with broad banks the herd could scramble down to get water.

Since none of them were sure whether or not the sheep would like fire, and anyway the group agreed they could do without, they contented themselves with sitting in a loose circle outside the entrances to their tents. None of them had brought more than a few days' worth of food with them, so for dinner they divvied up the last of their supplies, supplemented with wild greens foraged along the road during the ride and as they'd set up camp.

It wasn't the best meal, but it filled them up enough to sleep. It also served as a motivation to finish the trek the next day so they could have a good dinner back at home. Lewis wasn't sure whether Matt would make his way back to them after letting the town know they were coming, and if he did whether he'd bring food. Either way he could handle a day going hungry. It wouldn't be the first time.

He slept well that night, all things considered. Judging by Jane's alertness when he shook her awake the next morning she seemed to have slept well too, and they both wasted no time getting their shoes on and leaving the tent.

Only to discover the sheep had wandered off in the night.

Tom was already pacing the meadow following the tracks. "I shouldn't be surprised," he called. "No reason why they wouldn't do their own thing when we're not herding them along."

Pete glared at the few spots of trampled grass where the sheep had slept. "We should've had someone watching them."

The older man shrugged. "They'd have led us a merry chase wandering away in the dark while we tried to stop them. In a way it's almost easier to just follow them now and get them back going the way we want. They can't have gone far and their tracks are pretty clear."

"We should've had someone watching over them anyway," Jane said. She didn't look annoyed by the turn of events; just another thing to take care of. "They might've gotten attacked during the night by some predator and really scared off. Or maybe one person would've been enough to keep them from wandering."

They all looked at each other. "It's a learning process," Lewis finally said. "Let's get going."

It took about an hour to find the sheep, clump them up, and get them back to the road and on their way. The herd had meandered down the meadow instead of following the road in either direction, which made using their bikes more awkward. The second time Lewis had to head off a stray while jouncing over the bumpy terrain he found himself getting almost as irritated as Matt had yesterday.

They pushed the sheep a bit faster to make up for lost time, and after being herded all day yesterday the animals finally seemed to remember that this was something they'd done frequently with their previous shepherds. They trotted along the road with less deviation, and seemed more willing to be turned back when they strayed.

It helped that the way was mostly downhill at a steady slope. Lewis thought the herd naturally moved a bit faster with less prodding from them, and it took almost no effort to coast their bikes along at the same speed. They had to brake far more often than pedal.

Since they had no food they kept the sheep moving with fewer breaks, letting them water at the few places that provided an opportunity but keeping the grazing to a minimum. Lewis hoped that didn't put too much strain on the animals, but with any luck they'd make up for it that night with secure pens and all the grazing they wanted.

By late afternoon they finally reached Aspen Hill Canyon, where they met up with a winded Matt who'd finally come looking for them. There they stopped for a brief break to share the food he'd brought, enough for a small snack for everyone, while their friend caught his breath. Then, grumbling about being turned back so soon, Matt headed back down to make sure everything was prepared.

Their job herding the sheep got even easier once they started down the canyon, since there were fewer places for the animals to go aside from the road itself. Although the downside to that was that if one *did* stray, it disappeared into the undergrowth and was twice as hard to round up again.

The second time the most skittish of the sheep, which Lewis had less than affectionately named Bolt, decided to break away he finally lost his temper and did some shouting himself as he took chase. He managed to calm down again quickly, but he had to admit he'd be more than happy to be done with this and have the sheep secure in pens where they couldn't wander off.

That, or at least figure out how to better handle them, and maybe spend enough time around the herd that he was familiar and trusted so they'd be more manageable. He did want to have a herd of his own, after all, and wanted to do it right.

A bit of a crowd had gathered by the time they brought the herd out of the mouth of the canyon and along Center Street towards the heart of town. There were plenty of fenced in areas around the outskirts and even in Aspen Hill itself, many of which had held livestock before the disastrous winter forced the townspeople to eat anything that was available.

Thanks to that finding somewhere to put the herd hadn't been a problem.

According to Matt the townspeople had prepared the acre lot beside the Watsons' house for the herd. They'd painstakingly gone over the fence to make sure it was secure, as well as stretching a tarp over one area to provide shade next to a watering trough. Their friend had also been hard at work with his dad and brother-in-law salvaging scrap wood from fences and ruined houses to raise their own fenced in area beside the shelter, which he'd promised would be done by the time they reached town.

Catherine Tillman met them at the head of the crowd, coming out to meet them and accompany them the rest of the way. The Mayor was so overjoyed at the sight of the returning sheep that she hugged each of them, even an uncomfortable Jane. Thanks to her jubilant mood, when Lewis broached the subject of the pregnant ewes she immediately agreed that he and his wife could take one, as well as the young ram, for their contribution.

The other pregnant ewe was more of a question. Catherine was willing to also give her to a member of the group for the work they'd done, it was just a question of who. Tom and Alvin would be well on their way to starting their own herd with her as well as another ewe, and Matt had certainly earned consideration for all his contributions to the town, even if he'd returned early and arguably done less work in this case.

In the end, though, she agreed Pete should have the ewe and whatever lambs she birthed. The young man had been searching the longest, and while that extra work arguably hadn't been of much value since it hadn't produced any results, it at least deserved some acknowledgement. At the very least it had narrowed down places not to look. Pete seemed stunned by the offer, and once he was certain it was genuine he broke into his first real grin since finding the herd a couple days ago.

Everyone else was also satisfied with the arrangement. Matt, the Hardings, and Lewis and his wife had already agreed to combine their sheep to make their own herd, which now comprised of four ewes and a ram and whatever lambs were birthed. Pete also seemed eager to start his own herd if possible, albeit with a slower start, and Aspen Hill would have the remaining thirteen sheep, including the other ram.

In spite of the town's desperate need for food the Mayor had prevailed on the townspeople to not slaughter any of the valuable animals. It would take some time for the sheep to earn their value with wool and a herd large enough that some animals could be harvested for mutton, but everyone was willing to invest in that future bounty.

There was a lot to be hopeful about, and the mood in town was celebratory as they led the sheep into their new pen, snagging out the specific ones Lewis, Jane, Matt, Tom, and Alvin would be taking back to the shelter. Pete had arranged to have his ewe penned with the rest of the herd in exchange for doing some work caring for the animals, at least for now.

The five sheep clustered at the fence *baaing* plaintively at the others inside, at least until Lewis and his companions said their goodbyes to their neighbors and began shooing the animals along the road to the shelter and their new home.

At first the little herd tried to loop back around to rejoin the sheep they could still hear calling out to them from town, but after a few blocks they seemed to accept their fate and went along more meekly. Maybe they were as tired as the people herding them and just ready to get wherever they were going.

They found Matt and the others back at the shelter, and true to their friend's word they'd constructed a small pen between the two hills, at the foot of the shorter hill on the far side from the shelter itself. It wasn't a large space, which meant they'd have to let the herd out to graze, and there was no shade, but it was good as a temporary measure.

The sheep went quietly into the pen, making their way over to where a few of Lewis's large metal buckets had been filled with water and tied to the fence so they wouldn't accidentally get tipped over. As Matt secured the awkward gate the family had their own moment of celebration, with hugs and handshakes all around.

By that time the sun had set and Lewis was more than ready to wash up, enjoy a meal, and sleep in a proper bed. He had a few ideas for some lengths of wire fencing he'd been storing in the shed and that were now sitting outside. More of those things he'd purchased before the world went crazy just in case he needed them at some point.

It seemed like it wouldn't be too hard to tie together four of them to make a sturdy square pen that would be simplicity itself to move, keeping the sheep enclosed but allowing them new terrain to graze as often as they needed. They could also keep the ram separate from the ewes until he was a bit older and they figured out what to do about breeding.

All in all Lewis was in high spirits as he and Jane said their goodnights and headed for their shed. It was nice to be considering all these possibilities, since they represented a much brighter future. Between sheep, chickens, rabbits, their gardens, hunting, and foraging, the group at the shelter was in a good position to be self-sustaining before too long.

And then there were the bees, if he could figure out how to capture a swarm. But that was an opportunity for another day.

Chapter Five

Convoy

In spite of being exhausted every night and always feeling like he wasn't going fast enough, Trev had still been able to appreciate just how quickly he'd managed to travel on his bike on the way to Michigan. And the grueling 27 hour trip in the truck to get to Newtown had been unbelievable progress.

Pulling the handcarts and wagons, there was no word to describe their pace other than agonizing.

In every sense of the word. Trev had been afraid they'd overloaded themselves from the start, putting a burden on everyone so there was no chance to rotate people out to rest and make the trip easier. Instead for all of them, especially his parents and aunt and uncle who increasingly felt their age, each and every step they took required them to bring an endless burden along with them.

Rotating their positions on the carts and wagons only did so much to ease the constant burning strain on their muscles, and the first few days they rested almost as much as they walked. They decided to camp early the first day after Newtown when Aunt Eva abruptly dropped the handle of the wagon she'd been wrestling with all day and slumped down to the ground, breaking into tears of exhaustion and despair as she miserably apologized to everyone.

In truth none of them were in much better shape at that point, and she wasn't the only one who cried after pushing their bodies to the limit and beyond to put distance behind them. Trev felt bad thinking it, but it was impossible not to draw the comparison to when he and Lewis, stronger and in better shape, had been able to handle a trip like this. It wasn't that he'd overestimated his family's determination, more that he hadn't set a realistic expectation for what they could manage.

Although to be fair even he was giving more than he had available to pick up the slack.

Even on smooth, clear roads each mile was a battle. Making twenty miles a day was a pipe dream, and even fifteen miles taxed them beyond their limits. Trev hoped that with time everyone would get used to the exertion and their muscles would build up, and tried not to entertain the very real fear that exhaustion might lead to injuries that would further slow their current crawl.

Until then, all they could do was take each mile as it came and give it their all.

The third day after Newtown Lucas seriously broached the idea of leaving behind at least the wagons. Surprisingly it was his wife who vetoed him. "That's enough food to last all of us a month," she insisted. "That could be the difference between life and death down the line. And we've already carried it so far."

"We actually haven't carried it all that far," Linda muttered. She looked almost as worn down as her aunt. "And it won't be the difference between anything if we can't haul it.

Besides, I wouldn't mind having less wheat to choke down for a future meal."

Trev made a face. He wasn't sure he agreed with leaving behind food, but he was definitely getting sick of wheat. Their family had been boiling enough for three meals every evening when they camped, then dousing it with vegetable oil and spicing it as best they could. More than one of them had complained that the mess made them feel queasy after they choked it down. And they constantly had to get on Jim to finish his portion every meal.

Trev thought miserably about the candy bars he'd found, confiscated with all his other stuff by the Gold Bloc soldiers who'd captured him. They might not've been the healthiest thing to eat, but that simple treat would've done miracles to lift their spirits. Although truth be told, with the constant strain on their muscles he should've been wishing for some of Lewis's protein powder and homemade jerky, if anything.

With that in mind he kept his eyes open for anything he could bring down with his AK-47 to add a bit of meat to the nightly pot. He hadn't found any yet, but he kept up hope. They also searched for any plants worth foraging, using some of their precious energy during breaks to gather anything they found.

That was mostly dandelions and other weeds growing along the roadside. But even those represented something his family could shove in their mouths as they took one painful step after another, and hopefully would provide them with some of the nutrients they weren't getting.

On the fifth day it rained. Not a drizzle or a shower, but one of those infrequent thunderstorms that tore across the plains in a fury of sheet lightning and rain approaching like a gray curtain. They saw it coming for over an hour from the northwest and plodded in that general direction, trying to make the most of the time they had before they'd have to seek cover.

There was no way they could continue in that weather, no matter how determined they were. And deep down they were all a bit grateful at the chance to rest for some excuse other than because they didn't have the strength to continue.

The deceptively slow approach of the storm caught them by surprise when it finally came sweeping in, with barely a flurry before they were caught in the drenching downpour. With few other options they crawled under the low bottoms of the handcarts, grateful for the tarps that protected their possessions.

For the next few hours Trev huddled with his siblings and parents in the crowded space, soaked by the constant stream of chilly water that flowed along the road beneath him. Beyond the bottom of the handcart the sky was dark as twilight, lit almost continuously by flashes of lightning. They'd stopped along a part of the road where it dipped down lower than the surrounding area, and a stand of trees grew along a ditch with a stream not far away, but he was still worried about the cart being struck by one of those bolts.

With water flowing on the ground beneath them a strike would be extremely dangerous, but when Trev looked out at the fury of the storm he couldn't bring himself to go out in it to find a better solution. It was probably a bad judgment call, but he didn't remember ever seeing or hearing about lightning striking a car, and anyway he was so exhausted even that danger seemed distant. Nobody else brought it up, either.

He was tired enough that even in the awful conditions he ended up falling asleep a few times, usually woken by a particularly close crack of thunder. In the end he actually slept right through the tail end of the storm, as the front continued on to the southeast with its sheets of rain a gray fog in the distance lit by lightning arcing through the clouds overhead.

His mom shook him awake, and with a soft groan Trev pulled himself out from under the cart and helped the rest of his family slide out as well. Then they continued on, wet, chilled, bone weary, and thoroughly miserable. They camped early that night, when they reached a fairly dense stand of trees where they could scrounge for mostly dry deadfall.

The fire they lit was small and well concealed, but they all clustered around it gratefully to dry their clothes and warm themselves up. Then, depressed by the weather and the lack of progress they'd made, they crawled miserably into crude shelters built with tarps hung over twine stretching between tree trunks to sleep.

On the sixth day after leaving Newtown they heard the noise of approaching engines.

*****

At first Trev didn't recognize the sound as mechanical.

Absorbed in the grim task of pulling his cart with Linda beside him and Jim pushing from behind, his thoughts were on the lunch break an hour or an eternity away, depending on perspective. He wasn't sure if he looked forward to the same unpalatable meal or not.

He gradually became aware of the noise as a low, angry rumble in the distance to the east, and thought it was a last rolling wave of thunder from the storm that had hit them yesterday. The sound was too big to be a single engine, which was what threw him off.

As the rumble continued, far beyond even an extended wave of thunderclaps and far too constant, Trev finally focused on it completely. Only then did he pick up the slight mechanical tone in the rumble, and he felt himself stiffening.

It was the familiar noise of the interstate back when cars had still driven on it. The sound of dozens, perhaps hundreds, of approaching vehicles.

He stopped dead, holding up a hand. "Listen!"

His dad must've recognized it at about the same time, because rather than stopping he motioned sharply to Lucas and Mary and began pulling the wagon off the side of the road towards the only nearby source of cover. It was barely more than a low swell of hill overlooking the highway about twenty yards away, but it would have to do. Looking a bit confused, his mom and aunt began pulling their wagons that way too.

Trev quickly started again, throwing his weight against the ponderous load of the handcart to get it moving before he could begin turning it to follow the others. “What is it?” Jim asked from behind. Trev couldn't see his face but his brother sounded frightened.

“Engines,” Lucas answered grimly. He'd finally recognized it as well. “Lots and lots of engines.” He didn't say the obvious, but from the silence that fell over the group and the urgency they all showed in pulling the carts and wagons over the bumpy terrain everyone must've reached the same conclusion.

That many vehicles coming from the east could only mean Gold Bloc troops.

Trev felt like a snail racing a cheetah as he heaved on the cart with all his might, his back to the rumble of engines growing louder with every second. For a frantic moment the left wheel got stuck on a half-buried rock, and it felt like minutes rather than seconds that it took to shove the cart back and turn it enough to go around the obstruction.

Up ahead the other cart made it behind the hill and out of sight in a small hollow, and moments later his dad and uncle came charging back to help with their cart. Meanwhile Mary ran to help her mom pull her wagon, while Jim left everyone else with the cart to help their mom with the other one.

Within another minute they got the cart concealed beside the first one, and everyone hunkered down behind them. Trev noticed that, even though it was ludicrous to think the approaching vehicles had any chance of hearing them, most of his family were still doing their best to quiet their breathing. All except Mary, who he could hear humming a brave tune with a quavering voice over the sounds of the engines getting closer.

Not that he blamed the others: his last sight before ducking behind cover had been of a seemingly endless line of specks coming along the road in the distance. Even from that far away he could tell by the shape and coloring of the vehicles that it was a military convoy, with dozens of olive green or camouflaged trucks and humvees escorting two dozen or so semis in the middle. He wasn't sure, but almost back beyond sight some of the last specks in line might've been tanks. All in all he guessed there were a hundred or more vehicles in the convoy.

Together they waited for what seemed like an eternity as the rumbling engines got louder and louder, until they could feel the vibration of so many wheels on pavement in the ground beneath them and the noise was loud enough to make their teeth rattle. Due to the shape of the hollow they were in they could see down the road to the west while being concealed from the east. Because of that they saw when the first vehicles passed them and continued on down the highway without slowing.

Lucas stiffened. "Those are ours!"

Trev nodded. He'd hoped as much with that brief glimpse, even from a distance, but now it was clear: the convoy was definitely US military. He didn't see any sign of FETF markings stenciled on any of the vehicles, which suggested that the purpose of the convoy was combat, not relief efforts. Although the six semis hauling boxy trailers and the twenty or so hauling fuel tank trailers suggested their purpose might be resupply.

"They could've been captured by Gold Bloc forces," his dad argued.

Trev shook his head. A few of the troop transport trucks had folded back the canvas tarps normally covering the back, giving him a view of soldiers wearing the familiar standard issue uniforms riding inside. "They look US."

"Which doesn't change much," his uncle said. "Either way we keep hidden."

That was something Trev could agree with. They had no reason to distrust the US military, and it was even possible they might receive some help. But at the same time they'd already lost so much and were barely hanging on with what they had. Not to mention they'd had bad outcomes before with people they otherwise should've been able to trust. Why risk that on the chance they might get a friendly wave from some passing soldiers?

It turned out the choice was taken out of their hands. From the other side of the rise they heard the crunch of tires on gravel as one of the vehicles pulled off the road, followed by a voice shouting orders at a volume raised over the noise of the vehicles continuing to pass them by.

Trev risked ducking around the cart and scrambling the few feet up the rise to peek over, and felt a sick feeling of dread in his gut when he saw one of the troop transport trucks parked there. The soldiers in the back had hopped down and were fanning out towards where he and his family were hiding, weapons at the ready.

"Come on out!" the noncom officer at point position bellowed. "We saw you bolt for cover, we know you're there!"

Trev ducked back down, biting back a curse. With no other obvious options available he unslung his AK-47 and set it aside. Then, motioning to his family to stay still, he reluctantly stood with his hands raised high.

A dozen weapons immediately turned his way, and Trev swallowed hard and did his best to keep his voice steady as he shouted over the racket of vehicles passing on the road. "We aren't looking for trouble. We're just trying to get home."

He thought a few of the soldiers might have lowered their weapons slightly, looking relieved, but the officer's tone stayed sharp. "I need to ask everyone in your group to come out where we can see you, so we know you're not a threat. Don't worry, none of us want to hurt American citizens. This is just protocol . . . can't be too careful these days."

The rest of his family began popping up, starting with Mary and followed soon after by Jim. Linda followed her brother up, looking exasperated at his recklessness, and Trev's parents and aunt and uncle quickly stood as well, after his dad and Lucas had taken a moment to set aside their own rifles.

At the sight of women and children the soldiers relaxed further, and all lowered their weapons. The officer finally lost a bit of his hard edge, nodding slightly at the group in general and ambling towards them so he wouldn't have to shout so loud. "All right, how about we chat until the convoy's well past?" To punctuate his words he gestured curtly, and a soldier behind him talked into some sort of radio headset to report in.

"Where you headed, if I could ask?" Lucas asked, alternating watching the soldiers and the trucks passing by.

The officer grunted. "The Rockies. Don't know if you've noticed but there's been a lot of Gold Bloc aircraft flying overhead, or at least there were a hundred miles ago. That's cause the nuclear war took out most of the satellites in orbit, so they have no easy way to find us. We're going to station up in the mountains and try to hold the line in a place where the roads are easy to defend, or take out if necessary so the enemy can't get at us. The blockheads will have a tough time digging us out there."

Trev glanced at his uncle, who was looking grim and didn't seem about to say anything more. So he spoke up. "It just so happens we're headed that way ourselves. Central Utah, near the Manti-La Sal National Forest."

"Never heard of it, but then again I'm a city boy from Baltimore." The officer gave Trev a sharp look. "You wouldn't happen to be trying to hitch a ride, would you?" Trev shrugged and the man swore, but in a half-friendly way. "Well I don't blame you. The blockheads aren't exactly advancing fast, but even so they'll catch up to a group on foot before too long. Especially if you're hauling goods."

Like they needed reminding. Staying ahead of the invading enemy had been on all their minds since leaving Newtown. "Is that a yes? If you have room, I mean," Trev added. "We could pay you with some of our wheat."

The officer snorted. "This morning we passed an abandoned town with silos full of grain. Tons and tons of the stuff. We've already loaded up as much as we can carry."

Trev felt his heart sink. "Yeah, that's Newtown, where we got ours." He glanced at his uncle. "What about gold? We have a bit we could pay you."

"Gold is just shiny metal these days," the man said, spitting off to one side. "I'd rather cram in a bit more wheat." He hesitated, looking over Trev's group again. "Although I'm not a fan of the idea of leaving a bunch of women and children to the blockheads, so I might be willing to take a bad deal . . ."

There was a long pause as the officer turned to watch the convoy pass, then he shrugged. "I suppose eight people and a few cartfuls of stuff doesn't take up too much space. Better than having you on my conscience. The blockheads have been slaughtering Americans indiscriminately in some places, payback for what our former leaders did to their homes. I wouldn't want to leave decent seeming folks like you to that."

He motioned to the parked truck. "I suppose you can all squeeze in the back, out of our way. You can stow your stuff in your foot space and on your laps, or sit on it if you have to. As for the carts, we can see if it's possible to tie one onto the back, but we'll definitely have to leave at least the other one behind."

Trev couldn't help but grin at their good fortune, and his family's shoulders all slumped at once as if in a collective sigh of relief. "We don't know how to thank you."

"You can thank us by paying your way, like you agreed. Don't worry, the price will be fair. For now let's get you loaded in." The officer waited for a moment, then abruptly turned to the soldiers with him. "Did I sound like I was talking to myself?" he barked.

The soldiers exploded into activity, slinging their rifles over their shoulders so they could haul the carts over to the truck and lead Trev's family up into the utilitarian interior. Mary, Linda, and his mom and aunt squeezed down at the end of the benches while Trev and his dad, brother, and uncle accepted the sacks of wheat and other things the soldiers handed up to them, including the two smaller wagons. The 3 AKs and body armor the soldiers held onto out of caution, promising to return them once they dropped the family off.

It took a bit of doing to load all of that into the cramped space allowed, and they all ended up sitting on three piled sacks with their knees drawn up to their chests to allow for more piled even higher in the foot space, spilling out into the foot space the other soldiers would occupy almost to the back of the truck. Luckily in spite of their grumbling the soldiers didn't really seem to mind, and even took care to cover the sacks with a tarp so their boots wouldn't get them dirty.

In spite of the worries about space, in short order the soldiers had the carts emptied and everyone piled in, pulling one of the carts up behind them to tie in place across the back of the truck. It would block the exit from the vehicle, so they'd have to untie it or cut the ties if they needed to get out, but in an emergency they could hop over the sides instead.

Trev was slightly overwhelmed by the lengths the servicemen had gone to accommodate them, making their already cramped conditions downright claustrophobic and inconveniencing themselves every time they'd have to enter or exit the vehicle. He hoped it wouldn't cause them too much trouble, and as far as he was concerned whatever the officer, who introduced himself as Sergeant Ethan Davis of the Marine Corps, asked in payment was well worth it.

While they worked the family took the time to introduce themselves as well. Trev couldn't help but notice that even in her travel-worn state Mary drew admiring looks from a few of the soldiers, although they did their best not to be obvious about it. Even so his cousin must've noticed as well, because she was humming in slight embarrassment as she took her place at the end of the bench next to her mom.

Everything was done before the last tanks at the end of the convoy passed, giving the truck plenty of time to fall in at the back of the line. As the vehicle rumbled into motion everybody settled onto the benches as best they could. It was a tight squeeze, and a few of the soldiers grumbled good-naturedly, but Trev wasn't about to join the complaints no matter how uncomfortable he was.

They had a ride. The Rockies was a fairly vague term, but wherever it was these troops were going it would still bring them most of the way home, and more importantly away from the advancing blockheads.

Davis, seated just to Trev's right, stretched his legs out as much as possible over the sacks of wheat and around the legs of the soldier across from him. After a bit of shifting he leaned back against the tarp behind his head. "Don't suppose you guys are one of those musical families? Or any other entertainment type family act, you know?"

Trev smiled wryly. "After a winter of playing I can do a dozen or so songs on my harmonica, good enough you should be able to recognize them."

The sergeant snorted. "Son, if you start playing a harmonica next to me I'll shove it where the sun don't shine."

Down at the end of the truck Mary burst out laughing, then hastily put her hands over her mouth. Looking a bit embarrassed, she began humming a tune so quietly Trev could barely hear her.

He shrugged good-naturedly. "Lucky for you I lost it with all my other stuff a while back. Guess that's the end of my musical career."

*****

Once they got going there wasn't much to do but talk. Luckily it seemed like in spite of his slightly gruff exterior Davis was the talkative sort.

According to the sergeant the convoy had come from the east coast, where one of the few remaining refineries had been doing its best to pump out fuel at increased production ever since the Gulf burned. They'd initially been sent to Michigan to form a supply depot for US forces mobilizing to fight the Gold Bloc invaders, but after the Retaliation all bets were off.

In the confusion at least two high ranking officers, General Lassiter and General Erikson, had managed to break through the chaos on official airwaves to relay orders to any remaining forces to fall back to the Rockies, on foot if they had to, to regroup and mount a more organized defense in a setting where the terrain favored them.

When he learned about this convoy Lassiter had them swing by and pick up him and his remaining troops in northern Indiana, using the fuel the convoy brought to run dozens more vehicles for the long move west. Since then they'd been pushing hard along the highways south of I-80, using Trev's same reasoning that it was better to avoid the interstate itself. Their progress was spurred on by reports of Gold Bloc advance units taking the base the General had recently evacuated.

Along with information on the convoy itself, Trev and his family finally got news on where exactly the nukes had hit. Although nobody knew the exact details of the hours before the nuclear war, Sergeant Davis could at least offer some insight on what had gone down based on what he'd heard from the military bases where the higher ups had kept the US Armed Forces running as best they could.

By now it was fairly common knowledge that the Gold Bloc countries had been almost completely obliterated, destroying not just population centers but also blanketing lower population areas to make them unlivable. But the sergeant also had solid facts on where nukes had landed in the US.

The east and west coasts were almost completely gone, which wasn't much of a surprise. The Gold Bloc forces had been avoiding those areas and pushing south farther inland anyway, and since those locations still had a fairly sizable population they made prime targets. Other places all over the interior of the US that still had large populations had been nuked as well, which the Gold Bloc was able to determine thanks to still having intact satellites that could give them highly accurate data.

Military bases had also been targeted, even abandoned ones. That included Hill Air Force Base up near Ogden in Northern Utah, and news of that had the family exchanging worried looks. The site of the blast should've been far enough away to not threaten their friends and family in Aspen Hill, and the prevailing winds should carry the fallout in a different direction, but it was still too close for comfort. It also almost certainly meant that the Great Salt Lake was now irradiated, and northern Utah in general was best avoided.

Trev could only hope that any people still living there had managed to get away, at least out of the fallout zone.

Another target for the Gold Bloc's retaliatory nukes were the US's nuclear silos; it looked like future nuclear strikes were off the table, at least for the countries that had been hit. And last of all, the few deep underground military installations where the higher ups effectively ran the military were targeted, and if the blasts didn't destroy them outright then they were pinned down below ground for good, likely without adequate air filtration and with radioactive water seeping in from above.

In total the deaths of a hundred million or more US citizens were estimated, either immediately or shortly afterwards due to lethal doses of radiation in the fallout zones. In spite of that horrendous death toll only a surprisingly small area of US soil had been hit and irradiated, the strikes surgically planned to take out large numbers of people without making too much of the land unlivable.

It looked like the surviving Gold Bloc forces wanted to keep the US intact so they could take it, now that their own countries had been destroyed. They obviously planned to sweep through and wipe out the scattered, isolated pockets of citizens who'd survived both the winter and the nuclear strikes.

"What do you think of the decision to launch nukes?" Trev asked.

Davis scowled at him. "Judging the actions of my superiors is above my pay grade. But I will say I think this situation could've been handled better. We warned the Gold Bloc we'd nuke them right from the start, and warned them and warned them again. That's the problem if you ask me. We went straight to the nuclear option the moment it looked like the Gold Bloc would enter Canada, even though they'd been invited. Then we didn't have the ba-"

He cut off and gave the women sitting near the cab a sheepish look. "That is, we didn't make good on our threat, which just made us look weak. Then we made the *same* threat with our ultimatum for them to pull out in a month and didn't make good on it then, either. I'm not saying we're entirely to blame, and the Gold Bloc *did* invade us and give us no other real option, but we might've avoided all this loss of life if we'd just taken a stronger stance when it really mattered and not thrown all our cards on the table when the stakes were low."

"You ask me, I say the blockheads got exactly what they deserved," a soldier seated on the bench near the back muttered. "They invade our country, steal our stuff, and put all our people in prison camps, even though they were warned again and again what would happen if they tried it. Not to mention they blew up our refineries in the first place and started all of this. You ask me, they all deserve to melt in a mushroom cloud."

Davis barked out a sharp order, and the young man stiffened to attention where he was seated on the bench. Trev couldn't help but notice that the other soldiers were murmuring in approval, though.

The sergeant certainly didn't approve. "I don't care if they're our enemies, son, that's a billion or more people, mostly innocent civilians, who lost their lives when the nukes launched. You could spend the rest of *your* life counting that high. After what I just heard I'm tempted to make you."

The soldier stayed at attention, but he looked sullen. "No offense, sir, but we've lost a lot ourselves. And they're the ones who started it."

The sergeant abruptly leaned back, looking tired. "Nobody should be celebrating this one, boys. The world came to a standstill after the Middle East Crisis, the first use of nukes as weapons since World War 2, and the aftermath of it should've been enough to fuel all our nightmares for centuries.

"Instead we ended up in the middle of a global thermonuclear war orders of magnitude greater than even that tragedy. We're looking at a sixth of humanity dead in an eye blink, and even the most generous estimates predict another sixth or more will follow thanks to radiation and nuclear winter. It could've easily ended up with nukes flying from everywhere to everywhere, ending life on this planet. There's never been a disaster like this in all of human history, and I pray to God there never will be again."

Uncomfortable silence settled for a long while. Trev spent it trying in vain to picture the unimaginable death toll, and he was sure he wasn't the only one. The news footage coming out of Israel and Iran after the Middle East Crisis had truly been horrific, showing death and suffering on a nationwide scale. Field hospitals treating survivors suffering terminal doses of radiation, frantic evacuation of fallout zones, massive refugee camps full of people who wouldn't be able to go home in their lifetime, and perhaps not in their children's or their children's children's lifetime, or even longer.

And seven days ago the same event had happened on a global scale.

Finally his dad cleared his throat. "Will there be a disaster like it again?" he asked quietly. "Us and the Gold Bloc weren't the only ones with nukes, and you haven't mentioned how the rest of the world is responding to this."

Davis didn't seem to hear, eyes straight ahead, although after a moment he answered. "From what I've heard the rest of the world has written both us and our enemies off. They don't intend to send relief efforts or engage in hostilities, they're more concerned with their own survival now that all the major suppliers and refiners of oil are gone."

He sighed, looking older than his thirty or so years. "But if there's one silver lining to all this it's that we completely took out the Gold Bloc silos and their retaliatory strike was fairly restrained. For better or for worse, if the blockheads can't manage to conquer what's left of the US they won't be able to just pull out and finish the job of nuking us into oblivion. It's the one thing giving us hope as we prepare to fight back, that some kind of victory might be possible."

"Is it really possible?" Linda asked from Trev's other side.

Davis straightened up a bit and gave the young woman a reassuring smile. "It is if we've got anything to say about it. General Lassiter's promised to turn the Rocky Mountains into a killing ground, make the blockheads bleed for every square foot they take. We'll keep fighting them until they either retreat back across US borders and end their invasion, or take out every citizen willing to hold a weapon to resist them." His words drew strong support from his men, who whooped and cheered their approval.

Trev liked the sound of that, but he had his doubts. From the situation Davis had presented things weren't looking great for what remained of the US. From what the sergeant had told them about what the military had been able to find out after the Retaliation, the Gold Bloc invasion forces hadn't been hit nearly as hard as they could've been. That was because even though those in command hadn't really feared a full nuclear strike on their countries from the struggling US, they'd considered a more restrained strike on the military camps in Canada likely enough to justify evacuating them.

The evacuations hadn't been complete and tens of thousands of soldiers and civilian staff had been killed, but thanks to that precaution the bulk of the armies and most of their equipment and supplies had escaped undamaged.

That left the US facing over a million enemy soldiers with vehicles, helicopters, and even a few fighter jets, as well as enough fuel to prosecute a war for who knew how long. Meanwhile what remained of the US military was in shambles, their remaining citizens scattered in small groups with any significant population center destroyed by the Gold Bloc retaliatory nukes.

This very convoy, which represented one of the larger forces, had just over a thousand people, and of the thousands more soldiers ordered to assemble in the Rockies it was anyone's guess how many would make it.

It seemed fairly hopeless, but the small silver lining to the cloud was that if the enemy force could be dealt with the war would be won. There were no reinforcements coming for the Gold Bloc armies, no resupply, and no chance to send them home on leave to recover from the horrors of war.

The enemy had to win this war fast, while simultaneously caring for the few million settlers they'd already brought over and had waiting in Canada for their chance to move into intact US cities and make use of existing infrastructure.

"This full scale invasion can't last long though, can it?" Trev asked. "Without any resupply they're going to run out of steam fast."

The sergeant grimaced. "They're not entirely cut off from supply. From what I've heard Canada is providing them the aid they need to keep going."

"Canada?" Linda burst out in disbelief. "What do they have against us! We've been friends from the beginning, haven't we?"

Davis shook his head. "Yes and no. On the one hand they're pretty pissed that we nuked them. Sure, our only targets were blockhead military bases, but they were still on Canadian soil and a lot of them were near major cities like Toronto that are suffering from fallout or were even within the blast radius. That's going to make serious enemies.

"On the other hand the Gold Bloc army and its settlers are heavily taxing Canada's resources, and the country was already struggling to begin with. Plenty of Canadian citizens were growing more and more hostile to Gold Bloc occupation from the start. Aligning with the Gold Bloc in the first place wasn't a popular idea for the average Canadian, and the move was pushed by the Prime Minister and his Cabinet in spite of strong opposition."

"Not strong enough," one of the soldiers down the line muttered.

Instead of coming down hard on the man Davis just shrugged. "That opposition grew when people learned that the Gold Bloc had plans beyond simply securing Canadian oil fields and stockpiles from the US military remnants and driving US soldiers back south to their own country. When rumors started of a Gold Bloc invasion into the already struggling States many Canadians began openly protesting. The majority of the population didn't want their country hosting warmongers or offering them any sort of assistance in an act they were strongly opposed to. Those protests grew even more heated after the invasion actually began."

The sergeant snorted. "Of course, after global thermonuclear war and nukes landing near their biggest cities all bets are off. No saying what the average Canadian thinks about war with the US these days."

Lucas nodded. "Their military isn't all that big compared to what we had just a year ago, but it still exists. And since the Gold Bloc's been giving them aid ever since the Gulf attacks Canada's been much better off than us. They can provide supplies, staging areas, and other support to our enemies if they choose to."

"I never thought I'd see the day when we were engaged in hostilities with Canada," Trev's mom said, shaking her head in disbelief. "The world's gone completely insane."

"The biggest countries in the world being reduced to radioactive slag wasn't enough to tip you off to that?" the sergeant muttered. Clair shrugged uncomfortably, and after that an uneasy silence settled until Trev's dad cleared his throat.

"I know plenty of Canadians and on the whole they're decent, peaceful people," he said gravely. "Regardless of the circumstances, I have a hard time believing they'll get fully behind this war whatever their leaders say. They might even openly oppose it."

Davis shook his head. "Maybe, but I wouldn't hope to see Canadian insurgents joining up with us to fight off the blockheads any time soon."

There was another grim silence. "You never know what the future will bring," Lucas finally replied with a shrug.

"Although for the moment *my* future involves zombieing out for a while. It's been a rough week." He put his arm around his wife and leaned back against the metal frame the tarp was tied around, and true to his word instead of closing his eyes he just stared blankly up at the tarp overhead.

Trev didn't blame him. After breaking his back towing a handcart all this time riding in a vehicle, even one with poor springs and sitting on piled sacks of wheat crowded by people to either side, felt like pure bliss. Almost without realizing it he found himself staring blankly up at the ceiling too, at least until his eyes started drooping.

His last vague thought before falling asleep was that if he wasn't careful and slumped to his right, he'd end up falling off the sacks he was sitting on and landing on Sergeant Davis. To avoid that he leaned the other way into Linda. He could recall road trips when they were all a lot younger when his sister would throw a screeching fit if he so much as scooted a bit onto her part of the seat, but this time she didn't complain.

Spared his eardrums being blown out by a volume only teenaged girls could manage, he quickly drifted off to sleep.

Chapter Six

A Few Final Steps

With a bit over 600 miles to Aspen Hill Trev didn't expect the trip to take long. Especially since, according to Davis, General Lassiter was in a hurry to get the convoy to the Rockies. The General was motivated more by his desire to reach the mountains and begin organizing their defensive positions than by any desire to stay ahead of the Gold Bloc advance, which even at the speed the blockheads were moving was still a snail's pace in comparison.

Although for a line of over a hundred vehicles the notion of haste wasn't exactly what Trev would hope for. Which was why it had taken the convoy so long to catch up to the head start Trev's family had managed with their truck before Newtown, along with the much more modest distance they'd covered on foot in the six days since.

For one thing the logistics of moving so many people and vehicles was complex, even when there weren't breakdowns or other delays, and working at its best the convoy still took a while to get going again after every stop, and it ended the trip early most nights so everyone would have plenty of time to set up camp and do all the necessary tasks like cooking and vehicle maintenance.

Another reason was that the convoy didn't change its route to avoid any towns it passed, which felt odd to Trev after so long giving population centers a wide berth. Since it was in a hurry to reach the Rockies it didn't go out of its way to seek towns out, either, but whenever it found one that still had people living there it would stop briefly to give the warning about the approaching Gold Bloc forces and advise citizens make preparations or, better yet, flee entirely.

A warning was all they offered; no matter how the people in each town begged or cursed, Lassiter refused to give out any supplies or take on refugees. It was an ironclad stance he didn't waver on, no matter what sort of suffering the convoy encountered. The best the General would do was volunteer his soldiers to help with any heavy lifting or major tasks that needed to be done for a few hours, while the convoy's handful of doctors and medics offered what medical aid they could without permission to use any military supplies.

To be fair the convoy did bring on a few people from each town, although not out of charity. While Lassiter spoke with the town leaders his recruiters were out in force, looking for anyone willing to pick up a gun and join the fight against an approaching wave of enraged blockheads. Especially anyone with previous military experience.

The General's recruiting offer wasn't great, compared to what the Armed Forces had been able to give enlistees before the Gulf burned. But when the recruiters gave a blunt breakdown of the situation the country was in, emphasizing the need to defend friends, family, and fellow citizens thousands of miles away alike against an enemy that had a tendency to kill anyone they came across - that was enough to net a few volunteers with every stop.

Although the prospect of steady meals was probably the better recruiting tool, even if it came with the risk of getting shot at.

Seeing so many people refused a ride made Trev all the more grateful to Davis for making an exception to the rules and picking up his family. Even though they'd had to give the soldiers a few hundred pounds of wheat in exchange he considered it more than fair, and he didn't envy the people they left behind in those towns.

Lassiter wasn't entirely without heart, however. One of his main purposes for stopping to talk at each town was to let them know that, even though the convoy didn't have room to take on anyone but recruits, the townspeople should make their way to Utah and Colorado. If they did they'd be welcome where Lassiter and Erikson were setting up their defenses.

It was a recruiting tool, although a more subtle one. The military would need civilian workers as much as soldiers, and possibly in even greater numbers, if it wanted to effectively fight a large scale war against the invading enemy. At the same time the townspeople couldn't stay where they were under the threat of the approaching blockheads, and Lassiter's offer provided hope of safety and possibly even a better future.

The General certainly painted it that way, of an abundant, sheltered haven in the mountains.

A few of the towns they left were packing up by the time the convoy rolled out, getting ready to follow them as best they could. Others were more hesitant, debating whether to go or arguing for the need to take the time to properly prepare for that sort of long journey with so many people. But only one town flatly refused Lassiter's offer, insisting that trying to travel so far would be death, so they'd stay and hope for the best.

The convoy reached Cheyenne by that evening, rolling into the city without hesitation. Trev had his doubts about the wisdom of that, until he learned that not only had the convoy been in communication with the city beforehand but had sent scouts.

There was a modestly large National Guard unit there, who'd come with FETF at the beginning and managed to restore order after the initial riots. The situation in the city wasn't great, and starvation was claiming more of the population each day, but no violence broke out when the convoy arrived and began setting up camp.

Davis dropped Trev's family off at the campsite, inviting them to set up their tents near where his squad had been assigned to set up theirs. Then the sergeant and his men drove off to help escort one of the fuel trucks, which would be topping off vehicles the National Guard unit had prepared so the few hundred soldiers could come with them, along with a surprisingly large number of recruits.

Or, considering the starvation in the city and the fact that the only stabilizing element was about to leave, maybe not so surprising.

Once again Lassiter gave his speech inviting the remaining citizens to make their way down to where the military was setting up their defenses in the Rockies. Trev and his family weren't there to see it, but from scuttlebutt around the camp it sounded like the reception among the good people of Cheyenne hadn't been great, although with few other options they'd probably come anyway.

The next morning dawned chilly enough to drop a few flakes of snow on the convoy as they broke camp and prepared to roll out. That was a good reminder that even though it was getting on towards late spring, the weather could still turn cold if it wanted.

"Is this nuclear winter?" Linda asked, shivering as the family broke out their cold weather clothes in preparation for a ride in the drafty tarp-covered back of the truck.

The question drew uncomfortable looks from soldiers close enough to hear it, and Lucas paused in putting on his coat. "That's a hard question to answer."

"You mean you don't know?" Mary translated.

Lucas gave his daughter a slightly annoyed look. "I mean that since it hasn't happened, the best predictions we can make are models based on much smaller phenomena, like firestorms or volcanic eruptions. Even the Middle East Crisis, the largest nuclear exchange in history, amounted to roughly the equivalent of 50 Hiroshima-sized explosions. Most of the nuclear winter effects of that exchange were localized to the Middle East, with a drop of less than one degree Celsius worldwide. The old models and forecasts imputed what we learned from that, but didn't have time to really flesh out their predictions before the Gulf burned."

The blond young woman hummed for a few moments, a song Trev didn't recognize. "Then what do all the experts guess, Dad? In words people besides you can understand, please."

Trev's uncle gave them all a long-suffering look. "It means that given the scale of the Retaliation, the temperature could drop anywhere from 1 to 20 degrees Celsius. Maybe even more. We just don't know."

"Celsius?" Linda complained.

Their dad was frowning slightly in concentration. "A change of 20 degrees Celsius would be 36 degrees Fahrenheit, if I'm remembering my conversions right."

Trev frowned as he did his own math. With a drop that severe the previously hottest day of summer would drop into the 60s in most places, like spring. Spring would become winter, and winter . . . would be brutal.

"So is this nuclear winter or not?" Linda asked, a bit impatiently.

Lucas blinked. He'd obviously been lost in his own grim thoughts about the future. "Probably not. I'm not sure exactly how long it would take for nuclear winter to set in, but I don't think the ash in the upper atmosphere has had enough time to spread far enough to really begin affecting things." He pointed at the sun peeking up over the horizon. "The sun doesn't seem any darker. I'd say this is just spring in Wyoming."

"Thanks for the lesson, Professor Scientist," a dry voice said from behind them. Trev jumped slightly and turned to see that Davis had made his way over to their camp. Satisfied he had their attention, the sergeant jerked a thumb towards the truck. "Time to pack up. Convoy probably won't be ready to leave for another half hour, if we're lucky, but the General wants everyone good to go *before* then. Just so that the inevitable delays aren't added to by idiots slowing us all down because they decided to drag their feet when they didn't need to."

As Davis turned to walk away Trev's dad hurriedly caught up to him. "The convoy's going to reach where it's going today, isn't it? As long as there aren't any delays?"

The sergeant paused and gave them a broad smile. "Why yes, yes we are. But that depends on where "it's" going. We're splitting up, sending about half the convoy south to Denver to begin setting up defenses for the portion of the Rockies that stretch through Colorado. The other half, including General Lassiter and my squad, will continue on into Utah. Salt Lake City, to start with, although well south of the fallout zone near Hill Air Force Base. It'll be a good starting point, as we get the lay of the land and begin gathering up survivors and sending them to safe places."

Trev felt his heart sink. He'd made that hike before, and that had been when FETF and the Armed Forces assisting them had been patrolling the roads. Going now, with his family dragging an overloaded cart and wagons, the trip would be even more slow and dangerous. "We're closer to central Utah."

Davis's smile widened. "So you told me. Luckily the General was looking for volunteers for a scouting detail to break off from the convoy and head south down Highway 191, following it to Highway 6 and from there to Provo."

"You're kidding!" Aunt Eva nearly shouted. "191 meets 6 just north of Helper. That takes us within 10 or so miles of Aspen Hill!"

The sergeant looked a bit surprised. "It does? Wow, I figured I was doing you guys a favor getting you a bit closer, but I didn't realize we'd be going *that* close." His grin returned. "Never say I didn't do anything for you, I guess."

"A favor?" Trev's mom replied, looking a bit overwhelmed. "You're a godsend!"

Davis shrugged, embarrassed. "I was just looking for something a bit more interesting than riding along with the convoy, and it happened to help you too. Don't read too much into it." He turned and started back towards his squad's camp, snapping an order to one of his soldiers. But after a few steps he turned back. "Pack up. I want the camps down and everyone in my truck in ten minutes."

*****

They continued west, traveling more and more on I-80 over mountainous terrain where there was no room for smaller highways or roads to run alongside the interstate. A few of the soldiers seemed worried that the blockheads would suddenly swoop down on them from the north like a tide, but the area was remote enough that that didn't seem likely.

Davis continued to be more than forthcoming about the military's plans for the Rockies, although he was conscientious and didn't go into too much specific detail about locations and other sensitive information.

The idea was to take and hold the passes and high country in the ranges of the Rockies going through Utah and Colorado. Those passes would create natural choke points and easily defensible positions that would not only let them hold the mountains but, with any luck, defend the lowlands in between. That would give them a reasonably large territory in eastern Utah and western Colorado for civilian populations that they had some hope of defending.

If it turned out they couldn't defend that entire area, say if a significant enough attack came from the north or south, then as a last resort they'd pull back to whichever section of the Rockies was suffering the mildest attacks by the enemy and hunker down in the mountains there with whatever civilians they could escort to safety.

In that situation the Gold Bloc would find it almost impossible to dig them out or mount any successful attack, but the downside was that they'd have to surrender pretty much the entire rest of the country and abandon any hope of staging a significant counterattack. They'd be effectively besieged and forced to wait out their besiegers.

Ultimately the strategy cooked up by the two generals was pretty straightforward: delay the enemy, hold easily defensible territory and withdraw only when necessary, and if all else failed find the most remote, difficult to reach places up in the mountains and hopefully hold out until the Gold Bloc forces ran out of supplies and were forced to withdraw.

It wasn't the most inspiring plan, but outnumbered and outgunned it was the best they had. Davis confessed that part of the hope was that the invaders would be facing pockets of resistance all over the country in the territory they'd already taken, making those areas difficult and unsafe to hold and requiring constant attention to keep under control.

Facing a determined holdout in the middle of the country acting as a barrier between Russian and Chinese forces easily joining up, as well as small groups of insurgents striking targets of opportunity throughout the conquered regions, eventually the blockheads would fail just like every conqueror did when trying to deal with a well-armed, unruly populace.

It would be bloody, savage, and ugly, and US citizens all over the country would suffer terribly, but eventually the enemy would have no choice but to withdraw back to more securely held areas of the US, at which point the remaining US Armed Forces could go on the offensive and keep pushing until the enemy was driven all the way back into Canada.

Trev had to admit that it was a little disheartening, when even the most optimistic plan painted a grim picture. But he was glad someone was fighting back: at this point there wasn't much choice but to beat the enemy by pure stubbornness.

The convoy took almost 7 hours to reach Rock Springs, arriving in the midafternoon. Not far beyond that Davis's scouting group split off on Highway 191, half a dozen vehicles and two motorcycles. The smaller group traveled a bit faster than the convoy as a whole, making better time.

They stopped four times along the way. The first was soon after splitting off from the convoy, to investigate a fire a few miles off the road while idling on a hilltop, using their binoculars to see if it posed a threat. There seemed to be no human presence near the fire, so although the circumstances were suspicious they continued on.

The other times were at the few towns along the highway that still had people living in them. The scouts didn't do any recruiting, but they did inform the residents of the general situation. Since all the towns were nominally in the area the military intended to try to protect Davis didn't try to persuade the people to leave.

He did alert them to what was going on, however, as well as handing out a few shortwave radios and giving information on how to contact the military on them. Last of all he asked them to consider what they'd be willing to do to help the military protect their homes and their loved ones the next time a convoy specifically came to visit the town.

The sun wasn't far from setting by the time the scouts reached Highway 6, after about six hours of driving from Rock Springs. Trev could've probably done the math on how long it would've taken his family to walk that distance, even going the slightly faster route through Denver, but just thinking about it made him tired.

Besides, even though they were almost home they still had almost a full day's journey ahead of them, of awkwardly hauling over a ton of grain on a single handcart and two wagons.

The scouts stopped for a break at the junction as Davis's Marines helped take down the cart and load it up, piling it until the tires began to sag. Trev sincerely hoped it could take the weight, and briefly considered slinging a couple sacks over his shoulders as a precaution. He quickly dismissed the idea, realizing it wouldn't do much other than exhaust him and keep him from being free to help pull the cart.

"Well, from your expressions it looks like you've got a bit of a walk ahead of you," the sergeant said, standing with the family watching as his men worked. "Sorry we couldn't drop you off any closer."

"Are you kidding?" Trev asked, grinning ruefully. "You gave us help when we really needed it, which might've saved all our lives. I can't thank you enough."

Davis shrugged. "Well we had extra room and you paid your way." He hesitated, then continued. "Listen, at some point we're probably going to be setting up in this area, and if we do General Lassiter will want to contact the remaining towns around here. To offer our protection, but also for recruiting and other aid from the locals that we'll need if we want to beat the blockheads. Where's this Aspen Hill you're headed to?"

Trev opened his mouth to answer, then it was his turn to hesitate.

The sergeant scowled when he saw it. "Seriously? If you can't trust us at this point-"

"It's not that," Lucas cut in hastily, stepping over next to Trev. "We can certainly trust you, and we're in your debt. It's just that my nephew's been through a lot . . ."

Trev spoke up, a bit annoyed. "Actually it's not that, either. I'd be happy to tell you if it was just us, but I don't know if it's my place to speak on behalf of the town. We've had more than a little trouble since the Gulf burned, and some of it came from . . ." he trailed off, realizing that mentioning the trouble with Ferris and FETF probably wouldn't get a good reception with the sergeant. He found himself regretting even bringing any of it up.

Davis sighed. "Listen, I don't blame you for looking out for your people. And I certainly don't want to sound like we had an ulterior motive for giving you guys a lift. But did you wonder how I justified doing that when the General's been refusing to take on refugees at every town we've visited?"

Trev hesitated. "I didn't really," he admitted. "Mostly we're just grateful you did."

"Well listen. When we heard you were heading home to a town in Utah we viewed it as an opportunity. Like I said, we're going to need the support of the locals when we get to the Rockies, and we also need to coordinate with them on using nearby roads without having potshots taken at us. Not to mention making arrangements so they can contact us for aid if they come under attack."

The sergeant shrugged. "We just figured that you could let your town know the situation, see if anyone wants to join up with us to defend their homes. And once we get set up and seek you out you can sort of be an intermediary for us. Small price to pay for giving you a safe, speedy ride for 600 or so miles."

That was all pretty reasonable. And anyway Davis already knew the name of the town and it would show up on any map of the area. It really wasn't worth alienating the soldiers who'd soon be fighting for their lives to protect them over pointless paranoia.

Lucas had been nodding throughout that entire spiel. "If you've got a map I can show you, and we'll definitely make sure the town knows what your help means and that you can't do it alone."

"Fair enough." Davis got out his map, grunting in surprise when Lucas marked a dot on an area a bit northwest of Carbonville. Aspen Hill was too small to show up, but the location was accurate.

"According to my nephew the signs pointing you to town along Highway 6 were taken down to deter refugees," Lucas finished as he handed the map back. "But the roads are easy enough to spot, and there are three of them if you miss the first couple. I imagine you'll want to visit Helper, Carbonville, and especially Price as well. We'll contact them on the radio and let them know what to expect."

"Appreciate it." The sergeant abruptly noticed that his men had finished piling the sacks of wheat on and around the cart. Heading to the back of the truck, he retrieved the three AK-47s he'd temporarily confiscated. He also motioned to one of his men to retrieve the body armor and few other crowd control tools the family had been carrying.

As the soldiers piled back into the vehicle Davis made his way over and handed rifles to Trev and his dad. He then offered the last rifle to Lucas, but didn't immediately let go when the other man reached out to take it. "Listen, have you considered joining up with us right now? We got your family safely home, and from our conversations it seems like you and your nephew might be up for fighting back, especially if it means you can help protect your loved ones and reclaim our country."

Lucas hesitated as the sergeant finally released the AK-47, then shook his head as he slung it over his shoulder. "We're worried about just surviving."

"So is everyone else," Davis replied with a snort.

"We also have our friends and family to worry about," Trev's dad cut in. He looked slightly irritated at being excluded from the offer. "We can't ignore our responsibilities to them."

The sergeant nodded. "I get it. If you want to hide and look out for just yourselves until the blockheads finally find their way to your doorsteps that's your decision. But just consider whether you want an existence constantly on the move fleeing pursuit, struggling to survive as everything around you burns, or if you want to help rebuild this country's future."

The officer glanced at his men, then straightened stiffly. "I'm just a noncom with my boots on the ground, but forgive me if I see something worth saving in the United States of America. Something worth fighting for, even dying for if need be."

Shame was a powerful tool, and Trev realized he sounded a little defensive as he spoke up. "The town might want to send some of our defenders to help, like you asked. But right now we've got to go see how things are there before we can decide anything."

"Fair enough." Davis offered handshakes all around, then brusquely took the few steps over to his truck and hopped into the back. A moment later they heard someone banging on the back wall of the cab, and the idling vehicle started off with a crunch of tires on gravel until it pulled onto the highway. The rest of the scouts, waiting ahead, pulled out to follow it as it headed northwest towards Spanish Fork.

After watching them drive out of sight his mom straightened her shoulders. "Well, we've been sitting around resting for most of the past two days. What do you say we figure out how to pack this wheat and try to get some distance before dark? It's a good opportunity to stretch our legs."

Linda groaned. "Stretch them right out of their sockets," she complained. But there were no other arguments to the suggestion as the family got to work.

They ended up piling the wagons with another 100 pounds. That left the sacks stacked absurdly high, with the wheels almost bending outwards from the extra weight, and they had to use cord to tie them firmly in place. The rest they managed to fit in the handcart, although it was also stacked absurdly high and needed to be tied.

With one less cart that left three more people to help with the one that remained, but Trev wasn't sure that was a good tradeoff. His dad and uncle took the wagons while the others helped him with the cart, but even so Trev almost groaned when he threw his weight against the push bar and it barely budged.

To his relief it got a bit better as everyone else got their backs into it and began pushing along with him, but even so it was much more difficult than it had been. There was also the fact that the people pushing from behind kept naturally lifting as they pushed to deal with the added weight, which ended up shoving the front of the cart down.

Trev felt like his back would break and his arms would be torn from their sockets each time they did that, and he had to constantly remind them to push down slightly rather than up. It was more difficult for them, he could tell, and a few times they overcorrected so much that the push bar nearly banged against his chin as he struggled to keep the front of the cart down, but after about fifteen minutes they got it figured out.

They moved even slower than they had been with two carts, but by the time they began looking for a place to camp before it got too dark to see Trev was satisfied that they'd made it over half a mile.

In spite of their weariness everyone was in a great mood as they set up their tarp-and-line tents from the cart to a handy tree. They'd gotten a bit closer to home on foot, and with any luck they'd reach Aspen Hill sometime tomorrow afternoon. Everyone was looking forward to reuniting with Lewis and reconnecting with old friends, but mostly the idea of the trip being nearly over had everyone practically singing. Or in Mary's case humming.

The next morning they set out almost as soon as waking up, after eating half of the extra pot of wheat they'd boiled the night before.

On Trev's advice they steered clear of Helper, and although they were sure the town's defenders saw them nobody tried to cause trouble. That might've been due to the fact that all in all the people of Helper were decent human beings, or that even a small well-armed party was a deterrent. Or maybe they hadn't been seen after all.

Despite the appearance of safety Trev kept his eye on the town receding into the distance behind them as they kept going south, their laborious steps light with the knowledge that home was always just over the next rise.

Ten miles was nothing compared to the hundreds they would've had to travel without the convoy's timely aid. Even so, that "nothing" took a while when they were going barely over one mile an hour hauling their burden of grain. It was nearly noon by the time they reached the road leading off towards Aspen Hill.

At the sight of it a spontaneous cheer erupted from the family, and they managed a burst of energy as they pushed the last of the distance to reach it, eagerly talking about what they'd do once they finally made it to the shelter.

They'd made it. They were home.

Chapter Seven

Homecoming

On Trev's advice they took care to walk down the middle of the road stretching the last few miles to Aspen Hill, their weapons safely put away and showing no threatening signs. Just in case one of the defenders on patrol was feeling jittery.

Trev didn't really think any of his neighbors would shoot at a group with women and children without some pretty major threat to justify it, but it never hurt to be cautious. Although in that same spirit of caution they also kept their weapons within easy reach, in case the unthinkable had happened and the raiders had managed to take the town.

The cart didn't feel as heavy walking on ground he'd covered numerous times before, and he almost felt like he could count the steps left to reach home. After all his time patrolling and taking shifts at the roadblock, Trev knew exactly which of the rises they climbed up over and the bends they went around would give them a view of town from the road.

Although the northern road they were on wasn't the best for that, since with the layout of the land they'd be almost to town before their first view of it, atop a rise well within the patrol radius. He fully expected them to be stopped before then, and as they started up that last slope he felt the hairs on his neck prickling at no sign of any patrols.

"I should go ahead and see if there's a problem," he said.

"No way!" Linda protested. "I want us all to get our first look at town together."

Lucas gave him a concerned look, understanding his reasoning. "You're right, Trev. I'll go with you. Everyone else stay here, and stay alert."

Ignoring his previous suggestion about presenting themselves as harmless, Trev retrieved his rifle and slung it over his shoulder, then handed his uncle the one he'd been using. Moving cautiously and with his eyes panning the landscape in all directions, he led the way up the remainder of the slope to the rise. He saw no signs of danger as he looked ahead at the town.

At his first sight of it his spine went rigid with shock and dismay, and he felt like he'd been punched in the gut.

Aspen Hill looked like it had been shelled. Shelled after being a war zone for an extended period of time. The perimeter had been reinforced with roadblocks, fences, and earthworks, but most of those were in shambles along with just about every house near the edge of town. Some of the dwellings sported blackened, gaping holes, while others were completely collapsed or burned to ash. Even Main Street itself hadn't been spared the devastation, with a small apartment building half destroyed and the remainder sagging into the wreckage.

"Oh no," Lucas whispered, coming to a stop beside him.

Trev stared at the ruined town in horror, feeling sick. This was what he'd left his friends to deal with?

He'd worried about the town through most of his trip to Michigan, and on the trip back that worry had been building with every mile closer to home they got. Even so, he'd half expected to get here and find that the raiders had just given up and left, probably not too long after he started east.

Once again, just like when he'd first left, he found himself torn in two by conflicting guilts. He knew objectively that if he hadn't gone looking for his family Lucas might not have found them, and if he had they might not've been able to escape during the chaos after the nukes flew. He'd done what he needed to do, and because of it his loved ones were all alive and safe.

And returning to a scene of devastation.

He jumped slightly at a hand on his shoulder, his uncle awkwardly trying to offer some comfort. “We knew this was a possibility,” he said, looking tired.

“I left them to this,” Trev answered, tearing his eyes from the ruined town to look towards the two hills the shelter nestled between. He couldn't see it, but for all he knew it was a blackened crater, too.

Lucas's grip tightened. “Remember how we all used to get on Lewis's case about trying to put responsibility for everything on his own shoulders?” Trev nodded and looked back towards the grim sight ahead, although he couldn't think of anything to say. He got the hint, he just wasn't sure how much it helped.

To his relief his attention was drawn from the town towards a figure hurrying their way from the south with a gun slung over one shoulder, waving wildly. He was far enough away that Trev couldn't make out his features, so he got out the binoculars he'd purchased in Newtown.

It was Rick Watson, his thin and slightly haggard look offset by the huge grin he wore. He was holding his own binoculars in one hand and had obviously seen them, and it seemed that Trev's worry about not being spotted by a patrol before now was because his friend had been at the southernmost end of his route.

Trev found his own grin, relieved that the younger man had made it through whatever nightmare had left the town looking like that. He waved one arm over his head in response, then broke away from his uncle to meet his friend halfway and shake his hand.

Rick wasn't having any of that; he went right past Trev's hand and pulled him into a crushing hug. "I can't believe you made it, man! When we heard that a nuke hit northern Michigan we feared the worst."

"I don't blame you. We got a good close up view of the mushroom cloud." Trev stepped back, losing his smile as he looked over Rick's shoulder at the halfway demolished town. "I left you guys in a mess, didn't I?"

His friend lost his own smile and nodded grimly, also turning to inspect the damage. "I'm used to the sight so I've forgotten how shocking it looks."

"How bad was it?"

"Bad." Rick squared his shoulders and turned to look at him, forcing a smile. "But we cleaned it up. We wiped the raiders out and sentenced the ones who surrendered to death, including Turner."

"Turner?" Trev nearly shouted in disbelief. "Lewis didn't get him?"

His friend opened his mouth to answer, then paused and stepped forward to offer his hand past Trev to Lucas as he arrived. "Mr. Halsson! Last I heard you were in Norway. I wish I could see Lewis's face when he finds out you're here."

Lucas accepted the handshake, a bit of tension going out of his shoulders. "He's all right?"

The younger man's grin returned. "He's doing great, all things considered. In fact, he just got-" he cut off with a slight cough, looking embarrassed. "Actually, that's probably his news to share."

Trev exchanged glances with his uncle. "Good news, right?"

Rick's smile turned a bit mischievous. "Maybe not the best for you, Trev, since from what I hear you kind of, um, well . . ." he trailed off and glanced back towards town. "Actually I can't think of any way to finish that without spoiling the surprise."

"Uh, okay." Trev gave his uncle a confused look, and Lucas shrugged.

His friend hastily continued. "Anyway I radioed in your arrival. I'd expect to see your cousin and Matt and everyone stampeding down the road any minute now."

*****

They'd named the lambs Sunny and Snowy, a male and a female respectively.

When the time came Lewis had been afraid there'd be complications he wouldn't be able to handle, although he'd done his best to study up on the process. Thankfully Daisy, the mother, looked like she'd birthed lambs before. She handled things well and there were no complications, so the births went surprisingly smoothly, with Snowy born last just before dawn.

A recently awakened Sam immediately fell in love with the adorable newborns, and was at the fence for half an hour cheerleading them through every moment of their first awkward steps, spindly little legs splayed out and trembling. Aaron and Paul joined her for most of it, asking nonstop questions and trying to sneak into the pen to pet the animals.

Jane was slightly more pragmatic. She just as happy and excited as her friend, but her focus was on helping Lewis go through the checklist they'd prepared to make sure things were going smoothly and they were ready to help with any possible complications, not only as the lambs were born but in the vulnerable time afterwards when other problems could arise.

All in all the mood of the group was jubilant over breakfast at the shelter, with yet another step taken towards being fully self-sustaining, and the good mood continued as everyone worked at their morning chores.

By the time lunchtime rolled around the celebratory mood had faded somewhat. In spite of that Sam still wanted to go into town and give Matt the good news about the lambs, since he'd taken a rare overnight shift covering for Chauncey, who'd come down sick the day before.

Lewis wanted to go into town anyway and talk over what he'd observed from the lambing with Pete, as well as offer his help when his friend's ewe finally birthed her lambs. So he asked Jane if she wanted to go for a bike ride with him before they continued the day's work.

"Sure," she replied, swallowing her last bite of the roast rabbit and wild greens they'd had for their meal. "That'll take us in the direction of the garden anyway, so we can do the watering and weeding and check on the traps."

Decided, they cleaned their dishes and got ready to leave. Lewis was just checking over Daisy, Sunny, and Snowy one last time before they went, to make sure everything was all right, when the radio crackled with Rick's voice.

"We need to rework these patrol routes," their friend complained. "Or at least change up the roadblock shifts to have people farther out watching the roads. I was on the southernmost leg of my route, and by the time I got back around to the northern road I found some folks within shooting distance of town."

Lewis had been raising the radio to ask if there was a potential problem when Matt's voice came on, asking the question nearly word for word.

"No, I recognize the family." Rick's voice had an odd edge to it. "Lewis, I'm guessing you'll really want to come meet them."

The comment sent a jolt of electricity through him, and Lewis finished raising the radio. "You're kidding. Trev and his family?"

"Them too." His friend abruptly laughed, unable to contain his excitement. "You're going to lose your mind."

Lewis exchanged a confused look with his wife. "What does that mean?"

He could almost hear Rick's grin in his reply. "I don't want to spoil the surprise."

"I'll meet you out there," Matt said into the silence following that cryptic comment.

Lewis had already fumbled his radio back onto his belt and grabbed his bike. Jane was just a heartbeat behind him getting on hers, and he was about to tear off when he remembered Sam. "Go!" she called, wheeling out Matt's bike. "I'll meet you out there too."

She'd barely finished the first word before Lewis was off, Jane close behind him as he tore down the gravel road leading past the shelter at borderline unsafe speeds. He couldn't help but whoop a few times.

Trev was back. He'd managed to survive a round trip of almost four thousand miles and bring his family home. And holy cow, had he done it in record time! Even on bicycles Lewis hadn't expected them back so soon.

The shelter wasn't far from the north road, and the road he was on actually connected to a street leading to the road outside of town. Thanks to that he and his wife came out on the road *behind* the rise overlooking the town, and he was able to see the group laboriously hauling an almost absurdly overloaded handcart and two wagons up to the top ahead of them.

How had they managed to bring a *cart* with them from Michigan so quickly?

Rick was right, there were more people than just Trev's family. Nine people in all, since Rick was there helping Trev pull the overloaded cart along with-

Lewis braked so hard he almost went over the handlebars, staring ahead in disbelief. Then, just to be sure his eyes weren't playing tricks on him, he fumbled out his binoculars and raised them to his eyes.

Trev, Uncle George, Aunt Clair, and his cousins Linda and Jim were all there. Along with Lewis's parents and his sister Mary.

He began pedaling furiously again, awkwardly holding the binoculars and handlebars with one hand. His brain couldn't comprehend how his family had got here from Norway, but at the moment he didn't care. He passed a confused Jane, who didn't understand why he'd stopped. He'd showed her pictures of his and Trev's families on his recharged phone a few times, but she didn't seem to have made the connection.

"It's my family!" he shouted over his shoulder as she hurried to catch up.

By the time she did he'd reached the cart, and he threw himself off his bike and lunged the final few feet to wrap his arms around his mom, who was laughing and crying as she hugged him back so tight it hurt. He was laughing and crying too, and had no idea what he was even saying as he babbled a confused barrage of greetings and questions about what they were doing here.

Moments later he was swarmed by his family. He pulled Mary into the hug along with his mom, while his dad hugged him from the other side, while Trev's family huddled close around them adding to the general din of the reunion.

Trev, he was grateful to see, had noticed Jane hanging back by herself and, while keeping a generous space, had delayed his own reunion to go over to greet her. That was good, because Lewis could clearly see the awkwardness in his wife's posture, and the sight of at least one other familiar face calmed her down a bit.

Given her nature she probably dreaded this meeting, but Lewis couldn't see how to navigate the reunion without coming right out with the news about the wedding that he'd kept from Matt and his other friends for weeks. He couldn't do that to his family.

Besides, Mary was already looking over at Jane, and from her growing excitement he could see she was putting two and two together. His sister always had been pretty good at staying back and observing what was going on between people, rather than taking part in it herself.

Lewis extricated himself from the family to make his way over to his wife, who gratefully leaned against him as he put his arm around her. Trev gave him a shocked look at that, and he had a feeling his cousin was rapidly doing the math as well.

"Everyone," he said quietly. "This is Jane. She's very reserved and a bit uncomfortable around crowds, especially people she doesn't know, so I hope you'll do your best to give her some space." He hugged her a bit tighter, noticing how tense her muscles were, but she turned and gave him a nervous smile and a nod, so he continued. "We got married a few weeks ago."

Most of his family had probably come to that conclusion by that point, but even so for the first few seconds after the announcement he could've heard a pin drop.

"Congratulations!" Trev shouted. Since he was closest he only needed a few steps to shake Lewis's free hand while grinning broadly at the two of them. Jane gave her new cousin a grateful look, probably more because he'd remembered what she was like and hadn't tried to hug them both or shake her hand than because of his congratulations.

After Trev broke the silence the rest of the family swarmed in. They made some attempt to respect his request to give Jane space, but in the excitement of the moment the two of them still ended up in the middle of a huddle of well-wishing. For her part Jane didn't take Lewis up on any of the openings he made for her to back off a bit, resolutely doing her best to not dampen the celebratory mood.

And, to him at least, it seemed as if his wife wasn't quite as uncomfortable as she would've been in a normal crowd, probably because everyone was family and it was impossible not to feel their warmth.

Mary, bless her heart, helped too. His sister interrupted their mom's lengthy hug with her new daughter-in-law for her own, much briefer, hug, mostly hugging Lewis with only a light hand on Jane's arm. After that Mary sidled over to stand on Jane's other side, giving her plenty of space, and acted as a buffer there to prevent crowding as the congratulations continued.

Jane gave her new sister a grateful look as well, and Lewis had a feeling that with that small act of thoughtfulness Mary had earned a new friend.

The reunion naturally shifted into sharing news, a disorganized jumble of questions and descriptions of experiences as Trev, Uncle George, and Lewis's dad led the way to the handcart and got the group heading back towards town.

On the way they met up with Matt and Sam, along with Mayor Tillman and a few other townspeople. The couple met Trev with their own hugs, genuinely happy their friend had made it safely home. And if Lewis's mom and Aunt Clair had been disappointed about not being able to shower Jane with their full enthusiasm, they found another opportunity when Matt introduced his new wife and the conversation got around to the child they were expecting.

Sam seemed to enjoy the unexpected flurry of hugs and well-wishes, and Matt endured the neighborly stories of his childhood mischiefs with good grace.

Catherine interrupted the amiable exchange of greetings to officially welcome the family back to Aspen Hill, and invited them to the town's weekly movie night the next day as an opportunity to reconnect with their neighbors. Then, with handshakes and hugs all around, the Mayor let them continue on their way to the shelter while she led the small crowd of onlookers back to town.

"She didn't bring up the elephant in the room," Trev mentioned, nodding at the precariously stacked bags of wheat they were hauling. "I'm a bit surprised, actually."

Lewis felt some of his good mood sour. Not at the sight of the wheat, of course; hearing that his family had risked and suffered so much to bring over a ton of grain home with them was incredibly good news, and a huge relief. He hadn't even considered that aspect of things during the reunion, but if eight people had showed up empty-handed that would've put an even bigger strain on everyone at the shelter.

They were struggling to make sure everyone was getting enough as it was, although on the plus side everyone in his family was resourceful and hardworking, definitely not useless eaters. Even in the worst situation they *could've* made it work if they needed to. He was just glad it wasn't necessary.

Uncle George must've been thinking along the same lines, because he spoke into the silence caused by Trev's comment. "I think one of the first things we need to do is figure out exactly how long the wheat we brought is going to last us, and how strictly we should ration it."

"I guess that depends on how much we want to donate to the town," Trev said. Lewis winced, and an uncomfortable silence fell as everyone stared at his cousin. Seeing it Trev hesitated. "What?"

Lewis cleared his throat. "I think we should be planning in terms of keeping it all."

His cousin gave him an incredulous look. "What? Didn't we have this discussion the last time the town came to us needing food and we agreed to sell the cache? I thought we'd decided that we can provide for ourselves enough to share a bit of what we have. I mean you told us you guys have chickens, sheep, and rabbits now, not to mention our gardens! And we can hunt and forage too."

"That was before the Retaliation," Lewis said firmly. "Now we're looking at nuclear winter, when we might *not* be able to provide for ourselves in any other way than making sure we have enough stored up for it."

"Not to mention from the sounds of it we've also got the Larsons and Jane's group to worry about along with our own family," his dad added. He glanced over at Matt and Sam. "No offense."

Matt held up his hands. "Hey, we're sincerely grateful you're including us in the consideration at all."

Trev looked around miserably, and Lewis felt a bit bad for him. Everyone was looking at him like he was crazy for even suggesting helping the town, when at worst he was just guilty of not properly thinking the situation through.

"I guess you're right," he said heavily. "It's just that from the first moment I saw those silos in Newtown I've had it in the back of my mind that the grain would help the town. I guess it would've, if I hadn't gotten our truck stolen and we'd been able to bring a full load in."

Aunt Clair rested a hand on her son's shoulder. "I know helping the town was one of the reasons you wanted us to get that grain," she said gently. "But think about how much we have, compared to how many people we need to provide for. It's not really all that much after all."

Trev nodded, and they continued on in a heavier silence. Nobody wanted to think about the people in town who needed this grain as desperately as they did, probably even more desperately. But Lewis wasn't about to give in this time; he'd had his doubts and regrets about selling the remainder of their cache to Aspen Hill to begin with, even though he was the one who'd argued for it, but this time he wouldn't second guess himself.

His dad abruptly shook his head. "If it makes you feel better you can remember that *I'm* the one who paid for all this. I would've been the bad guy and insisted we keep it even if everyone else had wanted to do otherwise."

The silence became even more awkward, until finally Matt cleared his throat. "What's this about a stolen truck?"

*****

By the time they reached the shelter everyone had caught up on their experiences, or at least the important details.

Lewis could barely believe his dad had managed to find a way to join the Gold Bloc invasion, and that his family had made their way back to the US in the enemy camp. The risks they'd taken had been enormous.

And escaping the internment camp! He tried to imagine making his way through a crowd of hundreds of thousands of people, a mushroom cloud in the distance and terrified and enraged guards shooting prisoners down by the hundreds. They'd taken a huge risk, stealing the truck so they could get away safe. But it had been their only option from the sounds of it, and they'd managed to use the confusion to their advantage.

He felt awful hearing the things Trev and their family had gone through, knowing that he'd left his cousin to deal with it on his own. And as he and Matt described the raider siege he could tell that Trev was feeling the same guilt about leaving them behind. Maybe it was some comfort that both had been where they needed to be, and against all odds things had turned out all right. Or at least better than they could've.

They reached the shelter and introduced or reintroduced themselves to the Larsons and Jane's group, who greeted them warmly but looked a bit worried. Lewis didn't blame them: conditions had been crowded already, and adding eight more people to the mix would only make that worse.

Lewis took them through a short tour of the underground structure, which his parents had seen soon after its rough completion but before he'd put in the finishing touches, and his aunt and uncle hadn't seen since the early days of its construction. They were all suitably impressed, but obviously saw the problem with overcrowding as well.

Less than five minutes later his family piled back outside and began pacing out spots to hang the crude tarp they were using as a tent.

"Hold on, there's plenty of room in the shipping container!" Lewis protested, although he felt a bit of regret at his and Jane's honeymoon period being cut short.

His family hesitated, although the Smith side of it looked reluctant. "We've upset things enough with our sudden arrival," Uncle George said quietly, "and we've got plenty of experience sleeping outdoors." He smiled. "Besides, it's warmed up enough to be pretty comfortable and it never rains much here. We'll be fine for a short time until we can figure out a better arrangement."

Surprisingly it was Jane who spoke up to insist. "That's ridiculous. You'd be just as crowded sleeping under a tarp as you would be in with us, and we've spent plenty of time sleeping in crowded conditions ourselves so we don't mind." She looked at Lewis. "I mean they'll be more comfortable and we won't feel guilty so it's better for everyone, right?"

Trev and Mary, who'd been holding up the tarp to hang it over the cord, shared a look and then dropped it. "Well if you insist," his cousin said dryly.

Lewis had initially bought 40 cots to go in the shelter, preparing for the most unlikely of conditions, so there were plenty for everyone. Arguably they could've all fit in the shelter itself if needed, although they would've been packed side by side. This was much more comfortable.

First things first they emptied the back of the shed and loaded it with the sacks of grain, piling them three high, or about knee height. Lewis had covered the bottom of the container with sheets of plywood to protect the original floor, and they put these on top of the sacks to make a slightly raised area that would fit enough cots for the Smith family.

With the sacks underneath them the boards had a tendency to shift slightly with each step, but they were stable enough that sleeping on them wouldn't be a problem. Jim had fun hopping on the end of one while Linda was testing her cot, jolting her up almost an inch, and when she chased him out of the shed screeching Lewis couldn't help but laugh.

It was almost like when they'd all been younger on a camping trip. He noticed Trev and Mary laughing too, while their parents looked a bit impatient. Although even they couldn't hide slight smiles.

It didn't take too much longer to get the shed set up to sleep ten people. As a finishing touch Jane worked on arranging their shared possessions in their new sleeping area while Lewis put up some partition curtains to give everyone a bit of privacy.

As he worked he kept an eye on his wife, trying to gauge her mood. Her expression was a bit wooden, like she got when she was doing her best to keep patient until she could get a bit of alone time. Seeing it, he hurried to finish up so he could go sit next to her on their bed and put his arm around her, and she leaned into him and put her head on his shoulder.

"Will this be okay for you?" he whispered quietly, aware that the curtain didn't do anything to block sound. "We can set up my tent outside if you want."

She looked up hopefully, but then immediately shook her head. "Everyone would feel like they'd chased us out."

"They'll be fine."

After a short hesitation she shook her head again. "It's . . . nice, seeing you around them. I can put up with a bit of awkwardness to give them a chance to get used to me. You've bent over backwards to let me be antisocial, but this is something I should probably do."

Lewis hugged her a bit closer, then bent down and kissed her. "Want to go for a walk?" he offered.

"Yeah." She stood, but put a hand on his shoulder to keep him from following. "I won't be gone long. This'll give you a chance to spend some time with our family without me being a buzzkill."

For some reason that hurt a bit, although it was reasonable enough on her part. Lewis reminded himself that he'd promised to give her space when she needed it, and it was part of who she was. Still, it was a bit painful to think that she sometimes needed space from *him*.

Once his wife was gone he also made his way out of the shed, slowing slightly near the door to catch Trev around the neck in the crook of his elbow and drag him along. "Come on, let's go get dinner. We can take the bikes."

His cousin yelped slightly and danced his feet for the first few steps until he could get his balance. "Hunting?"

"Traps set up around the gardens, actually. You can see how our crops are growing at the same time."

They spent a minute or so explaining where they were going to their confused and slightly disappointed family, insisting it would just be a short trip. Then Lewis hopped on his bike and started off down the gravel road with Trev pedaling next to him.

Chapter Eight

Settling In

"Did you and Jane have a fight?" Trev called to his cousin as they set a brisk pace towards the south end of town. They passed a few people on the way, and returned their excited waves, but didn't stop to chat with anyone.

Lewis frowned slightly. "No. She just likes her space. You remember."

"Yeah." Trev glanced back towards the shelter, although it was well out of sight and the view was even blocked by a few buildings now. "You guys actually go great together." His cousin gave him a flat look and he quickly raised a placating hand, wobbling slightly on his bike. "I mean that in a good way! I'm actually really happy that things worked out so well for you. It was looking pretty bad when I left."

"Yeah, they did work out really well," Lewis said, nodding thoughtfully. "For both of us."

Trev shook his head, thinking about Lewis and Matt's reports about what had happened while he was gone. "I missed some pretty crazy stuff. Everything with the raiders, and you and Jane. And the animals!"

His cousin turned to grin at him. "That's up there on your list of major events?"

"Well, I mean now you've got a herd of sheep, a flock of chickens, and a rabbit hutch. You've turned into a regular farmer since I left. Not to mention all your heroics defending the town."

"How about you, dodging a hail of bullets from a machine gun?" Lewis shot back.

Trev felt his smile slip and his stomach lurched slightly, remembering those horrible moments. "And pissing myself, as Linda was quick to point out. It wasn't nearly as heroic as you think."

To his surprise Lewis braked to a stop, turning to face him as he stopped too. "I know how it feels," his cousin said quietly. "I've been there. I don't care if Linda was trying to embarrass you, she doesn't understand."

Even though Trev had a hard time imagining his cousin ever losing control like that, he really appreciated the words. "I'm glad you're okay, man," he said, needing to clear his throat halfway through.

"Same for you." Lewis started pedaling again, slowly so Trev could catch up. "Hopefully all that's behind us now and we can get back to living life. You did the impossible and brought our families home, so there's no reason to leave again."

Trev sincerely hoped that was true. He sped up, silently challenging his cousin to a race like they'd done as kids, and Lewis's grin returned as he accepted the challenge and began pedaling furiously. The rest of the ride was a blur of breakneck speeds, which passed in silence aside from the roar of wind in his ears.

From his cousin's description of the attacks on the gardens he'd expected to see blackened craters, but the area had been cleaned up at some point. More than that, the plots where crops had been destroyed had been prepared for new crops.

Those seedlings were already coming up, but less far along than the surviving crops in a way that made it clear where the missiles had struck. In some plots the sharp contrast between the two growing practically side by side stuck out like a sore thumb, which Trev found strangely unsettling.

Even that small oddity served as a reminder of the violence the ground had endured.

The plot he and Lewis had planted was one of those with mingled original and new crops, the land a bit more torn up than the others because the surviving crops had been partially buried by debris and grown up through to reach the sunlight again.

His cousin spent a few minutes specifically naming the new seeds he and Jane had planted and which rows they were in, as well as refreshing Trev's memory on what their original crops had been. Thanks to his mom's gardening he recognized more than a few by the look of the plants, especially the distinctive ones like tomatoes and beans, but it was good to have his guesses confirmed.

After that he helped Lewis water their plot, drawing from the nearby canyon stream and carrying it back in a few of the ubiquitous plastic buckets. Then they spent another fifteen or so minutes doing a bit of weeding and thinning out a few rows of seedlings.

Trev felt surprisingly content as he worked, even though every time he bent and stretched the muscles he'd overworked hauling the handcart for so long complained loud and clear. The day was chilly but the sun shone bright to warm his back, and he could hear birdsong and the conversation of other gardeners in their own plots. A few came over to welcome him back and exchange pleasantries before returning to work, and all in all he couldn't imagine a more pleasant day.

A lot of that was working next to his cousin again. Trev had missed Lewis a lot on his trip to Michigan and back, especially when times were hardest and he didn't have his cousin to lean on. It had been a relief to have Lucas step in to provide that same calm, confident assurance and seemingly effortless competence, but that wasn't all of it.

He missed the easy familiarity of being with Lewis, sharing their thoughts or working side by side in silence. Of having the reassurance of that brotherly bond they'd always shared, but even more so after the Gulf burned and they came to trust each other with their lives.

He could tell his cousin felt the same way, although neither felt the need to express it any further than they already had.

Once Lewis was satisfied with the garden they made their way around the perimeter checking the traps. Several had catches, a rabbit or two but mostly various potguts, squirrels, and other small creatures. Trev helped Lewis dispatch these and clean them, then reset the traps. His cousin had a bag to carry the carcasses in, which he cleaned each day after use, and they stopped off at the river to wash their hands before returning to their bicycles.

Their first stop was in town, to hand over most of the meat. Scott Tillman, acting on behalf of the storehouse, didn't seem to mind them taking two of the rabbits for their share and leaving the less desirable animals for the town, explaining that most of the meat would go into the infamous soups with foraged greens and the little remaining leftover grain.

"Besides," the older man said with a smile. "Your work brought it in, so it's only fair you get first pick."

Trev wanted to stay and chat with Scott and the other townspeople, and particularly introduce himself properly to Gutierrez since his cousin and Matt had only good things to say about the man. But he also wanted to get back and make sure everyone was settling in comfortably and had what they needed, as well as get their dinner cooking.

Besides, now that he was home he'd have plenty of time to reacquaint himself with friends and neighbors. Especially if the town was doing regular events like tomorrow's movie night. So they said their goodbyes and headed out with their rabbits.

Although one luxury Trev *did* indulge in, since it was on the way, was to stop at the town spring and drink his fill of the cold, clean water.

*****

Lewis was in a pretty good mood by the time they reached the shelter. He hoped Jane's walk had helped her as much as hanging out with Trev had for him.

His guess would be it had, since as they braked to a stop in front of the shed he saw his wife sitting on top of the shipping container with her legs hanging over the side, Mary sitting beside her. Neither one of them was talking, although his sister was humming, but they both seemed content.

His dad and Uncle George were using measuring tapes to measure out the dimensions for some houses closer to the shorter hill. Behind them Matt, Ed Larson, and Tom Harding followed with a square, a level, a shovel, and some rope to mark the lines. They'd already outlined one house and were halfway through another, and Lewis wondered if they planned to go with a third as well. Maybe even more, one for each family so everyone could finally have some privacy.

He didn't see his mom and Aunt Clair anywhere, but from the sounds of conversation coming from inside the shipping container he guessed they were busy in there. Linda was over by the sheep pens with Aaron and Paul, trying to coax the newborn lambs to the fence so they could pet them. Off to one side of where the men were working Jim was hanging out with Alvin, describing the escape from the internment camp, which the older boy was only half listening to as he snuck curious looks over at Linda.

Trev went off to join the two young men when his brother called him over, which Alvin used as an excuse to interrupt their conversation, offering to show the two the ewe he'd earned for helping bring the herd down from the mountains. He was probably also hoping for a chance to talk to Linda, and maybe even impress her with his partial ownership of the herd.

Lewis wouldn't have minded joining them, but he decided he'd probably better offer a hand with the measurements. So he continued on to meet up with his dad and uncle.

"Great, you're back!" his dad called, waving him over. "You've got a bit of experience with constructing the shelter and we could use your professional opinion here."

That was, unfortunately, more than a little true. Lewis wasn't sure what their reasoning was for the dimensions they'd chosen, but working with prefabricated materials like plywood and two by fours placed some constraints on things. Builders could use any measurements they wanted with them, of course, but it would mean extra work; going by standardized measurements made working with them far simpler and less frustrating.

Of course, they probably wouldn't have those materials to work with so that was a moot consideration. They might even have to go up into the hills themselves and find a way to cut down trees and haul down the logs they'd need. But that would place even more constraints on building, since they'd have to work with whatever logs they could find and every one was likely to have a different girth and taper. In fact, it was probably better to get the logs first and *then* do the measuring based on what they got.

He started to detail his reasoning to the two older men, and almost immediately Uncle George raised his hands. "I'm out of my element here. How about you two figure this out while I stretch rope wherever you tell me to?"

Lewis wasn't sure whether his uncle really meant that, or was just politely ducking out to give father and son a chance for some bonding time. Either way he seemed more interested in chatting with Ed and Tom than setting any rope lines when he went over to join them.

His dad chuckled ruefully. "I'll be honest, I'm feeling a bit out of my element here too. I've done a bit of construction, but mostly just hammering or driving screws where the boss told me. This'll be my first time planning a building from the start."

"Yeah, well this is also a bit different from digging a hole and burying a corrugated steel shed," Lewis admitted. "We'll figure it out, though."

"We will," his dad agreed, then hesitated. "Speaking of figuring things out, I wanted to ask you . . . that is I'm, um, trying to think of a delicate way to put this."

"Oh boy." Lewis shook his head, smiling wryly. "Just hit me over the head with it."

"Okay." His dad took a deep breath. "Jane seems like a remarkable woman, and from the sound of it you couldn't have asked for a better match. I'm just a bit worried about the fact that she's willing to throw herself into danger right along with you."

Lewis shrugged, a bit defensively. "It's not easy to let her, sometimes. But she's capable and she's willing to face the risks, and honestly I'd rather have her at my back than anyone else."

"That's not exactly what I was getting at." His dad shook his head, partly amused but mostly embarrassed. "I mean I heard what you two managed to do defending the town against the raiders, and it was pretty incredible. Only, um, you two have been married for a while now, right? Have you considered how that all works if you discover that Matt and Sam's kid can expect a Halsson playmate?"

Ah. "You mean, would she be out there defending the town if she gets pregnant?" Lewis asked. That really was was a pretty serious concern. "Yeah, the last thing either of us would ever want is to put our child in danger . . . it's hard enough knowing something might happen to each other. Luckily it's not a concern."

His dad flinched, expression becoming grieved and sympathetic. "Don't tell me she can't-"

"What?" Lewis gave him an incredulous look. "No, Dad, not that at all. Holy cow. I mean I planned ahead there just like everything else. When we decide to have kids it'll be when the situation's a bit better for them. Until then we're taking the necessary precautions."

"Well that's a relief," his dad said with a sheepish grin. "And honestly I shouldn't be surprised." He reddened a bit in embarrassment. "I should've realized you'd be prepared on that front, too. I guess I just didn't expect that, um . . ." he trailed off, obviously trying to think of a polite way to say it.

Lewis gave him a lopsided smile. "You didn't think your son the preparedness hermit would need prophylactics?" He laughed easily. "I'll be honest, half the reason I bought them was for trade, along with toilet paper and other things people might not've thought of when it came to their own preparedness efforts. Although I'm certainly not complaining about having them for personal use."

His dad laughed too, although he still looked embarrassed. "Okay, okay! Since you've eased my mind let's go ahead and drop this awkward subject." He clapped Lewis on the shoulder, looking over to where Jane and Mary were still sitting on the roof of the shipping container with their legs hanging over the edge, not talking but just seeming to enjoy each other's company. "I'm happy for you, son."

Lewis also turned to look at his wife and sister, lowering his voice solemnly. "I wasn't sure I'd ever find someone, especially not after society collapsed. And especially not like her. I still have trouble believing my good fortune sometimes."

His dad pulled him briefly into a one-armed hug. "It looks like you two make a great team. One that can handle anything the world throws at you. And once things settle down and it's safe enough you'll be great parents, too."

"It's something to look forward to." Lewis looked back down at the house they were pacing, getting back to business. "You know, these things are going to be a pain to build without a reliable source of materials. If we get our own logs we're going to have to cut down trees, limb them, drag them a reasonably long distance in large enough numbers to make walls, figure out what to do for a roof, and chink the inevitable cracks. And that's not even mentioning the challenge of figuring out how to keep the walls stable so they don't come tumbling down on our heads."

"Right." His dad wearily rubbed at his eyes. "You've got a bunch of books on portable hard drives, right? Got any on frontier-style construction?"

"Probably, but there's no hurry." Lewis motioned over to the sack he'd left hanging from his bike's handlebars. "I've got a couple rabbits. How about we make some dinner?"

"A bit of fresh meat would be good," his dad admitted with a wan smile. "Even just a few bites. We've had nothing but boiled wheat drizzled with vegetable oil and a bad mixture of spices for over a week."

Lewis rested an arm on his shoulder to gently nudge him in the direction of the fire pit between the shelter and the shipping container. It had been there for years, his first way of cooking food back when he'd begun work on the shelter, but recently they'd taken some time to improve it after things became crowded enough that the stove wasn't always available.

"We can tackle this later," he said. "At any time, really. And if you want fresh meat and you're feeling up to it we can go hunting tomorrow. We've found some really reliable spots not too far from here."

His dad let himself be led away, looking almost relieved to not have to face the challenge of building houses right then and there. He may have been in better shape than the last time Lewis had seen him, and his hair even seemed to have regained most of its blond coloring from the silver that had been taking it over the last several years, but after his ordeals since the Retaliation he looked exhausted.

He was due a rest, and now he could finally afford to take one. Lewis hadn't worked all this time on his shelter just for himself; his greatest hope had always been that it would be there for his family if they needed it. And now by some miracle they'd made it all the way from Norway and here they were.

Like he'd told Trev earlier, now that they had their families with them there was no reason to leave. No more slogs up to the hideout in the mountains, no more bicycle trips across the country, no more fretting over loved ones they couldn't reach on long winter nights.

Sure, depending on what the Gold Bloc did in the future the situation might not be permanent, but for the moment they had everything they needed right here.

*****

Over the next two weeks the family settled in comfortably in the shipping container, able to get along in spite of the cramped conditions.

Although not quite as cramped as they could be, since Lewis and Jane began going out on almost daily overnight hunting trips. It was a thinly veiled excuse for the couple to give themselves the privacy and space they valued without making their loved ones feel like they'd pushed them out, but since the hunting trips usually brought back fresh meat and forageables nobody felt too strongly about bringing the issue up.

The couple's frequent absences also gave the family an opportunity to keep busy by taking on the duties they didn't have time for, including caring for the animals and the garden and cooking meals. Trev began volunteering for patrols again, since the need was still there even though things had been peaceful since the raiders were taken care of.

Mary volunteered for roadblock shifts, while Linda began watching the children in the group to free the adults for other duties. Jim refused to be babysat as part of that group, so they put him up in the observation post above the shelter most days to be a lookout, just in case. To prevent the almost-teenager from going insane from boredom, as well as to further his education, Trev loaned him his phone loaded with books and audio files from Lewis's collection to keep his brother occupied.

Whenever they could spare the time Lewis, Matt, Trev, Terry, and Alvin went up to the closest stands of trees in the nearby hills with Lucas and George to chop down trees using an assortment of saws and axes. After managing that exhausting feat they then had to limb the logs, then laboriously roll, carry, or drag them back to the shelter. That usually ended up being every few days, with whoever was available to go. In between those logging trips Lucas and George busied themselves constructing the first house.

It turned out to be far smaller than they'd planned, and looking even smaller because they dug the foundation a few feet belowground to reduce the number of logs they'd need for the walls. Instead of using nails or screws they held the walls up by burying three of the thinnest logs vertically on each side, arranged to hold a wall of stacked logs between two on either end and one in the middle on the other side, and finally using rope and cord to hold the crude system together. The end result was sturdy enough, and had the advantage of being very quick to build.

For the roof they simply pulled a tarp tight over a peaked framework and tacked it to the walls. It was watertight and provided shade, which were the main necessities, although in even the slightest breeze it tended to make a lot of noise flapping against the framework. Definitely a temporary solution, since over time sunlight would ruin the tarp, and before then the wind would fray it wherever it scraped or pulled and create holes and tears. Not to mention that once the weather started to turn cold again the thin material would provide almost no insulation and the house would be nearly as cold as outside.

Still, it was sturdy enough and quick to build, especially since for the floor and the dirt portion of the walls they simply placed another tarp, with the edges tucked up and around the first of the stacked logs and the corners weighted down with rocks. Within eight days the first house was ready to be moved into.

There was a serious discussion about who the first structure should go to. Everyone agreed that that should be the family that needed it most, so the main question was which family that was. Or not exactly a family, in the case of Jane's group of women and children.

Matt and Sam and Lewis and Jane immediately excused themselves from the running. Ed and Mona Larson similarly turned it down, as did Tom and Alvin Harding, as being more space than they needed. Jane's group admitted that the house was probably too small for all of them, and anyway they felt more comfortable staying together in the shelter. Although they certainly wouldn't mind it being less crowded in there and having more chances for privacy.

That left the Smiths, the Lynns, or Lucas and Eva and Mary as candidates. Somewhat confusingly, none of the families were arguing for themselves to be given it, although they weren't flat out refusing the opportunity either.

With five people the Smiths could arguably get the most benefit out of the house. But in spite of that everyone agreed in the end that the Lynns should have it. The Smiths and Halssons all insisted they were newcomers and shouldn't be first in line, not to mention that with everything Terry and April had contributed to the town, working long hours in the clinic with little compensation, they'd earned a house for them and their boys. It would also ease crowding in the shelter.

With things decided, the Lynn family wasted no time moving out to the new house.

Before construction could begin on a second house Lewis argued that they should prioritize other projects first. The most urgent of those was a proper latrine, since the modest facilities in the shelter were woefully inadequate for so many people and the hastily set up outhouse over on the other side of the hill hadn't been dug deep enough. Another benefit to having a latrine was that they could then begin using the shelter's bathroom primarily for the shower.

Everyone who'd been helping with construction showed a surprising amount of enthusiasm for the latrine project, probably because it involved digging as a first step and they were all sick of chopping trees and hauling logs long distances. Even if digging was equally backbreaking at least it provided a change of pace, and they didn't have to go anywhere to do it.

Aside from town events like movie nights there weren't many breaks from the work that needed to be done. But one thing they could look forward to on most days was the news Matt and Chauncey fed them about Gold Bloc movements, which was somewhat good but mostly bad.

The slight good news was that the invaders had prioritized taking the territory in the center of the country, between the Chinese and Russian forces to the northeast and northwest, with the goal of meeting up in the center to go from there. It meant they were mostly ignoring the states farther south and closer to the coasts, so the remaining US citizens there had time to flee or even prepare to mount some sort of defense.

Unfortunately, for Aspen Hill it was very bad news, because it meant the town was smack dab between two gigantic armies that were pushing hard to meet up practically on top of them. And while the gains in territory the Russians to the east and Chinese to the west were making seemed comparatively slow, since the blockheads were taking their time fully consolidating an area before moving on, they were also ploddingly relentless. It was only a matter of time before they got to Utah.

Matt and Chauncey also had plenty of news about the remnants of the military who were setting up to hold the line in the Rockies. Word came fairly regularly about the movements of General Erikson in Denver and General Lassiter in Salt Lake City, often from soldiers speaking on behalf of the men themselves to anyone they could contact on the radio.

The military had been reaching out to towns, but mostly ones east of the Rockies in Colorado, around Denver, or west of the Rockies in Utah, around Provo and Salt Lake City. The towns in Sanpete County west of the Manti-La Sal mountains also reported being visited by convoys and having regular radio communication with Lassiter's officers, but so far the General hadn't found the time to make his way down to Carbon County. Chauncey admitted that he'd spoken briefly to an officer over the radio, but the man had simply advised him to wait until they could get to Aspen Hill.

But aside from worries about the outside world things were looking better by the day. Conditions at the shelter were steadily improving, with various projects to make things less crowded and more livable. The crops were growing well in the gardens, the livestock they were caring for were healthy and promised future prosperity, and the hunting and foraging were enough to keep them fed and their diet varied without forcing them to use too much of the wheat purchased in Newtown.

For the most part everyone was healthy and in good spirits. There were a few issues with some people not doing work they'd committed to do, or being too lazy and uninventive to find a way to contribute at all, but although there were the inevitable squabbles nobody had proven unhelpful and argumentative enough to cause serious issues.

Anyone who did have copious amounts of spare time was encouraged to head to town to see if there were ways they could help, and between the reconstruction and other projects there always were.

Fifteen days after the family reached Aspen Hill, content that everyone was settled in and had established a routine, Lewis finally got everything ready to do a task that'd been occupying his thoughts since they went after the sheep.

Going after the bees.

Chapter Nine

Abuzz

Jane had been very squeamish about the idea of capturing a queen to start a hive of their own every time Lewis brought it up, and for his part he was intimidated by the thought of tackling the challenge alone unless there just wasn't anyone else who wanted to help.

He'd been pretty confident he could find *someone* willing to help him, at the prospect of getting some honey for their trouble. But he preferred to keep it in the family, or at least the families living at the shelter. After their family got back he had a new opportunity to broach the subject, and as he'd hoped Trev was immediately on board with the idea.

His cousin was eager to go after a new source of food, especially a sustainable one. One that he could take some pride of ownership in. And Lewis didn't blame him; Trev had been working diligently in the gardens, about the only venture he still had some stake in, but it obviously pained him that he didn't have anything to call his own like the animals the others had purchased, captured, or earned.

With that in mind Lewis was perfectly happy to let him take the lead in honey production if he wanted. If they managed to start their own beehive it would benefit from having someone's undivided attention, and Lewis already had enough on his plate.

Aunt Clair was interested in pitching in too, surprisingly. She'd known some local beekeepers around Greenbush, who she'd kept in touch with after initially approaching them with questions about pollination for her garden. She'd even toyed with the idea of raising her own bees, before deciding that the garden itself was enough work, especially when she could buy or trade fresh produce for raw honey from her friends.

Not only did his aunt want them to go after the honey and even try to capture a swarm if they could, she even offered to come along and help.

Decided, the three of them began planning their trip.

Capturing the queen from the large, well established hive he and Jane had seen in the tree probably wasn't going to happen, since it would be too disruptive to the bees. The best they could hope for there would be to collect the honey stores in a sustainable way and then leave it alone.

Luckily it was spring, and about the right time of year when new swarms split off to form their own colonies. That was better for multiple reasons: it would be less disruptive since the swarm was already positioned to move, the swarm would get up and running in the new beehive more quickly, they'd have a much easier time capturing and moving it, and it would have a better chance of surviving the transition. With some luck and a bit of searching they might be able to find a new swarm hanging on a tree branch, which would be the easiest time to capture it.

They took the necessary precautions before setting out, doing as much research as possible and making the required preparations in the fourteen days before the planned trip up into the mountains.

First and foremost was scrounging up clothing to cover as much of their exposed skin as possible, including ties around the cuffs and collars to prevent the small insects from climbing in. For capturing the swarm if they did their jobs correctly the covering shouldn't even be necessary, but for harvesting the honey they fully anticipated they might get stung at least a few times even with some precautions. As far as they knew none of them were allergic, so that shouldn't be more than a minor discomfort.

For the main hive, which they planned to harvest honey from, they brought a metal pail they could fill with green leaves to produce smoke and calm the bees. They also brought a sturdy watertight sack to put the honeycombs in.

For the swarm they brought a spray bottle filled with sugar water so they could mist the wings of the clump of bees, making them too heavy to easily fly when they shook or scraped the swarm loose into the small wooden container Lewis and Trev had made. The container was dark and comfortably enclosed, with a mesh screen for a lid, and they hoped it would safely carry the swarm back with them.

It may have been a bit optimistic but they also spent some time building a box beehive, complete with niches for screens, to house the swarm once they got back with it. Trev volunteered to find a secluded, out of the way place a reasonable distance from the shelter where they could put it, using the criteria Lewis and his mom suggested, and once they'd come out to approve the location he set up the box there.

There was mixed excitement and apprehension at the shelter over the prospect of having a beehive. More than one person was afraid of having bees around that might sting them, while Terry and April's two boys wanted to come along and see the hive up close when Lewis's expedition took it apart. But while a beehive might've made a few people nervous, no one had any problem with the idea of them bringing back the honeycombs they planned to harvest.

They planned to set out early in the morning. The ideal time to capture a swarm would be in the morning or evening, when the bees were less active, which for this trip meant evening. That meant there was no real need to leave *too* early considering the distance they had to go, even if most of it was uphill. But with the consideration of traveling at whatever pace Aunt Clair could manage they wanted to make sure they had plenty of time to get there. That way they could search the area and capture the swarm before it got too dark to see.

It would also be nice to harvest the wild honey that same day, if they had enough time, so they'd have everything done before setting camp and could get home as quickly as possible the next morning. If things went well they might even be able to travel part of the way home before stopping for the night.

Since there were quite a few things they needed to take with them for the bees they packed light for the trip, with just enough food for a few meals, sleeping bags, a tent large enough for all of them, and Lewis and Trev's rifles and some spare magazines, just in case.

Trev had left quite a bit of ammo behind when he set out for Michigan, .45 and .223 for his Glock and Mini-14. He'd also left behind some spare magazines for the rifle, as well as a few 1911 magazines left over from his first gun that was stolen, way back at that Spanish Fork roadblock during his trip up to Midvale with Matt.

With that in mind one of his first errands after coming home had been trading one of the AK-47s to the town storehouse for one of the M16s they'd captured from the raiders. Lewis had gone along with him at his cousin's request, to give him advice and inspect the weapons he wanted to buy. Their plan was to make it a straight trade, just the gun itself with no ammunition or magazines, since those could be used by the other two AK-47s their dads were still using.

It wasn't a great trade for the town value-wise, but Scott Tillman was fairly generous and didn't charge extra for it, considering Trev would be using it for patrolling. He *did*, however, charge for the 1911 Trev purchased, cutting down a hefty chunk of the town's debt for the food in the cache they'd purchased from him and Lewis. Since Trev still had a few magazines for the pistol Lewis suggested he only purchase a couple more, at least for now.

On the way home Lewis warned his cousin that he should probably do some practicing, since the M16 was a bit different from his Mini-14 and would take some getting used to. It was an unfamiliar shape and weight and it balanced differently, to begin with, and it offered a three-round burst mode as well as semi auto.

It was also intended to fire 5.56x45 ammunition, rather than .223. Thankfully the M16 could still handle .223, while the reverse wasn't the case and the Mini-14 would experience problems with 5.56. Because of that Lewis was glad his cousin had made the switch in weapons in that direction, or all his .223 ammo would now be useless.

After making the purchases Lewis helped Trev look both weapons over and thoroughly clean and maintenance them. Then, almost as eager as his cousin, he agreed to come along when Trev test fired them.

According to his cousin the new 1911 handled roughly the same as his original pistol. Once Trev was satisfied with that he emptied the rest of the magazine to re-familiarize himself with recoil and trigger control for dry fire practice, then holstered the weapon at his hip. He'd lost his underarm holster when he was captured by the Gold Bloc, and Lewis only had a hip holster to offer him.

He could tell his cousin missed the concealed carry holster by his impatient response when Lewis suggested taking the time to extensively practice drawing from his new holster. That seemed like a good opportunity to change the subject by suggesting Trev try out the M16.

It was immediately obvious his cousin got a kick out of burst mode, and Lewis had to convince him to resist the temptation to waste bullets playing around with it. He instructed Trev to focus instead on staying on target through each controlled burst, having him go through a single magazine to familiarize himself with the recoil and muscle movements for dry fire practice. His cousin reluctantly called it good at that, more than satisfied with his new guns.

The morning of the trip dawned clear and reasonably warm, hopefully good weather for swarming. As they made their final preparations to leave Lewis suggested they might do a bit of long distance target shooting while they were up in the mountains if they had the time, which was something to look forward to.

The precaution of bringing the weapons was probably unnecessary, up there on tiny dirt or gravel roads nobody used. Especially with the military set up to the west, which would discourage anyone with criminal intent in the area from getting too bold.

Still, Lewis couldn't imagine traveling anywhere these days without a weapon; he carried them when going to town, and sometimes even around the shelter. A bit of that was in case he spotted any game, but more of it was because experience had taught him it was better to be safe than sorry.

Lewis and Trev carried most of the gear, to keep Aunt Clair unencumbered so she could set a good pace, and as they hopped up on their bikes he motioned for her to lead the way. She obligingly moved out in front, although she looked a bit amused.

"You've done everything but toss me a line so you can tow me along," she complained. "I'm in my 40s, not my 90s."

Trev grinned back at his mom, not looking the slightest bit sheepish. "Tell you what. When we're halfway up the canyon we can see if you still object to the entire towing thing."

She made a shooing motion at them, then waved goodbye to the few family members who were awake at that early hour and had gathered at the front of the shipping container. They were all grinning at the banter, and Lewis grinned back as he waved goodbye to Jane, who stood a bit away from the others. "Sure you don't want to come?" he called.

His wife grimaced. "I've been shot in the gut. Now ask me how much I want to get stung a dozen times."

That was as close as she'd come to admitting how uneasy the bees made her, and seemed like a pretty final answer. Lewis had to admit he'd miss her, since if the trip lasted overnight this would be the first time since their wedding that they'd be apart this long. Another incentive to hurry things up. "See you tomorrow, then." With a last wave he stood on his pedals and hurried to catch up to the other two.

In spite of the good-natured ribbing Aunt Clair set a fast pace. Almost too fast, truth be told, as if to show she could keep up just fine. Lewis struggled to find a polite way to remind her about pacing herself for long distances, but before he could think of anything Trev did.

"Hey!" his cousin shouted, pedaling faster to catch up. "All joking aside, keep going like this and we'll all collapse before we're halfway up the canyon."

Clair stubbornly kept going for a bit longer, then reluctantly slowed down. She was breathing hard, but then again Lewis was a bit winded himself. After a stormy few minutes she braked to a stop, then took a deep breath and looked back at them. "I guess I've been a little defensive. I got mad at you for treating me like I'm in worse shape than you guys, but it's true, isn't it?"

Trev finally showed a bit of embarrassment and ducked his head without answering. "Not as much as you think," Lewis admitted, feeling a bit embarrassed himself. "I guess we've been driving that point home more than we needed to. We weren't quite this bad with Tom on the last trip we went on, when he was having a pretty tough time. I guess we just overcompensated to try to make it easier for you."

His aunt's expression softened slightly. "Well you have no reason to be embarrassed for being in good shape," she admitted. "I had all winter and spring to improve my physical fitness and didn't, and it ended up costing me when I had to haul that wheat for a week. And it made things harder for the rest of you, too."

She started up again, going at a reasonable, if slightly slow, pace. "I'll do my best, and I promise to let you know if I need a break."

"No worries," Trev called. "It's not a race. That's why we started early, right?"

Aunt Clair looked back, making a face. "It might not be a race, but we still have to reach the finish line."

They took the canyon at a more reasonable speed, stopping to walk their bikes several times. To be honest Lewis didn't mind too much, since they were wearing their protective beekeeping clothes and even the mild breezy day was making him sweat like crazy.

There was also the fact that a lot of their hurry last time had come from Pete zooming up and down goading them on. Without him pushing them to go faster they reached the top a half hour later, but with enough energy to set a much faster speed on the gentler slopes beyond. So it all balanced out.

And more than balanced out, since they saved hours on their trip without the detour down the road Pete had taken, then having to retrace their steps and follow Matt and the Hardings down the correct road. Thanks to that, and the fact that they had a shorter distance to go to reach the ravine, they got there in the early afternoon and coasted their bikes down the steep road leading to the bottom.

They'd stopped for lunch only a couple hours earlier, so after just a few minutes to rest they left their bikes behind and hiked up the stream to the copse of trees with its tangle of undergrowth. There Lewis pointed to the hive he'd seen, which buzzed with just as much activity as before.

"Do we harvest it now?" Trev asked, looking a bit uneasy now that the task was there in front of him.

Lewis exchanged glances with his aunt. "I think we should hold off on that," she said. "We still need to wander around this area and see if we can find a migrating swarm, and I'd rather we do that *before* we infuriate a bunch of bees."

"We can also keep our eye out for more hives to harvest," Lewis added. "This is a good location, and where there's one there might be others. Even though I sort of doubt we'll find anything, we definitely won't if we don't look."

"Okay." His cousin looked around, stretching slightly. "Should we split up? I'll circle left around the copse, mom can circle right, and you can shove your way upstream through dense undergrowth."

Lewis snorted. "Yeah, no." He looked around for a moment, then pointed to another nearby copse. "I'll go check that out." The other two nodded and started off, and he called after them. "Remember, migratory swarms aren't *that* common. This hive might've already sent one off weeks ago, or won't for another few weeks. Don't be too bummed out if we don't find one, since we know we'll at least be coming home with some honeycombs."

His cousin grimaced. "I'm glad *you* know that," he muttered, giving the hive another uneasy look. Then he grinned to show he was still on board and started off again. Aunt Clair nodded to him and started off too, so Lewis began picking his way up the hillside to the left of the stream to reach the copse halfway up.

He was the one who'd given the warning, but even so he was a bit disappointed when he didn't find anything in the small stand of trees. Well, he found *something,* forageable plants and signs of game he could hunt or leave traps for, but it wasn't what he'd come looking for.

After thoroughly inspecting the underbrush and deadfall beneath the trees Lewis went on to another nearby copse. By the stream he could see his cousin and aunt had met up and were picking their way into the denser growth of that copse. Hopefully they wouldn't waste too much time in that tangle and would start searching the copses on the other hillside next.

Over the next few hours they searched a wider and wider area around the hive down at the stream. Lewis didn't see any sign of swarms or of other hives, but stubbornness and the thought of Trev's disappointment kept him looking after he would've given up.

Finally, with the sun sinking low on the horizon, he called his cousin and aunt back to the copse. "We still have time to harvest this hive and make it back down to Aspen Hill to sleep in our own beds before it gets too dark," he offered. "If you want to keep looking I won't argue, but I think chances are pretty slim of just wandering through the woods and stumbling on a swarm at this point."

Aunt Clair sighed. "I suppose finding a migrating swarm is more of a discovery of opportunity than something you set out looking for. Maybe we can ask people to keep their eyes open when they're out hunting and foraging and let us know if they find one."

Trev nodded glumly. "I guess the day's not a complete waste with the honey we'll be getting. Let's figure that out."

Lewis nodded his agreement, and they spent the next few minutes gathering up green wood and leaves and gingerly piling them next to the tree below the hive, careful to not get too close to the insects or disturb them. It took a bit of finagling to get the fire started, especially with bees buzzing overhead, but Lewis did his best to stay calm and get it done quickly.

Finally thick acrid smoke began drifting, then pluming up from the growing fire. Up above them the buzzing sound diminished as the flow of bees coming to and from the hive slowed to a trickle. The smoke seemed to have calmed them, although there was no way to tell by how much until they actually dug in there bear-style to grab the honeycomb.

Since the wind was a bit uncooperative, blowing the smoke the wrong way half the time, they waited a bit longer to be safe. And also, Lewis could admit to himself, to build up his courage for the task ahead. But finally he took a deep breath and glanced over at Trev. "Ready?"

His cousin nodded, doing his best to look casual. "I've been stung before. Wasn't that bad."

They started forward, gloves tied over their long shirts and mosquito netting draped over their hats. Lewis carried his heavy knife for cutting open the hive, while Trev held the sack for harvesting honeycomb and the metal pail.

His cousin made straight for the fire, scooping a generous bunch of coals and smoldering leaves into the pail. Here the wind finally worked in their favor, blowing across the top of the small container and keeping the fire inside going strong. As thick smoke drifted up Trev gave him one last questioning look to see if he was ready. Lewis nodded, so his cousin lifted the smoking pail beneath the hive with one hand while bracing himself against the tree with the other, planting a foot as high up the trunk as he could for Lewis to use as a leg up.

His turn. Lewis clutched the knife in one hand and climbed the trunk, careful not to put too much weight on the foothold his cousin had provided him. With a bit of effort he managed to pull himself onto the lowest branch, which was dead and broken off after a few feet. The footing was unsteady there, so he leaned against the trunk almost right next to the hive as he took a deep, steadying breath.

Then he began cutting into a layer of rotted bark covering the main part of it.

Once he pulled the wood away he uncovered the neatly layered honeycombs inside, as well as an almost frightening number of bees. Many of which immediately began buzzing around. Thanks to the smoke they didn't get aggressive, though, and Lewis mustered the nerve to begin brushing them off the first honeycomb so he could cut chunks of it free to drop in the bag Trev held below him.

He worked fast, especially after a bee managed to sneak beneath the mosquito netting and stung him on the neck, giving him extra motivation. The old hive seemed to have endless layers of honeycomb going deeper and deeper, plenty to spare, but he didn't get greedy and left quite a bit behind. It was spring now and the bees should be able to manage with a small store, but he didn't want some freak event to kill the hive because he took too much.

It was a relief to finally call down to his cousin he was done. He wasted no time in hopping down, and with Trev close behind they made a beeline for where Aunt Clair waited.

"Nice," she said when Trev handed over the bag, which she had to use two hands to lift. After brushing aside a few bees crawling around near her gloved fingers she hefted it thoughtfully. "What does that feel like, 50 pounds?"

"Probably closer to 40," Trev said.

Lewis nodded in agreement. "Give or take a few pounds. Although not all of that is going to be honey. Still, not bad."

"Not bad at all, and we'll definitely find uses for beeswax too." His aunt patted him on the shoulder. "I saw you wince at least once. Was it too bad?"

He shook his head. "Just got me that once. Trev?"

"Came off scot-free. Of course I was holding the smoke and you were the one ripping apart their hive." His cousin gave him a sheepish look. "I guess next time it'll be my turn to do the exciting part."

"I won't argue." Lewis glanced up at the sky, then held out his hand to take back the honey. "Well we should still have plenty of time to make it home. Let's get going."

They set a brisk pace back downstream to their bikes, and moments later were pedaling up the steep slope to the top of the ravine. Once they finished that brief uphill jaunt the rest of the trip would be almost all downhill, and the only thing holding them back would be how reckless they wanted to be with their brakes and around corners.

Lewis had just reached the top and was coasting towards where the steep downhill slope began when Aunt Clair abruptly shouted and skidded to a stop. Biting back a curse, he mashed the brakes as well, and as soon as he was fully stopped began unslinging his rifle. Behind and off to the side Trev was doing the same.

Then he saw where his aunt was pointing, at a solitary young aspen tree off to one side that looked like a shoot from the nearby grove. On the lowest branch a fuzzy basketball-sized shape hung, heavy enough to make the limb droop, made up of tiny shifting specks with more coming and going.

A swarm.

"Well how about that," Trev said, taking his hand away from his rifle. "We wasted all that time down in the ravine, when all we needed to do was keep our eyes open a bit better on the way here."

Lewis slung his rifle again, hardly able to believe their luck. "Better late than never." He shifted his gaze from the swarm to the horizon. "I think we might have time to catch it and still get home."

Aunt Clair nodded. "Shouldn't take more than a few minutes to spray it down, then shake it into the box."

Trev immediately dropped his bike and started for the tree, reaching into his pack for the spray bottle full of sugar water with one hand as he tugged the mosquito netting down around his face and the back of his neck with the other. Lewis followed suit, although it took him a bit longer to untie the box they'd made to transport the swarm.

By the time he caught up his cousin Trev had already liberally doused the ball of bees with the water. Lewis slid open the box's lid and held it up beneath the swarm, and his cousin wasted no time giving the branch a single, heavy shake. The swarm almost completely dislodged, dropping onto the soft cloth they'd placed at the bottom of the box. Only a hundred or so bees remained clinging to the branch, waving their sodden wings but unwilling to take flight.

"Think we got her?" Trev asked, looking down into the confused mass of insects in the container.

Lewis held off on shutting the lid, keeping it in place below the branch. "We'll see in a second." If the queen had dropped with the rest of the swarm then the bees still on the branch would drop down to rejoin her, while if she was still on the branch the bees in the box would be trying to leave.

After the swarm's confusion settled a bit the bees on the branch began dropping down, and the ones in the box began reforming the swarm inside. Lewis waited to see if any scouts would return to rejoin the swarm, and after a couple arrived he closed the lid after them and fastened it tight.

Moving much more gingerly now, he carried their new bees back to his pack and tied it on, then carefully lifted it onto his shoulders and got on his bike. "Let's go a bit carefully," he said as his aunt and cousin returned to their bikes. "I wouldn't want to crash, or even bounce these poor guys all over the place too much."

Aunt Clair took the lead again, with Trev following behind and Lewis in the back. They all kept an eye out for bumps or unexpected turns, and from his position Lewis had enough time to react when he saw his aunt or cousin go over one they hadn't seen. In spite of their caution they made good time, and with half an hour until sunset he was fairly confident they'd reach the canyon by then, and get home well before full dark.

At which point, with an eerie feeling of deja vu, he heard the sound of a truck engine in the distance.

Chapter Ten

Upset

It has to be US military. I mean, it has to be, right?

Trev was the first one off his bike, rifle unslung and ready as he tried to pinpoint the direction of the noise. Surprisingly, in spite of the fact that Lewis was carrying a swarm of bees in a bulky box on his back he reacted almost as fast. Although his cousin's reaction was to pedal furiously for the nearest source of cover behind an outcropping of rock, heedless of the jouncing.

That was probably the more reasonable response to the threat, rather than abandoning his bicycle and whipping out his gun in the middle of the road like Trev had. Trev hastily picked up his bike again, still holding his M16 in one hand, and awkwardly hopped on and pedaled for the hiding spot.

It was only when he'd almost reached cover himself that he realized his mom didn't seem to have heard the noise. She was fifty feet farther on before she finally realized they weren't behind her, and as she braked as well she looked back at them in confusion. "What is it?"

"Truck engine!" he called back.

Even at that distance and in the fading light he saw her face tighten with worry, and she wasted no time wheeling her bike around to join them. While she was on her way Lewis tried to radio in a warning to Aspen Hill, but got no response. Not too surprising given how far into the mountains they were.

"What do we do if it turns out to not be the military?" Trev asked once his mom pulled her bike behind the outcropping and they were all as hidden away as possible.

"Or if they are but they're unfriendly?" Lewis shook his head grimly. "I'm not sure we can just stay hidden. Last time it turned out the vehicle was on another road that wouldn't take them anywhere near us or the town, but I don't think we're going to be as lucky this time. This is the only road in this area, and from the sound of it that truck is heading right for us."

"Which means it's also heading right for Aspen Hill," Trev said, putting two and two together. "So we can't just let them drive on past since we haven't been able to radio in a warning to the town."

They all exchanged worried looks. "It's probably the military though," his mom said.

In response Lewis shrugged out of his pack and began to climb the outcropping, making his way up to a spot where he could see a long ways up the road. The climb didn't look too difficult so Trev joined him, and together they watched the vehicle come into view.

It turned out to be a truck almost exactly like the ones the town had captured from the raiders. Trev got out his binoculars and peered through them. "Pretty sure it's US military," he said after a few moments.

"For what that's worth," Lewis answered. He had his binoculars out too. "Hard not to remember the raiders also driving those."

Trev hopped back down, landing a bit awkwardly on the uneven ground, and shrugged out of his own pack, handing it and his rifle to his mom. "Use the outcropping as cover until you can get back on the road, then head towards town and radio a warning." He looked up at his cousin. "Lewis, will you go with her?"

"What?" Lewis demanded, turning. By that point Trev was already out in the road, in plain view of the approaching vehicle. His cousin made an irritated noise, although now that he was in sight of the truck Trev didn't turn to look at him. At least until Lewis continued. "This spot is a good place to provide cover if needed, it would be a shame to abandon it. Do you think you can make it back by yourself, Aunt Clair?"

Tearing his eyes off the vehicle, which was now only a few hundred yards away, Trev risked a glance behind the outcropping. His cousin had settled back and was unslinging his G3, while his mom had left his stuff behind and was picking up her bike. She turned to give Trev a stern look as she started to hop onto it. "If you're going to do this then be careful."

With a last reluctant look at both of them, she began pedaling away using the cover of the outcropping.

Doing his best to hide his uneasiness, Trev moved a bit farther up the road. They couldn't let the truck just drive past down to Aspen Hill, and if the people headed their way *were* unfriendly Lewis would have his back pretty well. All that aside, there was no way he would've taken this risk, not just for himself but for the others, if he wasn't fairly confident he was looking at soldiers sent by General Lassiter's group. He'd made a promise to Davis, after all.

The approaching vehicle had slowed at the sight of him, and as it got within fifty yards it rumbled fully to a stop. Doors flew open, and several armed men poured out to train weapons on him.

Trev bit back a sigh and slowly raised his hands over his head. A person shouldn't have to look down the barrels of a dozen assault rifles in his *lifetime*, let alone a few times a month. That sort of thing was impossible to get used to, but he was definitely getting used to not being able to get used to it.

"I'm unarmed!" he shouted.

The weapons stayed up as the man who'd been in the passenger's seat, an officer, shouted back. "Why are you stopping us?"

"I'm from a nearby town. You were driving right for it, and I wanted to avoid any misunderstandings that would end in violence." Trev hesitated. "Are you with General Lassiter?"

After a moment's hesitation the officer barked out an order, and Trev felt his shoulders loosen as the soldiers lowered their rifles. "Corporal Kyle Williams, United States

Marine Corps," the officer answered. He started forward, motioning for Trev to do the same so they could talk without yelling. "Yes, we're part of his group."

"I'm Trevor Smith, from Aspen Hill," he replied, offering his hand once he was close enough. Williams shook, although he looked a bit cautious about a trick. "Did Sergeant Davis send you to contact the town?"

"Davis?" the corporal repeated. "Ethan Davis?" Trev nodded. Williams frowned slightly. "I read his report on his scouting run along Highway 6, but he didn't mention contacting the locals."

"Actually my family was with him on that trip, until he dropped us off close to home," Trev said. "I promised him I'd sort of be an intermediary for the town when you guys finally came around."

"Well that wasn't our plan," the soldier said, sounding thoughtful as he glanced along the road towards the canyon. "We were just sent to map out all these little roads and see how many of them lead down to the valley below. Although I suppose if your town's not too far there's no time like the present to stop by and get the ball rolling."

Trev grinned. "It's not far, as the truck drives."

The corporal didn't smile back. "You might as well hop in, then. We can give you a ride back to your town and you can introduce us around."

He hesitated. "Um, actually I'm up here with my cousin."

"So we'll give him a ride back too," Williams's eyes abruptly narrowed. "He's not hiding somewhere pointing a gun at us, is he?"

"I was!" Lewis called, coming out slowly from behind the outcropping with his hands raised. The soldiers immediately lifted their weapons to train on him. "At least until I knew you were friendly. That's how the world works these days."

Williams looked a bit annoyed as he motioned for his men to lower their weapons. "Anyone else?" he demanded.

Trev wrestled with options, but if the truck was making for town anyway then they'd catch up to his mom before too long, so there was no reason not to mention her. Especially since they didn't seem like enemies. "My mom was with us. We sent her ahead to warn the town in case you *weren't* friendly."

"Well I suppose we've got room for a third." Williams brusquely turned for the truck. "Pick up your stuff and get in."

"Hold on," Lewis called, when the corporal turned he gave their hiding place an uncertain look. "Do you guys mind if we brought some bees along?" One of the soldiers with Williams cursed and took a few steps back, and Lewis hastily continued. "We've got them in a sealed box."

There was a brief, uncomfortable silence. "Bees," the corporal said flatly.

"It's why we were up here," Trev said with a shrug. "We've got honey, too. And bikes. If it's too much we can meet you down there."

Williams sighed. “No, we've got room.” He gave Lewis a stern look. “You better make sure that box is sealed. If one of my men gets stung I'm kicking you to the curb, and you'll be lucky if that's all I kick. Go get your stuff and we'll pull the truck up.”

Trev hurried after his cousin to get his things, although as he went out of earshot he heard the officer muttering about yokels and chickens. The complaints were less than complimentary, and Trev decided he wasn't going to share any of his honey with the man.

They stowed the bees and their bikes in the back. Lewis agreed to ride back there with their stuff, while Williams offered to let Trev join him and the driver up front. Since Trev would have a better line of sight his cousin offered him the radio, so he could contact town when they got close.

During the exchange the corporal eyed their weapons. “Nice rifles,” he said. “Let's keep them on our backs with our hands well away from them, okay?”

That seemed fair enough, considering Davis had outright confiscated the AK-47s until it was time to drop Trev's family off. He and his cousin quickly agreed, and with that settled they all piled inside.

Williams sat in the middle, giving Trev the passenger window. As the driver started the truck and they rumbled forward down the road the corporal turned to him. “I'd appreciate it if you could tell me a bit about Aspen Hill so I know what to expect. And more importantly, what we can expect you to offer to help fight the Gold Bloc.”

"Sure. First things first, though, I was wondering if you could answer a question that's been bugging me and my friends for a while." The corporal gave him a curious look and Trev continued. "A few weeks ago my cousin and some friends were up here and they also heard a truck. Was that you guys?"

Williams took a while in answering, thinking it over. "It's possible," he finally said. "I know the General sent some preliminary scouts to assess the area before he even arrived, although my team and the others he sent out in the last few days are the first to seriously cover this ground. But I couldn't tell you for sure without looking into it."

Trev shrugged. "I'm not sure who else it could've been besides you, and it was a while ago. We were just wondering."

"Fair enough." The corporal motioned. "You were going to tell me about your town?"

"Right." Trev briefly outlined what had happened with the town over the fall, winter, and spring, although he left out Ferris and the FETF occupation. There was no way to know what Williams would think about anything that had happened with the administrator and his soldiers, then their later return as raiders, but that was a can of worms he didn't want to open. When he did describe the raider siege he kept the details of their specific identity vague there as well.

By the time he was done they'd reached the canyon and had begun navigating the steep switchbacks, and after he fell silent the corporal shook his head. "I've heard all sorts of stories of some pretty vicious fighting since the Gulf burned, but what your town went through sounds pretty nasty even so. I'm impressed you managed to hold your own." He gave Trev a sidelong look. "Your defenders could probably help a lot if you joined up."

"I let the Mayor know about you guys when we got back a couple weeks ago," Trev said. "She made a general announcement to the town about who you are and what you're doing in the area. I think you might get some volunteers."

The driver abruptly stiffened and began to slow. "We've got someone hiding ahead, hundred yards at two o'clock."

Trev squinted ahead, then felt a surge of relief. All he could see was a bit of a handlebar, but it was the bike his mom had been riding. "That's my mom. She must've hid when she heard the truck coming."

"Right." Williams nodded to the door. "Want to let her know what's going on?"

With a quick nod Trev hopped out of the vehicle and trotted down the road. "It's okay, Mom!" he called. "They're giving us a ride home!"

She came out dragging the bike, a look of relief on her face. "They're military?"

"With Lassiter," Trev affirmed. He helped his mom get her bike up into the back of the truck with the aid of Lewis and one of the soldiers, then pointed towards the cab. "If you want the comfy seat go ahead."

Williams was standing beside the passenger door waiting for them, and at this he cleared his throat. "Actually, Mr. Smith, you're the intermediary. I'd like you to be in front ready to talk to your people, just in case."

Trev glanced at his mom, and she nodded and motioned for Lewis to give her a hand up into the back. Trev trotted up to the cab and climbed in after the corporal, who once again took the middle seat. Almost immediately the truck rumbled into motion again.

About a minute later they reached a part of the road that overlooked the rest of the canyon and the valley below. Williams nodded to the distant view of the town. "I'd say you're close enough to radio in and let them know we're coming."

Right. The last thing he wanted was for someone on patrol to freak out and start taking shots at them. Trev lifted his radio. "Trev here, can anybody hear me?"

After a few moments Chauncey's voice came in strong. "I hear you. How'd the beekeeping go?"

"Great, but we can talk about it later. Can you get ahold of Mayor Tillman?"

Before the retired teacher could answer Catherine's voice came on. "I've been listening, Trev. What is it?"

Trev glanced over at the corporal. "We met a squad of scouts sent by General Lassiter up in the mountains. They want to visit the town and talk to us. We're halfway down the canyon now, driving a military truck."

There was a long pause before the Mayor answered. "Okay, we'll roll out the red carpet. Come on in."

*****

At the edge of town a group of well-armed defenders in body armor were waiting for them, clustered around a truck parked across the left lane of Center Street. The truck had one of the M2 Browning heavy machine guns they'd captured from the raiders mounted atop it, with Rick Watson in the gunner's spot. Beside the truck Matt stood awkwardly holding one of the TOW missile launchers.

At the sight of the defenders the soldier driving the truck slowed down and shifted uneasily. "Jeez, that's a Ma Deuce on that truck! Corporal?"

Trev's radio crackled to life. "Go ahead and welcome our guests to Aspen Hill, Trev," Matt said. "The Mayor's waiting to greet them at town hall, if they want to keep going."

"I guess that's that," Williams said. "Let's go."

The driver hesitated before accelerating again. "Or we could turn around, Corp. That dude on the ground has a missile launcher! What kind of town packs this kind of heat?"

"The kind that had it used against us," Trev replied. "I told you we captured the raiders' weapons." He turned awkwardly in the seat to fully face the officer sitting beside him. "And I can promise you that if there's trouble, it won't come from us."

Williams shifted his shoulders slightly, almost a shrug. "I suppose scouting isn't all driving around in sunny meadows. Keep going."

The driver reluctantly sped up again. As they passed the other truck it rumbled to life and pulled around to follow them, which might've been meant as an escort but certainly wasn't doing anything to calm the nerves of the soldiers.

"Seriously though," Williams said in a low voice. "Your town has a *lot* more in the way of armaments than it should. If all your defenders have that kind of gear then you're better equipped than half the remaining companies in the US military."

Trev had a sudden uneasy thought. "You're not going to try to confiscate anything, are you?"

The corporal hesitated. "I'll admit, the idea of civilians holding that kind of firepower gives me the heebie jeebies. But at the same time the last thing we need is to antagonize people on our side. Besides, it's usually not a good idea to disarm the people you're trying to convince to fight for you." He glanced uneasily out the passenger side mirror. "Although we may consider sending a squad to come work with the town to properly, and safely, use what you've got."

Yeah, we haven't had the best luck with that in the past, Trev thought to himself. Although he wasn't about to say it out loud.

True to her word Catherine met them on the steps of town hall, along with what seemed like half the town. Trev hadn't been sure what mood would greet Williams and his squad, although celebration wasn't high on the list all things considered. Wariness, maybe, and suspicion. Possibly even outright hostility.

Instead the crowd seemed more expectant than anything, waiting passively to see how things played out. That silence stretched on as Trev hopped out of the truck, followed by the corporal, while the other soldiers and his mom and cousin piled out as well.

He figured introductions were a good first step, so he cleared his throat. "This is Corporal Williams. Corporal, Aspen Hill's Mayor, Catherine Tillman."

"Ma'am," Williams said, nodding. He looked over the crowd, likely noting how many were armed. "I suppose you know why we're here."

The Mayor nodded as well. "We've been expecting a visit, or at least radio contact, for a while now." She turned towards the auditorium beside town hall. "Do you want me to gather everyone so you can speak to them?"

The corporal shrugged reluctantly. "I suppose. Although it would be more useful to talk to you and any other town leaders."

Trev winced slightly. That might be true, but Williams wasn't winning any friends with that attitude.

Catherine turned to him and he jumped slightly. "Trev, could you show the Corporal and his men to the clinic and find them some food?" She directed her words at the officer as she continued. "It shouldn't be more than a half hour. A chance for you to rest. And of course you're welcome to stay the night."

"Thank you, ma'am." Williams glanced at Trev and nodded, so he started making his way through the crowd to the auditorium as the corporal barked an order and the soldiers all fell in line behind him.

Trev knew where the communal soup pot was kept boiling, but it turned out he didn't need to go after it because Catherine sent in Scott with a pot and enough paper bowls and plastic spoons to go around. After the Mayor's husband introduced himself and handed out the soup the squad went off on their own to eat, grumbling about the awful taste and watery consistency. They still ate it, though.

All except Williams, who stayed behind and questioned Trev and Scott about the state of the town. He was willing to answer a few questions about how the military's defense preparations were going, although he was a lot less forthcoming than he could've been and always steered the conversation back to his own topics.

Before too long Catherine returned and led the soldiers and her husband to the seats set up on the stage. Trev made his way down to the auditorium proper and found his family seated halfway back on the left side. Mary and Lewis had saved him a seat between them, so he edged his way down the row to join them.

"Where's our stuff?" he whispered at his cousin as Catherine stood and introduced the corporal to those who hadn't been there at his arrival.

"We took it home then came back as quick as we could," Lewis replied. "Your bike's sitting out front with ours for when we leave."

"What about the bees?"

"I set them in a quiet place until we have time to take care of them."

Trev was going to ask about the honey, but Mary hissed quietly and poked his shoulder. He hastily turned to see Williams approaching the podium.

The officer didn't say anything for almost a minute, looking around the assembled crowd that packed the auditorium to the rafters. When he did speak, voice booming through the room, it was so abrupt that Trev jumped slightly, and he wasn't the only one.

"I'm not a salesman," Williams began in an even tone. "I'm not even a recruiter. I didn't come with a pitch to get you all on board. Frankly, given what we're facing I don't think I should have to convince you of anything. So I'm just going to give you a few facts and let you choose what to do with them."

He took a breath. "First off, numbers. Even assuming General Lassiter and General Erikson can gather all the scattered groups of soldiers, law enforcement, and other trained personnel we've contacted, and we can get enough potential recruits from nearby towns, we'll be lucky if we can scrape together a hundred thousand fighters."

A low murmur of confusion swept the auditorium, and Trev didn't blame them. That sounded like a huge army.

At least until the corporal continued. "At our last best estimate, the combined Russian and Chinese armies number over one million professional soldiers. Which means going on numbers alone they have us 10 to 1. Admittedly, they have to worry about defending the territory they've already taken and guarding their supply lines, as well as logistics for moving and supplying so many soldiers. But even so their numerical advantage is going to be very, very difficult to overcome.

"Now let's talk about equipment. All of our military bases were destroyed, either before or during the Retaliation, by nuclear strikes or more conventional bombing runs. We have a handful of aircraft, most of which are built for hauling cargo or passengers. We have less than two hundred tanks and other heavy armored vehicles.

"We have the supplies to feed the soldiers we've gathered for a month at half rations. We have less than a million gallons of fuel, which may sound like a lot so I'll put it in context: with what we have we can run all our vehicles continuously for less than three days. We have enough weapons to arm everyone who comes to us, barely, but for ammo we'll be lucky if each soldier has 1,000 rounds apiece. To last however long this war goes on."

Williams fell silent to let that sink in, then looked around, meeting the eyes of people in the crowd. Those who didn't look away, at least. "That's all that stands between you and an enemy that's been butchering every American they come across. An enemy vastly superior in numbers, equipment, and with access to at least one relatively stable and intact country for supplies, on top of what they brought with them.

"So if you'll excuse me, I'm going to go discuss some of the finer details with your Mayor. After we leave I'd like you to think very hard on what you have, what you can contribute, and who of you is willing to stand with us to defend your homes, your loved ones, and give what remains of the United States of America a slightly better chance of surviving."

Without another word he made his way over to where Catherine sat and leaned down to speak to her, then made his way off the stage. She gave the townspeople an apologetic look and followed.

Once she was gone the crowd broke into worried murmurs, the noise level increasing by the second. Thanks to Chauncey those who were interested in knowing already had a general idea of the grim situation, but Williams had definitely painted a pretty clear picture. At Trev's side Mary was humming a depressing song.

After a minute or so Scott stood and made his way to the podium. "I suppose while we're all gathered we can discuss how the town as a whole is going to respond to this request," he said. "Strictly volunteer, of course, but it really seems like it's in our best interest to volunteer all we can."

Trev immediately stood. "We're going to send people, right?" His question raised a few shouts of agreement and a bit of clapping, but also some uneasy murmuring.

The older man frowned. "Do we have anyone we can spare? I'm guessing the only people the military wants is our defenders, and the town can't afford to lose that protection."

"If the military is going to be protecting us instead we can probably do without a small army," Lucas said, speaking up from the row behind Trev.

Ben spoke up from the other side of the room. "Not to sound selfish, but as far as we're concerned it won't really matter if the military wins against the Gold Bloc if the town doesn't survive the fight. I hate to be the one to bring this up, but we're still losing several people a week to starvation in spite of our best efforts. We have to think of our immediate survival first."

A minor commotion broke out as dozens of people spoke up at once, some in agreement and others calling him shortsighted. Trev sat back down, unable to think of anything to add and not sure if he even should. If the military had food he might have argued that every volunteer the town sent would be one less mouth to feed. But the people who could be most useful fighting the Gold Bloc also tended to be the best hunters and foragers, so the town would be losing food in the deal.

He also had his own personal quandary to deal with. There didn't seem to be any way he could justify *not* joining up with Lassiter's group to defend his home and loved ones. He'd seen the Gold Bloc firsthand, watched them gunning down defenseless prisoners at the internment camp. Everything he'd heard confirmed that they continued to commit those kinds of atrocities, and he wanted to keep them far, far from Aspen Hill.

At the same time these last two weeks had been some of the best since the Gulf burned. In some ways better than before. He had his family around him, safe and sound, and they were well on their way to being self-sufficient and surviving the hardships to come. He'd traveled a lot these last several months, by foot, bicycle, and even in vehicles, but everything that had pushed him to leave home was here now.

He wanted to stay. He wanted to set up the beehive and work in the garden and patrol the town and be with his loved ones. But all the reasons that kept him here pushed him to go, too.

The hubbub of debate and argument continued for some time, until Scott finally tapped on the mic a few times, filling the auditorium with bursts of feedback. The few strings of Christmas lights hanging overhead actually flickered when he did it, even such a minor thing a strain on the basic system of solar panels and batteries they'd set up.

That got the crowd's attention. The auditorium fell silent as everyone turned to look at him, and he spoke in a moderate tone. "This is a serious decision, not one you make on the spur of the moment. I would encourage everyone to go home now and think it through overnight. Or even longer, if we're fortunate enough to be given more time to decide."

Catherine had appeared on stage as her husband spoke, coming over to stand beside him. When Scott finished she added her own words. "I agree. Corporal Williams's arrival was very sudden, as was his request for aid. We all need time to process it. But for any of you who have decided to contribute something or volunteer, come see me as soon as possible so I can begin making up a list and keeping everything organized."

She turned to head back through the center curtains into the clinic, then paused and leaned over the mic again. "Matt, Ben, could you come with me, please? I need your input."

*****

The meeting naturally broke up after that, but a lot of the townspeople stuck around to discuss the night's events or share the news of the wider world they'd missed.

Some of the family decided to stick around as well, but Trev and Lewis wasted no time leaving the auditorium and grabbing their bikes to pedal fast for home.

Trev felt bad about leaving the soldiers without even wishing them good night, considering he'd taken on the role of intermediary for himself. But Williams and the town leaders seemed to have things well in hand, and the Mayor hadn't specifically told him to join the town leaders in their discussion.

Which was a relief, since it would be long past dark before they got their work done and bed was still a ways away for him and his cousin. Attending the meeting had taken a lot of time, and it had interrupted what they'd been doing with the bees.

The sooner they could get the swarm into their new beehive the better, so that the bees could begin doing their thing. They also needed to squeeze the honey out of the combs and then strain it, and if it was too watery they'd have to take even more steps to prevent it from going bad, then seal it in jars for long term storage. They'd also need to clean the beeswax so it could be made into candles, among other uses.

In spite of his eagerness for the project up to this point, Trev had trouble drumming up too much enthusiasm as they sped home in the fading light. The hard dose of reality Williams had administered put a damper on everything.

"So I guess we're back doing this, huh?" Lewis asked, surprising him after the silence had gone on for over a minute.

Trev blinked and glanced over at his cousin. "What?"

"Splitting up again. I can't feel right about not going to join the people defending us, leaving them to fight and die to protect us while I stay home safe. Especially if they lose and there's no one left to stop the Gold Bloc from taking over and killing us all."

It was a bit surprising to hear that his cousin's thoughts had been following his. Or maybe not so surprising, even down to the fact that Lewis had come to the same conclusion about being the one to volunteer. "And we can't both go because our family is here and one of us should stay behind to watch over them," Trev concluded.

"Exactly." Lewis grimaced. "It's hard to forgive myself for leaving you to take the trip to Michigan alone, especially after everything you went through. So this time I go and you stay."

Trev was already shaking his head before his cousin had finished speaking, and he slowed down on his bike so they could have an easier time talking. This wasn't his ideal situation to have this discussion, but it was definitely necessary.

"You didn't leave me to do anything," he pointed out as Lewis slowed to match his speed. "I thought we were being rational here." It was his cousin's turn to look confused, and he continued. "We have to hope that whoever goes is going to survive, but if he doesn't then who would you rather have here looking after everyone?"

Lewis flinched as if shot. "Trev, don't," he started, expression miserable.

Trev continued determinedly. "You've got the knowledge and skills to help everyone build a future. And you've got a wife to think about. You need to be here, which means I need to go."

"Jane would go with me. We can handle ourselves."

"I know you can. And so can I. This way makes sense, just like when I went to Michigan." He couldn't help but smile. "Also you're trying to take responsibility for other people again. Let me handle this. I'd feel better knowing the two of you were watching over our family."

His cousin looked away, slowing down even more. "All three of us should go. We're needed there."

In spite of the words Trev knew Lewis's resolve was weakening. "All three of us can't. Also isn't that a discussion you should be having with Jane?"

Lewis sped up without answering, until he was going an almost dangerous speed along the rutted gravel road in the darkness. "Let's get the bees taken care of," he called.

Trev had no arguments there. He did his best to catch up.

Over the next hour they took care of the honey and beeswax, working in strained silence. Both tried to relieve it with banter, but neither seemed in the mood. Last of all they hiked out to the box hive to release the swarm into it. Lewis brought his night vision goggles to see, and Trev let him do most of the work while he helped as directed.

It wasn't his project anymore. Lewis would do a good job tending the hive while he was gone, probably better than he would've, so it was best he work on it from the start.

His cousin finally closed the lid of the new hive over the relocated swarm and left them to settle in. "I don't know about you but I'm exhausted," he said, starting back towards the shelter.

Trev did his best to walk beside him in the darkness, tripping over obstacles Lewis could see but he couldn't. "Yeah, assuming I can sleep at all."

Just as they were circling around the shorter hill across from the shelter Lewis abruptly spoke up again. "Remember up in the mountains last winter? Just the two of us, conquering everything that came our way."

He smiled. "Yeah. I'll admit I feel a lot more confident about things when I'm around you."

His cousin stopped to put a hand on his shoulder, the shape of his face with the goggles odd in the darkness. "Are you sure you want to be the one to go?"

"No, but I'm going to do it anyway." Trev shrugged, trying to ignore the discomfort of having his cousin able to see him through the goggles while all he saw was a silhouette. "Take care of everyone, okay? Jim needs someone to help him along like you helped me. And Linda . . . well, even after everything that's happened she doesn't seem mentally prepared for the world the way it is now."

"I will." Lewis squeezed his shoulder, then dropped his hand and continued on towards the shelter.

Trev followed, making his way to his bed in the crowded shipping container while his cousin sought out Jane. It was a relief to sink onto the cot and let his muscles relax.

As he'd predicted, he didn't sleep well.

Chapter Eleven

Volunteers

Matt was up early, dressed and ready to take his bike into town.

Although she usually got up later than him Sam was awake when he left, coming out to hug him goodbye. She kept the hug going for an uncomfortably long time, not saying a word but just holding him tight.

They'd talked for hours the night before, and she hadn't liked what he'd had to say. She hadn't disagreed either, though.

"Love you," he finally said, stooping down awkwardly to kiss his much shorter wife. "Be back soon."

Sam nodded, still not saying a word. He thought he saw a tear slip past the curtain of her dark hair as she turned to go back into the shelter, but that might've been a trick of the predawn glow. Probably not, but it made him feel a little bit better to assume that.

Last night Catherine had asked him to go around to everyone in town who was likely to volunteer and talk to them. Not to pressure them into any decision, or even to ask what they planned to do. Just talk.

It was a nice bit of self-deception, since she might as well have just come out and said she wanted him to do both. Why else would he need to talk to them in the first place? And with the request had come the unspoken assumption that he'd be going with any volunteers he drummed up. And when Matt had agreed he'd basically confirmed her assumption.

It was the last thing he wanted to do, but he was needed. And beyond that, if he stayed behind anyone who was on the fence about volunteering themselves might decide to stay behind too. While if he went others might follow his example.

Williams had said he planned to leave as early as possible, and sure enough when Matt passed town hall he saw that the scouts' truck was gone. The corporal had promised the military would visit again, although the intent behind staying in touch wasn't exactly altruistic.

Above and beyond the request for supplies and volunteers to join the fight, Williams had convinced the town to defend Aspen Hill Canyon and the surrounding foothills and mountain slopes, in the event the fighting ever reached them. It was vital that the enemy not secure any route into the Rockies, since holding the multiple choke points the mountain roads represented was one of the few advantages the military had going for them.

Luckily General Lassiter didn't expect the town to fight a war. Williams was going to report in and have the military send demolitions specialists, to rig explosives at an ideal choke point in the canyon to completely destroy the road and cut off all vehicle travel beyond that point. He just wanted Aspen Hill's defenders to keep an eye on the destroyed road and turn back any incursions on foot the blockheads made into the mountains if they could, or radio in and request help if they couldn't.

It was an important task, and even with the road destroyed more than a little dangerous. A good way for Aspen Hill to do its part without needing to go anywhere. Matt would've been interested in the challenge of scouting the foothills and ravines in the area, to figure out how to prevent anyone from sneaking up into the high country on foot. But since he was one of the volunteers he had a different job to do, and right now that job involved finding people to go with him.

He decided to start with Carl and Tam Raymond first, since the Mayor's own family should be an easy conversation.

Since Tam had fractured her ankle in their attack against the raider camp she'd been out of action, taking the opportunity to spend time at home with her daughter. Matt had visited her a few times to see how she was doing, and yesterday she'd been at the meeting walking normally so he assumed she'd healed well from her injury.

With houses in town so crowded the Raymond family had moved in with their parents at the Mayor's house, along with a few other individuals who'd been displaced from their homes. Even this early in the morning he heard activity inside, so he knocked softly.

Not too long afterwards Scott opened the door, his granddaughter Jennifer sneaking a peek around his leg. When she saw Matt she popped out and waved, and the older man obligingly stepped aside. "Come on in."

"Thanks." Matt leaned down to pat the toddler on the head as she ran off to go play, then slipped through the door. "I came to talk to Tam and Carl."

"Yeah. Catherine's task for you, right?" Scott sighed. "Carl's on patrol. I'll go get Tamara."

He disappeared up the stairs, and a moment later Tam came down, dressed for the day but yawning as if she'd just woken up. She kissed her daughter when Jennifer ran over to her, then shooed her up the stairs and headed for the door. "Let's talk outside."

"Sure." Matt was a bit worried that she wasn't meeting his eye. He followed her out and joined her sitting on the top step of the porch. "I suppose you know why I'm here."

"Yeah. Mom asked you to recruit volunteers." Tam gave him an uncomfortable look, then stared west towards the mountains bathed in early morning sunlight. "We're sorry, Matt."

He gave her a blank look. All through the winter, and especially during the raider attacks, he'd been able to rely on her like few others. He'd thought she'd be an easy sell. "That's a no from both of you?"

The auburn-haired woman gave him a fierce look. "That's right. We've done our best to be there when the town needed us. I didn't mind taking an injury doing what needed to be done, but I won't risk leaving Jennifer without a mom. She's barely started talking and most of her questions are about where her mama and papa are since we've been gone so often helping the town, leaving her to her grandma and grandpa to take care of. I was actually almost glad I fractured my ankle since it gave me a chance to finally spend some time with her."

She paused, then took a shuddering breath. "I can't do it anymore. I won't. Me and Carl need to get on with our lives for our daughter's sake, not go off and play soldier."

Matt nodded, disappointed but not surprised. "I understand. The town couldn't ask you for more than you've already done. We'll take care of things from here." He stood.

Tam stood as well, sounding almost pleading as he made his way down the steps. "We know how bad it is out there, but the town needs people to defend it too. We can at least help with that."

He turned to give her a miserable look. "I'm not here to guilt anyone. I wouldn't dream of it, after everything you've done for the town. I'm just gathering the names of people willing to go."

Leaving his friend on the porch, he returned to his bicycle and hopped on.

That had been a pretty depressing meeting, and it didn't leave him in high spirits as he continued on. A niggling worry began in the back of his head that he might be heading off to join the military all on his own.

He visited the Watsons next, and there the news was a bit better. Rick was already packing to leave, and so was Wes. The two were actually arguing about it when he arrived, and the younger brother immediately came over to Matt as he opened the gate into their yard.

"I can go, right?" he demanded.

Matt hesitated and looked at Rick, who glared at him. "You're fifteen, Wes."

"Sixteen in less than two months!" the young man insisted. "Besides, I helped against the raiders!"

Rick stormed over. "One of us needs to stay here for Mom and Dad, and anyway I'm not letting my kid brother go off to war. Besides, will the military even take people that young? We're more civilized than using child soldiers."

Wes went red in the face. "Are you trying to tick me off, bro?"

Matt hastily cut in. "Catherine did set the age limit at 18, Wes." He didn't mention that she'd realistically allowed for exceptions. Wes *had* done his part to help against the raiders, but never anything too dangerous. He really was just a kid.

The young man swore and stomped into the house, slamming the door behind him. "I'll talk things over with him," Rick promised. He shook Matt's hand. "I'm guessing you came around to sign me up. I'm ready whenever. How many people do we have so far?"

"You and me." At his friend's alarmed look he hastily continued. "You were my second stop. Still plenty of daylight."

"Right." Rick went over and began moving his things, scattered on the porch, back inside in a neat pile by the door. As he worked he called over his shoulder. "Want me to tag along?"

Matt felt a surge of relief. Not having to do this alone sounded awesome. "You bet."

Rick had his own bicycle, a smaller kid's bike that he still rode well in spite of the size. Together they set off, his friend looking at him for direction on their next stop. "We going to everyone in town?"

"Not everyone. Ben's going to be asking around with his people." The former refugees had almost completely integrated into the town, but there was still that slight divide there. Ben had done a lot to bridge it.

"So I guess that means Ben's going too. That's three of us."

"And the cousins and Jane," Matt added. He hadn't talked to them yet, but he couldn't imagine them refusing. "Let's go talk to Gutierrez."

To his surprise the former raider, still living in the small room above the auditorium, seemed a bit reluctant even though he immediately agreed. "Is something wrong?" Matt asked.

Gutierrez snorted. "You tell me. I'm technically AWOL."

"So are half the soldiers out there, right?" Rick pointed out.

The former soldier shrugged. "I said I'll go. I just hope it doesn't cause any trouble."

On the way out the door they ran into Scott. "Hey," he said. "Glad I caught you. You took off without talking to me."

"About volunteering?" Matt asked, a bit surprised. It wasn't that he didn't think the older man was capable, quite the opposite. Maybe it was Scott's age, or because he was so vital to running the town, but it hadn't occurred to Matt that he might want to sign up.

Scott nodded. "I've been partially on the fence about it, but I figure someone should be there who can care for the gear the town's going to be sending along."

Matt hadn't considered that. Scott had been running the storehouse so he'd make a good quartermaster. "Glad to have you."

The older man smiled wryly. "I don't suppose many of us want to go, but what we want wasn't usually what we got even before the world went crazy."

Scott agreed to tag along to help them visit everyone, and so Matt decided the next stop should be the gardens and other places people would be working. It might save a few stops for when they'd exhausted all other options and had to go house to house.

Lewis and Jane were working in their plot when Matt's small group got there. His friends waved, and Jane stayed behind to continue working while Lewis came over.

"Sam mentioned you were out recruiting," he said, shaking hands all around.

"Working on it, at least," Matt agreed. "We've got a lot of people to visit. But at least you and Trev live with us so that's one less visit I have to make." He paused. "Speaking of which, are either of your dads also planning to volunteer?"

His friend looked uncomfortable. "Actually, we've already talked it through. Trev's going to go."

The silence stretched on uncomfortably as Matt absorbed this news. "Just Trev," he said flatly.

Lewis nodded, slightly defensive. "We also have our family and everyone else at the shelter to worry about. Defending and providing for them."

"Are you kidding?" Rick demanded. "Do you realize how many people would feel better about volunteering knowing you'd be along?"

"No, how many?"

Rick hesitated. "Well, me for one! You and Jane are the ones who get impossible things done."

Lewis's smile had a bit of an edge to it. "I'm sure Trev would love to hear how enthusiastic you all are about him coming along."

"Oh come on, don't give us that," Matt snapped. He grabbed his friend's arm and pulled him aside a bit. "You know we need you and Jane," he said in a low voice.

"So does our family," Lewis replied. "And we'll be here to help the town in case anything comes up."

That was starting to sound like a flimsy excuse to Matt. "The town will be fine. They survived the winter, they survived Razor's gang, and they survived the raiders. We can survive this too, but we'll need to face it head on. That means getting as many people as possible out there defending our homes."

Lewis shook his head. "Yeah, only instead of 50 raiders we're facing a million professional soldiers, coming at us from either direction, and instead of machine guns and missiles we'll be facing tanks and aircraft. It's not completely unreasonable to keep people back to defend the town if that doesn't go so great."

Matt did his best to keep his temper. "Yeah, but instead of Aspen Hill the enemy will be facing the *entire* United States military and all its citizens. It's not as lopsided as you might think."

His friend hesitated, then shook his head slowly. "I'm not sure that's going to be enough." He hastily continued before Matt could erupt. "I know what Williams said about how we're all doomed if the military fails, and he's probably not wrong. But if we do lose this war and worse comes to worst I want to be here with my family trying to find a way to survive the aftermath."

"Well aren't you a ball of sunshine," Matt said sarcastically.

Lewis looked away. "I'm sorry, Matt. Our family's sending Trev, that'll have to be enough."

Matt pushed down his anger with a sigh. It wasn't fair to give Tam a pass and then tear into his friend, even though he really wanted to. He held out his hand to shake. "I'm going to be a jerk and pretend you're still thinking about it. If you happen to change your mind before we leave you know we'll all be overjoyed about it."

His friend grimaced. “Fair enough. But I'm not going to. I will give you my word, though, that I'll make sure Sam and the rest of your family are looked after while you're gone. You won't need to worry for them, at least.”

That was something he hadn't considered about Lewis staying behind, and it almost made up for his friend not volunteering. “Thanks. That means more than I can say.”

They shook, then Lewis headed back to his garden while Matt went around to the other gardeners to try his luck with them.

Not a single one volunteered.

*****

Over the next several hours they went to the other places people would be working and then from house to house, trying to get in touch with as many townspeople as they could. After they finished they tracked down Ben to see what kind of success he'd had among the former refugees.

Truth be told, the results weren't all that surprising, although they were incredibly disappointing. A large portion of the townspeople already volunteered as defenders, or had in the past, but of them less than a fifth wanted to abandon everything and go fight in a hopeless war. Among the townspeople at large only a handful more volunteered.

He wasn't sure he could blame them. Williams wasn't wrong to warn them about just how bad the situation was, and how much everyone needed to help if they were going to have any hope of survival. But at the same time it wasn't exactly the sort of thing that would encourage everyone to go off waving their guns and stampeding for the front lines.

He'd gathered twenty-three people. Sure, even if everyone in town volunteered that wouldn't do much to swing the odds in their favor against the enemy, but under two dozen felt like a drop in the ocean.

He supposed that even as big as the threat was, it was still remote enough that people could try to ignore it. Once it got more immediate, once things started looking really bad, more people might be jolted into action and join the fight then. Hopefully before it was too late.

Maybe they should've let in the younger men who volunteered, like Wes. Near the end Matt *had* made one exception there, for Pete Childress. The young man had practically threatened to hike up into the mountains looking for the military so he could join up if he wasn't let in. Pete had handled himself well against the raiders so Matt agreed to take him, although he wasn't sure how he felt about it.

When Matt got back to the shelter he found that Sam had packed up everything he'd need and arranged it on their bed. He would've been grateful for the gesture, and he was, but when he arrived his wife was sitting there next to the backpack with his coat in her hands, tears streaming down her cheeks.

When she saw him she immediately buried her face in the rough cloth, scrubbing her eyes with it. Then she raised her head and did her best to smile and pretend she was fine. "Oh hey. How did it go?"

Matt slumped down onto the cot next to her and pulled her into his arms, resting his chin on her head. "It could've gone better." She didn't respond, which was usually an invitation for him to go on, so he briefly told her about visiting everyone in town and the results they'd managed.

When he finished they sat in silence for a while. Matt was just about to get up and start checking through the things Sam had packed to make sure she hadn't overlooked anything when she abruptly spoke up. "Maybe Tam and Lewis and Jane and the others have the right idea."

He stiffened and pulled away slightly, looking down at her. "What?"

She stared back, eyes flashing. "Haven't you done enough, Matt?" she demanded. "After everything you've done for the town, can't you just say no for once?"

Matt gave his wife a wounded look. "You too?"

"Don't act like I'm being unreasonable!" At some point she'd started crying again, although she didn't seem to notice. "You nearly got blown up fighting the raiders. Chauncey lost his leg. Almost a hundred people died and about that many were wounded."

Sam hesitated, her anger fading to anguish. "And that was a fight we couldn't avoid, against a bunch of scruffy criminals attacking the town. Now you want to go pick a fight with professional soldiers? Seriously, Matt, haven't you done enough?"

Talking to Tam he'd felt disappointed, and with Lewis he'd been angry. With Sam he felt guilty. Sharp, deep down to his bones guilt. But that didn't change anything. "I'll have done enough when the town is safe," he said as gently as he could. "Somebody has to fight the Gold Bloc forces. If we all just worry about ourselves they'll steamroll the military and take the entire country unopposed. We'll all end up dead, or on the run and hiding for who knows how long."

His wife looked away miserably. "Why can't it be someone else? We've done what we had to for the town. But, well, it just doesn't seem like the town has done much for us in return. I work at the clinic with April and Terry day in and day out and at best we get the same bowl of watery soup as everyone else. You spend your time protecting the town when you could be out finding food or tending our garden and they don't feed you any better."

Matt wrapped his arms tighter around his wife, staring at the curtain in front of him. Her complaints weren't exactly fair, but they weren't exactly unfair either. They *were* giving a lot to the town for very little in return, that was true. But only because the town *had* nothing to give, which was why it so desperately needed help from anyone who was willing to give it.

He preferred to be proud of giving that help rather than resent it, and frankly he was surprised to hear Sam talk like that given her generous nature. This had all been harder on her than he'd thought, harder than he had any right to ask of her, especially when they had a baby on the way to worry about.

And now he wanted to leave her when she needed him most.

"You won't be alone when I leave," he said quietly, kissing the top of her head. "My family is here for you, and so is everyone else in the shelter. Lewis and Jane are going to be staying too, and they'll look out for you and the baby while I'm gone."

She shook her head, but her resolve seemed to be wavering. "It's not the same and you know it."

"I know. But I've already promised to go." Matt hesitated. "Although if things start looking really bad I'll come back." He lifted her chin up to meet her eyes, shining with tears, and felt a stab of anguish at the anguish and fear in them. "Please, tell me this is okay."

Sam met his gaze for a long time, as if searching for something, and then abruptly pulled away and began fussing over his things. "You'll probably want to take all your ammo," she said. "Is the town going to give you a truck to carry things? If so we won't have to worry about weight and you can take more."

It wasn't quite what he'd hoped for, but he supposed it would have to be enough. With a sigh Matt stood and joined her. "We'll have one of the raider trucks, and Williams gave us a bit of extra fuel."

That wasn't all the town was giving them. Each person who went would have the best of the gear they'd captured from the raiders, weapons and body armor. They'd also be taking one of the missile launchers, half the remaining missiles, half the grenades and remaining Molotovs, and one of the heavy machine guns with half of the .50 BMG ammunition.

That would leave the volunteers incredibly well equipped, while the town would still have the means to defend itself. And maybe it would be some consolation for Sam, to know that the town had done everything it could to make sure that he returned home to her.

*****

With one person shy of two dozen volunteers they decided to split into two squads. Trev was a bit surprised when Matt approached him to lead the smaller squad of 11.

"What made you choose me?" he asked.

His friend looked a bit sheepish. "Honestly? Until we know better what the military needs from us I'm setting up the first squad so all the seasoned defenders are in it, assuming it'll be the one seeing the most action. Your squad has all of our older volunteers, less experienced defenders, and the regular townspeople. I plan to keep you on the bench wherever possible."

"Well it's an honor to be picked for that," Trev said wryly.

His friend chuckled. "That didn't sound all that complimentary, did it? I picked you because you did a pretty good job of getting the roadblocks into shape back when you first came down from the mountains, and everyone likes you." He hesitated. "Also you and Lewis both have a bit of a reputation. Nobody has any complaints about taking orders from the guy who outran a machine gun."

That again. Trev wondered if the full story was getting out. It wasn't exactly his proudest moment, the one he wanted to get a reputation about. With a sigh he looked down at the list

Matt held out for him. Tom Harding would be along with him, which was a relief. Matt had probably shoved him into Trev's squad due to age, not lack of ability.

He also recognized some names from the roadblock, Rob Jonas and Hans Miller. Good men, but they hadn't struck him as very soldierly. Fred and Susan Donnell looked like a couple, or maybe brother and sister. Either way he didn't recognize them, which meant they were probably Ben's people.

He looked up again. "When are we leaving?"

"A week. Williams didn't seem to think there was any need to rush, although he did say the sooner we sent people the more help we could be with preparing defenses. We'd also have more opportunities to receive some quality training from skilled soldiers."

"A week, huh?" Trev said. He looked back down at his list. "Well, no time like the present to get started. If you need me I'll be at our shooting range, hopefully with as many of the people on this list as I can round up."

Matt clapped him on the shoulder, looking relieved. "Good luck, and thanks."

As many people as he could round up turned out to be everyone. It took a while for Trev to go around finding them all, especially since he didn't know where half of them lived. But when he did find his new squad mates most seemed relieved to hear he wanted to start training immediately, and quickly agreed to meet him at the shooting range in a few hours.

Trev directed everyone to find Scott at the town storehouse and get the weapons they'd be using, and even went with one of the townspeople volunteers to help him pick up his rifle and sidearm and familiarize him with basic handling and safety until he could be more properly trained. The man seemed hesitant with even the basics, but determined to learn. That was a good sign, Trev hoped.

He could understand that for the less experienced people the idea of going off to fight a war was terrifying, and his offer to train them promised some hope that they wouldn't just be tossed into anything they weren't prepared for. As he pedaled home to get things ready he only hoped he was up to the challenge of preparing them.

The shooting range was a hundred or so yards west of the shelter, facing northwest towards the targets in a little hollow with a bit of a rise to either side and a low hill in front. It had been carefully picked out as a place where the risk of stray shots escaping to hit anyone was extremely low. Lewis had set it up while the shelter was still under construction, and had used it frequently. At his cousin's invitation Trev had used it a few times too, but not nearly as often.

While he waited for his new squad to show up he patched up the targets, then got out the bundle of colored flags that would warn people away, to put up along the hill and two rises. The thin wire stakes were easy to drive into the ground, if slightly flimsy, but it made it easier to put them up and take them down for each shooting session. Lewis didn't want them up all the time drawing attention to the area near the shelter, and Trev fully agreed.

Tom Harding came by early, since he had the shortest distance to go, and they chatted as they waited for everyone else. As the volunteers he'd be leading trickled in Trev noticed other people had tagged along, friends and family members. Maybe in a show of support, or maybe because they were on the fence about volunteering themselves and wanted to be convinced. He noticed Alice Thornton was one of the spectators, which struck him as a bit odd because she didn't really know anyone in his squad; her friends among the volunteers were all in Matt's squad.

Trev didn't mind the onlookers as long as they weren't a distraction, and even offered to let them train, with the reasoning that knowing how to handle a gun was always a useful skill, and even more so these days. A few hesitantly agreed, but most seemed content to just watch. Hopefully they'd learn something useful even so.

After he'd gone around to all the volunteers, shaken their hands, and introduced them to each other he had them line up in front of him. "As you can probably guess, we don't have much ammo to spare for training," he began. "Which means we need to get the most training value out of every shot. Any guesses what we'll be doing the rest of the time?"

"Dry fire practice?" Tom asked wryly.

Trev grinned at the older man. "Right."

"Wait a second," Alice said from among the spectators. "Are you even going to do any shooting today?"

He turned to look at her, again wondering what she was doing here. "That depends on how well everyone does with the basics." She seemed to accept that, or at least had nothing else to add, so he turned back to his squad. "Now, I see the town has made good on their promise to give each of you the best equipment they have. That means we'll all be using standardized M16s and 1911s. For today let's focus on pistols."

Turning away from everyone at an oblique angle so they could still see his hands and weapon, he drew his new 1911 and unloaded it, making his movements slow and obvious so everyone could see what he was doing and how he was doing it. That meant removing the magazine, ejecting the round in the chamber (and catching it as it flew away), then doing a mag and chamber check. Then, to be absolutely sure the gun was unloaded, he did another mag and chamber check.

Once he was satisfied he holstered it again. "My weapon is now unloaded and ready for dry fire practice. Notice I say it out loud, to cement it in my mind. When I'm finished with dry fire practice and load and cock my weapon so it's ready for use, I'll tell myself it's now loaded out loud. Just to be certain I don't decide on a whim to do just one more round of dry fire practice and end up shooting anything by accident."

He drew his weapon again, holding it at the ready position pointed downrange. "My weapon is now unloaded, with no chance I can shoot anything with it. *What don't I point it at*?"

"Anything you don't want to shoot," Tom once again answered for the group, sounding a bit impatient.

Trev nodded. "Rule one of firearm safety. Loaded, unloaded, safety on, safety off, you never point the gun at anything you don't intend to shoot. That's the best way to guarantee that even the most careless person will never have a tragic accident. Rule number two is similar: keep your finger off the trigger unless you're ready to shoot. Rule three, keep your firearm unloaded until you're ready to use it."

He hesitated, looking around the group to make sure his warnings were sinking in. This was literally a matter of life and death. "If you're in a situation where you need to keep your gun loaded so you can be ready to use it quickly, which will probably be the case a lot of the time once we leave here, the rule is to keep your firearm holstered unless you're ready to shoot something or you need to inspect or maintain the weapon. Similarly, for those guns that have a safety always keep it on until you're ready to shoot, and put it back on as soon as you finish shooting. Any questions?"

Trev waited, but no one spoke. Most looked as impatient as Tom. "All right then. Everyone unload your weapons. Let me know if you need help. I'll be coming around to watch you all do a mag and chamber check to be sure there were no mistakes. Once we're all ready I'll walk you through the dry fire drill, which includes drawing, holstering, the various positions of readiness up to firing position, clearing malfunctions, and the actual dry fire itself."

"Question," Mason Priscott, a man in his 30s who'd lived in Aspen Hill for over a decade, said as he raised one hand. Trev nodded to him. "If we already know all this stuff do we still need to do it?"

"Short answer, yes," Trev said with a slight smile. "Long answer, yeeeeeesssssssss. Aside from live fire practice this is the best training you can do, and you can never get too much training. You don't just want to learn this, you want it deeply ingrained in your muscle memory. That way when you're out there with bullets flying all around you, and an enemy pops up and everything's going wrong, you don't need to think about what you're going to do because you've already done it thousands of times."

For the next few hours he ran everyone through dry fire drills and made sure they were all using the proper grip and finger placement on the trigger. Once he was sure they were doing things reasonably well he had everyone fire one full magazine, stopping them after each controlled pair of shots to correct any signs of the usual problems that threw off a person's aim and tended to get worse over time if not corrected.

Eight shots felt woefully inadequate to help accustom the volunteers to recoil and make sure they were acquiring a proper sight picture, but they really didn't have the ammo to spare. Hopefully they could make up for that with consistent dry fire practice, since they didn't have many alternatives. Last of all he taught them how to disassemble, clean, and reassemble their 1911s.

Trev sent everyone home after getting them to agree to meet back tomorrow at the same time. The plan for the next training session was to take them through a few full sets of dry fire drills on the pistol to keep them fresh in their minds, then move over to the rifle and work on that. A few of the volunteers wanted to ask questions or just chat with him as everyone else left, and as he talked with them he saw Alice waiting for him.

Most of the spectators had left after a half hour or so, when they realized they were just going to be watching everyone do the same thing over and over with empty guns. The few spectators that had remained to the end had already left with the friends or family they'd been waiting for, leaving the young woman one of the last people left at the shooting range. He saw now that she'd brought Chauncey's familiar rifle case with her, probably carrying his shotgun, and she had it slung over her shoulder.

He excused himself from the other recruits, encouraging them to make sure they were packed and ready to leave even though the departure date wasn't for a week, then made his way over to her. "Hey Alice. Did you need something?"

"Yeah. I want to join your squad."

Trev blinked. She'd said it so casually it took half a second for the words to sink in. "I, uh, wasn't expecting that. Have you talked to Matt?"

The young woman flushed slightly. "Matt's squad is full, so I came to you. You've still got a spot open, right?" Trev hesitated, and her expression darkened. "Is it because of my age? I turned seventeen last December. I'm older than Pete, and Matt's letting *him* go."

"You still need to talk to Matt," Trev insisted. Then he hesitated, feeling a bit bad for dumping an awkward conversation on his friend. He decided to be blunt. "And he'll probably say no. Pete might be a bit younger, but he's been through a lot more fighting and proven he can handle himself. Also he pretty much threatened to go off on his own if we didn't bring him along."

He'd been half afraid she'd explode in fury, but instead Alice assumed a determined expression. "And you think I won't? I don't know if Matt told you, but I joined the last fight against Turner's raiders. I could barely hold a gun but I had the guts to point it at the enemy and pull the trigger, even when they were shooting back. I'm ready to do that again."

Well this was unexpected. Matt *hadn't* told him Alice had been part of the last fight, although she was one of many who had and his friend hadn't taken the time to name them all. Still, he hadn't seen this spark in the blond young woman the last time he'd seen her, back when they'd made Molotov cocktails together the day Ferris and Turner's raiders first showed up.

"Why?" he asked quietly.

Her determination abruptly exploded into anger, but not necessarily at him. "Because I lost everything! Razor's thugs killed my dad and nearly raped me. My mom died of starvation. My best friend's dad was blown apart by raiders, and the man who took me in and has been almost a second father lost his leg and became a cripple. The world's become nothing but one person after another coming to take what little we have, and I'm not going to let them take anything else from me."

Trev looked at her in a new light. He'd heard of some of what she'd been through, and had been there to see how she handled her mother's death, but even so hadn't really appreciated the depth of her feelings. But even knowing all that, could he really justify letting her volunteer? On the other hand, if she was this determined could he justify refusing her?

As if sensing he was wavering the young woman straightened to attention, shifting her rifle case on her back. “I don't know if America's got a chance, but every time we make the blockheads pay for killing American citizens and stealing their homes that chance gets better. When I come back to Aspen Hill I want to do it knowing that nobody else is going to be coming for us ever again. So, can I join you?”

“Maybe. Just one thing.” Trev nodded at her shotgun. “You said you could barely hold a gun, but I assume you've practiced since then. Show me.”

Alice's fierceness vanished into an eager grin, and she quickly stepped up to the firing stand and unslung her case, removed the shotgun, then quickly assumed a firing stance and pumped a shell into the chamber. Trev let her fire off a couple shots, watching to see how she handled the recoil. The answer was not great, considering her small frame. But she properly couched the butt against her shoulder and was obviously used to how it kicked, so she recovered quickly.

Trev had her unload the weapon and put it away, then nodded to her. “Go find Matt and let him know you want to volunteer and I've agreed to let you join my squad.” He quickly continued as her grin widened. “I've got to warn you that if he says no I'll follow his lead, but I'm guessing he'll agree.”

“Thanks!” she said, turning and starting to run off down the road towards town.

“After you talk to Matt you'll need to head to the town storehouse and get your rifle and pistol!” he called after her. “And since you didn't take part in today's training you'll need to have someone work through the basics with you. If you need I c-"

"I'll ask Rick or Pete to give me a hand!" she called over her shoulder, barely slowing. Maybe she was afraid he'd change his mind if she stuck around.

Trev watched her go, wondering if he'd made a mistake.

Chapter Twelve

Joining Up

At Matt's urging the two dozen Aspen Hill volunteers set out early in the morning, cramming into one of the captured raider trucks with as many supplies packed around them as the town could spare, particularly their precious weapons and ammunition. As well as the body armor, night vision goggles, and the other gear that had made the raiders such dangerous enemies and would hopefully keep them alive in the coming fight.

They packed lightly where food was concerned, and for good reason. Williams had pointed them south to Huntington as the location where recruits from the area were gathering up. The corporal wasn't sure what they'd be doing exactly, but he thought it was pretty likely that the volunteers would be assigned to help cover all the roads leading up into the mountains between Huntington and Aspen Hill.

They'd be more familiar with the area, for one thing. He also assumed that there'd be less fighting along that stretch of land since the Chinese forces were to the west, on the other side of the mountains, and the Russian forces were to the east an entire state away, *and* on the other side of the Colorado Rockies.

Perfect duty for civilian volunteers, providing a potentially vital service but one that was low priority. It also meant they'd probably have plenty of opportunities to hunt the hills, fish Huntington Creek, and forage, relieving the burden of needing to feed them from both the military and the town. They might even bag more than they needed that they could send along to Lassiter's soldiers.

But that was just the corporal's guess, speaking as a fairly low man on the totem pole. For all they knew the military could hustle them right to the forward defenses, or even send them off to face the blockheads. Now that they'd volunteered their lives were in the hands of General Lassiter; Matt just hoped the man would use them wisely.

He'd spent the last week making what preparations he could, transferring his responsibilities in town to Lewis and Chauncey and his work in the garden to his parents and April's family. He also took plenty of time saying his goodbyes, particularly to a pregnant wife that was trying to be brave for his sake.

Matt also spent time mentally preparing himself for what was to come. As much as that was even possible. Responsibility for the volunteers was on his shoulders in a way he hadn't experienced before, not even while leading the defenders when the raiders attacked. Back then he'd had the Mayor and other leaders in the town to seek advice from and make their own decisions.

Of course, the military would almost certainly be putting someone in charge of him and his people. Matt wasn't sure if that lessened or increased the weight on his shoulders. He only hoped he could bring as many of his friends home as possible.

In a way it was almost a shock to reach Huntington only a bit more than a half hour after leaving, taking small roads around Carbonville and Price just to be safe, all the way to Highway 10, then following it the rest of the way to the small town on the junction between 10 and Highway 31.

Somehow he'd been planning for a major road trip, but the 25 or so miles they had to go wasn't all that far: a day of walking with backpacks, a few hours on a bicycle, and what felt like no time at all in a moving vehicle.

Huntington had been roughly twice the size of Aspen Hill before the Gulf refineries attack, but the influx of refugees had almost doubled that population again. Then winter hit and, from what Matt had heard from Chauncey's radio communications, hit hard; by spring the town had barely a thousand people left, and as soon as warm weather started touching the mountains to the west many of those survivors had headed up there in search of food.

The few hundred remaining people did their best to fish Huntington Creek and hunt game in the surrounding area. That meant many of the houses were unoccupied, and Matt wondered with bemusement whether his own overcrowded town shouldn't be considering moving some people down. Of course there were far more considerations than just space these days, and he wasn't sure how many Aspen Hill citizens would want to leave their community.

From the looks of it the military had set up camp in a field a mile or so west of Huntington, and Matt turned the truck in that direction. As he got closer he could see three official looking tents, two bigger ones for sleeping maybe twenty men at once, and a smaller one slightly off to the side. A bit beyond those tents several more had been set up, most no larger than four-man camping tents.

In spite of the early hour the camp was already bustling with activity, with maybe a dozen uniformed soldiers and more than twice that many civilians, probably volunteers. From the way they were entering one of the larger military tents and leaving with plates of food Matt guessed that one was being used as a mess tent. Although at the arrival of the truck most of the people in camp forgot their meals and stood to watch their approach.

Even though Williams should've sent word ahead by now that Aspen Hill's volunteers would be coming, the soldiers still went for their weapons. Matt hoped that was just a precaution as he braked fifty or so feet away and pounded on the rear wall of the cab to let everyone know they were here.

He hopped out, hands up. “We're volunteers from Aspen Hill!” he called to the soldiers, none of whom actually had their weapons raised and pointed their way, thankfully. “Corporal Williams said this was the place to meet!”

The soldiers relaxed. “A little radio warning would've been nice,” one of them shouted as the others slung their rifles on their backs or set them aside. Another ran towards the smaller official looking tent, probably to alert the officer inside of their arrival. The soldier who'd spoken ambled forward to shake Matt's hand as the rest of the volunteers hopped out of the truck and gathered up around him. “How many'd you bring?”

"Two dozen," Matt replied, returning the man's firm grip.

"Out of a town of hundreds, I bet." The soldier shrugged. "Not amazing, but you're practically patriots compared to the other towns we've gotten around to approaching in the area. Somebody made a dog's dinner of things here after the Gulf burned, eh? Made you all more than a little leery of authority."

Matt did his best not to feel insulted by any of that. "So what now?"

"Now we wait for Sarge to introduce you all." The man turned, motioning for them to come on with him to camp. As Matt and his volunteers moved to follow the flap to the smaller tent opened and the soldier from before emerged, closely followed by an officer.

At Matt's side Trev stiffened in surprise. "That's Sergeant Davis!" his friend told him.

The soldier turned to give them a surprised look. "You know him?"

"He gave us a lift," Trev answered. But by that time Davis was already making a beeline for them.

The soldier with them hurriedly saluted. "More volunteers, Sergeant," he said.

"Thanks for stating the obvious, Private," Davis drawled. His eyes were on Trev. "Looks like you decided to accept my invitation after all."

Trev nodded, then turned to gesture Matt's way. "This is Matt Larson, leader of Aspen Hill's defenders and of our volunteers."

Matt stepped forward and, following the soldier's earlier example, saluted. "I hope we can be useful."

"Don't salute, Mr. Larson," the sergeant said with some disgust. "You may be under my command, but you're not part of the US Armed Forces and certainly not in the Corps. You and your people are volunteers, irregulars."

"So, um, what should I do?" Matt asked, feeling stupid.

Davis swore with surprising volume. "Whatever I tell you to! And right now I'm telling you not to embarrass yourself and me by saluting."

Matt tensed as Gutierrez stepped forward and, completely ignoring the previous exchange, saluted stiffly. For a moment Davis looked like he was going to explode, but then he seemed to notice the man's rigid bearing. He gave Matt a questioning look as he saluted back. "You military, son?"

Gutierrez maintained his salute. "Private First Class Raul Gutierrez, Sergeant."

The sergeant grunted. "Army?" Gutierrez nodded. "Welcome aboard, then. Where were you stationed when things broke down?"

"Last fall I was assigned as an escort to the FETF convoy bringing relief to Carbon County, Utah." The former soldier hesitated, then assumed a determined expression. "Over the fall and winter, under the leadership of a FETF administrator my squad abandoned our duties and began robbing US citizens."

Davis's eyes narrowed dangerously. "Private, in just about any situation I can think of you just asked for unimaginably severe punishment. Possibly even the death penalty."

Matt did his best to shove down his rising alarm. Had Gutierrez really needed to bring all this up? What good would it accomplish but to cause trouble for a decent man? Then again, maybe as a decent man Gutierrez hadn't seen any other choice.

The former soldier's salute faltered slightly, but he kept his position. "I make no excuses for my behavior, Sergeant, and am prepared to accept the consequences."

"Well if he won't make excuses I will," Matt said, stepping forward to stand beside his friend. "Raul Gutierrez abandoned the raiders when it looked like they were going to attack Aspen Hill, and joined us in defending the town. He's risked his life on numerous occasions doing just that, and in the time I've known him his actions have shown his bravery and integrity."

Davis gave him a hard look. "This doesn't concern you, Larson."

"I'm not sure I agree, sir," Matt replied. "Gutierrez has been fighting under my command and I bear responsibility for him."

The sergeant said nothing, looking between them as the silence stretched for what seemed like an agonizingly long time. Behind them the other Aspen Hill volunteers were shifting uncomfortably, a few even murmuring to each other. Gutierrez's arm had begun to shake slightly from the effort of holding the salute for so long.

"At ease, Private," Davis finally barked. Gutierrez immediately dropped his arm with a quiet noise of relief. "I'll ask you one simple question. Did you harm anyone during your time as a criminal?"

The former soldier hesitated. "I did my best to help those we robbed and protect them from harm. In pursuit of that I hit a few people to quiet them down and keep them from receiving a harsher punishment from someone else. I never killed anyone."

"I see." Davis glanced over at Matt. "Do you vouch for him?"

"Absolutely."

"Then he's your problem to deal with." The sergeant turned back to Gutierrez. "We can't afford to turn down people willing to fight, so I've been ordered to look past a wide range of minor criminal activity in volunteers, provided they commit no further crimes. If and when order is restored and some sort of legitimate government is created you may be held accountable for your actions, but faithful service defending your country may be your way to a pardon."

Davis's voice hardened. "Don't claim to be a member of the US Armed Forces, don't use your former rank, and stay with the Aspen Hill irregulars until such a time as you are dismissed or the group is dismantled. Understood?"

Gutierrez nodded, started to salute, then hesitated and dropped his hand again. "Understood."

The sergeant grunted and turned to Matt, pointing towards an empty section of camp. "Your people can camp over there. Once you're settled in we'll have a longer chat about what your duties will be and what sort of discipline and behavior I expect from the people under my command." He turned and started back towards his tent, calling over his shoulder. "Welcome to the war."

*****

Most of the volunteers had portable one-man tents, either a gift from the town or what they'd already owned. A few, like the married Donnells and the brothers John and Tony Russo, shared tents, but for the most part everyone had their own. Trev thought that was a good way to do it, since it meant they'd be more flexible in their sleeping arrangements depending on what Davis wanted them to do.

Speaking of Davis, Trev had just finished setting up his tent and was making sure everyone else in his squad had a handle on theirs when the sergeant came stalking over to the camp.

"All right, people, listen up!" he bellowed. The few people who'd been too occupied with their work to notice him jumped and whirled around. A few of the Aspen Hill volunteers awkwardly saluted at his approach, forgetting he'd told them not to.

The sergeant ignored them. "Time to tell you all what you're going to be doing. It's very simple so I'm sure nobody will have problems understanding." He paused, staring into the crowd as an expectant hush fell, then abruptly pointed at the mountains stretching northwards and southwards behind him. "Our job is to prepare ourselves and this area to ensure that, should an enemy come, they will *not* find a way into the mountains. We have a twenty mile long stretch of ground to protect, from Highway 31 to just north of your own little slice of heaven in Aspen Hill."

Trev felt a moment's hope at that. If they had to protect the area near their town that meant they might be able to spend some time there. Maybe the goodbye hadn't been as final as he'd thought. He might even find the time to help his family out here and there.

His hopes were dashed as Davis continued. "Fortunately for us your town is even better armed than you are, and they've agreed to cover that area on their own. We're going to take them up on that offer, so in fact we have closer to fifteen miles to cover. Realistically though, we'll be stationed in the canyon not far west of us and hold Highway 31, or destroy it and block of any means of getting past if necessary, as our top priority."

He once again waved vaguely northwest. "Some of you I'm going to give assigned areas to guard. You are to go over every square inch of that area until you know the terrain by heart and can walk it with your eyes closed. Knowledge of the terrain is one of the main things that'll keep you alive when the blockheads pay us a visit. If you find time you'll also prepare defenses, especially if any roads leading up into the mountains are situated in your area. Those we need to be prepared to destroy as well, then defend from any troops they send on foot.

"The rest of you are going to either be patrolling or standing by as reinforcements. You will learn the quickest and quietest routes to get to the positions your friends are going to be guarding. You will learn how to spot the slightest sign of suspicious activity, and how to efficiently report it so we can respond as quickly as possible."

Trev had his own look at the mountains. They seemed so peaceful that it was hard to imagine Gold Bloc soldiers swarming up the tree-lined slopes and meadows. But with any luck there wouldn't be, because the blockheads to the east would be stopped in Colorado and the blockheads to the west would be stopped on the other side of the mountains.

To his surprise Davis's next words mirrored his thoughts. "Now mind you, at the moment it looks like we won't be seeing many enemies in our neck of the woods. Which should be pretty obvious, because if we *were* facing any sort of threat here we'd have more than one squad of Marines and 50 or so local hayseeds to work with."

He abruptly raised his voice to a bellow. "That does *not* make our job any less vital! If an enemy *were* to get past us they could hit our main front on the other side of the mountain from behind. The western defense would be surrounded and annihilated! So I will expect you to take your job seriously, and that includes training hard as well as learning the surrounding terrain.

"Believe me, we should have plenty of time to do both, and I am prepared to personally instruct you on the use and care of your weapons, as well as strategy and small unit tactics. I will also personally have a problem with anyone who does not take advantage of the time we have to prepare as much as possible, and you do *not* want me to have a problem with you."

The sergeant abruptly relaxed and waved at the two trucks by the command tent, one his own and the other brought by Aspen Hill, which the Marines had immediately commandeered. Trev didn't mind, since the town had intended to give the vehicle and supplies to Davis in the first place, but the way the transfer of ownership had occurred still kind of rankled.

"As you can see we have two vehicles. For them we have a little over 100 gallons of diesel available. Do not expect more. We will avoid using them at all costs so they'll be available for emergencies, so get used to hoofing it through hill, dale, and up cliffs if you have to to get around. Any questions?"

Trev spoke up. "Does that mean our squads will be getting split up?"

Davis glanced around the assembled volunteers, looking amused. "Formed into squads, did you?" He shrugged. "We'll have to see how it goes. We've got a decent number of people, but we've also got a lot of ground to secure. At the moment it might be better to split everyone up in teams of three or four so they can get familiar with their assigned areas, and maybe rotate shifts for different duties.

"Once the blockheads get a bit closer and it looks like we might be facing action at some point I'll probably reform the squads. I'll respect the military structure you've already chosen, though, and no matter what duties I assign you I encourage you all to train in your teams, squads, and working together between your squads as well."

The sergeant waited to see if there were any more questions, then turned to Matt. "You can spend the time until lunch settling in, as well as acquainting yourself to anyone in camp currently on downtime. The mess tent is open to your men, although we'll want you to contribute to both finding food and the cooking in the future. I want you and any other leaders in your group to come to the command tent after you're done eating . . . by then I should've figured out a way to make best use of you working with my people."

Trev spoke up again as the man started to walk away. "Any objections to us using the morning hunting and foraging?"

The sergeant looked amused again. "You mean to you doing work during your free time on your own initiative? Be my guest. Just remember you'll be sharing your bounty with the rest of the camp, and you'll still be expected to work hard on duty even if you squander your opportunities to get some R&R. You're part of a unit now."

Once he was gone Matt glanced around the group. "All right then. I guess first things first we should probably split the squads in to teams, just to be prepared. Trev, you've been training your squad and know them best, so I'll leave them to you."

*****

It was a relief to know they weren't going to be sent out to fight the Gold Bloc, but at the same time Davis had meant what he said about making the best use of their time.

Over the next couple weeks Matt and his volunteers, working together with Davis's Marines and the other local volunteers, ended up hiking several miles every day, learning the terrain of the mountains, foothills, and the valley below between Huntington and Aspen Hill to within binocular range of their home. It wasn't just jaunts, either; they spent grueling hours scouring the foothills and slopes for even the most difficult paths the enemy could take to get past them into the mountains.

They didn't just do it for their own familiarization, either. Davis wanted anyone who had a decent eye for distances and could draw a straight line to sketch detailed maps of the areas they passed through, which he then personally traced onto a larger map in his tent to create a fairly accurate topographical map of the entire region. He jotted everything the scouts learned about paths and other useful information on that map.

Including ambush points, which were one of the sergeant's main priorities. Even before they'd become fully familiar with the region they'd been assigned to guard Davis had everyone in his unit hard at work digging foxholes and emplacements in likely spots, as well as rigging up pitfalls from any handy rocky slopes or ledges. He'd also requested demolitions teams to come plant charges above the roads in suitable spots to completely block passage beyond those points, especially along Highway 31. They were still waiting on those teams.

When they weren't scouting or digging the sergeant pushed them through extensive training, constantly bemoaning the lack of ammunition that kept them from doing much live fire training. "We don't excuse waste in the Marines, but to do proper training you'd be expected to fire hundreds of rounds before you were done," he said at the end of one exercise. "And that would just be for basic competency."

In compensation for that he split his soldiers among the groups sent out hunting, getting double value out of having the volunteers train on the spot while shooting at game. It wasn't the best setup, but it worked well enough for what they had.

As for gear, Davis didn't have much more to work with than the volunteers had brought with them. But there were some useful things he could provide, to streamline everyone's efforts at coordinating with each other. Among the most useful of those were the sophisticated radios he gave out to Matt and Trev as squad leaders.

They were designed to carry on the belt, with a high quality long distance antenna that could be attached to the top of the backpack with a breakaway cable for quick removal. In combat the radio would usually rely on a smaller antenna on the device itself, which reduced the range a bit but not as much as expected. The radio came with noise canceling earbuds and a mic designed to filter out loud and high pitched noises for clearer speaking.

It would solve a lot of the communication problems the Aspen Hill defenders had run into against the raiders. It was encrypted, to start with, and with the earbuds communicating over it wouldn't give away a person's position. There was also a toggle on the radio itself to talk, which meant talking would be more hands-free in situations where you had to do multiple things at once. The noise-canceling feature also meant you wouldn't go deaf being around gunshots and explosions, and even at the loudest times would have a better chance of hearing people talking and picking up telltale noises around you.

They were fairly standard issue, and in an ideal situation every soldier would have one. But with equipment scarce and precious Matt considered himself lucky that he and Trev had theirs to work with. The rest of the squad had to rely on the radios they'd got from the raiders, which were encrypted and could be used to communicate with the better radios but didn't have all the perks.

Still, they were worlds ahead of the gear Davis's other local volunteers had, where they had any at all. At best most of those folks had the same sorts of walkie talkies Aspen Hill's defenders had been stuck with when the raiders attacked. The higher quality radios could communicate with those, but without encryption.

Matt made sure to warn his fellow irregulars of the vulnerabilities of those radios, describing his experiences with Turner's raiders and the problems unsecured communication which could be easily exploited had caused the town. At least the leaders among the other volunteer groups also had Davis's radios, which was a plus.

The sergeant mostly kept the volunteers in their own distinct squads, training together, but he also encouraged them to get to know each other and often had people from different groups do camp chores together. The locals were a bit leery of Aspen Hill at first, since last fall it had developed the reputation of being stingy with refugees, and more recently there'd been plenty of rumors about the town's turf war with the raiders, not all of them true.

The other volunteers got more friendly once they'd had a chance to hear Aspen Hill's side of things. As for the towns they came from, mostly Huntington and Castle Dale, they had their own horror stories to tell about events since the Gulf burned. It was something everyone had in common and served to further bond them.

All in all Matt was feeling pretty good about their situation. They had the lay of the land, and Davis had painted a fairly clear picture of just what they'd need to do if the unexpected happened and they were required to turn back a Gold Bloc attack in the area.

Thanks to the natural choke points and their superior positioning and preparations they should have the advantage even if they were massively outnumbered, to the point where just the several dozen fighters they had should be able to hold back an army until reinforcements arrived. In fact, the sergeant predicted that once the blockheads saw that there was no easy path into the mountains along this stretch they'd give it up entirely, and either try to go around or hunker down in the valley for a more extended conflict.

If they went around they'd run smack dab into the bulk of Lassiter's forces waiting along I-70, Highway 6, Highway 40, and I-80. Most of those larger roads also had decent choke points along them, but there was a large area to cover outside of those points, more open spaces where the enemy could get through too easily, especially if they were coming from both sides.

The lack of choke points in those places meant the General had to rely on numbers rather than positioning. And because those were the larger roads the military predicted that they'd see the fiercest fighting against the blockheads there. Davis *did* warn, though, that with I-70 not all that far away they'd probably see plenty of probes from Gold Bloc scouts searching for alternative routes or just keeping tabs on the area.

Thanks to the volunteers' specific role in the upcoming conflict they were less worried about the future. So much so that when word reached them over the radio in mid-June, sixteen days after they arrived in camp, that the Gold Bloc forces had finally arrived, they weren't as anxious as they might otherwise have been.

They'd all gathered in the mess tent to hear the news, listening to the stream of reports being passed on to them about Russian forces to the east closing on the area where Erikson and his men had set up in the Colorado Rockies. The first skirmishes between blockhead advance scouts and the military had already begun, and the General expected the fighting to become fierce within the next few hours as the vanguard of an army hundreds of thousands strong reached Denver and Cheyenne, then began searching for an undefended path farther west.

The military had known of that army's approach for over a week now, but they'd expected them to spend more time taking and holding positions in the Great Plains rather than pushing westward as hard and fast as they had. It left the enemy strung out and exposed with supply lines stretching back for hundreds of miles, something the US Armed Forces could've punished them for if they'd had any units in the area. Unfortunately they didn't, and the Russians had either known the bold play was a safe one or they'd taken a huge gamble to shave weeks off their timetable.

From the sounds of it the Chinese were just now beginning to gather over a hundred miles northwest of Utah, still days away from being any sort of threat even if they copied their Russian counterparts' aggressive move. Their progress would be further slowed by the fallout zone around Hill Air Force Base, which they'd have to swing far around to avoid, traveling along predictable routes Lassiter was prepared to defend.

Which meant that, for the moment at least, the fighting was all in Colorado. And from the sounds of it Erikson's men had caught the approaching blockheads by surprise and were decimating the scouting units with relatively few losses.

Things seemed hopeful, although the enemy forces hadn't even begun to arrive and truly engage the military to the east. But even with that consideration the threat felt remote to Matt, far away and not likely to get closer any time soon with the Gold Bloc butting their heads against the natural protective barrier of the Rockies. The other volunteers didn't seem all that bothered as they listened to the continuing stream of reports, either.

Not so with Davis and his Marines. They were all tense, expressions grim as they huddled closer around the radio. Matt could understand their feelings, since their brothers in arms were in danger and some of them probably had close friends among the soldiers fighting the enemy. And it was probably a good idea to remember that, as far away as that threat was, it was a massive one and it was headed their way.

The war with the Gold Bloc was about to begin in earnest.

Chapter Thirteen

Confusion

Over the next three days the fighting got fiercer and fiercer in Colorado, but judging by what Matt heard from Davis or over the radio it was going well.

General Erikson had put up a lot of vicious booby traps while waiting for the blockheads to arrive, anything from bridges and overpasses rigged with explosives to destroyed roads channeling the enemy towards minefields. He'd also been sending out Special Operations Forces teams to strike at targets of opportunity, including behind enemy lines.

The massive army closing on them had slowed down to a crawl in the face of the unexpected and violent show of resistance, especially after going relatively unopposed for so long, and their losses were growing more and more severe by the day. In comparison Erikson's soldiers reported far fewer losses, and were solidly entrenched along all the routes westward.

The only options the Gold Bloc's eastern forces had at this point were to either try to go far north or south around the Colorado Rockies, which would slow them down considerably and leave them exposed to attack along a much larger front, try to settle in for a long siege and hope they had more supplies than the US Armed Forces holding out against them, or try to brute force their way through with sheer numbers.

So far that latter option didn't seem to be working. It might once the Chinese threw themselves into the fray, since at that point there'd be no guessing how things would shake out. But for the moment things were fairly hopeful and spirits were high in camp.

They could also be somewhat optimistic about a siege, depending on how well the Gold Bloc could keep up their supply lines. One benefit of being the defending force was that they were mostly stationary, which ended up using far less fuel. Not only did the enemy have to use more just getting to them, but if their attack failed and they were forced to retreat they'd use even more withdrawing, then getting to them again for the next attack they tried.

It all added up, especially with Erikson's Spec Ops teams ordered to specifically target fuel depots and tankers if the opportunity arose. They had the perilous but necessary task of finding ways to strike at such valuable and well defended Gold Bloc resources, after which they'd hopefully get away clean and disappear into the countryside to hide from any attempts at retaliation. With any luck they could then reposition for another strike.

Matt didn't envy those guys that job, but if they were successful they would ultimately be the ones that won this war for the remnants of the US, by taking away the enemy's ability to wage war long term and eventually forcing them to retreat.

Another thing that could, and absolutely had to, be used against the enemy was that they outnumbered the US forces more than ten to one. While that was a horrific advantage it also meant they had ten times as many mouths to feed, which would make any siege cripplingly costly unless they changed up their tactics.

With the good news rolling in people in camp had even begun talking about the possibility of winning this war, which had seemed unlikely given how outnumbered and outmatched they were.

At the crack of dawn that day Davis had sent Matt and his team to Cedar Creek Canyon, the one just north of the canyon Highway 31 ran through, to double check the spot they'd scouted out as an ideal place to plant explosives.

It was in a narrow part of the canyon where the slopes to either side were almost steep enough to be considered cliffs. A particularly rocky stretch along the southern slope seemed like a perfect spot to bring the hillside down, which would completely block off the canyon from vehicles and make even trying to get by on foot a nightmare.

Especially with a squad of fighters up there in already prepared emplacements gunning down anyone who tried.

His team returned to camp in time for lunch, with Matt satisfied that a demolitions team could seal off the canyon with a relatively small blast. Once they actually arrived and placed those explosives. The Marine who'd gone with them to check the spot agreed and went off to report to Davis, while the rest of the team headed for the Aspen Hill camp to wash up from a morning spent climbing.

Matt was hungry enough that he only took the time to wash his hands and shuck his dusty jacket before heading to the mess tent. Without even that light layer of clothing, the chill wind blowing across his skin served as an unpleasant reminder that summer was nearly here and the weather wasn't getting much warmer. In fact, on some days it was actually getting *colder*.

With a shudder he increased his pace, nearly trotting the last dozen steps to the tent. He preferred not to contemplate the inevitable cold in the autumn months, when they'd have a new understanding of the term "nuclear winter". Anyway he had something better to occupy his thoughts; the prospect of news was almost as big a lure as the food, and he was eager to hear what was happening in Colorado.

When he ducked into the tent he saw he wouldn't be disappointed. It was mostly full with everyone in camp at the moment, most still just getting started eating their meal. Oddly enough the table with the radio had only a few people around it, while a slightly larger crowd had gathered at another table where a rugged looking laptop was flipped open playing a video.

He stopped halfway inside the tent, staring. The thought of this camp having internet was nothing short of ludicrous, so it had to be on the hard disk or a DVD. It showed a view of Earth from orbit, looking down on Asia and part of the Pacific Ocean. As Matt watched a tiny star burst into light on the continent below, then another, then dozens more in rapid succession.

Matt made his way over to join the crowd. "Is that a recording?" he asked a soldier near the back.

The man nodded. "Transmitted from Great Britain. They're hurting bad, but from what I hear they're the closest thing left to a first world nation. Our headquarters picked up this feed from one of their satellites, and a scouting patrol passing by yesterday evening dropped it off for us. Davis gave us permission to watch an hour or so ago, and the ten minute footage has been on replay ever since. This is my first chance to see it."

The soldier turned his attention back to the screen, and Matt joined him. Together they watched as the mushroom clouds bloomed on the continent below. Even from orbit they were clearly visible, and somehow more horrific for the sterility of distance and complete silence. It was hard to believe each one potentially represented millions of deaths.

Matt had seen this sort of visual representation of nuclear war seen from space in movies and games, and the similarity they shared to what he was seeing now made it all eerily surreal. As if it wasn't hard enough to accept the reality of the Retaliation sometimes.

He looked away, feeling sick. In a hundred years this satellite footage would probably be aired in schools the world over in memory of humanity's greatest tragedy, assuming the technology still existed at that point. And to the kids watching it might not have much more meaning than some movie. But for him, right now, it was too painful to watch the recording of so many lives snuffed out.

Turning away from the small screen, Matt continued on to the front of the mess tent to retrieve his meal, planning to join a few other volunteers from Aspen Hill at the table they'd found near the radio.

As he waited in line he abruptly noticed the somber, tense mood in the tent, and realized with a start that it probably wasn't from the satellite footage of the Retaliation. From what he could see less than half the people in the cramped space were watching the video or even seemed to notice it, and those who weren't were huddled in small groups talking worriedly.

He'd been so intent on the video himself he hadn't realized that it wasn't drawing the crowds it should've for a new tidbit of news and information. An hour wasn't long enough for interest to die out that completely, which meant some even more important news had drawn everyone's attention.

Matt hesitated near a table with an open space where one of those groups had gathered. In spite of Davis's efforts to foster cooperation between his Marines and the irregulars, a few of the soldiers were a bit contemptuous of the volunteers, even hostile. But Matt had worked with all of the men at this table, and for the most part they were pretty easygoing.

"Hey," he said. As a few looked up he motioned towards the empty seat with his tray.

The man sitting closest on the bench, a short, scrawny guy named Abrams, obligingly moved over a bit. "Have a seat, Larson."

"Thanks." Matt settled in, taking a mouthful of barely appetizing pudding as the other soldiers got back to their food. "What's going on?"

Abrams had mostly emptied his tray and didn't look interested in what was left, so he didn't seem to mind answering. "We just got word from Denver. General Erikson is pulling out."

Matt paused with a second bite halfway to his mouth. "The blockheads pushed him out of the city?" he asked in disbelief. Denver was Erikson's main staging area, so losing it meant a major defeat. "I didn't know the fighting had got that bad."

The scrawny soldier made an impatient gesture. "Not out of Denver. Our people in Colorado are pulling out entirely, abandoning the eastern arm of the Rockies and coming to join us in Utah. The only ones staying behind are a few Special Operations Forces teams, who are going to destroy every road and block every pass they can, then operate out of the high mountains doing as much damage as possible to blockheads moving through the area."

Matt tried to digest that news. "I thought the entire point of locating here was to hold both arms of the Rockies."

A solder down the table who Matt didn't recognize snorted. "Maybe they figured we don't have enough people to hold that much territory. Or maybe the blockheads won a victory no one's telling us about. Either way the higher ups are leaving Colorado to the Gold Bloc, which means we'll be seeing action a lot sooner than any of us expected."

No kidding. Without the buffer in the Colorado Rockies the Gold Bloc could push right through to the Utah Rockies and attack them from this side. Which meant the enemy would probably try to come up Highway 31, Cedar Creek Canyon not too far north, Aspen Hill Canyon back home, Highway 6, and every single other road leading up into the mountains from the eastern side.

Matt had expected that he and the other volunteers to be well away from the action, with most of the fighting over on the west side of the mountains or in the Colorado Rockies hundreds of miles away. Sure, he'd accepted that eventually they'd probably see some fighting here, too, but not any time soon and only if things went wrong somewhere else.

Only now Erikson was leaving the door wide open and letting the blockheads waltz right to them. They were about to be at the front in a war zone.

Then a frightening thought struck him. If these mountains were going to be the only place the military defended, holding the line between I-70 and I-80, that meant that all the towns east of here were no longer safe. Including Aspen Hill.

"Have the towns between here and Denver been warned?" he asked.

The soldier down the table shrugged disinterestedly. "Probably. If they haven't they're hosed."

Abrams shot his squad mate a dirty look. "Come on, man. The guy's got family out there." The other man had the grace to look embarrassed.

Matt clapped the scrawny soldier on the shoulder as he stood, picking up his tray. "Thanks. I should go let my people know."

A few of the soldiers offered goodbyes as he walked away. "Keep your gun close!" Abrams called. "You'll probably be using it before too much longer."

When Matt got to his table he learned that his squad mates there had already heard about Erikson abandoning the Colorado Rockies, and were in the middle of discussing the ramifications. Since he was still reeling from the news himself he used his food as an excuse to withdraw from the conversation and sink into his own thoughts.

Erikson had spent over a month preparing those defenses around Denver, and had already fought several bitter skirmishes to hold them. From everything Matt had heard those skirmishes had overwhelmingly favored the US forces, and the blockheads were nowhere close to dislodging them from those mountains.

So why had the General abandoned his position all of the sudden? There had to be a reason, and Matt seriously doubted it involved good news.

"We need to get word to Aspen Hill and the other towns in the area," he abruptly said, interrupting the conversation his squad had been having, which had turned to a recent skirmish near Cheyenne along I-80, and its possible relation to Erikson's decision to pull out.

His friends looked at each other. "I'm sure the military's thought of warning everyone," Rick said.

Matt shrugged. "Probably. We should still do it ourselves, just in case. If nothing else we can send along details they might not get otherwise, and it'll be a good chance to relay some personal messages to family too."

Before anyone could answer a commotion outside drew the attention of everyone in the mess tent: the sound of an approaching truck engine, which was finally loud enough to pierce the din of dozens of people eating and talking, as well as yelled greetings from the sentries on duty. Soon afterwards the truck began honking.

Most of the fighters around him abandoned their meals to go see what was going on, and Matt left his half-empty plate behind as well to join them. When he followed the crowd outside he saw a military truck pulling into camp, still honking. As soon as it screeched to a halt the soldiers in the cab hopped out, and Matt was startled to recognize Corporal Williams as the man who'd been in the passenger seat.

Williams immediately made a beeline for the command tent, where Davis was waiting for him. The two pushed inside, leaving the rest of the soldiers who'd arrived in the truck to be mobbed by the curious denizens of the camp. The Marines returned the friendly greeting, and didn't seem to mind sharing what their visit was about.

A demolitions specialist team had finally been sent their way, along with enough high explosives to fill the truck. Williams was in charge of the squad escorting them, and once they finished planting their charges on all the roads from here to Aspen Hill Canyon the corporal had orders to remain behind under Davis's command, to help hold the roads on the eastern side of the mountains.

The reinforcements also sent along word that more volunteers would be heading their way as soon as they could hike the distance from one of Lassiter's camps to the north. Matt liked the thought of extra help, considering that they'd soon be facing hundreds of thousands of blockheads pouring in from the east, but from the sounds of it the General was only sending another few dozen people their way.

That really didn't feel like enough, whatever Davis's assurances of a squad being able to hold one of these canyons against an army.

After about fifteen minutes of waiting around chatting with the newly arrived Marines Davis burst out of the command tent, Williams on his heels. “All right, people!” he shouted. “Time to stop slacking and really get to work!”

Matt bit back a groan. Nobody would call what they'd been doing “slacking” by any stretch of the imagination. Truthfully though he wasn't too inclined to complain, since it was a bit of a relief to see the sergeant looking confident and full of purpose in spite of the situation.

In short order the volunteers had been split up and assigned to make new camps along every canyon road between here and Aspen Hill, with Trev's squad posted in Cedar Creek Canyon just above the spot Matt's team had greenlighted for the demolitions team that morning.

All aside from Matt's squad, that was. They were going to be posted along Highway 31 with the two squads of Marines, in a new camp farther up the road that was well above the rocky slope Davis had decided was the best spot for taking out the road. At least that they were going to find that close to the canyon mouth. Matt had mixed feelings about the assignment, since it meant his people were going to be at the most dangerous location. But on the plus side they'd also be working with the trained soldiers.

Within ten minutes the camp was a whirlwind of activity as all the tents were taken down and people began packing up to relocate to their assigned spots. Since the trucks would need to move anyway Matt's squad was given permission to load their things into one, along with the bulk of the camp's supplies. It would save a bit of time and effort, which was nice.

Matt was in the middle of supervising the loading when Williams walked up. "Our demolitions guys' first stop is Aspen Hill," he said without preamble. "Your town agreed to hold that canyon, but we still need to help them rig the road to be destroyed if necessary."

"We'd appreciate the help," Matt agreed. "Want me to ride along? I'd like to alert the town to what's going on with Erikson's withdrawal. The sooner they start evacuating the better."

The corporal shrugged. "Probably a good idea. We'll be leaving soon."

"Right." Matt turned to Rick. "Get our people set up in the new camp and going on whatever work Davis has in mind for us."

His friend nodded, clapping him on the shoulder. "Got it. Give my family my love."

Matt nodded. "I'll make sure all our families know we're doing all right and have things under control. Stay safe."

He trotted over to where Williams and his people were already waiting in their truck. The engine roared to life as he hopped in the back, and seconds later they were off.

*****

After being away for weeks, missing his home and his family and Sam most of all, it felt almost surreal to cover what had felt like an insurmountable distance in a half hour. In no time at all Williams's truck was driving up Main Street, with the town looking the same as when Matt had left.

Although that wouldn't be the case for long, once the news reached them that they needed to evacuate.

Matt had radioed ahead to let everyone know they were on their way. Catherine didn't bother to send one of the town's trucks and some defenders to escort the Marines this time, and aside from a few townspeople waving there wasn't much ceremony as they parked in front of town hall. Matt and Williams hopped down to talk to the Mayor, leaving the other soldiers in the vehicle for the moment.

Catherine met them on the front steps and shook the corporal's hand, then after a bit of chitchat the two headed inside to discuss the need for evacuation, as well as coordination between the military and the town moving forward. Matt was left waiting outside, but he wasn't bored because within minutes he was swarmed by curious neighbors wanting to know what was going on.

Deciding it would be better if he left it to Catherine to break the news of the approaching blockheads to the town, Matt omitted those details as he described the general situation with the war, and in more detail what the volunteers were doing down near Huntington. He also sent along the requested messages to the family and friends of his absent squad mates.

All the while, though, he found himself looking over people's heads searching for the familiar petite dark-haired woman he most wanted to see. When Terry came out from the clinic to greet him Matt was disappointed to learn that his wife wasn't volunteering that day, and neither was April. And although it was good to see his brother-in-law, Matt was tempted to make his way out the shelter and leave Williams and his people to do their thing.

Before he could decide one way or another the corporal came back outside, after less than five minutes talking with the Mayor. As he started towards the truck he passed where Matt and Terry were chatting, and paused to pull Matt aside. "We're headed up the canyon to set the charges."

Matt wasn't surprised the man was in a hurry. There was a lot to do before the Gold Bloc reached them, and who knew when that would be. "All right. I can think of a few good spots to check out."

"No need. The Mayor and I got in touch with your buddy Halsson. It looks like over the last couple weeks he's thoroughly searched the canyon getting ready for us, and he'll be meeting us at the bottom to guide us to the spots he's picked out and see which works best for our needs."

Matt felt a surge of hope, although he tried to keep his expectations realistic. "Should I come along too?"

The corporal gave him a slight smile. "We should be a few hours, and I doubt we'll need you. If you want to take the opportunity to visit loved ones now's the time."

He didn't have to be told twice. In fact, he was about to bolt down the street towards the shelter right that moment when Terry called him back. "I've been using your bike," he said, somewhat sheepishly. "Or Sam has when she takes a shift." He pointed to the rack off to one side, where sure enough Matt's bike stood waiting.

Matt pulled his brother-in-law into a hug, just in case he didn't get another chance to talk to him before it was time to head back south again, then ran to his bike and hurriedly unlocked it with the familiar combination. Williams was just starting the truck to head out the the canyon when Matt zipped past headed north, pedaling for all he was worth.

He reached the pair of hills the shelter was situated between in record time, and felt his heart soar when he rounded the taller hill and found Sam doing laundry in the little space they'd set up for washing clothes beside the underground structure.

His wife was pinning up a shirt on the clothesline when he caught his first sight of her. Even through the fairly loose shirt she wore he could see the swell of her belly and their child growing within, and his breath caught in surprise; she'd barely been showing when he left, and even after less than three weeks it seemed much more noticeable.

Matt slowed to a stop and hopped off the bike, feeling a surge of relief and longing. Relief that she seemed all right, longing for how long he'd been away from her and how little time he had to see her now.

Before he could start forward again Sam paused to stretch and turned Matt's way slightly, hands on the small of her back. As soon as she saw him standing there she stopped dead, eyes widening with shock. Then joy spread across her face and she gave a happy shout and bolted towards him.

Matt barely had time to drop his bike and open his arms before she threw herself into them, nearly bowling him over in the process. He had to lift her slight weight so she could get at his face to rain kisses on him, doing his best to hold her tight while treating her like porcelain as he returned her kisses and tried to get a word in edgewise. "Are you all right? You and the baby?"

"We're fine. We're great," she mumbled, breaking off her kisses to bury her face in his neck and hold him tight. "We've just missed you so much."

Tears stung at his eyes as he held her a bit tighter. "Me too. Every day."

She spoke into his shoulder, sounding almost hesitant. "How are you here? C-can you stay long?"

"Just for a few hours. I came with some demolition specialists from the military."

His wife mumbled something inaudible, not seeming curious about what they'd come for, and held him even tighter. They stayed like that for almost a minute, as Matt let himself enjoy just being with the woman he loved, the familiar presence he'd dearly missed while he'd been gone.

Finally Sam pulled away slightly to beam up at him, eyes shining with her own tears. "There's so much to say."

Matt nodded. "How have you been? Is everything going all right?"

She shrugged. "Okay, aside from missing you. Things have been happening, but nothing too interesting compared to what you've probably been doing."

He leaned down to kiss her again, longer this time. "I'm super interested. Tell me all about it."

"Deal, as long as you return the favor. I want to know what it's been like for you since you volunteered." His wife abruptly looked away and bit her lower lip, blushing slightly. "But first there's something important I need your help with."

"Sure. What is it?"

Dark eyes looked up at him solemnly, although humor danced in them as well. "I've been missing my husband for almost three weeks. Take a wild guess."

*****

Lewis met the soldiers at the mouth of the canyon, loading up his bike in back before hopping in the front to sit next to Williams. "Good to see you again, Corporal," he said.

Williams nodded. "The Mayor says you're in charge of the town's defenses now that Larson's with us."

"That's right."

"Good. Then while we're taking care of planting these charges I can fill you in on what's going on with the war."

"I'd definitely appreciate it," Lewis replied, meaning every word. Chauncey did his best with the radio, but a lot of what they got was secondhand. Most of that was because the military was fairly closemouthed, aside from sending out calls for volunteers and contradictory messages indicating a bright future for the country if everyone did their part, and conversely just how difficult the fight against the Gold Bloc was going to be and the need for all the help they could get.

The corporal gave him an impatient look. "This isn't gossip, Halsson, it seriously affects your town. General Erikson is pulling out of Colorado and joining our forces here in the Utah Rockies."

Lewis saw the ramifications immediately, and fought the urge to curse. "So just like that Aspen Hill is outside the protected area."

Williams nodded curtly. "You'll need to evacuate up to the top of the canyon, at least. Probably even farther, although I expect your town to keep their promise about defending this area against any Gold Bloc attacks."

"You don't need to worry about us." Lewis took a deep breath. "So what's the exact situation?"

Over the next few minutes Lewis listened in silence as the corporal laid out what was going on with the war, particularly to the east where the fighting was already fierce.

Lewis listened intently, but it was an effort to ignore the sinking in his gut.

This meant he'd have to abandon his shelter. Again. And not just the shelter but the gardens. Maybe even the bees, too, unless he could think of a safe way to transport them and find a safe place for their new home. Then there was the hassle of relocating all their animals, and how that would disrupt their usual routine. And they'd have to transport all the wheat from Newtown, and somehow find a place to store it.

And his family had really been getting settled in. They'd just finished building the second house, which his aunt and uncle and cousins had moved into only a few days ago, and everything was more comfortable for everyone.

And the town! Organizing the evacuation was his responsibility, and he'd been preparing for it as best he could since just after the Retaliation. Thanks to that he knew just how overwhelming the task was going to be, and it was anyone's guess how much time they'd have. They would need to get started right away.

Williams finished with his terse breakdown of the situation and leaned forward to peer at the road ahead. "Where are these spots you scouted out?"

"We're almost there," Lewis replied, shaking out of his grim thoughts. He was leading them first to the most ideal spot he'd picked out, which meant they'd already passed a few less suitable ones.

This one was halfway up the canyon, where a crumbling cliff overlooked the road in a narrow spot. A few rocks had already broken away from it, littering the ground beside the road, and the rest of the cliffside looked as if it wouldn't take much to join them.

Williams nodded in approval as they piled out of the truck for a closer look. "This definitely looks like a good spot. We could probably do the job with half the charges here."

"I'm no expert," Lewis said, pointing, "but it looks like the weakest spots are there and there. That might be enough to bring the cliff down."

The corporal looked over at Graham, leader of the team of demolitions specialists he'd brought. The bulky man shrugged. "I'd want to look closer, but from this angle I'd say he's not wrong."

"Let's get to it, then." Williams turned to give Lewis an appraising look. "You've got a pretty good eye." Lewis started to shrug off the compliment, then realized it wasn't exactly one when the corporal continued. "How about you use it to keep watch down the canyon, just in case? We've got this covered."

"Sure. I know a good spot not far from here." Lewis turned and started down the road.

Williams called after him. "We'll let you know when we're done, but it may take a while. Think you're up to keeping watch for a few hours?"

You mean like I've been doing for months now? Lewis thought. But he just nodded. "No problem."

It was a bit annoying to be taken away from his duties in town for so long, not only the personal work he had to do but also leading the defenders. The Mayor had asked him to accept that responsibility after Matt left, and Lewis had agreed with the caveat that once Matt got back he could have the position if he still wanted it.

Those duties were even more pressing now that he knew they needed to evacuate. From the sound of it the Gold Bloc wouldn't be anywhere near this area for a week at the soonest, but it was better to start the evacuation now. That way they could make sure they had the time they needed, could move as many of their possessions as possible, and could get to work sooner on the location in the mountains he and Jane had scouted out as a suitable refuge until they could find a more permanent solution.

It was going to be a huge task, and the people of Aspen Hill would suffer immensely. Even after all the warnings he and the Mayor had given about the potential need for evacuation, he wasn't sure how many of his neighbors had prepared what they needed for camping, living on the move.

Which meant they'd probably need to do their best to rig up tents out of tarp and other materials. And people who were struggling to eat now would probably go hungry, and have to hope that the chill of the higher elevations and the stress of suddenly finding themselves homeless didn't lead to illness.

At the very least they could probably leave a few people behind until the last possible second, to tend the gardens and then harvest whatever they could before fleeing the approaching enemy. At which point they'd face the tragic need to torch the remaining crops to keep the blockheads from getting them.

Lewis sucked in a sharp breath and focused on his current duty as he reached his lookout spot. He knew he should spend this time planning, but the enormity of the task and its unpleasant necessities prompted him to put it off, at least for a few minutes.

At least there was one upside to acting sentry for Williams. Part of leading the defenders had involved taking less time to personally go out on patrols, because he had to be in town and available when issues came up. That didn't prevent him from doing chores in the garden or even at the shelter, with his bike handy to respond to any emergency, but he'd only gone on two shifts since taking over for Matt.

In a way it was almost nice to be out here on watch. The breeze was cool in the canyon and scented by the trees it passed through, and he could faintly hear the stream babbling along off to his left. The midafternoon sun was warm on his back, slowly pushing the shadows down the canyon away from him, and looking over that to the valley below made for a striking view.

Surprisingly content, Lewis settled back to the task of watching the mouth of the canyon for any approaching people. If Jane was here with him this would be just about perfect; he really did enjoy being up in the mountains, and it gave him a sense of freedom he just didn't feel at other times.

Although it looked like he'd have plenty of opportunities to enjoy these mountain surroundings soon, when he was living here and trying to wrangle hundreds of displaced people into some sort of orderly community.

That thought broke the mood, and with a sigh Lewis turned his thoughts to planning the upcoming evacuation.

About four hours later he heard the truck rumble to life farther up the canyon, and Lewis stood and stretched out a few kinks as he made his way back to the road. The vehicle drove into view not too long after that, and he moved over to the other side of the road so he could hop into the passenger seat as it crunched to a stop next to him.

"How did it go?" he asked.

It was Graham, behind the wheel, who answered. "Pretty good, I'd say. That cliff is rigged to collapse and bury the road beneath it, making a nearly impassable blockage." He looked over at Lewis for a moment and grinned. "I suppose the enemy could pick their way over the rubble on foot, but it'd make them sitting ducks. That's what you'll be there for, right?"

"Right."

Williams cut in, sounding a bit impatient. "We're done here, Halsson. All that's left is to drop you off and pick up Larson. Know where he'll be?"

Lewis nodded. "The same place I'm going. I'll point you the right way once we're out of the canyon."

A few minutes later Graham stopped the truck on the dirt road near the taller hill, and Lewis shook hands with the two soldiers and hopped down to the ground. As he was shutting the door behind him Matt emerged from the shelter, looking a lot more cheerful and relaxed than when Lewis had last seen him a few weeks ago. It seemed like his reunion with his family had taken some of the weight off his shoulders.

Williams called for him to hurry up and get in, but Matt ignored him for a second to come over and say his goodbyes, and helloes, to Lewis. "Sorry we didn't get a chance to really catch up," he said. "I wanted to thank you for taking care of the town while I've been gone, and for looking out for my family. You have no idea how much I appreciate it."

"It's the least I could do." Lewis offered his hand. "Be safe out there, and look out for Trev for me."

His friend ignored the handshake and pulled him into a hug. "For sure. And you take care of everyone here."

"I will." Lewis watched as Matt pulled himself up into the back of the truck and disappeared. He thought that was that, but then Williams and Graham, who'd hopped out too and were waiting by the hood, made their way over to him.

The corporal turned to give the canyon a thoughtful look. "Well, we've done as much as we can to secure that road. The rest is up to your town. If things start looking bad in the area we'll send some soldiers to help you out, and if you run into trouble at any point you can radio in. General Erikson's group will be in charge of the northern region when he arrives, specifically Colonel Grimes guarding up along Highway 6. He can probably get help to you fastest in an emergency."

Lewis appreciated the offer, although he had a feeling the town would be smart to assume they'd be on their own in a true emergency and prepare for the worst. "We'll do our best."

As Williams stepped away he nodded to Graham, and the demolitions specialist stepped forward holding a backpack. "Here's a few replacement parts for the wiring and detonators in case something goes wrong with them," he said. "Along with detailed instructions on how the explosives were wired and how the wireless receivers work, which will hopefully be enough for you to fix the problem."

"We'll figure it out," Lewis said, reaching out for the pack.

Graham hesitated giving it over. "The transmitter to set off the detonators is in there, too. I'd appreciate it if you'd put it in the care of the most responsible person in town. Ideally we want that road open for our own use until such a time as it becomes more a liability than an asset, so you should hold off on detonating the charges until blockheads are coming up the canyon itself, at the last possible moment." He snorted. "And if you're feeling daring you can wait until they're actually under that cliff and take a few of them in the explosion."

Lewis took the pack, holding it gingerly. "I think we can get the timing right." He thought of the truck full of explosives they'd sent into the raider camp.

"All right, then." Williams started for the truck, Graham following. Once the two were inside and had slammed the doors shut behind them the corporal called out the open window. "We'll be keeping in touch over the radio to let you know what the blockheads are up to, especially if they start nosing around this area. We won't let you get caught flatfooted."

"Appreciate it." Lewis lifted a hand in farewell. "Best of luck out there."

As he watched the truck drive off he debated who to entrust the demolition gear to. He was pretty confident he could handle it himself, but since he'd been entrusted with defending the town while Matt was gone he needed to focus his attention on that. As Catherine had told him, when she'd come close to ordering him to reduce the number of patrol shifts he was taking so he could focus more on organizing the other defenders, leadership required delegation.

He had no doubt Chauncey could've easily handled it, but with his leg gone he'd lost most of his mobility, and that would probably be really important when it came time to blow the charges. Scott was good with technical things but he was gone with Matt, as was Rick, who took after his dad and had been helping with the radios.

The obvious candidate felt a bit like nepotism, but Lewis had to admit his own dad was probably one of the most responsible people in town, and shouldn't have too much trouble figuring out the technical details. They could also keep Chauncey in the loop and get his expertise, so things should work out.

Since he'd taken on Matt's duties he'd stopped the overnight hunting trips with Jane, so they'd set the tent up in a more permanent spot in the shade of the shipping container. Thanks to that, when he went into the container itself to deposit the pack in a more secure location it was the first time being in there in a while.

It was a lot less crowded now, with Trev away and the rest of the Smith family in the second house. That left just his parents and Mary to share the elevated sleeping area in the back, while the front had been converted into a living space.

Lewis stowed the pack out of sight until he could track down his dad and hand it over. After he'd done so he stood staring at it, trying to imagine the explosion the transmitter in that pack could cause, and what it would ultimately do to the canyon road. He knew he should be getting to town to begin planning the evacuation with Mayor Tillman and the other town leaders, but he let himself take a few moments to stop and let everything sink in.

The blockheads were still all the way over in Colorado, but at the moment that didn't seem all that far.

Chapter Fourteen

Unpleasant Arrival

The next two days were a frantic flurry of activity as the town packed up to move, prioritizing the most important things first and saving anything that wasn't strictly necessary for later trips.

They didn't plan to go far, only an hour or so's walk away from the top of the canyon. Close enough that the defenders could patrol the area without having to hoof it too far back to camp, but far enough that if the townspeople had to flee from an unexpected attack they'd have the advance warning to get some distance before it was too late.

Lewis spent a lot of the time biking up to the site and back, coordinating with the few people who'd already arrived there and passing dozens more who were making the hike towing their possessions in whatever wheeled contrivance they had available or, with no other alternatives, lugging them on their backs. The number of people fleeing up the canyon increased by the hour, as the trickle became a flood.

The refuge he and Jane had found over a week ago was a shallow valley one slope over and upstream from the canyon, where a relatively flat meadow provided enough space for everyone. A tree-lined ridge not far to the west provided plenty of deadfall and trees that could be cut down for fires and making shelters, as well as signs of game that might provide some meat to feed the displaced townspeople.

He'd just come down from his third trip up and was going home. For the moment he was leaving his duties in the town to other people so he could focus on helping everyone living in the shelter pack up and get their own things out.

They had the handcart his family had brought, capable of carrying a surprising amount but woefully inadequate compared to what they had to take, as well as half a dozen wagons, including Lewis's own heavy duty one that had served him so well on the trip up and down from the hideout. They also had more than enough people to tow the wagons or carry things on their backs.

While Lewis had been scouting out their destination, preparing it for hundreds of people to set up camp and organizing the town's efforts in the evacuation, his dad and Uncle George had been tallying all their possessions and calculating how many trips it would take to bring them all up.

The last time he'd been down they'd been confident they could get all the most important things up in one trip, and another trip for things that weren't strictly necessary but would make life a bit easier and more comfortable up there. But to his dismay, when he parked his bike and went over to where they were loading the handcart his dad informed him that it would probably be two trips for necessities, and maybe two more total.

A lot of the issue came from the number of people living at the shelter, between his family, the Larson clan, and Jane's group. There were more possessions than expected split among that group, and their limited wagons and what they could handle on their backs just wasn't enough.

"I don't suppose Catherine would let us load some of this into one of the trucks?" Uncle George said hopefully, looking at the stack of cots off to one side. They were lightweight but bulky, which wasn't a great combination for traveling. "We could strap them on top and barely add any weight. The town could use the extras too, as added incentive."

Lewis shook his head regretfully. "There's a lot of stuff to take, and when it comes to wagons and carts we're better off than just about everyone so we're near the bottom of the waiting list. The town's gear all on its own will overload the trucks for one trip, and we're not sure how many we're going to get out of the fuel we have."

His dad sighed and knuckled his back. "Well then I guess we'll have to resign ourselves to a few days of trudging up and down steep roads hauling heavy weights. We've had a bit of practice with that."

"You guys more recently than me," Lewis agreed. He looked around at the dozen or so people hard at work around him, with as many inside packing. "Where's Jane?"

His dad chuckled. "Patrolling. She insisted somebody had to, when everyone else was running around like chickens with their heads cut off."

That was probably true, and reminded Lewis that he'd dropped the ball in that area while planning the evacuation. Unfortunately he was needed to help with the moving, or he would've gone to join his wife. Or at least patrolled another route, content knowing she was out there with him. "How are the Larsons coming with their preparations?"

"About like we are, I expect," his uncle replied, making it sound like that wasn't a great thing. "If you want to take over slinging sacks of wheat I'll go check on them."

Lewis hesitated. "I'll get the wagon loaded, but first I want to make sure Sam's got hers and Matt's stuff packed in and ready to go. I promised I'd look out for her."

The two older men exchanged looks. "Absolutely," his dad said. "You aren't the only one. We've been in a few times asking her if she was ready for us to load her things up, but she's dawdling at packing."

That didn't seem like Sam. From Lewis's experience she usually went overboard pitching in to help. Maybe she'd needed help with packing and had been too embarrassed to ask. Either way it made it more important he go check on her.

He made his way inside, nodding to Ed and Mona in the living area and fending off Aaron and Paul when the two boys ran over to pester him with questions about their new home in the mountains. Shooing them away, he made his way over to the curtained off area that was Matt and Sam's room and slapped the curtain to announce himself. "Sam?" he asked.

A moment later the dark-haired woman's head popped out around the curtain, smiling. "Hey, you're back!"

"Yeah." Lewis shifted his feet slightly, noticing her smile was forced as if she was making an effort to be cheerful. He hoped he wasn't intruding. "I just wanted to let you know we're packing things up now. Do you need help with anything?"

She disappeared back behind the curtain. "Sure, I'm just finishing up with this last box," she called. "Come on in."

He ducked inside to find his friends' "room" looking empty and forlorn, the two cots leaning up on one end against the wall and most of their things already packed up in one cardboard box, while Sam neatly arranged the rest in a smaller one atop it.

"Want me to get that one?" he asked, pointing at the full box.

The dark-haired woman nodded. "Sure, thanks." She abruptly made a face. "I can't believe we have to move. Again. It's just one thing after another."

Lewis shook his head wearily. "I know, we can't seem to catch a break. I really should've built this place up in the mountains."

"Would've been way better for you," Sam agreed, then hesitated. "Not so great for us or the town, though." She glanced toward the wall of the shelter and abruptly changed the subject. "Do you think he'll be all right?"

"Matt?" Lewis asked. She nodded. "We saw him just a couple days ago. I'm sure he's still fine."

The petite woman shook her head doubtfully. "Only now the blockheads are finally coming, and the military's not going to be protecting us on this side. Matt might be fighting them along 31 any day now."

"The point isn't to fight," he replied, doing his best to sound reassuring. "Their job is to make that route impassible, destroying the highway and nearby roads if they have to and putting down booby traps anywhere they can. They'll only fight if the Gold Bloc forces keep coming, probably on foot and walking into ambushes every ten feet. Matt and the others are going to be fine."

"If wars were that one-sided people wouldn't fight them," Sam said, slumping down onto the full box. She looked miserable, and he found out why when she abruptly changed the subject. "I didn't make it easy for him when he left. I told him not to go."

"A few days ago?" From what Lewis had seen Matt had been way too carefree for that kind of encounter when he headed off with Williams.

She gave him a slightly impatient look. "No, that went great. But it was a *visit*. Back when he actually left I really let him have it, and now that's probably all he can think of."

Lewis shifted uncomfortably. "That's not exactly unreasonable. You have the baby to worry about."

Her dark eyes flashed. "Yeah well I *was* unreasonable! I told him the town and the military and everyone was being selfish, expecting him to go when I needed him here. I made him feel guilty about doing what he had to do when I should've supported him. I shoved all my own burdens on him when he was already dealing with so much, and now whatever he faces down south is going to be that much harder for him."

The petite woman lowered her head until her dark hair covered her eyes, although not before he saw a tear slip down her cheek. "He'll be worrying about me when he should be worrying about himself. He might die thinking I was mad at him for abandoning me."

Lewis crouched down next to her. Blast, he wasn't good at this sort of thing. "I think you've got it wrong," he said quietly. "I think he understands what you really feel, no matter what you said to him when he left. You and the baby are the most important things in the world to him. You won't be a distraction, you'll be his reason to fight even harder so he can get back to you in one piece. And I'm sure he'll be thinking of the good visit he had with you, not whatever happened before that."

Sam sucked in a sharp breath, then abruptly stood. "I need to finish packing so we can get out of here," she said firmly. Still keeping her face carefully turned away from him in embarrassment, she bent over the smaller box and began neatly arranging the things inside once more.

Lewis straightened as well, bending down to pick up the big box. It was surprisingly light, probably mostly clothes and blankets. "I'll get this out on the cart. Let me know if you need help with that one." She nodded, and he hesitated for just a minute before ducking through the curtain.

In the living area Matt's parents were still doing their own packing, and his friend's mom paused to give him a grateful look. Of course they'd heard everything. He only hoped he'd found the right things to say for his friend.

It felt selfish to think it, but he was grateful Jane was always there with him when things got bad. It was awful thinking about something happening to her, but at the same time it meant neither of them would ever have to leave the other behind in a situation like this. Whatever they faced, they'd face it together.

Or at least he hoped.

*****

Lewis hadn't really paid attention to it before, but now that they were lugging heavy burdens up a steep road it was hard to ignore the fact that less than a third of the people in the shelter group were grown men, and of them only him and Terry were in their prime.

Everyone tried their best, of course, and there were enough people pitching in to get the job done. But it wasn't easy for anyone, and the farther they went up the canyon the more often they were forced to take breaks.

Linda summed up what everyone was thinking during the tenth or so break, when half of them were so exhausted they slumped to the road right where they'd stopped. "We have to do this *more than once*?" she complained. There were a few grumbles of agreement.

After taking the trip on a bike so often the slog seemed to take forever for Lewis, and in spite of the fact that they'd started in the early afternoon he was almost afraid they wouldn't reach the top by nightfall. Those fears turned out to be exaggerated, but the five hour trip wasn't fun for anyone.

Realistically they couldn't leave their most valuable stuff alone up there and all head back down. It wasn't that Lewis didn't trust his neighbors, but temptation was a tricky thing. It was hard to forget earlier in the year when Matt's family had come under attack in the shelter from former refugees, and many in the town were still in that desperate stage.

A surprising number of people volunteered to stay behind up in the meadow, to guard their tarp-covered possessions and begin setting up a more permanent arrangement for the group. Probably motivated by their desire to avoid another trip if they could get away with it. Lewis convinced his dad and Uncle George to stay as well to stand guard, while the rest determined to get back down to the shelter and pack up that night to make another trip early in the morning.

That one was going to be fun in its own way, since they'd be bringing the animals up. In a way it was good so many people wanted to stay in the meadow, since they could be put to work building a pen for the sheep. As for the chickens and rabbits, Lewis was almost tempted to toss the hutch and coop into the handcart and make an extra trip of it at some point.

It was a dispirited group that lugged their empty wagons down the canyon. Lewis could sympathize with Sam's frustration about having to move again, and he was sure they all felt it. He was glad he'd managed to convince her to stay behind with Mona and his mom and aunt to watch over the younger kids in the group and keep packing up. The move would be hard enough for her in her condition without having to haul a pack or loaded wagon.

The work of loading everything for the second trip up went by in near silence as everyone sank into their own gloom, and most seemed relieved when Lewis suggested an early night. Jane was already in bed after back to back patrols, and he wanted nothing more than to curl up with her and pass out.

Instead he hopped on his bike and made his way over to town hall to make sure the Mayor had all the help she needed loading the trucks and guarding them.

It turned out she didn't, not by a long shot. Lewis looked at what was going to be another major project and did his best to fight his growing dismay as he waded in. He had no idea how Matt had managed to juggle these duties for so long.

*****

Word had gotten around to all the towns in the area about the approaching Gold Bloc forces, and the last several days had seen a steady stream of people fleeing their homes and heading into the mountains, most taking the Highway 31 route. Some were specifically seeking out the military camps up there for shelter, food, and protection, while others just seemed to want at least some sort of barrier between them and the hundreds of thousands of soldiers headed their way.

In his small camp up Cedar Creek Canyon Trev hadn't had any refugees actually come his way, but he and his squad were close enough to see the line of people heading up 31 through their binoculars, towards Davis's camp higher up that canyon. Some among those refugees had signed up with the sergeant as volunteers, a few dozen total, but most passed through and continued farther into the mountains.

Trev wasn't sure he blamed them. Davis had assured them that the Gold Bloc probably wouldn't push too hard along any of these smaller canyons once the roads were destroyed and any easy route blocked, but that didn't stop his nightmares about thousands of enemy soldiers converging on his canyon and flooding the mouth, climbing the hills to either side, and flat out overwhelming him and his squad of twelve.

The sergeant had also assured them that once the new volunteers arrived he'd be sending out more fighters to each location, ideally so they'd have enough people to not only guard the canyons but also patrol the foothills and low mountains along this stretch. He'd already sent the few dozen new volunteers farther north to reinforce the farther away canyons.

As for Trev's squad up Cedar Creek, they'd have to rely on the relatively close by fighters along Highway 31 to send reinforcements if they ran into more than they could handle. At least for now. Davis seemed confident they'd see even more volunteers from the locals now that the Gold Bloc was headed their way and the situation was more real, and the first of those volunteers would be sent along to Trev's canyon.

Until then they'd have to handle it on their own.

To prepare the squad, as well as so his people would have something to do besides sit around worrying, he'd stepped up the training schedule in the three days since the news came about General Erikson pulling out of Colorado. He'd even let them start using some of their precious ammo for more extensive live fire practice.

Unfortunately he was all too aware that even the best training could only do so much to prepare people for the reality of combat. Once they were in that life or death situation they'd have to hope that they were physically and mentally ready for it. And while good training could take them all the way up to the point where they were able to expose themselves to danger so they could pull the trigger and shoot an enemy, it couldn't give them the courage and determination to do either.

Although that was no reason not to try, which was why this morning he was doing something a bit different: he had his squad engaged in a mock battle with an enemy coming up the canyon, manning their foxholes and emplacements and dry-fire shooting at targets he'd set up earlier down below. At his signal he had his people ready to break from cover and retreat to the fallback positions they'd set up, doing it in organized fashion with a few going at a time while the rest covered them.

He was watching closely, both how much they were exposing themselves to fire down the canyon from their emplacements and how well they managed their retreat. A lot of those retreating weren't moving as quickly and erratically as he would've liked, considering they were supposed to be getting shot at, and almost nobody was sticking to the low crouch he'd recommended, instead doing more of a hunched trot.

Trev knew it was hard to take a mock battle 100% seriously, especially when they were pointing empty guns at imagined bad guys like he'd done a few times as a kid. But doing it properly when it didn't matter would make it more likely they'd do it properly when it did, and when it mattered it would *really* matter so they needed to do it properly.

He was about to halt everything and have them start over, but this time make them military crawl when they retreated to their fallback positions to see if they'd take that more seriously. Before he could a warning came on the radio.

Surprisingly it wasn't one of the current lookouts, Alice or Hans, who were calling in. Instead it was Private Abrams, in his own advance lookout post in the valley five miles northeast of them, whose voice came through his earbuds.

"You there, Smith?"

Trev flipped his radio's transmit toggle. "I'm here. What's going on?" It took him a few seconds before he remembered with a start to flip the toggle off again. He was still getting used to using the radio, which included actually remembering to wear the thing half the time.

Abrams sounded urgent. "We've got a truck approaching. Gold Bloc by the looks of it. They're headed right towards Cedar Creek Canyon from the northeast, going at least 40 on a small road."

Nervous anticipation crawled its way down his spine. The main Russian force had barely gotten over the Colorado Rockies, clashing with Erikson's rearguard as the General retreated west. Trev really hadn't expected to see them any time soon, especially not a lone scout far behind enemy lines.

"One truck?" he clarified. Then he remembered he hadn't flipped the toggle and hastily did so, repeating the question.

"One truck," the soldier confirmed. "It'll reach you in less than ten minutes."

Trev looked around at his squad, most of whom didn't even have their radios with them. On the plus side thanks to the mock battle they were where they needed to be to set up an ambush. "We've got a truck coming our way," he called. "Enemy by the looks of it. Everyone back to the forward emplacements!"

As his people burst into action Trev radioed advance notice to Davis, who agreed to send people and ordered him to only intervene if the truck tried to go directly up the canyon. From the sounds of it the sergeant didn't consider even an approaching enemy vehicle to be enough justification to use one of their own trucks, so Trev's reinforcements would be coming on foot.

It wasn't a terribly long walk from the new camp up Huntington Creek's canyon, but it was far enough given how rough the terrain was. Unless whoever Davis sent really hoofed it Trev's squad would have to handle this threat on their own at first.

As Trev spoke to the sergeant he'd been making his way to the nearer lookout spot, where Alice was crouched tensely with her binoculars in one hand, her M16 held in the other in a white-knuckled grip. In the blond young woman's hand the rifle almost looked like it should be a toy, and he hoped she'd be ready to use it after her limited training.

"I can't see it," she said, voice shaking slightly. "I don't know where it is!"

He put a reassuring hand on her shoulder, glad he'd made it standard practice to have lookouts wear body armor and he'd had the rest of the squad geared up for the mock battle.

There was no way to tell whether they were ready training-wise, but when it came to their equipment they were as prepared as he could make them.

"No matter what happens with the truck, I want you to stay out of sight and keep watch for any other approaching vehicles," he told her. "That's your role in this fight. And if I tell you to break away and retreat entirely you go, along the same route I've had you practice a dozen times. Okay?"

She nodded, still looking tense as she searched for the elusive truck. Trev pulled out his own binoculars and joined her.

It took longer than he'd expected to find the vehicle, which was coming from a direction closer to north than northeast, driving on a road that wound in and out of view between the foothills. When he did he immediately recognized it as a Gold Bloc vehicle, the same type as the one his family had captured to escape the internment camp.

He toggled his radio transmitter. "Heads up, people. It definitely looks like an enemy."

His earbuds did a surprisingly good job of reducing the crackle of static as Hans replied. "So do we turn it into a colander as soon as it's close enough?"

Trev hesitated. It was probably a smart move, but he didn't like the idea of killing a bunch of people without properly identifying them or giving them a chance to surrender. For all he knew those could be defectors, or another family like his that had stolen an enemy truck and escaped.

Even if it turned out to be enemies the chance to capture the truck and all its fuel and gear intact, as well as some soldiers who could potentially be questioned for useful information or traded later as prisoners of war, presented an opportunity he didn't want to throw away.

"They'll have a hard time getting away from our ambush if they turn out to be unfriendly," he said. "Let me stick my neck out talking to them. If they decide to cause trouble hopefully my body armor will do its job, and then you can perforate the vehicle to your heart's content. Tom, you've still got the detonator?"

"Got it," the older man said, sounding a bit nervous.

"I hate to jump the gun with that thing, but if the truck somehow gets past the roadblock you blow it before it can get up the canyon. Got it?" Tom answered in the affirmative. "Everyone else in position and ready?" He waited until he heard acknowledgements from everyone in his squad, then slipped away from the lookout spot and made his way down to the road.

They'd set up a simple roadblock around a blind turn there, a sturdy log across the road braced by a stump on one side and a pile of stones on the other. It was enough to completely stop a vehicle at the ambush point, but at the same time it could be quickly moved if necessary.

The demolition charges Graham and his specialists had rigged were less than twenty yards behind the roadblock, on the steep rocky southern slope that was nearly a cliff. From what Graham had told him about the planned blast it would probably send an avalanche of rocks all the way to the roadblock itself, burying Trev along with it if things went wrong.

He'd just have to hope whoever was in the truck wasn't suicidal, although as he hunkered down in the emplacement they'd built behind the roadblock he couldn't help the sick nervousness he felt at the risk he was taking. He could already hear the rumble of the truck engine getting closer.

Maybe *he* was the suicidal one.

He caught brief glimpses of the vehicle as it entered the mouth of the canyon and started up the road, winding its way along the switchbacks beside Cedar Creek. Even when it was out of sight he could somewhat track its progress by the noise of the engine, growing louder and louder until it sounded like it was almost on top of him.

Trev took a deep breath, hefted his M16, and straightened to point the weapon towards the blind turn. Just in time as the truck barreled into view.

To his credit the driver immediately saw Trev and the roadblock and understood the danger, screeching to a halt and starting to back up. Unfortunately for him, part of the ambush involved dropping a tree across the road behind the truck, having prepped it beforehand by nearly cutting through the trunk so it was ready to fall with a good push.

Rob Jonas, in charge of felling the tree, had a covered path behind an outcropping to bolt back up once the task was done, and had probably made it to safety before the people in the truck even realized the impromptu roadblock had begun to fall.

Trev took a deep breath, then raised his voice to a bellow. "Shut off the engine, then come out slowly with your hands above your heads! I see anyone holding a weapon and we start shooting!"

The driver quickly complied, half ducking as if expecting to be shot at any moment. He was average height with brown hair, and had one of those familiar faces that everyone thought they recognized. Or at least Trev did. "Easy!" he shouted back. "We're Americans!"

"Then you won't mind us taking a few precautions for someone driving a blockhead truck!" Trev motioned with his rifle. "Get your friends out here, out of the back too if anyone's in there, and if you've got any weapons let's see you set them aside slowly and back away."

The passenger door opened and another man stepped out, wearing a cowboy hat with his lower face covered by his jacket riding up around his upraised arms. "We stole this truck from the blockheads!" he called, and Trev stiffened as he recognized the voice. The man continued. "Are you guys the ones we've been hearing about, the remnants of the military setting up to turn back the Gold Bloc in the mountains?"

Trev couldn't believe it. Out of everyone he'd expected to drive up his canyon, this had to be the least likely. But it explained why the truck was so familiar. He tried to keep his tone even as he answered. "What's your purpose here?"

"We want to join up. The enemy made us flee our homes, and we had a good life before they came. We want that life back if that's still even possible. We even brought supplies and weapons to help you out, more than we need ourselves. You can see for yourselves." The man awkwardly motioned towards the back of the truck with his raised hands, and the motion lifted his jacket enough for Trev to see the sheriff's badge on his chest.

Had he kept it as a memento or did he still cling to his role as an enforcer of law and justice?

More men were emerging from the back with their hands raised, slowly setting weapons on the road before walking up to join their leader. Fourteen in all, so the numbers fit there too. The man turned back to Trev. "Look, see? We're cooperating, we just want to join the fight!"

It certainly looked like they were cooperating, but that hardly mattered. Trev reached down and thumbed his radio. "Get ready to move in and take these guys prisoner," he whispered into his mic.

Then he raised his voice again. "Good to hear. But it'll be hard to join the fight when you and your men are under arrest for armed robbery, Fred Vernon."

Chapter Fifteen

Necessity

The former sheriff sighed and lowered his hands slightly, so the jacket didn't cover his face anymore. He looked a bit more haggard than when Trev had seen him last; the life of an outlaw didn't seem to agree with him.

"I was afraid you'd recognized me, Smith." He chuckled slightly. "Of all the luck, driving up the one canyon *you're* set up in. I'm impressed you managed to get all the way out here on foot in such a short time." He looked around. "But you're really with the military? You're here guarding this piss poor road for them?"

"You'll find out soon enough." Trev carefully stepped over the fallen tree roadblock, weapon still trained on the group of fourteen men. Although he tried not to specifically point it at anyone and he kept his finger off the trigger. "Is this everyone?" He already knew the answer since this was the number of men who'd betrayed Newtown, but the former sheriff might've picked up some friends since then.

Vernon nodded wearily. "There's no need to keep pointing that thing at me. Remember how we didn't go around waving our weapons willy-nilly when the situations were reversed?"

Trev grit his teeth. "Probably not smart to remind me about any of that." He motioned with the tip of his rifle. "Line up on your knees, hands on your head. My people are coming to tie you up, but you won't be harmed."

The former sheriff's people reluctantly complied, and didn't cause any trouble as Trev's squad converged on the road and cautiously moved up behind the kneeling men to search and bind them. Although they were obviously pissed; most weren't stupid enough to actually say anything to the people pointing guns their way, but there were plenty of glares and more than a few muttered obscenities.

Vernon remained calm through it all, even when Trev zip-tied his hands behind his back after patting him down to make sure he wasn't hiding any weapons. The man also kept his full attention on Trev as he stepped away a short distance, to radio in and let Davis know what had happened. He quickly explained that they were bringing in prisoners, and that the sergeant could recall the reinforcements he'd sent. Davis didn't seem overjoyed at the news, but he curtly told Trev they'd talk about it when he reached camp.

"What happens now?" Vernon asked as Trev thumbed the transmit toggle off and made his way back over to him.

"Now we take you to our main camp," Trev replied, pulling the former sheriff to his feet. "Normally we'd be looking at a hike to get there, but since you were kind enough to bring back my truck we'll be there in no time."

"So, what, we all pack in clown car style? There was barely enough room for us in there."

Trev had already considered that, but it wasn't the problem Vernon seemed to think. "Just me and a few guys to keep an eye on you. My squad was assigned to guard this canyon so we can't send too many people away."

Vernon nodded thoughtfully. Maybe it was paranoia, but Trev didn't like something about the man's expression. He stepped a bit closer, meeting the former sheriff's eyes. "If you think during the drive would be a good time to try something, think again. We'll shoot without hesitation."

In response Vernon shrugged his shoulders to indicate his bound arms, as if announcing his helplessness. "You know, me and my boys did what we had to do, but we weren't as eager for violence as you seem to be," he said quietly.

Trev had to laugh. "You're going to try to take the moral high ground here? Don't try anything and there won't be a problem." He tapped Vernon's shoulder to turn him around. "In the back."

Vernon went, although he took his time. "We came here to fight the blockheads, like I said right off the bat. You really want to lose our help over a petty grudge?"

Petty grudge? Did he actually have the gall to try to downplay leaving Trev's family stranded in Nebraska, forced to haul over a ton of food and other possessions the rest of the way to Utah with Gold Bloc soldiers at their heels? Not to mention abandoning the people of Newtown to fend for themselves.

"Do I need to gag you?" Trev shot back. The former sheriff shook his head, keeping quiet as he led his men up into the back of the truck.

Trev left them to get settled in with Rob keeping an eye on them and gathered the rest of his squad. "Tom, Mason, you're with me. Leave your rifles behind and just take your 1911s. And keep a good hold on them." He handed his M16 over to Fred Donnell.

Tom nodded, although he looked uneasy as he also handed off his rifle. "What exactly is going on, Trev?" he asked. "Armed robbery? Who are these guys?"

Right. He probably should've given his people a heads up about what was happening. "You heard about Newtown, right?"

The older man nodded. "The grain silo utopia you guys passed through." His eyes widened and he darted a glance at the vehicle. "Wait. *These* are the guys who stole your truck?" Trev nodded grimly. "What in the blazes are they doing here?"

"No idea. Last I heard they planned to make for Mexico, as far from the Gold Bloc as possible."

Mason snorted. "Joke's on them, then. They ended up where all the blockheads are going."

Trev wasn't in a laughing mood. "Tom, you're driving while me and Mason ride on the back and keep them covered. Keep it slow and avoid bumps so we don't get tossed off." He turned to Hans, taking off his radio and mic and earbuds and handing them over. "You're in charge here until I'm gone. Make sure to keep the lookouts alert; these guys were alone, but they may not be the only ones out there."

Hans accepted the radio and started hooking it to his belt. "Gotcha."

"Let's go, then." Trev led Mason to the back and hopped onto the fender, hanging on to the side of the opening and leaning in slightly. His squad mate copied his position on the other side.

"Looks awfully uncomfortable," one of Vernon's men said. "What're we going to do, head-butt you and fall face first to the road? Our hands are tied."

Trev ignored them and signaled a few of his people to move the tree Rob had dropped behind the truck. While they were doing that Tom started the vehicle, and less than a minute later they were bumping their way back down the canyon to take the side road to Highway 31. The ride on the back wasn't too bad, all things considered, but they were jolted around enough that Trev had to wonder if they'd even be able to do anything if Vernon and his men tried something.

At least they were going slow enough that if they got bounced off it wouldn't hurt too much.

Even though he'd radioed ahead that they were coming Trev still felt his shoulders crawl as they drove up the larger canyon, past the rocky slope Davis had rigged with explosives. It was ready to create a rockslide that would completely cover the road and the rest of the canyon, on a scale that dwarfed what Graham and his demolitions specialists had set up at Cedar Creek or other locations.

The sergeant always had at least one squad of sentries and lookouts up in emplacements along the slopes to either side, too. That included the M2 Browning they'd brought from Aspen Hill, set up in the emplacement above the rocky slope and pointed down the canyon.

If for some reason Davis *did* decide they were enemies the truck could be simultaneously buried under tons of rubble, blown to smithereens by one of the two TOW missile launchers, Aspen Hill's operated by Gutierrez and the one Davis had brought with him, and punched full of holes like a cheese grater by the .50 caliber heavy machine gun and assorted small arms fire. And Trev had no doubt the sergeant had taken other measures, like mining the ground along the sides of the road leading up to the slopes where his men waited.

Good thing they were friends. He only hoped that when their enemies came this way it would be enough to handle them.

He'd only been to the new main camp once since being assigned to Cedar Creek Canyon. It had grown a lot since then, including a section cordoned off as a temporary stop for civilians fleeing up the highway. The truck passed the section where Matt's squad had set up their tents, but it was deserted and his friends likely on duty somewhere.

Tom drove them right up to the command tent, where half a dozen Marines were waiting, including Williams. The corporal nodded at Trev as he and Mason jumped off the back. "We'll guard the prisoners, Smith. Sarge wants to see you."

"All right. Thanks." Trev started for the tent.

As he passed Williams the man caught his arm. "He's pissed," he warned in a low voice.

Trev wasn't surprised. He nodded his appreciation for the heads up as he ducked into the tent. Inside Davis stood hunched over the map table glaring down at the detailed map he'd cobbled together, but he didn't seem to be looking at anything in particular. As soon as Trev entered he lifted his head, glaring.

"Care to explain the stunt you just pulled?"

It took a lot to keep calm under that scrutiny, especially since Trev wasn't exactly sure what the problem was. "Stunt?"

The sergeant reddened slightly, but he kept his tone disconcertingly polite. "What else would you call arresting US citizens?"

Ah. "Fred Vernon, former Sheriff of Newtown, and his former deputies who aided him in committing crimes, are guilty. Just like I told you when I radioed in. I have eight witnesses who can testify to that, and that I had good reason to arrest him."

"You don't have the authority!" Davis snapped, finally starting to lose his cool.

"With all due respect, you confirmed my position as leader of my squad and sent me to guard that road however I could. I assumed I had a bit of leeway when it comes to authority. Besides, even citizens have the right to arrest suspected criminals and turn them over to law enforcement."

"And what should we do with them? Shove them in a big cage in the middle of camp and waste time and resources guarding and feeding them when we have a war to fight?" The sergeant rubbed his forehead. "How many men does Vernon have with him?"

Trev hesitated. "Thirteen."

"So that's fourteen well-armed and supplied men coming to volunteer in the fight against the blockheads, assuming that part of your report was also correct. You realize that's probably not happening now?" Trev had no answer for that, and Davis sighed. "Fine. Tell me exactly what they did that you just couldn't look past."

Trev quickly explained obtaining the truck from the Gold Bloc internment camp and the decision to enter Newtown for supplies, as well as Fred Vernon's highly vaunted reputation. Then he described having the truck taken at gunpoint and the "payment" the sheriff tossed at them as if it made it all okay, and Vernon and his men abandoning the town in the stolen truck.

Once he was done Davis shook his head. "Downright civilized compared to some of the atrocities I've heard about," he growled. "You realize we're fighting a better supplied, better equipped, better trained, and numerically superior enemy force and need all the help we can get? Is his crime worth canceling out the assistance he and his men could provide?"

"I-" Trev hesitated. "That's up to you to decide, sir."

Davis swore at him, then yelled for one of his Marines waiting outside. “Go grab our car thief.” The soldier saluted and left.

After a minute of tense silence the same Marine pulled the entry flap aside to let Vernon through. Aside from his hands still being bound the former sheriff didn't look much like a prisoner, with his shoulders back and his back straight. Even his cowboy hat was on straight.

Davis motioned to his soldier, who cut the zip ties binding the man's hands. Vernon nodded his thanks and rubbed at his wrists to restore circulation, and when Davis waved him forward he came to stand next to Trev without hesitation. Meanwhile the Marine settled into an at ease position near the entrance, eyes on the former sheriff and hand on his sidearm. So it wasn't all rolling out the red carpet.

“Fred Vernon, right?” the sergeant asked. Vernon nodded. “Mr. Smith has told me his side of things. Now I want to hear yours.”

The former sheriff glanced over at Trev. “I like to think I have a handle on Trevor's honesty. I'm willing to accept that he told you the truth.”

Trev took half a step back from the man, completely shocked. He didn't know what he'd expected, but it wasn't that.

Davis looked surprised as well. “You admit you and your men stole his family's truck and possessions at gunpoint, then robbed and abandoned the town you'd committed to protect?”

"Yes."

The sergeant glanced over at Trev, then back at the former sheriff. "Smith tells me you were headed south to Mexico. How did you end up here?"

"Only partly by choice." Vernon looked at the ground, and his expression actually seemed a bit haunted. "We got pretty close to Mexico and what we thought was safety, only to learn that the Gold Bloc already had an army there. Tens, maybe hundreds of thousands of soldiers."

"BS," Trev snapped. "We haven't heard anything about an army in Mexico."

Vernon glanced at Davis, who surprisingly hadn't reacted to the news. "Then you're about to have a very unpleasant surprise. The army's had the southern US in a massive cordon for weeks now, snatching up any refugees fleeing from the Gold Bloc forces coming down from the north. Those poor people are caught between hammer and anvil and from what I've heard it's beyond brutal. My men and I were lucky to get away ourselves, and we wouldn't have without the truck. We had to fight every mile of the way to break through to Utah from New Mexico."

Trev grit his teeth. "You know the people of Newtown are some of those "refugees" fleeing south, right? Deb, Clara, Max, even Westman and his barflies."

The former sheriff flinched, and his haunted expression became almost haggard. "I'd figured as much."

"Let's set that aside for now," Davis abruptly said. "You and your men want to volunteer, Mr. Vernon?"

"Yes." Vernon finally looked up, fighting to regain his calm. "I wanted to run with my men, but it looks like that's not possible. The only option left is to fight, so that's what we're going to do."

"You're dead right about that." The sergeant settled back against his desk, arms folded across his chest. "We could use everyone who's willing to fight alongside us. Especially people who can handle themselves."

"Wait, hold on," Trev said incredulously. "Are you seriously going to trust him? He told you himself he'd run if he could, and he's already proven it once."

Davis shot him a hard look. "The point is that he's here."

"Until he finds something better and runs off! This is the guy who abandoned the town he swore to protect as soon as he could steal a vehicle with fuel."

Vernon clenched his jaw. "He's not wrong," he said grudgingly. "I don't expect you to believe that I feel guilty about that, and for more reason than just because we couldn't run south like we'd planned. But whether you believe me or not I *do* feel guilty. I watched a blockhead convoy massacre a group of refugees and couldn't do anything about it, and I had to accept the fact that I'd probably left my friends and neighbors to the same fate."

"Well in that case welcome aboard," Trev said sarcastically.

"Give it a rest, Smith!" Davis barked. "I'm already pissed at you, don't give me a reason to really lose my temper."

Trev hesitated, then nodded and stepped back. He wasn't doing his case any good antagonizing the sergeant, and anyway he was starting to sound spiteful. Justice was on his side, he'd have to be content with that.

Davis gave him a final glare, then turned to Vernon. "Here's the deal, Sheriff. You and your men can join, and punishment for your crime is waived as long as you're with us, all the way to however this war ends. You will, however, return the truck and all remaining fuel to Mr. Smith, and anything else you took, at which point he will generously pass them on to the military until such time as we no longer need them."

The sergeant paused to look at both of them. Trev nodded, since he hadn't expected to get the truck or anything on it back in the first place, and Vernon nodded as well.

Davis continued. "The other supplies you brought with you from Newtown are likely also stolen, but that's just fine because you've already generously offered to donate them to the military. You can keep your weapons and other equipment as long as you fight with us, and once this war's over they're yours to keep."

Vernon glanced at Trev. "What about the gold I paid him for the vehicle?"

Davis slammed his fist down on the table behind him. "You can't pay for something you stole!" he snapped. "If Smith wants to return it to you that's his choice, but as far as I'm concerned that gold is a gift, or you could consider it reparation for the suffering and danger you put the man's family through." He motioned for the Marine waiting by the door to escort Vernon out. "Get your men settled, Sheriff. I'll talk to you more then, give you an idea of what we expect of you and fill you in on what you need to know. Oh, and welcome to the Rockies."

Once Vernon was gone Davis whirled to Trev. "You going to have a problem with that?"

Trev hesitated. He thought the sergeant was making a mistake, but if Davis had made up his mind then that was probably that. "If you think he can be trusted then I'll trust your judgment. I just hope you won't let your guard down with him. I certainly won't."

The sergeant swore at him again. "I like you, Smith. You're the kind of person I can respect, and you and your people do your jobs well. I don't even blame you for seeking justice." He pointed an accusing finger at Trev's chest. "But you and your Aspen Hill irregulars came in with a deserter from the US Army who'd spent the winter robbing innocent people! Remember that?"

"Yeah, I remember," Trev said reluctantly. And unfortunately it was a pretty good point.

"You expected me to look past that because Gutierrez had earned your trust and was trying to pay for his mistakes, and you were lucky because my orders *were* to look past it, if he was willing to fight for us. And you know what? I looked past it." Davis waved vaguely at the tent's entrance. "So do the same for Vernon and his people and don't let me hear about you causing problems. Understood?"

Trev couldn't think of a way to argue with that. "Understood. Hopefully he'll do the same."

"He better," the sergeant growled. "We ignore past crimes, we don't ignore current ones. Those we come down on like a ton of bricks." He reached behind him and absently tapped his map. "On the subject of keeping you apart, I hope you realize he was going to be your reinforcements at Cedar Creek. Next group of volunteers to show up, right? But I guess you'll have to wait a little longer for more fighters."

That was something he could've done without hearing. "Couldn't you reassign people from another camp and swap him out there?"

"No," Davis said, with finality. He rounded his desk to lean over his map again, obviously considering the meeting over. Trev stayed where he was, though, waiting patiently until the man finally looked up. "What?"

"Vernon was telling the truth about the army coming north out of Mexico," Trev said, "and you knew about it."

Davis set his jaw. "And?" Instead of answering Trev just waited in silence, and finally the sergeant growled in annoyance. "We haven't known about it for long. The blockheads managed to sneak it into Mexico without anyone on our side knowing. A hundred thousand conscripts from newly inducted Gold Bloc countries, who were just positioning themselves in Mexico to push northward when the Retaliation happened. Since then, as best we can tell they've taken Texas, Louisiana, Arkansas, Oklahoma, Arizona, New Mexico, and the parts of California that aren't irradiated slag. And from our reports Vernon's spot on about how they're treating the refugees fleeing their way."

A sudden realization struck Trev. "That's why Erikson pulled back to Utah. If the blockheads have a force that big coming up from Mexico they could've easily pushed right between the two arms of the Rockies where we'd set up, dividing our forces."

Davis nodded. "Yeah, that's right."

"So why didn't you guys tell us that?" Trev demanded. "We all thought either Erikson had suffered some major defeat you weren't telling us about, or he'd just retreated with his tail between his legs and put up barely a fight."

The sergeant's eyes narrowed. "Morale, Smith. Our soldiers are having a hard enough time fighting on against a vastly superior force that's already swallowed up most of our country. You want to tell them that on top of that there's nearly a hundred thousand more blockheads coming up from the south that none of us knew about? Who'd stayed so well hidden from us that not a single nuke targeted them during the Retaliation, leaving them completely intact with all their equipment and plenty of supplies?"

Unfortunately that wasn't the worst argument. Lassiter and Erikson had done their best to scrape together every single available soldier they could find all over the country who'd managed to survive the chaos, as well as recruit as many civilian volunteers as they could find, and their forces still barely numbered over 100,000 people.

If those brave defenders found out that the enemy that already outnumbered them 10 to 1 had a fresh army as large as their entire ragtag group that no one had even known about, that was about to flank them from an entirely new direction, that would be more than disheartening.

"That's why General Lassiter's got as many people here in the south as General Erikson is positioning up north, even though most of the blockheads we knew about were coming from up there," Trev guessed. "He has to hold our flank."

"If he can," Davis said grimly. He slumped down on the cheap metal stool behind his map table, vacantly staring down at the wrinkled paper. "The casualties in Colorado massively favored us, but the blockheads were still positioning themselves and hadn't even started really throwing bodies at us to try to break our defenses."

The sergeant sucked in a breath. "Once they do that here we'll be closed in, and the casualty numbers are going to get worse as they grind us down and we use up all our fuel and munitions. If we can't outlast them they'll bury us like a tide coming in, and that'll be it for the US."

Trev was a strong believer in the mindset of knowing the reality of a situation so he could deal with it. But at the moment he almost wished he wasn't hearing any of this. It made defending his little canyon seem a lot less useful to the overall war.

After a grim silence the sergeant finally looked up at him. "I could've done without you hearing all that from Vernon. I told you even more because I trust you can keep your mouth shut and, to be honest, it's nice to tell someone else." His eyes narrowed. "But I do mean it, Smith. Keep your mouth shut about this until the time comes to tell everyone. If it ever does."

"I will," Trev promised.

"All right then, dismissed. And keep away from Vernon!"

Trev saluted, forgetting that he didn't have to, and with some relief exited the tent.

*****

On Davis's orders Matt's squad had been on hunting and meat preserving duty almost nonstop over the last couple days.

There were plenty of good reasons for that. One was that for the moment, at least, the two squads of Marines were enough to hold the canyon. Another was that the sergeant wanted to store up as many supplies as possible before the enemy rolled in and occupied all their focus. There was also the fact that Davis felt like it was his duty to give the refugees coming up Highway 31 heading for safety in the mountains at least one meal to see them on their way, as well as a place to sleep if they needed it.

All in all it meant that no matter how much game they bagged each time they went out, it was never enough to satisfy their needs. And when luck wasn't with them, like with this current hunt, Matt almost felt bad returning to camp.

It didn't improve his mood much to see that while he'd been gone *another* section had been added to the permanent part of the camp, housing a dozen or so more volunteers. Not that he had a problem with having more people fighting with them, just the opposite, but it meant more mouths to feed.

Who knew, maybe Davis would send the new guys out in hunting parties too.

Matt set Rick and Pete to cleaning the few varmints they'd managed to find while he headed over to the new camp to introduce himself. He'd only made it halfway there, though, before Graham intercepted him.

"Probably don't want to go over there," the specialist said.

Matt frowned. "Is there a problem?"

"Only with you guys." The soldier shrugged. "Your buddy Trev brought those guys in. Under arrest."

"What?" Matt demanded, incredulous. "What did they do?"

Graham shrugged again. "Stole a truck from him or something. But whatever they did, Sarge has pardoned them and let them join up. He doesn't want trouble so you'll probably want to keep your distance, just to be on the safe side."

Matt looked over at the camp and the few unkempt men in view around the tents. It wasn't possible that was the sheriff Trev had told him about, the guy who'd robbed them in Newtown. Was it? "I'll give them a wide berth," he told the specialist. "Although if Davis let them join up and wants me to keep the peace there wouldn't be any trouble from my end either way."

"That's the spirit." Graham clapped him on the shoulder and walked away, so Matt turned to head back to his camp and help his friends with their work.

He'd only gone a few steps when there was a burst of laughter, not quite friendly, from the camp behind him. He looked back to find a few of the newcomers staring his way and grinning like he was the butt of some joke. One of them flipped him off.

Terrific. He kept going, ignoring more laughter from behind. He'd been hoping Davis might put the new guys on hunting duty to help his squad out, but under the circumstances maybe he didn't want a bunch of armed pardoned criminals who apparently had a grudge against the Aspen Hill volunteers roaming the forests with his people.

He hoped Davis knew what he was doing.

It turned out that only a few hours later the arrival of Vernon and whatever tension it was bound to cause became the least of his worries. That was when word reached them that the fighting in Colorado was mostly done. Erikson had broken away as cleanly as possible and his force was making a beeline for northern Utah, to take over the defenses there as planned. Meanwhile Lassiter's troops that had been stationed to the north made their way south to cover central and southern Utah.

Less than a day behind them, the Gold Bloc forces were in close pursuit. Equally alarming, to the west the Chinese army had finally sprung into motion in a big way. They seemed to have some intel on the way the US Armed Forces in Utah were reorganizing, and were trying to race Erikson to northern Utah to take it first. And from the looks of things it was going to be a close one even though they had to go around the fallout zone.

But as dire as those events were, they were a distant concern compared to the warning Davis's Marines and the volunteers soon received that directly concerned them.

A Gold Bloc army had materialized out of nowhere in the south, pushing up hard towards Utah. It was smaller than the other two forces but much more mobile, and expected to be in position to attack days ahead of the Russians to the northeast and Chinese to the northwest. By some reports it would engage Lassiter's position along I-70 as early as tomorrow afternoon.

If the General turned them back, as everyone desperately hoped he would, that was a mixed blessing for Matt and his volunteers. It meant the enemy would be heading their way next.

Chapter Sixteen

First Strike

For the rest of the day Davis led everyone in frantically making final preparations for whatever came their way. Matt and his squad worked hard, but were always partially distracted by listening intently to radio chatter hoping for news.

There was plenty of that as afternoon turned to evening, none of it good. It looked as if Erikson would barely make it before the Chinese, and Lassiter had redirected thousands of his soldiers heading south back to their previous positions to hold off any of the enemy's advance units. That left the south weaker than the Generals would've liked when it came to the army headed their way along I-70, but there was no help for it.

Things were going FUBAR, as the Marines put it, and the next few days were going to be critical. Needless to say Matt didn't sleep very well that night, and he doubted anyone else had either.

The next morning Davis gathered everyone in camp together. "We're 99.9% certain the enemy will attack us today," he began bluntly, "along at least one front and possibly along all of them at once. So from now on all our other duties take a distant second priority to manning our positions, which we'll be doing 24/7 starting now. I suggest you get used to sleeping in foxholes and eating lean, at least until we solve this current crisis and things settle down a bit."

He fell silent for a few moments, letting that sink in, then abruptly barked out, "This, ladies and gentlemen, is US soil! We do not let any enemy trespass on US soil. Highway 31 will *not* be where the blockheads break through into the mountains. Is that understood!"

The Marines responded enthusiastically, while the volunteers were more subdued. Matt did his best, but he was too nervous to get swept up in a pep talk.

Davis seemed to notice it. He gave the volunteers a slightly impatient look and gestured down the canyon. "Everyone to your emplacements!" he snapped. "Take what you need to stay there for a few days, assuming you'll be fighting that entire time. Including a change of pants if you think you'll need one; I don't care how scared you are, I don't want to see *any* of you abandoning your posts on my watch unless I give the order to fall back!"

As motivational speeches went that left a little something to be desired, but it got them moving. Matt had his squad pack up and lug their gear to the emplacement they'd set up, on the other side of and slightly up the canyon from the rocky slope Davis had rigged to bury the road.

Aside from Williams's squad across the canyon they were the farthest forward position, but it wasn't all bad because it was also one of the more inaccessible ones from below. The enemy would have a hard time getting to them through a dense thicket of scrub oak closer to the road, and this emplacement was also situated next to a slope thickly treed with spruce and Douglas fir.

If they had to fall back they'd almost immediately be in the cover of those trees, which would offer close to complete protection from anything but the luckiest stray shot. They'd cleared a good path to the fallback position ahead of time as well, which would allow them to quickly relocate and begin firing from their new spot.

Matt got his people situated in the shallow trench behind the line of sandbags they'd set up over a week ago, which was lined with branches and other forest debris for camouflage and extra cover. Everyone looked tense, and Carl Mitchell actually threw up from nerves. Matt put them to work checking their gear, not just because it was an important task but also to occupy their minds. Once they were busy with that he got in touch with Davis to let him know they were in place.

"Good hustle, Larson," the sergeant said.

"Thanks. What do we do now?"

Davis snorted. "What do you think? Wait until you're needed, and find that balance where you somehow manage to stay sharp for long periods of time without turning into a complete basket case." His tone sharpened. "Keep an eye on the area around us, too. I may have scouts out to give us advance warning, and General Lassiter has people even farther out, but that's no reason you shouldn't keep watch too."

"Roger, Sarge. We'll keep our eyes open." Matt thumbed the transmission toggle off.

"Oh, and the enemy is really hoofing it. Last word was they'll be here hours earlier than expected, maybe even before noon. Davis out."

Matt exchanged worried glances with the rest of his squad, who'd gathered around him as the conversation began. "They got here sooner than we expected," Pete said. He looked almost excited by the prospect.

"The early bird gets the worm," Rick replied, sounding half joking, half dour.

Matt knew it was probably good for morale, but he wasn't in the mood for banter. "And the early worm gets the bird," he shot back with finality. "Let's be the bird, guys. We'll make them regret showing up at any time. Everybody get your gear in order and remember your training."

His squad burst into activity, hastily moving back to their assigned positions and setting up there for the wait.

*****

Twelve volunteers. A dozen people to hold against whatever came their way.

Davis had finally spilled the beans to everyone about the army coming up from Mexico, right before that army leapt down their throats. Not the best timing, but better late than never.

Trev thumbed his radio toggle. "Two rules, people: be alert, and no heroics. We're not here to fight the enemy, we're just here to take out this road if it looks like they're coming up the canyon. If they continue to come on foot in small numbers we drive them back, otherwise we fall back ourselves and wait for Davis to send help."

His squad gave their acknowledgements, sporadically and with more than a little trepidation. They'd been set up in their positions since last night, since Trev wanted them to get used to the idea of staying there, although he'd let them pitch their tents outside their emplacements for a more comfortable sleep. He also wanted them to be as rested as possible for whatever happened.

Still, twelve people, and the less experienced of the volunteers from Aspen Hill. Not to mention that most of the toys the town had sent along with them were with Matt and Davis in the other canyon. Realistically he knew Cedar Creek Canyon's road wasn't ideal for the enemy, and they weren't far from the main camp along 31 if they needed help.

In spite of all that he felt like he and his people were standing in the doorway just before the start of the Running of the Bulls, while everyone else was safe behind the barricades.

He had to hope it wouldn't be as bad as he feared. They'd prepared their positions to have escape routes with fairly good cover, so if his people needed to run they could do it safely. He also had Molotovs and grenades captured from the raiders in case things went wrong and they needed to cover their escape with more than just small arms fire.

And while he wouldn't have minded having the .50 caliber heavy machine gun or the missile launcher, he could accept that Williams's and Matt's squads along 31 needed them more.

Matt's voice came over his earphones. "You guys set up, Trev?"

He toggled his radio. "Yeah, since last night. You?"

"Ready as we'll ever be." His friend paused for a few seconds. "Be careful out there."

Before Trev could answer Davis's voice barked in his ear. "Keep the airwaves clear! We've already caught sight of the blockhead forward scouts, and their main army should be in sight of our far lookouts any minute now."

Trev sighed and settled back in his emplacement, moving his shoulders to loosen the tension in them. He'd trained his squad the best he knew how. They'd spent weeks preparing this canyon for ambushes. They had the best gear Aspen Hill could provide them. Reinforcements were available if they really needed them.

Still, a dozen people. Against a hundred thousand. Not entirely accurate, but it was hard not to think like that. They could end up facing however many soldiers the blockheads decided to throw at them, and that could be a very, very big number.

*****

They received radio warning long before the Gold Bloc forces ever came into view.

First that a large portion of the enemy army had split off onto Highway 6 well to the east, heading towards Price. They only knew about it because the convoy of hundreds of enemy trucks was nearly to the abandoned county seat and had been spotted by lookouts up there. Which meant that their families back in Aspen Hill could soon be in danger.

The second warning came soon afterwards of the main convoy's first sighting along I-70, then of another large portion of those forces splitting off onto Highway 10, which branched off northward from the interstate and ran just east of the mountains, allowing the blockheads to scour every potential canyon between Emery and Huntington.

The enemy was met with resistance at every one, including some heartening accounts of several trucks being crushed beneath rock falls and rockslides. For the moment it seemed they weren't in the mood to abandon their vehicles and try to secure any of the canyons on foot, instead continuing on to the next potential road to test it out. Each one delayed the blockheads, and those delays added up, but it was only a matter of time before they reached Huntington.

Matt definitely appreciated the advance notice, but it had its drawbacks too. Now that they were set up in their positions all that was left to do was wait, sitting there in a tense silence that was half fear and half anticipation. Which seemed to last forever while they watched to see whether the enemy would try to come up Highway 31 or pass them by entirely.

He was doing his best to keep his cool under the pressure of that interminable wait, but not everyone was managing it. "There's no way they'll take 31," Rick said for maybe the tenth time since the squad had settled into their emplacement hours ago. "It's too small a bottleneck."

Even though Matt wanted to do his part protecting what was left of the country, it was hard not to hope his friend was right. But he had to be the voice of reason. "There's only so many ways to get through this range, and 31 is one of the most reliable. We'll probably have to turn back scouts if nothing else, and if General Lassiter or our people up near Spanish Fork Canyon hold the blockheads back like we're all hoping, that means they're going to start really looking for another way past. Like it or not, we should expect to see enemies coming our way."

"Let them come," Pete said, hefting his M16. "We didn't spend all this time climbing around and digging on these steep hillsides for the fun of it."

Matt was glad the young man had control of his fear, although he wasn't sure if he should be. Pete had been on edge ever since his dad died, and during the fight with the raiders Matt had been afraid a few times his friend might lose it. Like when he'd clocked Turner with the butt of his rifle. Other reckless behavior, like when he'd gone riding off on his own while going after the sheep, only added to Matt's worry.

He'd probably want to pull his friend aside for a talk once things settled down a bit.

News continued to reach them over the radio during the interminable wait, and his squad eagerly listened to every tidbit. For the moment most of that was from down south, but the northwest and northeast Gold Bloc armies continued to close on northern Utah like a nutcracker that could begin the squeeze at any time from hours to days.

Along I-70 Lassiter had ordered his people not to engage the enemy until the blockhead convoy was in the mountains. Part of that was to draw them in as far as he could so his attack would do the most possible damage, but another part of it was that many of the towns in Carbon and Emery counties had refused to evacuate until the last second when they were sure it was necessary, and their people were still struggling to get to safety.

The General was afraid that anything that slowed the enemy convoys might give them a reason to spread out and begin searching the area, which would put civilians in harm's way. Given the brutality the blockheads had shown since the Retaliation, even to innocents, that was something they needed to avoid at all costs. Especially since the convoys would be even less reasonable with anyone they caught if they'd just been turned back by a surprise attack.

Like they'd be unreasonable if they successfully managed to come up 31 and took any of the fighters there as prisoners. Yet another grim reminder that Matt's squad and the rest of Davis's people needed to hit them hard and turn them back, since if anyone got caught they couldn't expect much mercy.

Word finally reached them that Lassiter had engaged the convoy moving along I-70, and the fighting turned brutal. First reports had thousands dead on both sides within the first ten minutes. And still Matt and his friends waited for the enemy to reach their own ambush in the mountains.

After what seemed like an eternity their advance lookouts confirmed sighting the convoy coming up 10, then began booking it for the safety of the mountains as quickly and stealthily as possible. Not long after that Williams, with his 2nd Squad on the north slope of the canyon, confirmed sighting the enemy nearing Huntington.

Matt heard some of his squad mates begin grumbling as their companions on the radio described what they saw. From their vantage point on the south slope his squad's view was blocked by the spur of the ridge to the east of them, and even Huntington to the southeast was barely in view. The convoy was pulling into the town itself before Pete stiffened and shouted that he saw the enemy trucks.

Everyone around him went absolutely still and silent, as if hardly daring to breathe for fear of alerting the vehicles in the distance. The reflexive action was completely irrational, and also completely understandable.

The trucks kept coming, one after another. By the tens, and finally by the hundreds. There were even a few tanks in the middle of the column, looking unwieldy but menacing navigating through the small streets of Huntington.

"That's a lot of people," Rick said quietly. The younger man looked at the rocky north slope where Graham's specialists had hidden the explosives, as if imagining dozens of trucks and the hundreds of soldiers inside all being buried in the rockslide.

"A lot of corpses, if they keep coming," Pete shot back.

Matt winced at his friend's words, as well as his tone. He could've done without that sort of bloodthirstiness. Yes, the Gold Bloc troops were their enemies, and after massacring every single innocent US citizen they encountered if anyone deserved to pay for their crimes it was them. But it was a necessity, not something to look forward to.

He couldn't see how anyone could have a taste for bloodshed after the unimaginable number of people that had already died in such a short time since the Retaliation.

"They chose to attack us," he said, trying not to sound too harsh, "but we can't let ourselves enjoy killing them. If they come up that canyon they'll leave us no choice but to fight, but it's not something to be happy about. What happens after that will be on their heads."

"Literally," Pete muttered, glancing at the rocky slope across from them. He didn't seem too abashed by the gentle rebuke.

For a moment Matt considered calling the young man out, but now was a bad time to get into something like that. So he kept quiet along with the rest of his squad as they watched the line of vehicles continue to converge on the town.

It was soon apparent that Pete would get his wish, as the lead trucks in the enemy convoy turned onto Highway 31 and began making for the canyon. Behind them the following vehicles stretched all the way through town and out of sight along Highway 10, a seemingly endless line that kept on getting longer and longer.

Rick was right, it was a lot of people. And even if his head was in the wrong place Pete was, unfortunately, probably also right. Matt tried not to think of all the people he'd already been forced to kill to protect his friends and family in Aspen Hill, which would seem like minor skirmishes compared to what was about to happen.

If the blockheads turned back from the trap it would be a disaster, in its own way, but he found himself hoping they would even so. Hoping they'd turn back altogether, just go back to wherever they'd come from and stop all the senseless killing.

Only they couldn't really, since they didn't have any homes to go back to.

It didn't take long for the lead trucks to make their way up the canyon towards the ambush. Everyone around Matt went perfectly still as the vehicles came to within twenty feet of the rocky slope rigged with its charges. Then ten feet, then five, moving at a cautious pace the entire time.

Then, as if in answer to his wish, the two trucks stopped entirely, their front fenders even with the first few boulders on the slope. Moments later soldiers poured out of the backs, rifles in their hands, and began forming a defensive circle around the vehicle, calling to each other.

Beside him Pete stiffened. “Why are they stopping?” he hissed. “There's no way they could know!”

Matt motioned sharply for him to shut up. The soldiers below were hundreds of yards away and shouting at each other in Russian, so it was almost impossible they'd heard something that had barely reached his own ears. Still, better safe than sorry.

It was a good question though. Why stop there, in front of an innocuous rocky slope beside the road? You could find those all over the place, so it wasn't like it stood out as suspicious, and Graham had done a good job concealing the explosives.

Was it just paranoia? If so it was understandable that they'd be cautious, since this convoy had already been ambushed several times as they probed into the canyons between I-70 and here. And if they were in contact with their main convoy fighting Lassiter, and had heard how vicious the fighting was, they'd have even more reason to be wary.

Unfortunately their caution included metal detectors and German shepherds, likely trained to sniff for bombs. Matt watched in dismay as enemy soldiers picked their way up the slope through the boulders sweeping every square foot, dogs wagging their tails as they scrambled on ahead with their noses to the ground.

This was more than just the timid probes reports said they'd done in the canyons to the south. It seemed like the blockheads wanted 31, and they were going to put some serious effort into making it secure.

"Davis is going to have to detonate, even if we can't drop the hillside on the convoy like we planned," Rick mumbled, almost too quietly to hear. He did a good job suppressing the "s" sounds that normally carried, too, and Matt made a note to do the same the next time he needed to talk quietly.

Which wasn't right now. There was a chance the soldiers across the canyon would miss the explosives, and he didn't want to blow it with a stray noise carried down to them. If the enemy gave the all clear and the convoy continued forward the ambush could still go as planned. It was a faint hope, but they couldn't afford to detonate early and pass up the potential damage they could cause.

Then one of the dogs began barking furiously, shoving its nose between the rocks at one of the locations where a charge had been set up. Soldiers called warnings to each other, some running towards the explosives as if planning to try to deactivate them, while most ran the other way.

At which point Davis decided to detonate.

*****

The series of shaped explosions vibrated the air around Matt, and across the canyon the entire top of the rocky slope became a cataclysm of rock and flame rushing down the hillside, catching more rocks and the bodies of men and dogs with it in a massive rockslide. Boulders weighing more than Matt himself were hurled dozens of feet by the initial blasts, shattering as they struck more rocks below and speeding the slide.

Before the two idling lead blockhead trucks could even begin to back away they were physically lifted off the road and hurled across the canyon by the cresting wave of debris. Half a dozen trucks in the line behind them were hit by dozens of boulders larger than his head, spinning them across the road as they crumpled like they were made of foil.

Matt had seen explosions, and he'd seen large fires, and he'd watched Turner destroy dozens of houses. But that rockslide seemed beyond the hand of man, a primal force of nature that kept going and going, until the entire bottom of the canyon was buried in boulders and loose earth and shattered and uprooted trees at least ten feet deep. The noise alone would've been deafening without his earbuds, and around him his friends were covering their ears with pained expressions.

He didn't think anyone was considering the fight to come with all of that happening, too focused on the devastation. As he watched the shifting mass of rocks gradually begin grinding to a halt, seeing it through a thick haze of dust, he almost forgot why they'd set off the rockslide in the first place.

Then Davis shouted in his ear. “All squads, open fire!”

Matt gave a start and jerked his eyes away from the settling slope of debris that completely barred the way farther up the canyon. He expected to see the convoy hightailing it out of there with tires squealing, but to his alarm instead he saw soldiers boiling out of the backs of trucks all down the line.

He couldn't see how it was possible they weren't panicked by the explosion and landslide, but if so they didn't show it. The growing press of soldiers moved with good coordination to fan out on either side of the road.

At least until the M2 Browning, manned by one of Williams's people on the opposite slope, roared to life and began tearing into the packed enemy soldiers. It was quickly joined by 3-round burst fire from the Marines in that emplacement.

At that point the blockheads' coordination broke, enough that they bolted for cover before doing their best to return fire. Other enemy soldiers somehow managed to ignore the gunfire once they reached cover, and began slipping up the slope searching for ways to get at their enemies. Or at least looking for a better vantage for firing.

Meanwhile the empty trucks in the convoy had begun backing out and turning around in a coordinated fashion to escape the ambush, only to find themselves the target of the heavy machine gun as its hail of .50 BMG rounds walked back towards them in a devastating line. Several were taken out before the others got moving, and then the heavy gunner's attention was diverted by the hail of return fire coming his way.

All that happened within the first half minute, and even though the fight already seemed to have gone on for much longer Davis was still relaying specific instructions to the outer emplacements about dealing with any soldiers trying to flank them. Which on Matt's side of the ravine was a squad of volunteers positioned on the ridge above with a good view of the hillside all the way down. Their squad leader acknowledged the order, and moments later gunfire sounded from above Matt.

At about that time he realized that just about everyone in the canyon was firing, while he and his squad were gawking at the bright lights and loud noises. He grit his teeth and lifted his M16, shouting for his squad to do the same.

Things were already ugly, and they were about to get uglier. There were hundreds of blockheads down there, and if they were able to kill or drive away Matt's squad and Davis's other forces they'd be free to begin clearing the road, and would probably call for reinforcements to come and help secure a way into the mountains.

General Lassiter might not be able to send help in time, and before they knew it the enemy would have a foothold behind the lines and would be that much closer to attacking the remaining US forces from behind.

There was also the fact that Matt and his friends would probably be dead by that point, and his family and friends from Aspen Hill would be pinned down with enemies on both sides. They had to hold here, whatever it took.

Pete had already begun firing, and Matt hurriedly sighted in on the soldiers nearest the road. They were searching for better cover farther off the road, but that still left far too many easy targets as he began squeezing off shots.

It was a long distance, shooting at moving targets hundreds of yards away, and the man he'd been specifically aiming for managed to reach his new spot of cover without taking a hit as far as Matt could tell. Which hardly mattered because two of the men around him went down to Matt's shots.

Explosions downslope meant that the enemy soldiers had managed to find the few mines Davis had scattered across the hillside, and he heard screams and flashes from below. Matt ignored them and kept shooting, determined that he wouldn't be distracted again, and for his effort was rewarded by seeing another target drop to one of his shots.

There were plenty more enemies to shoot at after that, and he and his squad were relatively well concealed behind a good embankment in case they took return fire. At some point they might come under determined attack and have to fall back to another position, but for now he just focused on squeezing off as many shots as possible and doing his best to make sure he hit something.

A minute passed that seemed like half an hour, and in that time the road below and any cover within twenty feet completely emptied out aside from dozens of bodies. The trucks that had been disabled by the rockslide or M2, around fifteen in all, lay scattered like abandoned and stomped on toys, while the rest of the convoy had cleared out to a safe distance. It was now creating a fortified position just outside the mouth of the canyon.

And the fight had only begun. The rocks, trees, and undergrowth below swarmed with enemy soldiers, and flashes of gunfire seemed to come from everywhere. So far his people seemed safe at their position, but Matt was keeping a close eye on the slope below them. If the enemy got too close they'd have to run.

Their own return fire was far less effective than it had been during those initial moments. Enemy soldiers were still dropping in large numbers, but he also heard shouts for medical aid from their side over the radio. Then there were the distant booms from the blockhead tanks just now pulling out of Huntington, although if the shells they fired were hitting anywhere close to the ambush site Matt couldn't tell.

In spite of the fierce blockhead resistance the casualties had to favor Davis's ambushers at least 40 to 1. Why had the enemy decided to deploy their soldiers in such a vulnerable position and cut and run with their trucks? It made no sense, not when there was no hope of clearing the destroyed road even with a week of work, especially not while under fire.

So why were they sticking around?

His firing pin clicked on an empty chamber, signaling the need for his third reload since the fight began. Matt released the empty magazine onto the ground beneath his knees and fumbled for a full one from his flak jacket pocket, distantly aware that he only had two more after that before he'd need to go for his pack.

As he slammed the loaded magazine home Matt suddenly felt the hairs on the back of his neck begin tingling, a subconscious warning of something he hadn't yet realized. He paused, looking around and straining his ears to hear past the roar of gunfire from the rest of his squad. It was easier with the noise canceling earbuds, but at the same time the sounds he heard through them were deceptively muted or amplified in odd ways.

It took a while, and in the end he didn't hear the noise that had caught his attention *over* the sound of gunfire. In a strange way the low, rhythmic thumping cut beneath all other noise, growing steadily louder, and in the heat of the moment it took him a few seconds longer than it should've to recognize it.

A helicopter. He darted his eyes to the east and caught the glint of sunlight reflecting off something high in the sky, the glare distorting the dark, insectile shape of the aircraft.

That was why the blockheads had stuck around . . . they were holding out for air support. Matt bit back a curse and fumbled at his belt for the transmit toggle. But before he could shout his warning Davis's voice thundered in his ears. "All units, scatter!"

His squad mates, obviously confused by the abrupt order, hesitated. Matt raised his own voice to repeat the order even as he broke from their position to one of the nearby foxholes they'd dug. Those were more fallback positions, set up in case the enemy turned any serious firepower on them and they needed to relocate, but things weren't bad enough to force them to retreat entirely along the forest path they'd cleared to the secondary emplacement.

The next few seconds were a blur as he crossed the slope in a scrambling crouch, expecting to be hit from behind by the enemies below even though rationally he knew the angle was bad for them. He reached the foxhole he'd dug himself and dove inside, landing awkwardly with his rifle skittering away as he came down on top of it.

It took a while to get himself right side up so he could duck down and retrieve the weapon in the cramped space. Once he managed it he poked his head up out of his new source of cover, checking to make sure everyone else had gotten away clean and no one needed covering fire or other assistance.

His people had scattered in all directions, keeping well apart to reduce losses in case of whatever threat prompted them to scatter, and a few were still scrambling to their own foxholes. Matt saw Gutierrez poke his head out of the one nearest their original position, and to his relief he saw that the former soldier had kept hold of the squad's TOW missile launcher.

Matt thumbed the toggle. "If you've got a shot take it, Raul," he whispered.

Before Gutierrez could answer a small streak of brilliant flame speared out of the sky to the east and slammed into the other side of the canyon, almost on top of 2nd Squad's position. The air and ground both shook around him as the hillside across from them became an almost blinding fireball, and Matt winced and ducked away from the explosion.

The helicopter had missiles of its own, and had rightly identified the location of the heavy machine gun as the greatest known threat. Matt could only hope Williams had gotten his people into their scatter positions in time. Although even scattered, it seemed impossible that a blast that big hadn't claimed a few lives. He felt a surge of relief that his squad's position hadn't been hit, then guilty for feeling that way.

From farther up the canyon came the bright streak of a TOW missile heading the other way in response, fired by 1st Squad's launcher, but Matt's hopes were dashed when he saw it fly off into the afternoon sky and explode brilliantly nowhere near the approaching chopper. The return enemy missile, which shrieked up the canyon towards the spot where Davis's attack had come from, confirmed that the helicopter hadn't even been fazed by the miss.

Matt ducked slightly at the explosion farther up the canyon, gritting his teeth. "Raul?"

"Give me a second," Gutierrez snapped. "I mostly know how this thing works, but I wish you would've let me fire at least one missile so I knew what to expect. Learning on the fly against a fast-moving object in midair is going to suck."

Matt found himself also wishing he'd let his friend practice at least once. At the time aiming the wire-guided missiles had seemed simple enough, and they'd expected that Gutierrez would be using them against large convoy targets like trucks and pick it up pretty fast. At the time, from a shortsighted perspective, it had saved them the waste of using one of their few precious missiles just for training.

Now he could see that the opposite was true. If Gutierrez had to shoot a chopper out of the sky it seemed impossible he'd manage it in one try, and even missing once made not letting him practice beforehand a bad call.

Worse yet, if he fired and missed he'd almost certainly make himself a target, and he might not get a second shot. Matt's decision to be stingy might cost more than the missiles themselves, it might cost his friend's life. All their lives possibly, since they were close enough to be hit by the explosion too.

"Take your time," he said. "Make it count."

The former soldier abruptly ducked and cursed in Spanish. "It'd be easier if you'd do something about the people shooting at us from below."

Right. Matt hastily lifted his rifle. "All right, people. Resume fire."

Some of his squad mates hadn't needed his order, like Pete, but Matt didn't wait to make sure everyone else had heard before sighting in on a flash of gunfire from the trees below and squeezing off a 3-round burst. In the lingering dust haze from the rockslide he wasn't sure if he'd hit or simply spooked the enemy soldier off, but the muzzle flashes stopped so he began searching for another target.

A moment later his world went white.

It was more the force of the explosion than any reaction on his part that caused him to collapse down into his foxhole in a ball. He felt a wall of noise and heat roaring over his head, singeing the hairs on the back of his neck, and the sheer force of it rocked him hard against the dirt wall to his left. For a moment his ears rang, but the earbuds shielded them from the brunt of the noise, same as with the gunfire.

This experience wasn't nearly as bad as during his disastrous attack on the raider camp about two and a half months ago, when a missile had struck nearby, but his second brush with a nearby explosion still wasn't anything he'd want to get used to.

Once the noise and heat faded Matt forced himself to stand, peeking out of his foxhole at the devastation. To his relief he saw that the missile had hit the hillside below their original position, just about the only place where no one in his squad had dug a fallback foxhole since it would've put them in the enemy's line of fire.

"Aspen H-" he coughed as the wind blew smoke and dust into his face, then covered his eyes and mouth with his elbow as he tried again. "Aspen Hill squad, report any injuries."

His ears were full of chatter, shouts and curses and conflicting information and orders, as well as a few screams of pain and pleas for help. Over which Davis's ignored shouts for everyone to clear the airwaves only added to the confusion. But before he could make out any replies from his squad in that mess he became aware of the insectile black shape hovering over the mouth of the canyon, several hundred yards away.

The helicopter. It had some sort of heavy machine gun spooled up and emptying rounds into a spot higher up the canyon, closer to where Davis and 1st Squad were set up. Matt wasn't sure if it was out of missiles or just reloading, or maybe even still had some ready to go and had switched to the gun for some other purpose. Whatever the pilot's reasoning, he was holding the bird steady so he wouldn't throw off the gunner's aim.

Matt thumbed his radio. "Now or never, Raul." As he spoke he sincerely hoped his friend was still alive, and not just so he could take this opportunity to bring the bird down for good.

To his relief Gutierrez almost immediately popped out of his hole, missile launcher propped on his shoulder. His face was grimy with dirt, with a dark stain on one temple that might've been blood, but his arms were steady as he aimed the unwieldy weapon at the hovering helicopter.

A moment later the missile streaked away on a tail of fire, with Gutierrez carefully guiding it towards the chopper. It moved so quickly Matt almost didn't see what happened next, but he thought the bird banked to one side at the last second. That, plus the fact that his friend's aim was slightly off, caused the missile to miss by a dozen feet and quickly overshoot its target.

The explosion rocked the helicopter in the air, and its gunner abruptly ceased firing. Over in his hole Gutierrez swore loudly and ducked out of sight, hopefully to load another missile. Because of that he didn't see that his efforts were unnecessary.

The helicopter veered away, banking into a sharp turn that sent it thumping to the northeast away from them. At the sight of it a few cheers erupted, both from his squad mates and over the radio.

Matt didn't cheer. He was relieved to see the biggest threat flying off, but the canyon was still full of enemies, some of whom might've been sneaking up to his squad's position right at that moment. He thumbed his radio toggle. "Fight's not over yet, guys. If you're not already firing time to start again."

He suited his words by raising his rifle and sighting down the scope towards the valley below, listening as the gunfire from his squad started up again around him. Oddly enough he didn't see any muzzle flashes from the enemy, but he did catch a few glimpses of movement in the scrub oak below. He aimed at one and focused on keeping his gun steady as he squeezed the trigger.

Just before he got the shot off his earbuds abruptly vibrated with Davis's thundering voice. “Everyone cease fire! Cease fire!”

Chapter Seventeen

Aftermath

Matt cursed and yanked the end of his rifle up as his finger finished squeezing the trigger, sending the shot flying harmlessly into the slope where the rockslide had swept through across the way.

"What?" he demanded.

"You heard me, Larson!" Davis snapped, and with a start Matt realized he hadn't toggled his radio off after his last transmission. "Cease fire! Haven't you noticed the enemy's already stopped?"

Even as the sergeant spoke Matt lowered his M16 and repeated the order in a shout to his squad, although they all had their own radios and should've heard it. The racket of gunfire around him fell down to near silence, allowing him to hear the last few stray shots from other squads on the hillsides.

And Pete. In spite of Matt's shout the young man kept firing, and when he finally stopped almost ten seconds later the near complete silence in the canyon suggested he'd been the last to obey Davis's order.

Speaking of which . . . Matt was just about to ask what was going on, but before he could Davis kept going. "That's right.

We've agreed to a ceasefire with the enemy. Everyone disengage and head for the fallback positions until we can get this sorted out."

Matt wasn't sure when or how that arrangement had happened, but after almost getting blown up he wasn't complaining. He finally toggled off his radio, slung his rifle over his shoulder, and climbed out of his foxhole, crawling towards the small trail they'd cleared through the woods that headed farther up the canyon. As he did he called to his squad. "You heard the Sergeant! Let's get out of here while the getting's good."

His people followed, and Matt did a quick count to confirm they were all still alive. By the lack of complaints it looked as if they'd all avoided getting hit, or at least not seriously. Which was a huge relief; things had gotten pretty hairy back there, and they were all lucky to have made it through.

He paused when his count came up one short, although he could immediately see it was because Pete was still in his foxhole, aiming down at the enemy soldiers below. "Pete!" he snapped.

The young man glanced over his shoulder, then reluctantly began shimmying backwards until he was on the trail. Matt gave him a shove to get him going after the others, then followed at a trot at the back of the line while they made for their fallback position.

It didn't take long, since the second emplacement was only a few hundred feet away at another good vantage for shooting down at the road below. Once everyone was safely hidden behind cover Matt made his way around to personally make sure no one had been badly hurt.

Then he stomped over to Pete and caught the young man's shoulder. "What are you doing?" he demanded.

His friend gave him a confused look. "What are you talking about?"

"The ceasefire! You heard Davis, the blockheads gave us a chance to end the fighting. And good thing they did, because they had that helicopter ready to rain down fire on us."

Pete snorted. "Yeah, to keep us from killing any more of their troops after we nearly blew up that helicopter and forced it to run." The young man glared at him. "Why are you getting on my case about any of that?"

Matt hesitated. Pete's shot hadn't come that long after Davis's order to cease fire. It had been the last one fired, sure, but not by too much. It was possible his friend just hadn't reacted as quickly as everyone else, or he'd been caught up in the moment.

Still, that shot could've fouled up the ceasefire and kept the violence going. He felt like he needed to say something about it, but he wasn't sure what he could say without accusing the young man.

Before he could decide whether or not to push the issue Davis's voice crackled over his radio. "All right, people, the blockheads are gathering their dead and pulling back. That gives us a bit of a breather, so now's the time to get our feet back under us. Williams, anyone unhurt in your squad will stay behind just in case they're not true to their word.

Everyone else head back to camp, and I want a debriefing from the other squad leaders as soon as you arrive."

Matt stared at Pete, his friend staring back defiantly, then sighed and toggled his radio. "Larson here. Understood; pulling my squad back to camp." As he lowered his radio he gave the young man a warning glare. "Next time you're given an order, obey it immediately." He turned and started calling for his squad to pack up.

"I did!" Pete shouted behind him, sounding outraged. Matt ignored him, content to let the matter drop for now. Although it bothered him as he led his volunteers on down the trail towards camp.

Davis had thought ahead towards the location of his main camp. He'd put it close enough to the ambush site that they could reach it quickly, but far enough away that it wouldn't get dragged into the fighting unless things went seriously wrong. Most importantly of all, he'd situated it around a bend in the road so it was well out of line of sight of the canyon below.

When they passed 1st Squad's emplacement at that bend, where Davis and his men and been fighting, they saw for themselves how important that precaution had been. The helicopter's missile had been a direct hit, obliterating the sandbag fortifications. Judging by the three bodies neatly arranged well clear of the blast site, not everyone in the sergeant's squad had managed to get clear in time.

Matt and his squad paused to observe a moment of silence for the fallen Marines, all aware that could have been any one of them if the circumstances were just slightly different. Then they continued on to camp, where the mood was subdued. Matt sent his people to help with the camp chores, however they could on short notice, and continued on to find Davis.

The sergeant was with the seven men who'd been wounded in the attack: two from his squad, three from Williams's, one from a volunteer squad covering their flank to the north, and one from the new volunteers who'd just arrived, Vernon's people. When Davis saw him coming and turned towards him Matt saw that the number was actually eight, since the sergeant's sleeve had been torn away so his upper arm could be bandaged.

The officer led him a short distance away from the wounded to talk. "I'm sorry about your men," Matt said first thing.

Davis blew out a weary breath. "Could've been worse, considering. Could've been better too. Shame about your town's Ma Deuce. We could've got a lot more use out of it."

Under the circumstances losing the M2 seemed like a small consideration. "What about the gunner?"

"Jenkins?" The sergeant fell silent for a moment in respect. "He tried to shoot down the chopper instead of obeying the order to scatter. Full points for courage, although it's possible he just made it easier for the bird to find 2nd Squad's emplacement and land a missile on target." He rubbed at his forehead. "Hindsight. I'll stick with the bravery angle when we remember him, and quietly add avoiding return fire to the tactics training."

Matt wasn't sure what to say, so he just nodded.

After a moment Davis straightened with a soft grunt. "Anyway, back to business. Your people did a good job."

"Thanks." Matt glanced north. "Speaking of my people, has Trev reported in?"

"Yeah. A dozen or so blockhead trucks drove right past his canyon without even trying to peek their heads in, and that's all the excitement he's seen. It seems like the enemy wants 31 so they're parking the bulk of the convoy in Huntington. My guess is they'll try to secure this entire area on foot so they can move in and start clearing the road."

Matt could've done without hearing that thousands of enemy soldiers with tanks and possibly even a helicopter were going to be a recurring problem for them. "What are we going to do?"

Davis spat off to one side. "Get more people, for one thing. I've called in for more reinforcements, along with the ones that were already coming. Then we just fight them off like we planned, hope eventually it gets too costly for them and they go away."

The sergeant glanced down the canyon. "I wouldn't expect to get much sleep for the next little while, Larson. Are your people good to get back to your emplacement? Even with the ceasefire I feel a bit antsy leaving just one partial squad watching the blockheads."

"We're in good shape," Matt said. "We got lucky with the missile they sent our way." He hesitated. "If you don't mind me asking, how exactly did that ceasefire happen?"

"Greed." Davis sighed. "Once your guy chased off the bird they probably realized the fight wasn't going to get any easier. They offered the ceasefire so they could get their people and vehicles out with all the equipment intact so it didn't fall into our hands. The alternative was that they'd commit to a full attack, including bringing the tanks up to start shelling us. I figured buying some extra time would help us more than them, so I agreed."

"How long?"

"They didn't say. And I'm not sure I'd trust them if they had. I barely trust this ceasefire to begin with, even if they're sticking to their end of it so far." Davis clapped him on the shoulder and turned him toward the command tent. "Send your people back to the emplacement. You can join them after we've talked through the attack and settled on how you can do better in the future."

Matt went along, although he still had one last question. "Have you heard from Aspen Hill?"

The sergeant hesitated, then sighed. "Yeah. Sorry to say it, but it looks like they're in the same boat as the rest of us."

*****

Lewis stood beside his dad, uncle, and sister on an overlook at the top of Aspen Hill Canyon, watching grimly as dozens of Gold Bloc trucks rolled into Aspen Hill in the valley below. Even through binoculars the vehicles were small and the houses only a bit bigger, but he could practically feel the ground rumbling beneath his feet as their home was invaded.

Smoke rose from the south end of town, although that had nothing to do with the blockheads. Or at least not directly: two hours ago he and Uncle George had torched the gardens to prevent them from providing food for the enemy, then hightailed it back up the canyon on bikes.

It had been just the tiniest bit soul crushing to watch the plants they'd worked so hard to nurture go up in flames, especially when he was the one lighting the match. At the very least the town had harvested every scrap of edible plant matter from the gardens during the final stages of the evacuation, so while they'd lost a lot they hadn't lost everything.

A flash of reflected sunlight in motion turned his eyes from that smoke plume, and he caught sight of the lead trucks in the convoy turning down Center Street in their direction.

He wasn't the only one who'd noticed. "We knew they'd eventually check out the canyon," George said heavily, swinging his rifle around to inspect the road below through the scope. The road the enemy would likely soon try to take, just one of many options they were pursuing to get behind the stubborn force of US soldiers and citizens determined to defend their country.

Chauncey had been passing on any reports of the day's events he could glean, and from the sounds of things the fighting was getting brutal in multiple places. Including along Highway 31, where the blockheads had tried a full on assault and been repelled.

Lewis hoped his cousin and friends were okay.

To his right Mary was humming a depressingly fatalistic song, and he half didn't blame her. He felt like the world was ending too as he watched some trucks in the convoy below briefly stop, so soldiers could pour out to scour the town and confirm for themselves that it was abandoned.

That left the bulk of the convoy inching on towards the canyon. A part of him wondered why they didn't set the town on fire behind them or something of the sort, but then he figured they might want to use it for a staging area or something.

Besides, from what the others had told him about Michigan the invading forces didn't destroy anything, just emptied places out for their own use. If news from Canada was correct there were hundreds of thousands or even millions of Gold Bloc colonists, now refugees, who needed someplace to settle. The blockheads would have an incentive to keep the existing infrastructure intact.

His dad finished radioing in another report to Chauncey back at the temporary refuge the Aspen Hill townspeople had made, who would pass it on to Colonel Grimes up along Highway 6. The retired teacher also promised to send more defenders down, just in case the surprise Williams and his demolitions team had set up in the canyon wasn't enough.

As for Grimes, from the sounds of it he had his own problems, in the form of a fierce fight that had already claimed hundreds of lives and was only getting started. That fight was over thirty miles away, but that didn't feel all that far with trucks pulling into the town below.

Lewis had to hope they wouldn't need help that might be late, if it came at all. According to Chauncey's last report the Gold Bloc was now stopped all along the Utah Rockies, the Chinese to the north and west, the Russians to the east, and this new army to the south all halted by one of the last knots of US resistance remaining in the country.

Since the enemy had just barely found themselves being turned back along the major roads it was no surprise they'd started checking the smaller roads for anything that would let their trucks through, but it was way too early for them to be trying any forays on foot once a potential route was blocked or destroyed. Especially when they had no idea just what sort of resistance they were facing.

Which meant that once they saw that the canyon was useless for their vehicles they'd give up for the moment. Hopefully.

“Godspeed,” Chauncey said before signing off. “Davis and Grimes entrusted the defense of this canyon to our town. Let's not fail them.”

They watched in silence as the trucks below approached the canyon. But instead of entering its mouth and continuing up the road towards them the enemy vehicles began splitting off, taking the nearby roads to scout the area around the town. Two trucks *did* stop a cautious distance away, however, to let out a few dozen soldiers with dogs and metal detectors.

“They're not going to take their vehicles anywhere close to the canyon?” Lewis said in disappointment, watching the small group of scouts cautiously approaching the canyon mouth. He'd hoped to catch a few trucks beneath the cliffs when they blew them and took out the road.

His dad nodded grimly. "They've probably been burned too often on other approaches and don't want to risk walking into another trap. By this point they must've realized that there aren't any unguarded roads into the mountains."

"So what now?" his uncle asked, lowering his rifle. "Do we just blow the road so they know the canyon's not an option and go somewhere else, or do we let them scout it and hope they don't find our explosives and give it the green light? If we can lull them into bringing some vehicles up we'll be able to do the most damage with our explosives."

"I don't think they'll be bringing those trucks anywhere near the cliff," his dad said. "And we have to consider that the evacuated townspeople aren't too far away. We don't want to let enemy troops wander around freely and possibly discover them."

"So we blow it now?" Mary asked.

His dad and uncle glanced at each other and nodded. "I've been waiting to see some fireworks," his dad said with a slight smile.

"Let's give it a bit," Lewis said. "We've got nothing to lose from waiting a bit longer, and a better opportunity might come up. If nothing else we might get a chance to take out some of those scouts."

His dad looked down at the approaching soldiers, who were moving extremely cautiously and letting their dogs go well ahead of them. "I suppose it couldn't hurt," he said with a shrug.

As they settled back to watching the canyon and valley below Lewis turned his binoculars to their shelter. Like with the raiders, he'd buried the entrance and they'd hidden anything they couldn't take with them in the escape tunnel, as well as locking the shed and covering it with a thin layer of dirt over the top. As far as he could see the blockheads hadn't found the place yet, but given how thoroughly they were scouring the area it was only a matter of time.

He had to admit that even though he'd willingly abandoned his home to escape the threat, the thought of enemy soldiers taking it over and using it for themselves seriously pissed him off. Although to be fair, since the shelter was so far from the rest of town and he knew every square inch of it there was a good chance he could severely punish them if they tried trespassing.

After a few minutes of watching the enemy below Lewis heard the noise of an approaching truck engine from behind. He turned to see the reinforcements Chauncey had promised, driving one of the raider trucks with the town's remaining M2 Browning mounted on the top.

Lewis hastily radioed Carl Raymond, who was driving the truck, to tell him to cut the engines, then turned to Uncle George, who'd been following the progress of the scouts with his scope. "Did they hear that?"

"Doesn't look like it," his uncle replied.

Carl and Tam hopped out of the parked vehicle and continued on foot, joined by Wes and a dozen other defenders. That was probably the most they could scrape together on short notice; with the volunteers with Davis to the south, ten defenders a time on patrol in the nearby hills scouting for any Gold Bloc troops sneaking their way, and all the sentries and patrols taking shifts around the refuge itself, not to mention the people off duty taking what rest they could, the community's manpower was stretched a little thin.

That included Jane, who had spent the last 24 hours either sleeping or as one of those 10 on patrol. He missed his wife, especially now when it looked like there might be trouble soon.

“Have they come up the canyon?” Tam called as they got closer.

“They're sending scouts,” Lewis replied, “but even those are still tiptoeing around the mouth of the canyon.”

“I guess I wouldn't be in any hurry either if I had hundreds of thousands of friends behind me and ambushes in front,” Carl said. “They've got all the time in the world to feel us out before committing to anything.”

The group joined them, and the new arrivals looked down into the valley with the scopes or binoculars they'd brought, or if they hadn't then shared what was available among them.

After a few minutes Tam lowered her scope. “Hmm. Looks like they're setting up in town.”

Lewis nodded, eyes also on the vehicles moving to secure the ruined perimeter of the town while the rest of the convoy pulled into the center and parked wherever they could find a place.

"Seriously?" Mary asked. "They're going to set up in that dump?"

Wes glared at her. "Hey, that's our home you're talking about!"

Lewis's dad gave them both a long-suffering look. "They might just be camping there for the night, or they might be planning to use it as a more permanent base of operations. Either way it's too close for comfort. We should probably be cautious and call in to tell Catherine, see if she wants to move the townspeople farther into the mountains just in case."

"And if they decide they want to be Aspen Hill's new residents?" Uncle George asked. "We were ready to destroy the road and maybe discourage any attempts to explore up the canyon on foot, but this is more than we can handle alone. We should radio Grimes and see what he wants to do about it."

Lewis's dad frowned down the canyon. "Whatever we decide, I think it's about time we blew the road." He hesitated for a moment, then carefully withdrew the detonator from his pocket and thumbed off the safety cap.

"Wait," Lewis blurted, mind racing. Everyone turned to look at him, and he did his best to pull his thoughts together. "That road is the only way up the canyon."

The others gave him blank looks. "Um yeah, that's the idea," Mary said.

"But they're not the only ones with vehicles."

There was another uncomfortable pause. "Please tell me you're just talking about keeping the way open if the military wants to bring people down for an attack," his dad finally said.

"Them too, if they have anyone to spare. But we can do plenty by ourselves." Lewis looked down at the cluster of intact buildings in the midst of the ruined town, where the enemy soldiers had begun to ferry things from the trucks while more set up a perimeter along the fortifications he'd helped build. "We defended that town for weeks against a determined enemy, and at the moment we're pretty well equipped. I've got a good idea of the sort of attacks they'll have trouble dealing with, and I know every square inch of the area."

Uncle George shook his head emphatically. "No way, bud. We promised Williams we would hold this canyon. Nobody said anything about trying any heroics against professional soldiers. Besides, the longer we delay blowing the road the greater the risk they'll take it."

Lewis did his best to hide his frustration. Didn't they see? "This is *our* road! We're the ones with the explosives set up to detonators. We can come and go as we please along it, and if they try to follow us they'll get buried under tons of rubble. That's a huge advantage, one we should use."

Tam gave him an uncomfortable look. "Come on, Lewis. The town lost almost a hundred good people fighting the raiders, and what we'd be facing down there is a hundred times worse. This isn't our fight. Let the military handle it while we worry about our own survival."

"It'll be our fight if the military fails and we find ourselves surrounded by blockheads we can't do anything to defend ourselves against," Lewis shot back. "Every small victory means we're that much closer to ending the war for good."

Almost everyone stared at him doubtfully, although Wes was nodding in agreement. Hardly the best recommendation. He hurried to continue. "This is *our* town we're defending. Our terrain, our opportunity to make a difference. At least give me a chance to see if I can round up some volunteers."

George and his dad looked at each other, then his uncle sighed. "He's right about one thing, that for the moment the road offers options we shouldn't be in a hurry to eliminate. We can always sit on the detonator for a while. Who knows, they might slip up and send a vehicle up the canyon after all and we can do some damage."

"What about the scouts?" Mary asked. "They're going to actually head up the canyon at some point."

"It would be a good idea to take them out if we can," Lewis replied. He turned and looked thoughtfully at the truck.

"No," Tam immediately said. "We're not sending the truck roaring down the canyon, firing blindly at trained soldiers that'll have heard us coming from miles away and set up to punch us full of holes the moment we're in range."

"Just hear me out," Lewis said.

His family and the defenders exchanged looks. But he *was* in charge of the defenses. And he liked to think he'd had enough good ideas that they'd be willing to give him a chance.

Nobody spoke up, so Lewis outlined his plan.

*****

It took almost an hour for the scouts to move half a mile up the canyon. They'd stuck to the part with gentle slopes, far from any sign of cliffs or steep rocky inclines, and they continued to send their dogs out a hundred yards or more ahead at all times, sniffing for whatever they'd been trained to sniff for and ears pricked for danger.

The enemy was moving slow, but they *were* moving. Eventually even at their pace they'd make their way to someplace they could be a nuisance.

Lewis didn't intend to give them that chance.

The first step had been greasing the truck's axles as best they could to prevent any squeaking. The vehicle had been well maintained to begin with so it didn't make much noise, but even so they hadn't taken any chances.

Then, forty-five minutes ago, he, Tam, Carl, and Wes had coasted the truck down the canyon to the spot Lewis had carefully picked out. It was hidden out of sight from below by a thick stand of trees and a bend in the road, and well out of earshot of the scouts at the time.

Once in place they'd waited patiently while the scouts made their painstaking way to them, with his dad, Mary,

Uncle George, and the other defenders up above keeping tabs on the enemy movements and relaying that information to them.

The idea was to let the blockheads reach a gently sloping meadow just around the bend from where the truck waited. There was no way up the canyon aside from crossing that open expanse, and they hoped that eventually the enemy would take the chance.

At which point the truck would coast the rest of the way to the bend and park at a ledge that overlooked the meadow.

"Now," his dad whispered over the radio, the signal they'd been waiting for.

In the driver's seat Tam released the brakes, while along the back bumper Wes and Carl began pushing hard. With barely a squeak the vehicle started coasting down the road, slowly picking up speed.

Heart thudding beneath his body armor, Lewis checked the M2 one last time to make sure everything looked good. He'd oiled the mechanisms with the special lubricant before they'd set out, and he'd also made sure the belt-fed ammo looked clean and didn't have any visible flaws that might cause jams. Having the weapon jam on him while he was in the sights of dozens of blockheads would be a bad thing.

The truck reached the bend, and Lewis spun the heavy machine gun on its mount to point at the meadow and hunkered down behind it. Down below he heard dogs begin baying their presence. "They know you're there," his dad warned, unnecessarily.

The meadow came into view around the bend, two dozen enemy soldiers ranged halfway across it in a cautious formation, completely exposed and far from the trees below or the ridge above. With the truck moving nearly silently he heard he heard the warning shouts, saw some of the scouts drop to the ground, a few turn to run, and the rest raise their weapons to fire.

Lewis fired first.

He'd never shot the M2 Browning before, and without doing so there were few ways to adequately prepare himself for the experience. Even sturdily mounted to the truck the recoil was incredible, vibrating the gun almost painfully in his grip; compared to it his reliable G3 was a pop gun. Wearing his noise-canceling earphones it sounded like nothing so much as the world's largest woodpecker, but without them the volume would've been close to deafening.

It took him a moment to get control of the weapon, and then he sent the line of bullets walking across the meadow in a zigzag to hit every blockhead he could see.

He'd watched this machine gun chew through brick walls when Turner used it against them, and what it had done to the townspeople unlucky enough to be caught in the open still haunted his memories. So even given that he was shooting at enemies in standard issue body armor, overkill didn't begin to describe it. He did his best to avoid seeing the aftermath.

The truck roared to life beneath him, and even as he finished his first sweep and ran the line of bullets back across the meadow, towards any enemy that was still moving, Tam slammed them into reverse along the road and back around the safety of the bend. Lewis had stopped firing not long after the vehicle started moving, when aiming became too difficult, and at that point he dropped down into the bed of the truck to avoid any enemy return fire.

If there were any enemies left.

He stayed that way until he heard the slam of the passenger's side door as Carl and Wes piled into the cab, then cautiously stood to a crouch. Tam was pulling them around in a three-point turn, and he soon had a view of the road behind them as they roared back up the canyon towards safety.

There wasn't much to see back there, since the scouts hadn't gotten past the meadow and nobody else was around. More useful was the constant stream of information his dad fed him over the radio. The upshot of which being that if anyone had survived back there, they weren't taking the chance of moving just yet.

"What about the blockheads down in the valley?" he asked. "Are they giving chase?"

There was a long pause. "No," Uncle George replied. "I've been watching them. The pattern of the vehicles patrolling around the town changed after you hit the scouts, but none of them are heading towards the canyon. They must still be wary of traps. Probably even more so, now."

Lewis nodded and settled down on his back in the truck bed, staring up at the sky above and the sun overhead. Still midafternoon, but it felt like the day should be almost over. He didn't want to think about what had happened back there.

Maybe there was still time to find Jane on her patrol and join her. That's where he should be anyway.

"Is everyone okay?" his dad asked.

He listened as Tam replied that she, Carl, and Wes were just fine, then lifted his radio. "I'm unhurt."

There was a long pause before his dad responded. "Good job, everyone. I don't think the blockheads will be sending anyone else up the canyon any time soon."

Lewis lay clutching the radio, feeling the vibration of the truck beneath his back. It matched the tingling in his hands from holding the machine gun. He lifted the radio to his mouth. "Then we'll have to go out after them, and keep on going until they give us back our town."

Chapter Eighteen

Reassigned

The fighting continued through the day and into the night, but not along the mountains near them.

Trev's squad sat in their prepared emplacements, alert for the approach of enemies with their weapons in easy reach. As for Trev, he spent most of the time manning one of the lookout spots, keeping the detonator close by so he could destroy the road leading up the canyon at a moment's notice. Even though no enemies came their way the tension still built up in him as the hours dragged by, making it impossible to really relax.

Part of that was because even though the enemy kept their distance there was still plenty to see in the valley to the east. The swift-moving southern army had tried to push into the mountains along multiple routes, including Highway 31, and had engaged Lassiter along I-70 and Colonel Grimes along 6 near Spanish Fork Canyon.

But while they'd likely hoped for a quick victory somewhere, their main goal had been to bottle the US forces in the mountain defenses they'd set up. Once that was accomplished they were perfectly content to withdraw and dig in, while behind them the valley slowly filled with seemingly endless waves of Russian soldiers coming in from the northeast.

From their place in Cedar Creek Canyon Trev and his squad had been able to hear the fighting the next canyon over, including the massive rockslide that had shaken the ground even where they were. He'd watched the helicopter approach, watched it exchange missiles with Davis and Matt's squad up the canyon, and finally watched it retreat to safety.

He didn't know whether to be relieved that his people hadn't had to deal with the same threat, or frustrated that he'd had to sit and watch while his friends and fellow fighters faced the danger. But one thing he did know was that the reinforcements Lassiter was sending their way couldn't come soon enough.

Even setting aside the consideration of whether his squad could handle holding this canyon on their own, there was also the fact that they'd basically been on duty for days now, and most of them had been awake for over 24 hours. Even if they could just get spelled for 8 hours to get some solid sleep without having to jolt awake at every noise, Trev's squad needed someone to come take over for them for a while.

Which didn't seem like it would be happening any time soon, as the night grew later and later. The valley below had been a patchy carpet of campfires during the evening, and even through the night lights would spring up as new waves of enemy troops arrived and set up their camps.

Trev sent most of his people to bed and doubled the number of lookouts, having them trade off with the squad's two pairs of night vision goggles and keeping their shifts to two hours so no one would fall asleep on watch. Davis's earlier ceasefire and the apparent relaxed attitude of the blockheads in the valley didn't fool him, and he wanted to be ready in case any enemies tried to sneak their way on foot under the cover of darkness.

That meant his lookouts had to be extra vigilant, panning the valley below and the slopes to either side for the slightest sign of anything unusual. They couldn't just count on telltale headlights or the sounds of engines to alert them to danger, and making that mistake could get them all killed.

Arguably Trev was making his own mistake, staying up into the night manning a lookout post and letting each squad mate who took a shift with him catch an extra nap while he hogged the night vision. But he felt surprisingly alert in spite of the lack of sleep, able to focus on his duty without the slightest weariness sinking in. He'd been like that on road trips, too, able to keep driving and focus on the road without ever nodding off no matter how tired he got.

He'd pay for it later, when his exhaustion caught up with him, but for now he was fine. Better one person sleep during the day while the rest of the squad was rested and awake. It meant four less people who'd have to wake up halfway through the night to take a shift, then return to their beds and try to get some quality sleep afterwards.

Sure, it was something he'd never ask one of his people to do, not only for their sake but because it was an unnecessary risk. But he knew himself, so it wasn't really a risk.

In spite of his fears he saw no sign of blockheads sneaking towards them, which he sincerely hoped meant there weren't any, and neither did the lookouts at the other spot. Better still, a bit before sunrise Davis's voice came through his earbuds.

"Have your squad pack up their things, Smith," the sergeant said, "you're getting reassigned back to camp for now."

"About time," Trev muttered to himself, then toggled the radio. "Copy that, Sarge. When are the replacements coming?"

"We're on our way," Davis replied. "See you in ten minutes."

Trev woke up his squad and got them organized and ready to leave, keeping the lookouts at their places and making sure their things were packed for them. He was glad Davis had finally acknowledged Cedar Creek Canyon's need for a change, although he hoped his people weren't being taken from the frying pan and tossed into the fire.

They'd go where they were needed, though, and hopefully their replacements here would be in a better position to defend the canyon.

In spite of their unexpected awakening and short notice, Trev's squad was ready to go by the time Davis jogged down the canyon, leading half a dozen of his Marines from 2nd Squad. And Fred Vernon and his men.

"Get your camp set up," the sergeant ordered the former sheriff, then turned to his soldiers. "Higgins, get with Smith's squad and get a rundown on how they've been guarding the canyon and where all their emplacements are. Smith, with me."

Trev followed Davis a short distance away. "You've got to be kidding me," he told him once they were out of earshot of the others.

"No, I don't," Davis said flatly. "Vernon's got well trained and experienced men. He's more than capable of holding the canyon. And in case you think I'm a complete idiot, you'll notice I've got half of 2nd Squad here to keep an eye on them."

"Is an eye going to be enough? If they bail on us, our main camp could get attacked from behind by blockheads who walked right past our defenses along 31."

"Smith," the sergeant warned. Trev clammed up, and the man continued. "I hate to be the one who tells you to get over it, but it was a truck. A truck you stole in the first place. I've talked to Vernon and he's got a lot of admirable qualities. Ones that aren't diminished by one moment of weakness."

"Yeah, I thought he was the most noble guy around too. Right up until he betrayed me."

Davis looked like he was doing his best to hold in his temper. "Go brief my Marines on the defenses here, then get your squad back to main camp," he snapped. "I'm giving you the morning to sleep and unwind. After that your irregulars will have new duties, ones I'm confident you're prepared for."

Since they were civilians the sergeant didn't like it when volunteers saluted, and he *really* didn't like being called "sir". So Trev just nodded and went to get his squad. He spent ten minutes or so hiking around the canyon to the various vantages, showing the soldiers what they'd done. Once that was finished he circled his squad well around where Vernon's people were setting up camp and led them up the path Davis had just come down.

On the way Tom came up to walk beside him. "Got to say I appreciate Sarge's thoughtfulness. He assigns us back to camp, and just to be sure there's no trouble he sends those criminals out here so we never have to be in the same place together."

Trev hadn't considered that. And in spite of his misgivings about Vernon he *was* a bit relieved he wouldn't have to be around him and his men. "There's that."

He took it easy with the pace to give his sleep-deprived squad a break, so they'd reach the main camp in twenty minutes of walking instead of ten jogging. After all the traveling he'd done it felt like a trip to the mailbox, but there was no point needlessly tiring anyone.

But in spite of the easy pace he *did* stop at the first bend in the trail that gave them a view of the camp ahead, although that was more to gawk than to rest.

Davis had failed to mention that the reinforcements had finally arrived. The camp had already held hundreds of people, the last few stragglers who'd managed to make it to safety ahead of the enemy convoy. But now it held at least a hundred more, judging by the tents set up where the rest of the volunteers were camped. He also saw enough uniforms to easily fill two squads; with the sergeant and half of 2nd Squad back at Cedar Creek that could only mean more soldiers had arrived as well.

A few dozen of the new arrivals were bunched up near the Aspen Hill camp, and Matt was there with Rick and a few others from his squad talking to them. Trev guessed that Davis had asked them to fill in the new volunteers on how things were run here, as well as what they'd be expected to do.

His friend broke away from the meeting as soon as he saw them coming, though, pulling Trev into a crushing hug. Which Trev returned wholeheartedly. "It's good to see you're still in one piece," he said. "It sounds like things got pretty crazy here."

Matt's smile faded somewhat. "Yeah, we had a few close calls, and we were the lucky ones." He nodded to the rest of the squad and shook Tom's hand, since he was the nearest person. "How about you guys? Has it been quiet all night?"

"Nothing but crickets," Alice said.

"Good." Matt jerked his head towards their camp. "If your people can get set up without you, Trev, I could use a hand whipping these guys into shape. You did a good job with your squad."

Trev glanced at Tom, who nodded and led the squad on towards camp to set up their tents. He noticed Alice just dropped her backpack off and went over to where Rick and Pete were sitting in front of their tents cleaning their weapons. The young woman gave both of her friends hugs and immediately pulled them into an animated conversation, which from the sounds of it involved Rick describing the worst parts of the previous day's fight while Pete boasted about how many blockheads he'd shot.

"All right, people," Matt said, clapping his hands and turning back to the volunteers gathered nearby. "Get anyone in your groups who's never held a gun before, or who's been out shooting less than five times. My friend Trev here is going to give them an introductory gun safety course and then work them through some dry fire practice that will very likely save their lives."

His friend took a breath and continued in the same loud voice. "Everyone else come with me. We've got enough ammo to let each of you demonstrate your aim, and from there I'll decide if you need to join your friends training or if you're ready to pitch in right away. If you are, I'll send you along to Corporal Williams to assign you where you're needed. So be prepared to have your groups possibly split up, and consider how you want to do that if asked."

The gathered people, who seemed to be leaders in their groups of volunteers, nodded and dispersed to their camps to get their people situated. Matt turned towards him. "You okay with that?"

"Sure," Trev said, although Davis had technically promised them the morning off. "I'll have my squad help out, since the training's still fresh in their minds and I've drilled it in until it's practically second nature. Although I think you should at least run everyone through the rules of gun safety and the most important firearm handling and shooting procedures just to be safe. It couldn't hurt to run them through all the dry fire drills so they can practice on their own time, too."

"Good point." His friend clapped him on the shoulder. "For now just get together everyone you're going to be training and set up a time and location for getting started. That's probably all the time we'll have before breakfast."

Trev perked up at that. He'd put thoughts of food out of his mind along with sleep, and was suddenly aware of the hollow pit where his stomach should be. Of course it reminded him of his exhaustion, which chose that moment to come crashing down, but he thought he could hold it off until the late afternoon if need be and still stay kind of in sync with his squad's sleeping schedule. "Deal."

He headed over and gathered up his people, including a reluctant Alice, and quickly explained the situation. They seemed to like the idea of passing on their knowledge, although a few looked nervous at being tossed into the instructor role. Trev assured them they'd just be doing more of what they'd already been doing for weeks, only with an audience, which seemed to help.

After a brief confusion as the new volunteers got separated between him and Matt, Trev stood in front of about forty people. That was less than he'd expected in some ways, although more than he would've liked for recruits who'd come to join the fight against the Gold Bloc. He introduced himself and his squad, then did his best to go around and get everyone's names and where they'd come from.

When he mentioned splitting up and meeting after breakfast the group balked slightly, preferring to stay with him, so Trev led fifty people towards the mess tent, biting back a yawn with every step. He hoped the civilians who'd volunteered to help cook in lieu of actually joining up wouldn't be too slammed by that many people all at once.

Just to be sure he left his people in the growing line in front of the mess tent and went in to check, weaving through a crowd of soldiers, volunteers, and refugees to get to the front. He was almost there when someone spoke up abruptly from a table off to his right.

"Hey, I remember you. You're the candy bar guy!"

Trev didn't even consider that the man was talking to him, and ignored the call as he started to round the food tables to reach the cooks serving food behind them. That is, until he saw the man stand up from his table and hurry towards him wearing a broad grin. "Trev, right?"

"Right." It took a moment more for recognition to kick in, but when it did it was a pleasant surprise. "Trent Lincoln. I met your family west of Newtown."

"I'm surprised you remember." Trent held out his hand, and when Trev accepted it shook vigorously. "Man, those candy bars you gave us were the highlight of our trip."

Trev returned a lopsided grin. "Yeah, the blockheads who captured me were pretty stoked about them too." Trent blinked at that as he continued. "But how did your family end up here in the mountains? I never thought I'd see any of you again."

Trent's smile faded. "Well it wasn't our plan, but there weren't too many other options with blockheads rampaging across the west coast. We were traveling farther north and ran into some of General Erikson's scouts making a beeline for Utah, and they convinced us it would be a bad idea to keep going into Oregon."

Oregon, huh? Back when he'd met the Lincoln family neither side had offered information on where they were headed. But he supposed it was a moot point now with the state almost completely occupied. "Sorry to hear that," he offered with genuine sympathy. "Did you have family there?"

"No, it was just a place we'd heard might offer a new start for anyone willing to work hard. Things east of the Mississippi were too crowded for us, too many violent confrontations and close calls." Trent turned to look northward with a gloomy expression. "Now my family's up in Erikson's civilian camp, which is growing by the day and already has tens of thousands of displaced refugees. They're doing their best to scrape together what they can to survive, but it's hard going. I should be with them, but with blockheads hitting the area from both sides I figured starvation was the less pressing threat."

"Yeah, I'm pretty much in the same boat." Trev motioned towards Trent's table, which seemed to be a collection of strangers who happened to be sitting together rather than a group. "I've got to get my people fed, but you're welcome to join us if you want. We can catch up, swap stories."

The other man looked tempted, but shook his head. "Sorry. I've already been assigned to an irregular group stationed a bit farther north. I was supposed to leave with them this morning, but they let me eat with the promise I'd catch up afterwards. I don't want to make them wait too long, but I really did need a good meal."

Trev felt a sinking sensation in his gut. He only knew of one irregular group that had gone anywhere that morning. "Fred Vernon?"

Trent brightened. "Yeah. Hey that's right, you must've gone through Newtown and met him too. His people had a really good reputation there, and they're getting a good reputation here in camp, too. Real professionals. I was lucky to get assigned to them."

For a moment Trev debated whether to warn the man about what he was getting into. Trent seemed like a good guy, and he'd definitely done a good job of protecting his family and catching Trev by surprise when they'd first met. He deserved better than to be lumped in with criminals who abandoned their own people at the earliest convenience.

At the same time it probably wouldn't do any good to poison the well against Vernon with Trent, especially not when the man had been assigned to his group and would be fighting alongside them. That was the sort of thing Davis had basically ordered him not to do, and would probably royally piss him off if he heard about it.

Besides, if they were all going to be working in the same area it would be nice to have at least one friendly face in Vernon's group. Trev offered his hand again. "Makes sense. If you catch a moment before you leave come say hello and I'll introduce you to my squad. But either way best of luck with your new assignment, and best wishes for your family."

"Thanks, same to you." Trent shook his hand firmly, then made his way back over to his table and the plate he'd abandoned.

*****

Considering they had a massive enemy army camped only a few miles away and every fighter counted, Matt figured there was no time like the present to get started testing the new volunteers. There was grumbling from some of them, as well as among his own squad, at the thought of a delayed breakfast, but it looked as if the mess tent was slammed and could use a bit of a break anyway.

“Think of it as an incentive to get this done quickly so you can eat,” he called with a slight smile. “In the meantime it can't hurt to get used to going hungry, since we can't be sure what our supplies are going to look like day to day.”

“We've already had plenty of practice going hungry,” one of the volunteers muttered, and by his gaunt features it seemed plain he had.

Ah, right. So that hadn't been the most motivational thing to say. Good thing Vernon's truck had brought plenty of wheat with them to pad out the camp's stores. Wheat stolen from Trev's family, sure, but at least now it was being put to good use.

As he gathered up everyone to lead farther up the canyon to the camp's impromptu shooting range, he pulled Pete aside and had him run to the mess tent to let them know that they had a bit more time to prepare food for his squad and the volunteers, but he'd like it ready when they got back.

His friend seemed more eager than usual to run the errand, making Matt wonder if he was planning to sneak some food while he was there. Then he noticed the young man veering over towards where Alice waited in line out front with the others, and realized he'd used it as an excuse to visit with her some more.

Matt glanced over at Rick, walking not far behind him, and saw that his friend was glaring that way. Okay, so he hadn't realized that *that* was going on between the three. He hoped it didn't become an issue.

It turned out to be too much to hope for. After giving the speech about basic gun safety and starting off with a few basic but important pointers, Matt divided the volunteers among his squad mates and had them begin taking shots downrange with their M16s.

Davis had enough extra rifles and ammo for those who'd shown up, barely, but if they got more recruits they were going to have to either set up an armory and begin issuing weapons to those on duty or scrounge around for more weapons. No wonder the sergeant had been so annoyed about the blockheads using the ceasefire as an opportunity to drag the dead with their equipment away yesterday.

Pete had returned by that point, and he and Rick had their own line of volunteers to assess. But less than five minutes after they'd started Matt's attention was drawn from his own volunteer, an older man very slowly and deliberately focusing through the scope to make the most of each of his three shots, by the noise of shouting off to the side.

He turned in time to see Pete punch Rick squarely in the face, sending the taller young man stumbling. Rick recovered fast and started forward, his own fists up and looking ticked off, but Pete didn't give him a chance and tackled him to the ground before he could land a punch.

A few of the volunteers stepped forward hesitantly, unsure whether to step in, but Matt had already crossed the distance to his friends. He grabbed Pete by the shoulders and hauled him away, sending him staggering a few steps as he pushed him back.

Pete immediately bounced back, half looking like he was going to punch Matt next before trying to slip around him to get back at Rick. For his part Rick was up again, blood streaming from his nose, and he took a step forward like he was perfectly happy to keep the fight going too.

"Hey!" Matt snapped, stepping directly between the two. "Both of you stop, now!" For a long second he was afraid they'd ignore him, but then Rick stopped where he was and Pete reluctantly backed away. Matt looked between his two friends, aware of the crowd of onlookers. "What's going on?"

Sullen, Pete pointedly ignored Rick and didn't answer, while Rick gave Matt a slightly embarrassed look. "Nothing."

"That didn't look like nothing," Matt shot back.

Pete glared at him in annoyance, like starting fights in the middle of training was none of his business. "Rick's right, it's nothing."

"Well we're going to have a talk about it once we're done here. Until then I don't want to see either of you doing "nothing" again." Matt pointed. "Rick, take your volunteers over to the other side of the range."

"Why me? He's the one that-" his friend trailed off at Matt's glare, then nodded and got to work ushering his people away.

Matt waited until Rick had relocated and got his people sorted out, then turned to face the crowd. "Let's continue." He suited his words by returning to the older man, who was still patiently standing and holding the rifle in a carrying position.

They took a break about midmorning, and Matt had Scott use that time to instruct the volunteers on field stripping the M16 and clearing misfires. While that was going on he planned to take his friends aside to talk to them, but before he could Rick sought him out and pulled *him* aside.

"Hey Matt, we need to talk," the younger man said, expression serious.

That was for sure. "Okay. Talk to me."

His friend couldn't quite meet his eye. "I've decided I'm going to join Trev's squad."

Matt bit back a sigh. "If this is about your argument with Pete, there's other ways we can work this out."

Rick shuffled his feet. "No offense, but I'm not sure we can. Nothing against the guy, but he's obviously losing it." His friend finally looked at him. "It's not really that, though. The argument just made my mind up about something I've been thinking about ever since we decided to volunteer. Gave me a good excuse to actually do it."

"You want to be with Alice?" Matt guessed.

"Yeah." Rick flushed slightly with embarrassment. "I don't know if you know this, but we had a pretty big argument after I heard she'd joined up. A lot of shouting, and she's been a bit frosty with me ever since. But I still care about her, and anyway I feel like I should be looking after her since my family took her in."

"Right. And your fight with Pete?"

"Wasn't exactly about that," Rick admitted. "But I guess you could say it kind of was."

Matt waited, but his friend didn't supply any further details. "Let me think about it."

Rick nodded, and they moved to rejoin the group. At which point it was Pete's turn to single him out, although he was a lot more blunt and didn't even bother pulling him aside. "I want to swap with someone in Trev's squad."

Matt bit back a groan, motioning for Rick to keep going. His friend was slow to comply, and he obviously had a problem with what Pete had just said. Once he was out of earshot Matt turned back to the young man. "Care to explain why?"

Pete glared Rick's way. "Maybe I like the company better."

"Thanks, that's great to hear," Matt said wryly.

His friend gave a start and looked at him. "I don't mean you. Or anyone, really. I just think I could use a change of scenery."

Matt gave him a knowing look. "I know exactly why you want to transfer. No need to beat around the bush."

The young man flushed with embarrassment. "Right, I guess Rick told you all about our fight. It's not my fault he thinks he has a shot with her just because his family took her in, but he can't grow a pair and just tell her how he feels. Then he gets mad every time I spend time with her and tries to keep us apart."

Pete's flush started to look more angry than embarrassed. "It's actually really not cool. Alice has been one of my closest friends for years, and we even went on a date before the Gulf burned. He had that punch coming, and I'll hit him again if he keeps thinking he can decide who she gets to talk to." He took a deep breath and met Matt's eye determinedly. "So can I join Trev's squad?"

"Maybe. Go help any of the volunteers who're having trouble with Scott's lesson and I'll get back to you, okay?"

Pete nodded and trotted off, and Matt rubbed between his eyes as he watched him go. What was he supposed to do now? His friends were putting him in the middle of their nonsense, but unfortunately at this point it threatened to affect the rest of the squad if he didn't do something about it.

If he sent them both over to Trev they'd almost certainly keep fighting, and probably even worse with Alice around. If he kept them both in his squad they'd resent it and keep up the fighting there too. If he split them up then whoever he didn't send would resent him, and probably feel like he was acting matchmaker and playing favorites.

He also had reservations about Pete and wanted to keep him close, especially after watching him lose it earlier. Rick he wanted to keep around for a different reason, since the younger man was one of his best people and he relied heavily on him.

Gah, what a mess. As far as Matt was concerned none of them should be worrying about this when they had more important issues to deal with. He almost wished Trev hadn't convinced him to let Alice volunteer, although then that wouldn't have been fair to her. And speaking of fair to her, what if *she* had a problem with any of this and it was a further source of contention?

Matt mulled it over during the rest of the break and as they finished testing the remaining volunteers. Ultimately he decided that only a dozen or so of the sixty men and women were ready to get tossed right into the fray, while the others either needed to join Trev's group or start an intermediate group that required a bit less training but still desperately needed some. For the moment it looked as if the Aspen Hill volunteers would have training duty, which was fine with him. He only hoped he could get these people in shape for what they were about to face.

It was closer to lunch than breakfast by the time they headed back to camp, and Matt felt a bit bad about making everyone miss a meal. A lot of the new people looked like they'd already missed too many as it was. He gave Ben permission to get a bit of extra food, which they would give out during a break from training as a midafternoon snack between lunch and dinner.

To his irritation he found Pete and Rick waiting for him after he'd lined everyone up at the mess tent. Judging by the tension in the air it was obvious they'd been arguing about each's decision to transfer. "Well?" Pete burst out as Matt led them aside.

There were no good solutions here, but there was what Matt felt was the necessary one. Keeping the two together after this was just asking for trouble, and Pete was too hotheaded and could do with some watching. If nothing else he could trust Rick to keep his head on straight and not do anything irresponsible. “I've thought it through. Rick, you'll swap places with Ted Benson in Trev's squad.”

Rick burst into a grin, while Pete's expression darkened. “What about me?” he demanded.

Matt was tempted to give some excuse, like not destabilizing the squads too much, but his friend deserved better than that. “You're staying with me,” he said simply.

The young man looked like he was going to explode, but somehow managed to contain it. “I should've realized you'd take his side,” he snapped, then turned to glare at Rick. “You're stupid if you think spending more time with her is going to improve your chances.” Without waiting for a response he stormed towards their camp.

Fantastic. No matter what he'd decided there'd be trouble for at least one person, and most decisions would've caused trouble for the squads too. If he'd sent Pete instead he'd be dumping a potential problem on Trev's head, and he wasn't about to do that.

Rick was shuffling uncomfortably. “I didn't mean for this to be an issue,” he apologized.

“I don't want it to be, after this.” Matt offered his hand. “Good luck in Trev's squad. He could use another experienced person. You'll join him training the new guys after lunch.”

"It's almost lunch now, I'll go find him." Rick immediately broke away from the line and headed for where Trev had spent the morning running his volunteers through dry fire drills.

Matt hesitated, looking longingly at the breakfast line, then moved to follow so he could give Trev a heads up about how he was upsetting his squad. He supposed it *was* almost lunch, so he might as well eat then.

*****

Trev had to admit he would've planned things differently if he'd known he was going to be spending the day training people. He supposed that was one of the reasons soldiers took regular shifts, so they wouldn't push themselves too hard and be complete wrecks when they were really needed. It wouldn't have strained his squad mates too much more to take some of his shifts so he could sleep, and he would've been much better off for it.

He needed to be smarter about things, or at this rate he was going to hit Lewis levels of sleep problems.

It wasn't fair to let the people who depended on him suffer for his mistake, so Trev did his best to give it his all even though he was almost nauseous from exhaustion. But by midafternoon his vision was starting to swim in the bright sunlight and he had that lightheaded, sweaty feeling that came from insufficient sleep, and at that point willpower just wasn't enough.

Thankfully Matt had given him Rick, although the details of exactly why were unclear. During lunch he'd heard a few of his squad mates talking about a fight that morning, but he'd been too focused on staying awake to pay attention.

Either way, he didn't feel too guilty about leaving the younger man to take over the training while he went and crashed. Hopefully if he got some good sleep today he'd be able to push through and get his sleeping schedule back in line by tomorrow.

It was probably his current state that made him extremely annoyed when Davis saw him passing the command tent and called him inside. He did his best to fight that as he followed the sergeant in.

"Looks like you jumped right in helping Larson train the new recruits," Davis said, nodding his approval. "If you have no arguments I think we'll keep you doing that for the foreseeable future. In fact, once we put Larson's squad back in action you'll probably take over his training duties too."

Trev nodded. "I can handle that. Starting tomorrow, once I've had a chance to crash."

The sergeant gave him a closer look, frowning. "Yeah, do that. I shouldn't have to state the obvious, Smith, but sleep is a soldier's most important friend. You should be taking every opportunity to get as much as you need, so you're alert when you have to be awake in a crisis."

Yes, that was obvious. Unfortunately sometimes obvious things were the easiest to miss. "Speaking of crises, is there any news?"

Davis sighed and moved around behind his table, leaning on it to stare down at his cobbled together map. "Nothing but news," he said. "Lassiter and Erikson have been fighting nonstop since the blockheads arrived yesterday. The death toll is already in the thousands. We're punishing them hard for their aggression, but they've got enough bodies to throw at us that they can keep this up indefinitely until they wear us down and stomp right over us."

His expression sharpened. "Which gets us back to getting sleep whenever possible. More blockheads are arriving in the valley by the hour, and at this rate we're going to have our own little Thermopylae in every canyon from I-70 to I-80. You need to teach our new irregulars which end of a gun to point at the enemy as quickly as possible."

Trev nodded wearily and exited the tent, passing through the bustle of the ever growing camp without noticing it as he made his way to the Aspen Hill camp. He still had to put up the tent he'd failed to prepare that morning when the rest of his squad were doing theirs, but thankfully long practice let him set it up quickly, and he almost groaned in relief as he crawled inside.

He had a lot to do tomorrow.

Epilogue

A Closer Look

Lewis had been wanting to spend more time with his wife ever since she'd started working overtime on patrols, while he concentrated on evacuating the town and organizing the defenses. It felt like he'd barely seen her at all the last few days, where even their sleeping schedules were different a lot of the time.

Although to be fair, taking a circuitous path down into the valley below along one of the game trails Jane had found, so they could spy on the enemy and decide whether they wanted to take the fight to them, wasn't exactly an ideal outing.

The blockheads had left their fallen men where they lay in the canyon, unwilling to take the risk of retrieving them. That had given the Aspen Hill defenders an opportunity to risk going back down themselves to gather their gear. Which they'd done, with lookouts posted at every vantage point with a good view of the valley and prepared to flee at the slightest activity from below.

Capturing that equipment had been an unenviable task, with more than one pale face among the volunteers who'd gone once they returned. But they'd picked up a lot of decent gear from it, which helped replace what they'd sent along with the volunteers.

A clear win, one that better prepared Aspen Hill's defenders for any future fighting, but even so Lewis wasn't willing to get too cocky when it came to using the canyon. He was certain the enemy constantly had eyes on it, so if they tried to sneak into the valley by that route they'd almost certainly get caught.

On the plus side this roundabout route along the game trail would also swing them around well north of the town, letting them look at things from that angle. It meant climbing down about twenty feet of cliff at one point, but there were plenty of handholds and footholds and the cliff was facing away from the town so they wouldn't draw any unfriendly eyes.

"What do you think about trying to besiege the town?" he asked his wife as they hiked down the narrow path.

Jane gave him a slightly confused look. "You already asked me that."

"I know, and I'm glad you agreed it was something we should try. But what do you think about actually doing it?"

"Pretty much what you said. We've been on the other side of things and we know how Turner made life difficult for us. With a bit of luck we can use the same tactics against the blockheads. As for specifics?" She shrugged. "That's why we're going down there to look around, right?"

"Right." Lewis hesitated. "Only, we thought it was just going to be a few hundred blockheads occupying the town, but more are coming by the hour. I don't want to bite off more than we can chew."

Jane slowed to a stop and turned to look at him. "Even if we do, and things go badly for us, the rest of our people should be safe after we blow the charges and block the canyon. A few dozen defenders can guard every approach up into the mountains for miles, at least long enough for the military to send in help, so it's only our own lives we're risking. And we're risking them with the chance of making a real difference that could help us win this war."

"All right then." Lewis affectionately bumped her shoulder with his and continued on, feeling a bit better about things.

When they reached the cliff he found a good vantage overlooking the valley and kept watch while his wife climbed down. Once she reached the bottom she returned the favor, finding her own lookout spot so Lewis could descend.

Even though the climb was relatively easy he was glad he'd packed light, since he felt as exposed as a bug on a wall with a flyswatter hanging over his head as he worked his way down. He wasted no time, and even jumped down the last few feet.

While catching their breath they spent a moment looking at the nearby town and the valley beyond, but with the angle here the view was actually worse than from the top of the canyon. Anyway the point was to get in close, to pick up details that they couldn't get from far away even with quality binoculars. So as soon as they were sure there weren't any patrols deviating from their observed routes they began circling north around the town.

It took a couple hours to get to the spot they'd agreed on, which was actually near where the raiders' north camp had been and had a good vantage for observing the town. Once there they settled in for some extended watching, paying special attention to the places where vision was obscured from the canyon above, and more specific details about the soldiers and their movements, including their weapons and other equipment.

They appeared to be well supplied, which is to say they had standardized weapons and body armor and uniforms in good repair. They weren't exactly the walking array of high tech gadgets and useful tools that gave US soldiers, particularly Special Operations Forces, so many small but significant advantages in combat.

But from the looks of it they were disciplined, well organized, and most importantly there were a whole lot of them.

"What do you think?" he whispered after about a half hour.

Jane took a while to answer, still looking through her binoculars. "I think they're packing even more people in there than we had," she answered. "And you know how Turner had a field day with us once he got set up on that east hill."

Lewis nodded. "We're going to have trouble doing the same. Turner completely controlled the area surrounding the town, so it was hard for us to get at him. The blockheads control the town *and* the surrounding area."

"And they're watching the canyon road." She frowned. "We could try coming in fast with a vehicle and firing off a few missiles from a safe distance, and maybe strafing the more crowded areas with the M2, then get out before they have time to respond. Or we could try sneaking people in to create a distraction to the north, south, or east and then set up for a real attack."

For several minutes after that he concentrated on his own inspection of the occupied town, feeling a leaden weight sinking in his gut. In spite of his earlier confident words about learning from their fight with the raiders to bring the same headaches to the blockheads, he was now facing serious doubts. The situations weren't the same at all, and the enemy seemed to hold every advantage.

After a few more minutes Jane tapped him on the shoulder. "Seen enough?"

He nodded and began packing up his binoculars, then followed as she shimmied out of sight of the town and slipped back the way they'd come. The initial plan had been to circle far around and approach from different angles to get a good idea of what they'd be facing, but given the heavy enemy patrols on foot *and* with vehicles, as well as the sheer number of blockheads in the area, Lewis didn't blame his wife for heading straight back to the trail they'd come down.

Maybe Uncle George was right. This might be way beyond what the town could manage and it would be better to just focus on holding the mountains, letting the military win the war for them. It was certainly the safe option. Then again, staying hunkered down in town while the raiders circled outside had also been the safe option, at least short term.

Whatever they did, they'd need to spend a long time thinking it over first.

Once they reached the cliff Lewis paused behind cover to check and make sure they hadn't been spotted, as well as cover his wife's climb. When he did he noticed an odd sight, and he motioned to Jane to come take a look too. She paused in her preparations to scale the rock wall and joined him.

It took her a while to spot it, since what he was looking at was beyond the town and slightly obscured by the same east hill they'd been talking about earlier. Lewis had been watching the whole time, as half a dozen troop transports disgorged a crowd of disheveled young men and women in filthy clothes. Once they were free of the trucks the troops began herding them together and sitting them down on the ground.

"Civilians," she said thoughtfully. "Some of their settlers, maybe?"

Lewis watched one of the blockheads slam the butt of his rifle between the shoulder blades of a young woman who was favoring a hurt leg and moving too slow for his taste. From the haphazard way the vehicles were parked it also looked like they'd come from the south and were headed northward. "I don't think so. Prisoners."

Jane gave him a worried look. "I thought they didn't take prisoners."

He'd thought that too. Those poor people were all in their twenties and looked fairly strong and healthy, all things considered. There were no signs of elderly or children.

"Whatever their reasons, I doubt they're sparing them out of kindness."

That suspicion seemed confirmed by the callous way the soldiers went on to feed and water their charges, passing out pails of what he guessed was water from the town spring for them to share around, as well as what looked like scraps of leftovers or castoff food that the prisoners dug into ravenously. The blockheads also lazily curtained off a latrine area, not even bothering to dig a hole or put in a toilet seat or provide anything like toilet paper, and gave each person a limited time to use it.

Trev and his family had described the way they'd been treated at the internment camp, and while it had been impersonal and degrading in many ways it seemed like Southern hospitality compared to the treatment these poor people were receiving.

While those soldiers were doing the minimum to supply the barest needs of their charges, other soldiers had been refueling the transports and doing quick maintenance checks. In less than a half hour everything was done and the prisoners were crammed back into the trucks, packed in so tight he doubted they even had room to sit. Then the vehicles rumbled off towards Highway 6 and continued northward.

Lewis watched them go, feeling a deep sympathy for their plight and an even deeper frustration that there was nothing he could do to help them. Once the trucks had passed out of sight Jane abruptly sucked in a shuddering breath. "How soon can we hit them?"

"Soon," he said grimly. "Let's figure it out."

She nodded, and as he continued to watch the valley she began climbing back up the cliff.

*****

Debra Rutledge nervously clutched her revolver as she sprawled in the ditch with a dozen other Newtown refugees. She didn't know what model it was, and only knew it shot .38 Special through the trial and error of fumbling through various boxes of bullets until she found ones that fit the 5-round cylinder.

Kind of sad, really. She'd spent months working at that store without ever learning about the guns on display. Clara or Max had always handled those customers. She supposed a better reason to learn would be if she actually needed to use one, like right now for instance, but she'd always expected that Fred and his deputies would protect the town.

So much for that. The only consolation she could think of there was that the man and his fellow thieves and traitors had been heading south well ahead of them and were probably dead. Which served as an unpleasant reminder that they might be joining them before too long.

Farther down the ditch a little boy was whimpering while his mother did her best to comfort him and quiet him at the same time. That probably wasn't an issue, right? After all, Deb could barely hear him over the sound of the vehicles passing down the road on the other side of the hedge, so surely anyone in the vehicles themselves wouldn't be able to hear either. And the leaves mostly blocked out the headlights, leaving them in darkness, so they wouldn't be randomly spotted. Especially if they didn't move.

For the most part the others were doing a good job of staying still and silent, although more than one was shivering. From fear, since even with the unseasonably cool weather the summer nights were warm this far south.

She was glad the townspeople had decided to split up into smaller groups to avoid detection. It had been a hard decision, and everyone felt more vulnerable without the safety of numbers, but so far it had kept them from the notice of the enemies roaming freely through the southern states. It was probably the only reason they were still alive.

Even so, she missed Clara and Max and some of her other friends from the General Store. It must be nice to have family to stick together with, although it hurt a bit that none of them had asked her to join them. For all the talk of keeping a strong community, people had gotten a lot more selfish after Fred and his cronies took off on them.

Although maybe being with this group wasn't the worst thing, since as far as she knew they were the only ones still alive. They hadn't seen anyone else from Newtown since splitting up and had no idea if anyone else had even survived. It seemed impossible, considering how many heart-stopping close encounters Deb had faced in the last few weeks.

It had been so long since they'd seen anyone but enemies, with day after day of hiding and trying to snatch hours of fitful sleep and night after night of furtive creeping, that she was starting to feel like this was all some sort of nightmare that never ended.

Or she supposed she meant the blockheads were the only *living* people they'd seen.

Just in case they were tempted to let down their guard or surrender, they stumbled across the remains of less fortunate refugees often enough to remind them of the consequences. And often enough to make Deb certain that if she did see a blockhead, she'd be able to point her revolver at him and shoot him full of holes to escape the fate that had befallen those poor people.

The trucks kept passing, the general rumble broken by the nearest ones getting louder from the left and then quieter to the right. How big was this convoy, anyway? It felt like they'd been here half the night, and even though she wasn't keeping count she could confidently say that hundreds of vehicles had passed them by this point. Those sorts of convoys weren't all that common, but the enemy made up for it by using plenty of scouts that searched even the smallest roads and lanes.

It seemed like the entire world was filled with nothing but blockheads and the corpses of their victims.

South was supposed to mean safety! They'd pushed so hard since Newtown to escape the blockheads coming down from the north, at times with the enemy close behind and once even passed by a convoy on a nearby road as they scrambled to hide and prayed they'd be ignored. Day after day of desperate grind, fighting exhaustion and injury to get miles behind them as their bodies broke down and the pace they set never seemed to be good enough.

And then they'd started running into people fleeing the other direction, warning of enemies coming from the south. The weary refugees from Newtown could only give their warning in turn that enemies from the north weren't far behind them.

They were trapped, with nowhere to go and enemies all around. Their only hope was to head due east, away from where most of the blockheads seemed to be going, and pray that eventually they'd find a place where they'd be left alone.

Deb shouldn't have done it, but she was just so exhausted that the repetitive noise of passing enemies less than fifteen yards away eroded her alertness. The next thing she knew she was being awakened by a deafening roar from somewhere in front of her, quickly followed by screams from the rest of her group.

She lurched into a sitting position, heart pounding so hard it was almost painful, and scrambled around to find the pistol that had fallen from her limp hand. She couldn't see flashes of gunfire in the darkness but there was light trickling through the hedge, along with the whine of bullets passing overhead.

They'd been discovered.

The mother farther down the ditch was one of the people screaming, and as the gunfire continued she turned and bolted the other direction, leaving her child behind in her panic. She only made it a few steps before stumbling, and from the limp way she fell Deb had the terrible feeling she wouldn't be getting back up. The young boy, sobbing and babbling confused questions, crawled over to her and started to shake her.

Deb turned away from the awful sight and lifted her pistol, noticing that even though she wasn't the only armed person in the group she was the only one who'd thought to use her weapon. The others were either cowering in the ditch or trying to crawl away. She pointed the revolver uncertainly at the hedge, wondering if she should even bother to fire.

The blockheads were firing dozens, maybe hundreds of bullets, and so far they'd only hit one or two people. Would she have any better luck firing blind with her five?

The question became moot a moment later when the deafening racket abruptly ceased and bullets stopped flying all around her. Deb immediately took the opportunity to scuttle over and wrap her arms protectively around the boy, gently pulling him away from his mother's body.

Around them the rest of the group was starting to slip over the other side of the ditch and flee, but before she could follow she heard harsh voices shouting in an unfamiliar language beyond the hedge, then a moment later the leaves rustled with the sound of large bodies pushing through.

Almost immediately dogs burst into view and fell among the group, snapping and snarling. One of them came right for her and the child, terrible jaws snapping down on the spindly arm the boy held out protectively in front of him. The child screamed as he was torn out of her grip and thrown to the ground with the snarling animal on top of him.

Deb screamed as well and pointed the gun at the dog with trembling hands, so weak from hunger and fear that her finger barely seemed to have the strength to pull the trigger. Max had told her about pulling back the hammer with her thumbs before each shot so the trigger pull wouldn't be as difficult, but in her panic she'd completely forgotten about that until now.

The shot seemed deafening in the night and the German shepherd leapt away, snarl turning into nearly a yelp. She didn't know if she'd hit it, was terrified that she'd hit the boy by accident, but all that mattered was that it was farther away, now. She scrambled forward, screaming at the dog to stay away, and scooped up the child in one arm while she pointed her pistol one-handed.

She wasn't sure she could even pull the trigger, and her arm was trembling so much she'd probably miss even from a few feet away. And that was only if the dog didn't suddenly leap and knock her to the ground before she even had time to react.

Thankfully the animal stayed away, making a low dangerous noise in its throat. Deb kept screaming at it and slowly backed along the ditch in the other direction, struggling to keep her hold on the limp little burden she held.

More bodies had joined the dogs in crashing through the hedge, soldiers in uniforms and full body armor. They were shouting orders to the animals in their unfamiliar language, and gathering up the people in her group who the dogs had already subdued or taken down.

Maybe it was luck, or some random fluke, but she made it ten feet in the confusion without being spotted. Then she heard a crashing from the hedge directly in front of her, along with what was obviously cursing even in another language. Another soldier was fighting through clinging branches to get at her.

Deb turned and shoved the boy away, catching him by the shoulders and leaning close to his pale, frightened face.

"Run!" she hissed. The boy stared at her blankly, clutching his hurt arm close to his chest. "Run, and don't hide! The dogs will find you if you hide, so run and keep running until they stop chasing you!"

He didn't seem to understand, at least until she shook him and then shoved him away. The boy stumbled, made a heart-wrenching keening sound, then turned and bolted into the darkness.

Almost at the same time the soldier broke through the branches, shining a light directly into Deb's eyes. From the way he held it she had a feeling it was attached to his rifle. She grit her teeth, thinking of the boy fleeing behind her, and raised her pistol. And just like she'd prepared to do for weeks now she pulled the trigger over and over. She wasn't even aware she was still screaming until the sound of the shots drowned out her voice.

The blockhead staggered and the blinding light swung away as a hit threw off his aim. She fired half a dozen times more, barely aware that for the last few the only noise that came from the gun was a hollow *click*.

In that silence the soldier, apparently unharmed, darted forward. She saw the light on his gun swing around wildly, and a moment later stars burst behind her eyes and pain exploded across her face.

She went down hard, mind blanking for a moment. The only thing she could think was that now she was dead. She'd either missed or her bullets hadn't been able to get through his flak jacket, or maybe they had but hadn't done enough to stop him. At any moment she expected to feel the cold jab of the rifle's muzzle against her face, then the end.

The seconds dragged by, each one an eternity, until she finally recovered her wits enough to open her eyes. She saw the soldier standing over her, gun pointed down at her chest, but he didn't fire. And he didn't fire.

She was alive. He hadn't killed her.

The man saw her open her eyes and screamed an order, taking one hand from his gun to motion wildly. He kept repeating the gesture, growing more and more angry and impatient, until Deb's dazed brain finally processed the unspoken command and she painfully pulled herself to her knees. Immediately the man moved around behind her and roughly grabbed her arms, slapping handcuffs around her wrists.

Then he hauled her to her feet as easily as if she weighed nothing, which unfortunately these days wasn't all that far from the truth, and began shoving her towards the hole he'd torn through the hedge to reach her. Deb stumbled forward with her path lit by his wildly waving light, awkward without her hands to balance her or prevent her from running into branches.

One poked her face less than an inch from her eye and made her stop and duck away with a yelp. The soldier behind her cursed impatiently and slammed his rifle into the small of her back, knocking her forward through the hedge on her knees so she tore through a dozen branches that all scraped her skin and caught at her clothes.

Deb allowed herself to be pulled back to her feet and pushed forward again, trying to focus through her pain and misery. Blood trickled down from a cut on her cheek where the man had hit her with his gun, dripping off her chin onto her filthy clothes, and her face throbbed as it began to swell. Her back throbbed with a dull pain of its own, and her skin had fiery lines of pain from the branches that had scratched her. But beyond all those distractions was the confused reality of the situation.

He was taking her prisoner. Only the blockheads didn't take prisoners. That was one of the few things all the conflicting reports agreed on, that the invaders shot any Americans they found on sight. Deb's panicked mind tried to think of any reason why she hadn't met the same fate, and all the answers were too unpleasant to contemplate.

The soldier marched her towards the back of a truck, and to her relief Deb saw that the rest of her group had also been taken prisoner, including the men. So maybe what the blockheads had in mind for her wasn't what she'd feared.

After all, they'd started out the invasion taking everyone prisoner, relocating them to massive internment camps but by all reports treating them fairly. Maybe they'd finally gotten over their rage at the Retaliation and had stopped killing people on sight. They had to have some human decency left, didn't they?

It sure didn't seem like it. The soldiers who weren't occupied handling prisoners seemed to be amusing themselves by beating and taunting Derrick, the oldest man in her group, while he cowered on the ground and begged for mercy.

The only other mother in the group cried in protest as her seven year old daughter was torn from her grip and prodded away from the huddle of prisoners. The soldiers shouted at the confused girl and waved their hands in a shooing motion, until she finally seemed to realize what they wanted. She turned and bolted into the night, disappearing into the darkness beyond the lights.

A few others were pushed out of the group, people in their thirties or older and a boy in his early teens. Then the soldiers began herding Deb and everyone who remained towards the back of the nearest truck, which she saw was packed with even more filthy and frightened prisoners.

She tried to catch one last glimpse of the rest of her group as the blockheads made her scramble up into the crowded truck with the others, but all she saw was soldiers and snarling dogs. Everyone who came up into the truck was about her age, less than half of the group she'd been with. She didn't want to think about what would happen to the others.

Then again, she didn't want to think about what would happen to her.

The press of unwashed bodies was so tight that no one could sit, and the stink of it made her stomach heave. It was like the worst mosh pit ever. When the truck lurched into motion a few minutes later the packed mass of people barely shifted.

Deb slumped against the prisoners around her, who were all slumping as well. Not quite sitting or crouching, but all leaning against one another to take the weight off their legs.

It wasn't very comfortable and she had trouble breathing, but there was literally no other choice.

To her surprise another emotion had joined her grief and despair. Relief. She was caught, and the enemy might have a terrible fate in store for her, but at least she didn't have to run anymore. Didn't have to hide, cower, and spend sleepless days and nights evading pursuit. Events were out of her hands for the moment.

She could finally rest, at least until she found an opportunity to do something about her situation.

End of Book Four
The story continues in Determination,
Fifth and final book of the Best Laid Plans series.

Made in the USA
Middletown, DE
17 December 2022

18999737R00257